O

BIRDLAND

Published by Fish Out of Water Books
Ann Arbor, MI, USA

www.fowbooks.com

ISBN: 978-1-947886-05-6.

Library of Congress Control Number: 2021936700.

Realistic fiction (YA and Adult) — creative nonfiction — memoir
coming of age — music — culture shock — pop culture

Michigan via Manchester, England.

We are all fish out of water.

Cover design by Bailey Designs Books: baileydesignsbooks.com.

Also available from Fish Out of Water Books

- ***Peach*** by Wayne Barton
- ***No Sad Songs*** by Frank Morelli
- ***Love & Vodka*** by R.J. Fox
- ***Awaiting Identification*** by R.J. Fox
- ***Life, Liberty, and the Pursuit of United*** by Gary B. France

For further information, visit www.fowbooks.com.

ON THE WAY TO

BIRDLAND

Frank Morelli

"A must read for everyone trying to find their way back to what matters most."

—Adrienne Kisner, Author of *Dear Rachel Maddow, The Confusion of Laurel Graham,* and *Six Angry Girls*

"On the Way to Birdland ***shows us what's possible."***

— Angelo Surmelis, author of *The Dangerous Art of Blending In*

"A classic tale of choice and chance, with more twists than a Virginia mountain road."

— Valerie Nieman, author of *To the Bones* and *Backwater*

To the birds, whose salient songs quench
the parched depths of our humanity.

Alone

Second period. Humanities. We're four days into our personal TED Talks. Mrs. Haynes told us the project would be "a creative outlet to express our passions." Yeah. Right. The only thing I've seen that came anywhere close to passion was when Margaret Downes paused mid-speech, took out her phone, and blew a kiss to her boyfriend on video chat.

I don't know. Maybe I'm being unfair. Maybe I'm just out of it because I didn't get enough sleep. I mean, it's not like I get a ton of sleep on most nights. But last night was not a normal night.

Because last night was the night before today.

And today is special.

It's so special my heart rattles against the front of my chest the second Mrs. Haynes glances in my direction. And then my palms go all slick and sweaty.

Mrs. Haynes gives me her trademark wink and my tongue goes all flabby and dry. I start to think my only means of speech for the rest of my life will be through this overcooked steak that now flops around in my mouth.

"Mr. Wheaton?"

Every head in the classroom, in each perfectly-lined row, turns to face me. Mrs. Haynes stares me down with expectation in her eyes, but I don't know how she expects me to distill the entire life's work of one of the greatest musicians who ever lived into one fifteen-minute presentation. Because this happens to be my passion. It might not be a popular one, but I'm not worried about popularity. It's mine and it means the world to me. And I'd like to think that John Coltrane has already taught me more about life than any of these fools in my high school will ever know. But it's not like anyone would ever know that, because no one ever has a thing to say to me. To them, I'm just some know-it-all kid who lives in his brother's shadow.

I guess if I'm really being honest, preparing for this project has kind of been a welcome distraction from all of the recent weirdness in my life.

So then why am I so damn nervous?

And why do I keep having these…moments? Weird ones, where my heartbeat gallops off without me and my vision goes blurry and the whole world falls into a hush. This blunt, hollow chamber somewhere deep in my mind where I can hear them. My thoughts, I guess. Or maybe something else:

Can you hear me?

Cordell.

Cordell?

Then the fog clears in a flash and I'm right back in the classroom, like it never happened. It has to be my nerves.

"Cordell?" Mrs. Haynes says sternly. Her use of my full first name tells me her sense of expectation has boiled down to frustration. "Are you going to keep us waiting forever?"

I can't manage to push a single word past the back of my throat, so I stall and fan through the stack of index cards in my hand as I inch my way to the front of the classroom. I turn around. My hands shake so hard all the notes I'd written on my cards last night—about Charlie Parker, Miles Davis, Dizzy Gillespie, and John Coltrane—look like they're in the process of being electrocuted. Or like they're trapped in a perpetual earthquake. In other words, I can't read a single, damn word. I guess I'll have to wing it.

"Hi!" I say much too loud and squeaky to be considered a normal human being in a high school such as this one. "Well," I continue, "you all know me as Cordell…and…and I'm…"

"A dork!" comes a quickfire response, accompanied by a few snickers from the back of the class.

That's when I remember what had made me nervous about presenting in the first place.

David "Spud" Murphy.

A mountain of muscle with a creepy, little excuse for a mustache and the perpetual desire to do harm to others by any means necessary.

Both Spud and his mustache wink at me. I feel the frown form on my face before I can hold all the muscles tight and hide it from the entire class. I'm about two seconds away from shitting my pants right there at the edge of Mrs. Haynes's desk. But I take a deep breath and swallow hard. I get myself composed.

And then I continue to fall all over myself.

"Err...as I was saying...my name is Cordell, and..."

"Wind instruments give me wood!"

The entire class erupts in raucous laughter, like the kind you'd expect to hear at a comedy show. Except in this show, I'm the punchline.

Spud leans back in his chair, with a self-satisfied grin on his face. He blows a kiss from under his filthy, half-cocked mustache. And that's when I lose all control. That's when the words "shut it...asshole" leap from my mouth.

My hands clasp tight over my lips as I fight to stuff the words back in. But it's too late. The whole class hears them. Spud hears them and his mustache does too. The worst part of all is that Mrs. Haynes doesn't miss a syllable.

The typical *oohs* and *aahs* of a hijacked high school humanities lesson swirl around the classroom and my head starts to spin. The posters on Mrs. Haynes's wall—the one of Winston Churchill and the classic Uncle Sam Wants You poster and good old Rosie the Riveter—swirl together like a foamy wash of soap suds as they circumnavigate the drain.

Somewhere in the background, Mrs. Haynes's tinny voice screams out, "Murphy! Hallway! Now!" Spud fires daggers at me as he rises from his desk and strolls out of the classroom with all the cockiness of a mafia kingpin. He delivers a single, mustachioed parting shot before he hits the doorway.

"You're dead, Wheaton."

It's more than enough. He's made his point. But will I accept it? That's the real question.

In my normal life—the one before my brother, Travis left home without any warning—Spud's ice-cold threat would have been enough to put an end to the matter. To cool off my fuse. Because let's face it—I'm not exactly what you'd call "equipped" to tangle with a kid like David Murphy. But ever since Travis hightailed it, I've started caring less and less about consequences—and even less about keeping my mouth shut.

Travis used to say that I was a happy-go-lucky kind of dude. I'm not sure what he meant, but I can tell you I no longer feel happy, and I'm definitely not lucky. These days, the only emotions I seem to feel are anger and rage. Or maybe it's fear and confusion? What do I know? All I can tell you is, before I have time to think better of it, the following words escape my mouth and they land squarely in Murphy's stupid, mustache-ridden face:

"Just try it, you overgrown prick!"

The look on Murphy's face as he exits the classroom tells me one thing with complete certainty: oh yes, indeed, I am a dead man walking. But Spud's look of shock and surprise isn't the worst one I get. That comes from Mrs. Haynes, the tigress, who spins around on the tips of her heels and snarls, "You too, Wheaton. Out! Now!!"

My head starts to throb and the classroom lurches around me in a psychedelic swirl as everything starts to turn red. With rage. With frustration. With all the little pricks and pins piled up before me. All the barbs from the Spud Murphys of the world who don't care and could never understand what it's like to be part of the Wheaton family. Folks who don't understand what it means to lose something precious.

I can't quite recall what happened next, but my knuckles are sore and I have a pretty nice cut under my left eye. And, now, I'm fully aware of the consequences.

You see, David "Spud" Murphy left school today with a broken nose. And I left school today with no earthly idea of who I am anymore.

Sitting here. Home. Suspended for the rest of the semester—which essentially means the rest of the school year. According to Principal McDowell, I'm lucky I'm not facing criminal charges.

So now I'm truly alone. With all the time in the world on my hands. With nothing to do but think. About life. About my only real friend: my brother, Travis. And about how on Earth I'm ever going to fit in without him, here in High Point, Nowheresville, USA.

The Low Point

I'll never forget the night Travis left. It plays through my mind on an old film reel, all sepia-toned and littered with static. The opening shot is a flat, white ceiling staring down at me as I lie on my bed and clap my hands over my ears to drown out the shouting. Their voices ring out from the kitchen and knife right through the paper-thin walls that partition our house into rooms and wriggle through the microscopic spaces between my clenched fingers. Directly into my ears. Directly into my brain. And my heart starts to pound each time the memory respools and runs itself through the film projector in my mind.

Each time I hear the same remarks, the same piercing words fired from Travis's mouth. And each time they hit their bullseye: my father. First come the warning shots. The "You have nothing to do with this, so why feel shame?" and the "For God's sake…how many times do I have to say it? I haven't done anything wrong!" See, Travis always finds a slick way to bring God into the argument just to push Dad's buttons.

And it worked. Every time.

Because those warning shots are always followed by a back and forth volley of nuclear proportions. First comes Dad's familiar responses: "You're a disgrace to the family!" and "Son, I brought you into this world and I can take you out!" Then Travis: "I'd like to see you try it, old man!" That's the precise moment when Dad swipes something off the table and there's an epic crash of silverware and ceramic that spills out over the kitchen floor. Travis fires back with a simple, "forget it…I'm outta here." And the next thing I know, the door to our bedroom swings open and Travis stands there with a distant look in his eyes and an empty duffle bag draped over one shoulder.

His hair is no longer secured in a neat ponytail, and it splays across his forehead and cheeks in sweat-drenched tentacles. I sit up on my bed, alarmed, but Travis doesn't acknowledge my presence. He just starts tossing old t-shirts, underwear, and assorted odds and ends into the duffle. When the bag is stuffed to its capacity and zippered shut, he stands upright, saxophone in hand. His prized possession. His life. His soul. The one thing in this world that defined the type of person my brother was meant to be.

He pushes his hair back off his face and takes a deep breath like he's ready to dive off a cliff into the swirling whitewater below.

"What the hell are *you* looking at?" he asks when he notices I've been staring at him with my jaw dropped open for the past five minutes.

"I don't know," I say. "Why don't *you* tell me?"

He doesn't respond. Just stares off into the distance, shakes his head, smirks and throws the strap of the duffle over his shoulder. He pops open the old, cracked-leather saxophone case he bought with his birthday money at Mel's Music down on Main, and carefully pushes the instrument into its foam cutout. He stares down at the sax for a moment with his eyes burning bright. With the memories of him and I listening to Coltrane in our room playing across his forehead like clips on the film reel long after Dad had passed the jazz gene down to us. Long after Dad's corny stories about his days discovering new musical acts and playing trumpet in a local cover band had grown old and tired. Long after the well of Dad's affinity for America's supreme art form had gone dry and his two sons tried to keep it alive on their crappy record player without him.

Then Travis's eyes go dark and flat. He snaps the sax case shut, lifts it off the surface of our desk, and turns toward the door—but not before I try to stop him. Not before I try my best to talk sense into him. "Travis, man, where the hell are you going?"

"Cordy...I've had enough...I'm following the sound," he replies.

When my eyebrows crease in the middle of my forehead, Travis realizes he owes me a deeper explanation. "You know," he continues, "kind of like Trane when he outgrew all the small-town talk and small-town people...when he decided his destiny, and his vision lay elsewhere. Dude, there's more to life than High Point, North Carolina. You'll figure that out for yourself someday."

Then he left. Just like that. Gone.

And that's how my last memory of Travis ends every single time, over and over again, and there's nothing I can do to change it. And there's nothing I can do but feel like I was the one to blame, the one who sent him away. To wherever he went. That it was my fault. That I could have stopped it all from happening if I would have handled things differently.

If I would have known.

Travis did send me a few messages, so I knew he wasn't lying in a ditch somewhere. Four texts and two photos, to be exact. Not much to go on in six months. And the texts all sounded the same; generic crap like, "luv you bro. Mom too. I'm ok" and "still doing well, hope ur good too." I'd be halfway through my reply to him before the chime on my phone was done ringing, but he would never respond. They were one-way conversations. The kind Travis prefers.

The photos Travis sent were a little more helpful, though I'm not sure how much he meant them to be. The first one was your basic selfie, a downward facing shot with his right arm stretched to the limit over his head. There's not much to see in it, other than him sitting on a set of dilapidated steps under the overhang of an old row home. There's a crooked smirk on his face, so it seems like he looks happier, I guess, but maybe it's all in my mind. Maybe that's just what I want to see. Who knows?

What I do know is the second pic Travis sent is the one that makes me certain that he bolted for Philadelphia. It took me a while to figure it out, because it was just another picture of a beaten-down, old townhouse. I had no idea what the picture was supposed to mean, or even if the text itself was meant to be sent to me. But then I got all technical and popped it into an online image search. And that's when at least a million pics of the same house popped up. That's because it happens to be John Coltrane's house…in Philadelphia. Good old 1511, North 33rd Street. Domicile of a legend. Or, at least, it used to be before that legend moved to New York City and played at Birdland and became the greatest saxophonist of all time.

So I guess it's true that Travis never told me specifically where he was headed, but, in a way, he did. In a way, he told me *everything* I needed to know, because Travis and I are telepathically connected. We always have been, and I think he was pretty sure I'd know what he meant when he told me he was "following the sound" and needed to seek his destiny and then sent me—whether by accident or not—a picture of his hero's now-historic house in Philadelphia. I mean, it all seems to add up. Of course, I don't *truly* know for sure. I guess my whole theory is more of a brotherly hunch, and one that has me thinking—as I've been known to do.

Ever since Travis told me there's more to life than High Point, North Carolina, it kind of feels like my hometown is a tortoise shell. Those may sound like the words of a lonely philosophy nerd, but they're true. If I stay hunkered down inside the shell, I'm *safe*. And the people on the outside? They admire my shell. They think there's something beautiful about it. They make it easy for me to carry it around and dive down inside when I come across the things I'd rather not see or hear. Things that scare me. Things I want to avoid.

But, after a while, the shell feels more like a cage—one that I keep mindlessly carrying on my back.

Sometimes it grows heavy.

Sometimes it suffocates.

Most times, I want to escape.

I'm not trying to be dramatic about my hometown or anything. Travis once told me my whole existence verges on drama. But Travis is gone—my best and only real friend—and now that I've been kicked out of school, and I'm sitting alone in what used to be *our* bedroom, I'm finding it pretty damn hard to avoid being dramatic.

Fact is, I live in High Point, North Carolina, which is about two hundred notches below Wisdom Tooth Removal on the fun scale. I don't know if there's such a thing as a fun scale. If not, I think they should invent one so you can know ahead of time if the channel you're about to select or the webpage you're about to load or the town you're about to move to is gonna suck. I also never had my wisdom teeth removed. I guess I'm lucky. I mean, I'm not quite seventeen yet, so it's not like I'm about to throw a party over it or anything. All I can say is I heard Mom complain about getting her wisdom teeth removed when she was young. She made it seem like getting teeth yanked out of your face fares almost as lousy as High Point, North Carolina on the fun scale—whenever they get around to inventing one.

I didn't always think my hometown was just a desolate stretch of tractors and highways between real civilization. A glorified truck stop. I didn't always lie around in my room with my curtains drawn and my finger scrolling, scrolling, scrolling through my social media feed, searching for that single, hot take that would somehow make my life matter. I didn't always notice the tortoise shell propped on my back until recently. Like, within the last year. Since the shit hit the fan and Travis took off. That's when the shell started to gain weight.

At least when Travis was around I had someone who didn't think I was a total lost cause. To my high school classmates, I was just the kid with the ginger crewcut, the spaghetti-strap arms, and what Travis sometimes referred to as "an acute case of verbal diarrhea." I think he was talking about my mouth, and how I could never keep the damn thing shut. He was right. It's probably why I'm holed up in this shell all alone since he left. Because there aren't many people in High Point who like to find out from an almost-seventeen-year-old they're wrong most of the time.

Well, I'm through with talking. Now I get up in silence and sit around in silence and stack my dirty clothes in a wrinkled-up pile on one side of my bed and my clean clothes in a folded pile of slightly-less-wrinkled stuff on the other side of the bed and once in a while stare out through a gap in the curtains to watch the mockingbirds swoop down through the myrtles.

I watch the news sometimes, when I'm in the mood for deeper depression than usual. On those days when it doesn't seem like anything I do holds more meaning than a half-digested stalk of hay in a pile of horse manure. Excuse me if I "verge on the dramatic" without Travis around, but those stories about people fighting and countries shooting rockets at each other all over the world don't help me see possibilities outside of the shell.

I mean, that kind of stuff doesn't happen in High Point, North Carolina and I still feel alone. Worst thing we see here is people separating themselves by choice. Not even attempting to understand the folks standing right beside them. You got the poor people and the rich people and the church people. Through the sheer force of physics, they intersect in so many ways it's impossible to keep track, and yet I don't often see them make an effort to intersect with each other on purpose. That's been my experience since Travis left and the whole town started avoiding us—as if a father and a son can't have a disagreement without it infecting the whole town. As if they think an addiction is some kind of contagious disease. As if a whole family can somehow be forever tainted by the actions of one member. I don't know if the folks in Dad's congregation are embarrassed *for* us or embarrassed *of* us, but I can tell you it gets pretty old when some of the people you've known since you were born would rather dive behind the tabloids rack when they see you in line at the grocery store than just nod their heads and say a simple hello. It's to the point where I doubt the turkey vultures would circle around if I ended up as roadkill on Route 40.

Maybe I wouldn't be so pissed if my dad—the one and only Maynard T. Wheaton—wasn't so apologetic to the people who think we're now a family hellbent on eternal damnation. It's like my father stood on the altar so many times to preach to his congregation that he somehow turned into the church itself and became incapable of explaining how my brother's problems were also the town's problems. How everyone contributed. Every single man in his summer seersucker suit and woman in her Sunday dress that lined those pews. All of them. They played a part in my brother leaving because they turned tail on him when he needed them most. They pretended nothing was wrong. They didn't put a stop to it. At least I can admit my guilt. At least I can admit that I pretty much ruined Travis's life. Everyone else out there on Sundays? They blame Maynard, because he's the head of the family. The one who's supposed to have control.

And old Maynard T. never says a damn thing in return.

He never will.

That's why I lie here in a pile of toast crumbs I'm too lazy to clean off my sheets, and why I stare at a jagged crack in the plaster of my ceiling and a wayward barn spider perched on a web in one of the corners where the ceiling meets the wall instead of listening to a single word from the news anchor about whatever is happening as the closing bell rings at the stock exchange. My problems are much closer to home. And they're even bigger than getting suspended and nearly murdered by Spud Murphy.

I take a deep breath and gather my strength to sit up in bed and allow the gunked-up soles of my Chucks to touch down on the planks of the bedroom floor. The news anchor's vacant eyes stare at me from the screen as she scribbles a fake note on a blank transcript and tells the world, "Soybean futures are looking bright, up two percent in Asia this morning." I hit the "power" button on the remote and watch her brown curls fizzle into blackness and silence. I can't see how the future of some beans can "look bright" in any market unless you can make a batch of ben dip out of them.

While I'm pondering the future of beans, I hear the front door open and shut. Maynard's boots sound in the front hall. Listening to my parents through the walls of my room has accounted for ninety-five percent of the child/parent relationship we've shared since Travis left. It feels kind of weird to eat waffles at the breakfast table and talk about a Duke versus UNC basketball game that doesn't take place for six months after you've been through something like us Wheatons have. But that's not the important thing. The important thing is we're not a family anymore. Dad wanders out like a zombie at 7:45 each morning to fulfill his shift at one of the last woodworking shops in a town once drowning in furniture. He shouts, "Ginny, I'm off," as he lumbers through the kitchen and closes the door. And each afternoon, he returns at exactly 5:15.

Our remaining interactions take place through the sheets of drywall that partition our small bungalow on Brookside Drive into five rooms—two bedrooms, a bathroom that barely holds a washtub, a shotgun kitchen at the back of the house, and a living room crammed in between the front door and everything else. Sometimes we eat together in silence, but most of the time we retire to separate rooms and do it all over again the next day. About the only other interaction we have is when my father keeps us awake at night with his persistent and annoying cough. I've lost count of the number of times I've wanted to run into their room to tell him to please, *shut the hell up*! But that'd take actual communication, so instead I cover my head with a pillow and try not to suffocate.

On this particular Tuesday afternoon, as soon as my father steps inside and closes the door I can tell something is wrong. For one, it's 3:24. And he's stationary. And quiet. His first stop is usually the kitchen, where he grabs a beer from the fridge, and I hear the trademark cling of bottle on bottle. Today, however, he drops his tool bag on the floor near the door and I hear the shuffling of much lighter feet—Mom's—traveling in the opposite direction, from the kitchen to the front door. I strain to listen.

"So, what'd he say?" I hear in a shaky whisper. Then nothing but the sound of soft whimpering for what seems like minutes but is probably closer to seconds.

"How long?" Mom asks in a voice that's recovered more weight.

"I don't know," Dad says in the static voice of a robot.

"He must have some idea," I could hear Mom reply.

"Ginny, will you just leave it, please?" Dad sounds agitated. After a moment or two, he calms himself and finds his voice. "Look…he said there's nothing they can do. It's in my lungs. Up to God now." The room lurches on me. My brain feels like a thousand-pound boulder hatching from my skull.

I want to run to him. I want to tell him I heard everything he said and that I won't let him give up. I won't let him leave us. I won't let him die. But how do you do any of that when you've spent the past year having a relationship with your father through your bedroom wall?

Instead, I collapse on my crumb-encrusted sheets and bury my face in the pile of pillows and lose myself in the touch of warm tears as they run down both cheeks.

I don't know how long I'm there…

The room is dark. Familiar. I remember the cold concrete. The stench of motor oil. The sting of rope fibers. The serpent-like twine tied so tight on my wrists the blood oozes out between sections of knot. I remember the double-barrel touch of steel behind my head. The blunt CLICK! that vibrates behind my ear like a twenty-two caliber mosquito. And the fear. Oh my God, the fear. So thick and rancid it bubbles through my pores ...

My Favorite Things

"Cord-ELL DAARlington WHEATON!"

My eyes pop open. I'm face down on the pile of soggy pillows. The door to my room shakes off the hinges under the weight of my mother's fist.

"Cordy! I've been calling you for ten minutes and—"

"I'm here!" I wipe the fog from my eyes and cough up a furball. Probably a face full of Ritz crackers from the bedsheets.

I open the door and Mom blabbers away without notice. "I've been knocking for ten minutes! Sometimes I don't know if you're alive or dead in that room." She adjusts the wire glasses on the bridge of her nose and pushes a tuft of auburn hair off her forehead. That's what she does when she's said too much. And saying the word "dead" around her kid when she still hasn't told him his dad might be dead soon fits the description of "too much." But we don't say a word about Dad. Not without a wall or a shell or a protective force field between us. Not without Travis.

"You plan to eat something?" she asks, as if dinner is somehow a cure for my father's terminal illness.

"Not hungry," I say.

"Holed up in this room day and night," Mom says. She tugs the front of my t-shirt as if the technique is a medically proven factor in determining body mass. "Sun never touches your skin. You're disappearing." She sighs and shakes her head. "Eat some chicken fried steak before we can slip you through a cheese grater."

"I'm. Not. Hungry." My eyes shoot laser beams that burn through Mom's forehead. She doesn't flinch, but a scowl flashes across her lips so I know I'm not making an ally. I feel a wave of guilt wash over me. But I don't apologize because I know Ginny Wheaton won't say a word to me. Fighting's not her style. She's yet to challenge me on the Spud Murphy incident and for getting my ass suspended. I don't think she's even mentioned the word "Travis" since he left. That's Ginny Wheaton.

Anything to keep the peace, even if it means losing the war. And now I'll never know how that war may have played out for Travis, because no one had the courage to say a damn thing before it was too late. Not Maynard. Not me. Not the town of High Point, North Carolina. And certainly not Ginny Wheaton.

"I'll leave a plate in the fridge," she says. It's so predictable I have to chew back a laugh, but before I can close the door and resume the normal course of my unraveling, a hand pushes through and stops my progress.

"Mom, I heard you," I groan, "Food's in the fridge. I get—" but the door creaks open and it's clear I'm no longer talking to Mom.

"Come and eat supper with your mom and me," Dad says.

His lips form a horizontal exclamation point under the swirling lines of hard work and worry on his face. His piercing, green eyes meet mine and the warmth begins to well up below my eyelids.

I want to hug him around the waist and walk around with my feet on top of his and pretend we're a robot like when I was four years old.

But I can't.

That would show weakness and Dad has never been good about giving in to weakness. It's why Travis took his bags and went to Philadelphia, and why we're here in High Point pretending Travis is still with us and Dad will be here forever. And why I try to pretend I wasn't the one who set this all in motion. That it wasn't my fault. That I'm not the villain.

But I can't.

"Later," I tell him, because it's all I have the strength left to say.

Dad nods and closes my door.

I feel like going to sleep and not waking until they invent the damn fun scale, which would be a long time, but I woke up five minutes ago and it wasn't from a place I'm interested in going anymore. To the nightmare. The one I've had so many times since Travis left I've lost count. The one that scares the ever-loving shit out of me.

So I try to forget it. Push it way down. I do what people do when they're not ready to face life or reality or their parents or High Point, North Carolina or even Travis. They pace around and think about the past. About how things used to be.

I grip the ragged laces of a baseball that's been sitting on the desk so long it has its own dust imprint. I remember tossing it for the first time with Travis and his friends at the wide-open lot on the corner of

Brookside Drive. Not too far from John Coltrane's old house. Some don't know, but John Coltrane grew up right here in High Point. Travis and I used to think it was the most exciting piece of news we'd ever heard. I still do. When Dad delivered this news to Travis one morning at the breakfast table, my brother saw it as an omen. He saw it as a miracle. He saw it as God speaking directly to him. That he could take his musical talents, because my brother was a musician—and I hope he still is—to the top, even if the starting point was High Point, North Carolina. If John Coltrane from Underhill Street could do it, why couldn't Travis Wheaton?

Some folks around here say Coltrane was the greatest saxophonist who ever lived. Travis said he was more than that. He liked to use one specific word to describe his hero, and he'd use it all the time. To Travis, the words "John" and "Coltrane" were synonymous with the word "visionary." To Travis, they were one and the same. This was how Travis turned me onto another of my great passions in life—Greek philosophy. I doubt he'd ever remember it, because it's not like learning philosophical teachings were Travis's thing. But he told me something once, about Coltrane and his vision. About how the ancient philosopher, Plato, believed the rhythm of music should follow the rhythms of a life that is orderly and brave. Travis believed Coltrane was living out the purest form of humanity in his music and that he'd dug deep down into the past to find it and blow it out in sweet notes from the mouth of his sax.

Travis believed that was what it meant to be a visionary, and that always stuck with me. It made me hungry for more, so I became obsessed with Greek philosophers, because I figured they had a better chance of explaining Travis and Coltrane to me than anyone else. After all, it was Plato who also said a musician is someone who is "temporarily engaged in works of peace." I like that. It's how I like to see my brother, Travis. Not like the way my father sees him. As a failure.

I drop the ball on a dust-free spot on my desk and rifle through the stray pages of nonsense strewn across its surface. I like a little bit of clutter. It makes me feel free in a way, but I also can't find anything, which is one of the less freeing experiences in life.

Under a stray tissue I find an old photobooth picture of Travis and me wearing fireman's helmets and donning stick-on mustaches each thicker than push brooms. A tear threatens the corner of my eyelid, but I'm all out of tears and patience. I have nothing left to give. I drop the photo on the desk and watch it slide overboard and behind, to the crevasse of the unknown, where paper clips and thumbtacks go to die a humiliating and tackless death.

It's fitting.

Watching the last good memory I have of my brother spill off into the abyss of my room as if dumped by a giant garbage truck into an endless landfill. But then I'm down on my hands and knees under the desk pushing empty soda bottles and crinkled up papers out between my legs like a dog digging for his bone until I have the picture in my hand. It's stuck to another page. A crinkly page that's not quite tissue paper and not quite paper-paper. I flip it over. It's sheet music. Travis's sheet music for the song "A Few of My Favorite Things"—but not just any version of the song. It's Coltrane's version. The *only* version, according to Travis.

Back when Travis's bed was bunked above mine, my brother would sit on the corner of his bed and practice this song on his alto saxophone four or five hours a day. It got annoying to hear that fool squeak and squawk his way through the song, but he got it straight. Played the song his sophomore year at the spring jazz concert. Penn Griffin School, which happens to be Trane's alma mater.

Trane.

That's what Travis and I call John Coltrane. Well, not just us. Pretty much everyone. In fact, Travis and I were among the last to learn of the obvious nickname. But it didn't stop a college bigwig from one of those fancy universities in the Northeast from noticing Travis and giving him an audition. I think the school was named after some lady in New York. I think Travis told me it was called the Julie Yard School or something like that. I can't remember.

It's also about the same time Travis caught the illness everyone around here seems afraid of catching. I know it's not, like, a mark of the devil or anything because John Coltrane had the same illness and people here in High Point built the man a statue in the center of town. See, people don't often build statues in honor of folks who terrify them. Maybe that's why they're not in a rush to build a monument to my brother, Travis, any time soon. Maybe it's because they see him as a dope addict and nothing else. That's what Dad calls Travis. The dope addict. The kind of person who can't make it through a day without a handful of pills or a bottle of cough syrup or something far, far worse. The same type of addictive personality that almost sunk John Coltrane.

But here, in this version of High Point, I can't worry about statues or sheet rock or tortoise shells. I can't leave my room without my real problems staring me in the face through Dad's green eyes. I can't close my own eyes at night without the flashes reminding me. I can't imprison myself in my room without Travis not being there and without his absence bringing me back to what I know is reality. Our stark reality. That Maynard Wheaton will leave this world. Soon. And he'll do so without his first-born son knowing he's gone.

I need a plan.

A good one.

One that will get me to Philadelphia, the very place where jazz legend, John Coltrane, found the soul within the man. The city that taught Travis's hero how to dig himself up from six feet under and resume his life. The same place I knew, and Travis knew, could be my brother's only rescue.

I dump my school books from my backpack onto the floor and toss a t-shirt or two and a few pairs of jeans in their place along with some underwear and the forty bucks I have left from mowing lawns and washing cars last summer. I grab a pen off my desk and scribble out a quick note to Mom and Dad. Nothing that'll have them on my tail, but enough so they won't think I've simply evaporated off the face of the Earth. "Gone to find something important. Be home soon. Please, don't worry. Love, Cordy."

Travis would be proud.

I fold the note in half and place it on the surface of the desk. A wave of sickening nervousness cascades through my insides.

But I know I *have* to do this.

I swallow hard and inhale a deep breath. I let the breath wash from my lungs, taking with it some of my doubts and fears—at least, for the moment. Then I slip through the bedroom window and slink off into the darkness.

Friend or Foe?

Been standing out here for hours. Since the cars along Main Street stopped buzzing past, and the sidewalks turned to barren stretches of cement, and the hum of the streetlights became the only sound in town. Right here. In the earliest hours of the morning. The ones that open their eyes long before daybreak. In front of the Coltrane statue. Travis always said it was *his* statue. That if he ever did become as famous as the mighty Trane, he'd have one erected next to his hero, on the spot where High Point's legend of bebop, jazz, and soul juts up from the brickwork along Hamilton Street.

I know those kinds of music probably don't amount to much for most, especially in my age group. But for me and Travis, there was nothing better than the brassy voice of a wind instrument. Nothing better than the rat-tat-tat of the hi-hat. Nothing more human than music that came straight from the soul. Sure, you might find a few acts out there today who have the vision, like Trane, to reach deep back into the human experience, grab a handful of beats and rhymes and various rhythms, and blow them wistfully back at us like a palm full of flower petals. But nobody could do it like Trane. And I suspect no one ever will. That's why the man has a statue in his hometown, and that's why Travis and I visited it every chance we got.

Travis and I would grab a carton of chocolate milk after school, and he'd walk me downtown past the furniture showrooms with their Scandinavian throw rugs strewn halfway across the sidewalk, and past the antique shops and the old hotel perched like a sentry atop Main Street, and on down through tobacco-stained alleyways until we were crouched together on the bench beside the statue. His statue. And we'd stare at Trane; Travis with his sax case on the sidewalk, and the legend with a suit jacket draped over his shoulders and the glare of eternity glinting off his bronze-cast face.

They were cool cats, Travis and Trane, even though they couldn't have looked more opposite if they tried: Trane, a smooth mocha brown with an expression that somehow captured and combined all the strain and serenity in the world; and Travis, the scrawny ferret with a ratty goatee and a brown nest of curls tied back in a ponytail. Trane, the man who could step beyond his limits and then draw back before he got lost. And my brother, the kid who never had a sense of self control to begin with. It's why he and Dad always clashed. Why they never combined to form a tune worth hearing. Why the only notes they could ever seem to strike were filled with discord.

Maybe that's why I'm here.

To stand in the shadow of Trane.

Or, at least, in the shadow of his statue.

The one Travis loved so much.

Maybe I didn't make it more than a mile from my house, but I made it to this spot. And sitting here, staring at Trane makes me realize something: I need to drill some sense into people's heads. It's up to me to be the voice of reason. To make sure the people I care about can live or die without regret.

I mean, I guess if I can make it to Philly, I can find Travis. And if I can find Travis, maybe I can help him remember the musician he used to be instead of whatever it is he's become. And, if I can do that, then I might be able to convince him to patch things up with Dad before…well.

Only problem is, once I got out here and smelled the sweet gums in the air and snagged a coffee and a plate of eggs and grits over at Alex's House, the town luncheonette where Travis and I used to hang, I realized I don't even know how I'll get Travis to talk to *me*, let alone Dad. Let's face it, I don't have much of a plan. At least not one that'll get me from High Point to Philadelphia on forty bucks, a sheet of music, and a few tufts of lint at the bottom of my backpack.

I guess that's another reason why I ended up here in front of the statue. Maybe it's because I miss Travis, and this place makes me feel as close to him as I can be from five-hundred miles out. Maybe it's because I'm lost. Totally and hopelessly lost in the dead-center of my hometown. Or maybe I just need a guide. Some advice.

From the legend.

Maybe Trane's been standing here all along, just waiting around cast in bronze so he can pass an important message to one Cordell Wheaton, town nobody, aged sixteen and five eighths. Who knows? Maybe Trane's been the answer all along.

I pull the sheet music from my pocket and trace the folded seams between my thumb and forefinger. My eyes zero in on the brooding eyebrows of the legend, which cast equally brooding shadows over his bronzed-out eyes.

"So…what should I do?" I ask. Just for the hell of it. I mean, it's not like I expect a response. It's not like I've totally lost it.

But then I hear it. In a deep whisper, with just the right amount of rasp to come from an actual, come-to-life statue, I hear, "Do what's in your heart. It's what my daddy would say." Every follicle of buzz-cut tingles with razor sharpness on my head. A jolt rushes down my spine. My jaw locks up and my legs go wobbly, because that's what happens when a giant hunk of bronze on the side of Hamilton Street wakes up and speaks to you.

"W-w-what did you, uh, say?" I squeeze out through clenched teeth. Then I hear a chuckle.

"Ah…didn't mean to startle you," a gentle voice says from behind the statue. He steps into the light. A tangled beard stretches down over the frayed collar of his flannel. His boots are caked in grease. I start to step back, but something changes my mind. He smiles and there's something friendly about him. Granted, he's the only person in High Point awake and roaming the middle of town at this time of morning—which is kind of weird—but his soft, brown eyes and round cheeks tell me I should hear him out.

"Name's Joe Crowley," the old man says. "Guess I'm domestically-challenged, some would say." He tips the brim of a mesh ball cap with the words "Tucker Parts" printed on the front.

"Nice to meet you," I say, trying not to sound freaked out.

"Well…what's a young guy like you doing out here at this time?"

"I'm not exactly sure," I tell him.

"I see," he says. "That why you came here?" I nod. "It's a good place to come when you don't know where you're going. Why I'm here ever' night!" The old man lets out a deep roar of a laugh that is both jolly and fearsome. He laughs so hard his insides might burst out of him at any moment and then he stops suddenly as if there was nothing to laugh at in the first place. "He's a good man. Best there is." He pats the Trane statue on the rump like they're lifelong pals.

"He's my brother's hero," I tell him. "Mine, too."

"You fellas got classy taste. Cause this here's a classy gentleman. These streets right around you made him the man he was. Lots of people don't know that about him. Think he was a Philly cat or some New York cat."

"But he's a High Point cat," I interject, and old man Crowley gets a kick out of it. He bends over at the waist and cackles like a madman. He slaps me on the shoulder as if beating the hell out of someone is the only way to let them know they made you laugh. As if the laughing part wasn't enough of a clue.

"He suuuure was, my friend. Through and through." Old Joe takes a deep breath and diverts his attention from the statue. His eyes fall on me. "You strike me as someone who's lookin' to get on outta town for awhile. Like Trane himself done."

"But he never came back."

"Oh, he never left, son. Just cause someone's not standing in his own backyard don't mean his backyard ain't standing in him. My daddy told me that one too. But I 'spect Mr. Trane understood that better'n anyone."

"But I don't have enough money to get where I need to go."

"Well, if you need to go bad enough, you'll find a way." A sly, crooked smile rises under Joe Crowley's raccoon tail of a beard. As if on cue, a train whistle echoes in the distance. The old man raises a bushy eyebrow and winks. "You have a good one, you hear?" I nod and watch old Joe slog past in his patched-up shirt and grease-stained dickies. Before his shadow melts into the darkness, my new plan is formed.

A *real* plan.

I'll hitchhike. Stowaway. Ride the rails if I have to, like in those silent films where bumbling cops chase clever hobos from boxcar to boxcar. I'll find Travis, and when I do I'll convince him to take the next leg of the journey with me and I'll remind him about the saxophone and his days playing alto in the Penn Griffin marching band. And I'll remind him about Coltrane and tell him how cool it'd be to travel to the birthplace of jazz. To Harlem in the great city of New York and to Birdland, the legendary jazz club where Trane cut his teeth. I'll have my forty bucks saved up from all the hitchhiking and rail-riding and food-begging, and I'll lay it down at the ticket counter for two tickets. One for Travis and one for me. And, after I help Travis find his identity, there's no way he'll choose the pills over coming back home to High Point and to Mom and

Dad. And then I can feel like I've done all I can. That I didn't abandon him. That it wasn't my fault. That I didn't derail Travis's entire life on a sunny afternoon in High Point.

The train whistle draws closer. I follow its call south on Main Street, back past the furniture galleries and the rundown theater that went out of business before I was born, until I arrive at the only train station in town. The only one I've seen in my life.

It's a classic, little station. The kind you'd expect to see under a Christmas tree. The tall, oak doors contain two rectangular windows and a thick, brass door pull that dates back to the early nineteen hundreds. Only problem is both doors are locked. My only option is to search further on down the track.

If you need to go bad enough, you'll find a way.

I stalk down High Street and find a break in the chain link fence meant to guard the lower tracks against pedestrians wandering in from the bordering neighborhoods. In other words, idiots like me. A low rumble builds in the track. A distant beam of light glows up ahead. The chain link rakes at my back. The gravel chafes my chest as I squeeze under and crouch down behind a patch of the deep South's living version of an invisibility cloak: *kudzu*, an invasive vine that swallows up anything that stands still on a roadside for more than a few minutes, including sign posts, telephone poles, rusty fences, abandoned vehicles and, in this case, a terrified human being.

The groan of a train whistle vibrates in the cavity of my chest. Loose pebbles close to the tracks shift and slide across each other until the cannon of another whistle blasts a rush of air through the kudzu. The locomotive rumbles past, leaving a thick, diesel fog and the clanking onslaught of boxcars in its wake.

I emerge from the kudzu and watch the metallic dragon wind its way down the tracks, hauling flatbed train cars stacked with desert-camo military vehicles and wooden crates filled with ammunition. I watch fifty of these things whip past, stacked with enough military might to take over a small country and wonder how many iron serpents slide across tracks under the blanket of dark. I wonder how many train cars a country needs to stack with arms so we can have places like High Point, North Carolina and Birdland Jazz Club and create people like John Coltrane and Travis Wheaton.

But I don't have time to solve the world's geopolitical problems because I see my moment approaching up ahead: a line of covered boxcars.

In every silent film I ever saw where a hobo rides the rails, they always steal a ride in the same exact way. Without fail. The guy gets a running start beside the tracks and waits for the right boxcar to catch up behind him. Then he swings up inside, sits himself down and starts to puff on a soggy cigar. That's it. Easy as pie. Even though I've never learned how to catch a pop-fly and I've never been able to do a single pullup in gym class. I kind of hang there until Mr. Gaylord says, "That's enough, Wheaton."

I'm sure I can do this. I have to. Fact is, I don't have another option.

And I have to act now. Like, *right now*! The boxcars rattle past in a line of thirty sleeping powder kegs. I burst from the kudzu and break into a sprint beside the tracks. The rumble of the iron wheels pulses through my bones. Gravel kicks up like tiny pieces of buckshot, pelting my shins and thighs as the train gains on me. Fast. Like I'm being pulled out to sea on a riptide. My lungs burn with fire. My eyes bounce out of focus with each step.

And then I see it. A rope.

A single strip of twine dangles from the door latch of a boxcar two lengths back. I quicken my pace and feel the train settle into a rhythm with my step. Like a jazz song, all herky jerky and crazy one moment, then smooth and uniform the next. I feel the rope approach over my shoulder, see its shadow, feel the burn in my thighs and the quiver in my step. I reach up and lift off. No more gravel under my feet. I dangle there for a moment, then swing wide and nearly clip a tree branch as the train whips around a curve with the station ahead.

One thing I never learned from the hobo flicks was how to get the boxcar door open, because nothing I do, either push or pull or twist or spin, gets me any closer to safety. Up ahead, the station draws closer. It dawns on me that it might look fishy if a train blew threw with a kid hanging off it like a June apple.

With my hands giving out and a chance I might get smeared across the Main Street Station platform, I think about giving up. I'll just let go of the rope and tumble through the gravel and dust myself off and go home before Mom or Dad know I was gone. Before they ever see my note. But then I think of Travis. And I think of Trane, and I know there's no way I would have been standing in front of that statue if Trane hadn't followed his heart way back when. So, I lift myself on the rope and I heave and spin and swing with all my weight—which isn't much—and, lo and behold, the door slides open. I swing through the open cavity in one motion like a scrawny, Southern Tarzan and I roll to a stop below a stack of wooden crates.

It takes a few seconds to suck the wind back into my lungs and find my bearings in a pitch-black boxcar where the only light shines in when a passing streetlamp winks through the open slider. Almost immediately, I have one of those moments where it feels like I'm not alone. The hairs bristle on the back of my neck. I bounce to my feet so quickly I upend the whole stack of crates and watch them topple to the floor.

"Remind me never to rob a bank with you," says a voice from the darkness. A girl's voice. It's followed by a slight crackle and a single, orange ember that burns in the corner of the boxcar beneath a thick plume of smoke. Cigarette smoke.

"Those things'll kill you," I say to the stranger.

"Oh yeah? That coming from a guy who could barely scale Mt. Caboose?"

She takes another drag of her cigarette and exhales, blowing a huge cloud of smoke in my face. I cough.

"Geez, you're a real iron man. You sure you're not late for snack time in Ms. Crabapple's class about now?"

"Who's Ms. Crabapple?"

"Forget it."

"In fact, who are you?"

"I'm the girl who just saved you from becoming railroad salami for every vulture from here to Charlotte." She flicks a lighter and ignites the wick of a small candle she'd pulled from the breast pocket of her unbuttoned flannel. Now that I can see her face, I can tell she's not a monster. Just an ordinary girl. About my age. Brown hair cut short so her ears poke out. Thin lips that are permanently frozen in a pout.

She sits there and stares at me like she's waiting for some grand introduction. "So, you're not gonna thank me?" she asks. "Did we forget about Southern hospitality up here in the North?"

"The North? Last I checked, the Mason Dixon Line is still in the same place. And thank you for what?"

"I meant North as in North Carolina. I'm from the *real* Carolina. Columbia. And you should thank me for saving your stupid, little life."

"Saving me?"

"Yeah. I mean, you don't think you flexed everything you've got under that size extra small t-shirt and swung this heavy door open all by yourself, do you? Didn't happen. What happened was I saw you wriggling around on that rope like an itty-bitty worm at the end of a hook and I opened the door. With *these* bad boys." She flexes in the candlelight like she's about to wrestle in the main event.

"You really think you're something, don't you?" I say. She shrugs and takes another drag of her smoke.

"Well, I got myself all the way up to…where am I now?"

"High Point, North Carolina."

"Got myself to High Point, North Carolina without a dime in my pocket and it only took two weeks."

"Two weeks?!"

"I know it doesn't sound like much, but it's rough out here. People don't give things away, you know. You *do* know that, right?"

"Of course I know that."

"You gotta watch your back out here or you'll get yourself attacked, abducted, arrested, raped. You name it. You could get your throat cut if you're not careful." She gives me this weird look where her nostrils flare and the skin on the bridge of her nose wrinkles before she continues. "Something tells me you're not really cut out for this. Like, you're out here cause your parents won't buy you a new convertible and you threw a tantrum long enough to get you half a mile outside of town so they can come pick you up in their plush, little Suburban."

She blows a fat smoke ring.

"I know what I'm doing," I reply, flatly.

But my voice cracks when I say it and I'm not even sure if I believe it myself.

"Sure. So where you headed, kid?" she asks.

"My name's not kid. It's Cordy. Cordy Wheaton. And I'm off to Philadelphia."

She snorts and hacks up her entire drag of the cigarette.

"Shit, kid! I hope you packed lunch."

"Maybe you should worry about yourself, Miss Universe."

"It's Emma Rose, actually. Those are my first and middle names. I don't have a last name. Got rid of it."

"What? How do you get rid of a last name?"

"You wake up and realize it reminds you of shit, and then you do what you do to shit. Flush it."

"Makes sense."

"Besides, I'm not going anywhere in particular. Just anywhere that's not where *he* happens to be…and no, I don't want to talk about him."

"Good. Cause I never asked you."

"Good. Well…have a pleasant trip to Philadelphia."

"Have a pleasant trip to nowhere in particular."

"I plan to."

"Good."

That's when the boxcar ride starts to seem like a bad idea. That's when we section ourselves off from each other between two stacks of crates, and sit in complete silence, with only the rat-tat-tat of the train cars on the track to break the monotony.

My phone vibrates as I navigate through the three o'clock riptide of Penn Griffin students. It's a message from Travis:

Meet me @ the spot. Got a surprise.

The "spot" was the Trane statue. The only place we ever met. The surprise? I can only guess, so I take the long walk downtown and cut up a side street lined with bungalows and tulip poplars. A lone car inches up the lane, but otherwise the street is quiet. The way I like it. Just the single car.

That's when the engine roars and there's a squeal of rubber on asphalt.

Adrenaline rushes from my head to my toes. The car speeds up beside me. Its brakes screech and my legs go numb. A tinted-black window winds open and a man in a leather jacket smiles at me.

"Hey! You know how to get to Lexington Avenue?"

My jaw relaxes. I can breathe again. "You're on it," I say, relieved to be giving basic directions instead of being kidnapped.

"Hmmm." The man's eyes are red around the edges and glazed over. His eyelids are heavy and swollen.

I continue up the street in the direction of Travis's spot. The lone car revs its engine and rolls a few more feet before the brakes click down on the wheels again.

"Say, kid?" I turn around. "You the preacher's boy? Old Maynard Wheaton?"

"He's not a preacher," I say. "He just preaches sometimes."

I barely get the words out before the car door swings open and he's on top of me with all of his weight, whiskey vapors wafting from every pore. I try to kick and swing and scratch, but his forearm locks down on my neck. The wiry hairs on the back of my head scrape the sidewalk.

A car door slams shut and a fresh set of footsteps approach.

I'm choking. Almost blacked out. "Help!" I scream. "Hel—"

"Shut up!" the stubble-faced man shouts. He and his associate scoop me off the ground and rush me to the car.

"Help!" I manage once more, but the two assailants toss me in the trunk. My hip collides with the spare tire and the wind gets all trapped in my chest.

The last thing I see before total darkness is a row of rings approaching my face and then...

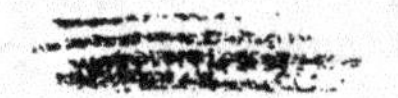

Homeward Bound?

"Kid! Wake up!"

I'm drenched in sweat and being shaken halfway to hell by a teenage stowaway.

Kid? Again? Just who the hell does she think she is?

The candle sputters in the corner of the boxcar. It casts waves of dim light off the angled surfaces of corrugated metal. The wooden crates are stacked around me to form a private nook, but my privacy has been invaded by Emma Rose—no last name—who hovers over me with an expression of pure shock on her face.

"What do *you* want?" is the first thing that comes to my mind.

"Talk about rude awakenings," she says. "Man, you really have something against saying 'thank you.'"

"Ugh. That again? What could I have to thank you for this time? I was asleep."

"For starters, I'm pretty sure I saved you from some pretty serious Freddy Krueger shit…and then there's the whole incident where you were literally dangling by a thread before I strapped the old cape on and did what I do."

"What are you talking about?"

"Let's see. You…very stupid. Hang from train on tiny rope. Me… very smart. Save stupid monkey hanging from vine."

"No. I mean the Freddy Krueger stuff."

"Oh. That. Well, you were screaming like a stuck hog. Nearly made my heart stop because I'm not in the mood to get snatched by rail patrol."

"Rail patrol? That's not a thing."

"Oh, it's a thing. Especially on these military loads."

"I don't believe you."

"That's your choice, rookie. Just don't go thinking any of these train conductors want to carry extra cargo cause, believe me, they do not."

I unzip my backpack and pretend to search for something among the three or four articles of clothing I packed. Anything to get me out of a conversation with this know-it-all who thinks she has the right to call me "rookie" after spending a grand total of two weeks on the road.

Emma Rose lets out a sigh of disgust and starts back to her corner of the boxcar. But then she stops and stares at me and I smell the gears heating up in her head.

"So," she says with a smirk smeared across her face, "care to share what had you screaming in your sleep like some horror queen?"

I stare at her good and hard and with zero change of expression for ten long seconds before she simply says, "Well?"

"No!" I say. Flat out. Just like that, which should have been enough. But nothing seems to be enough for Emma Rose, no last name.

"So, you're afraid to tell a total stranger who you'll never meet again for the rest of your life what almost made you soil your shorts in your sleep?"

"I didn't come close to soiling anything. It was just a stupid dream. That's all."

She moves in close and sits cross-legged on the floor beside me as if I have some sick desire to continue the conversation.

"First time you had the dream?" she asks.

I release my own strategic sigh of annoyance.

"I said it was nothing. Can't you just leave it?" My voice echoes back off the metallic walls.

"I'll take that as a no."

I shoot daggers at Emma Rose until she gets the message that my dreams are off-limits. She decides to change the subject, although it's not much better of an option. "So, what's got you running then, rook?" she asks in this bright, gleeful voice you'd expect to hear from a crazed circus clown.

"Who says I'm running?" I reply.

"On the road, everybody's running from something," Emma Rose says. "For me, it's my male parental unit. I refuse to call him Father anymore. I made that promise the night I left."

"Why would anyone run from their own father?"

"First of all: parental unit. Second, he's a monster. That's the only way to describe it."

"What could he have done to make you take a hacksaw to your last name?"

"You want the short version or the long, agonizing one?"

I think about asking for the long, agonizing version, but something about the quiver in Emma Rose's voice and the look of defiance in her eyes tells me I'd be wise not to.

"Let's go with the short one," I say.

Without pause, Emma Rose slides her flannel and her t-shirt down off her shoulders to reveal a network of bruises that is so deep and painful looking it might contain every color in the rainbow.

"That's the short of it," she says bluntly. "The long of it is much more sinister and disgusting than a few bruises."

Emma Rose pulls the shirt back over her shoulder. She winces and, for the first time since she saved my life, I can see she's not made of sheet metal like the four walls of this boxcar. She's out here on the road, like me, because she's completely destructible and she's desperate not to get destroyed. Like me, she knows her flight might be the only way to find normal.

"Your turn," she says. I swear, this girl never lets up. "I broke the ice. It's only fair." I give her my jagged look again, but this time it gets me nowhere. "Come on. What are you running from, Cordy Wheaton?"

After what Emma Rose had just shared, I feel obligated to tell her my story.

"I'm not running from anything. More like *to* something," I tell her. "To my brother, Travis. He needs to clean up his act and my father—" but that's as far as I get before we're shaken back to reality by the clomp of boots outside on the metal gangway.

Emma Rose scrambles to her side of the car and crouches behind the crates. I do the same on my side, as Emma Rose blows out the candle and blankets us in darkness.

The footsteps are right outside the door and we're on the other side of a few sheets of metal like a couple of trapped rats. The latch on the door rattles. Then it slides open. The sharp beam of a flashlight floods the boxcar. My eyes go blurry for a second and I hear it again. Like an echo that crawls to me from some far-off place. A voice:

Cordy?

Cordy?

Can you see this?

Can you follow it with your eyes?

Can you...

What the hell? I shake my head and my vision clears. The patrolman's flashlight assaults my eyeballs as I squeeze in between a crate and the wall, hold my breath, and pray he sucks at his job and decides to catch a smoke in the next car.

But he doesn't suck at his job. He whips his flashlight around and moves further into the boxcar. Toward me. There's nothing I can do but move in the opposite direction, keeping a stack of crates between myself and the patrolman, trying not to make a false move as the patrolman sweeps his light from left to right:

Cordy?

Can you see *this light?*

Can you move *your eyes?*

Left to right...

I shake off the fog again and look up at the patrolman just as he surveys his surroundings until—CRACK!

I gasp and try to move my leg, but the heel of my sneaker is jammed between two slats in a wooden crate. The patrolman's light swirls around the boxcar as he moves in on the sound. I'm trapped. I think about what it will be like to have Mom and Dad spring me from some police station in one of the tiny burgs surrounding my hometown. But there's another loud crash. A whole row of wooden crates spills over me. The patrolman grunts. The flashlight smacks the metal floor and sparks out:

Cordy?

CORDY!!

He's just not ready yet...

I'm pretty damn freaked out now as I shake the blur from my vision and the echoey voice trails off, but I have no time to make sense of it because I'm trapped under the crates. The patrolman is two steps away and moving in.

But then I see a dark form flash across the outside light as it pours through the sliding door and, with ultra ninja quickness, the form scuffles up the door frame and lifts off to the roof of the boxcar. The patrolman catches sight of the dark form and tromps off through the sliding door in hot pursuit. I hear two sets of footsteps clomp their way overhead. Then silence. The ordinary chug-a-lug cadence of the locomotive some fifty cars ahead. Thank God for Emma Rose, though I expect she'll claim she saved my life a third time after this.

I crawl out from under the mountain of overturned crates and lift my backpack from the rubble. There's something small and square and made of leather leaning against the side of my sneaker. I reach down and pick it up. It's a wallet, probably the missing remnants from a certain train inspector's back pocket that slipped out with the same kind of quickness as Emma Rose when the poor fool tried to chase her into eternity.

I flip the wallet open and squint my eyes to make out a fuzzy image of a man with a bushy beard and soft, sympathetic eyes. Officer Harrison Smith from Colfax, North Carolina. The goofy grin he wears in his driver's license photo makes him look about as dangerous as a butterfly floating on the breeze. I might even feel kind of sorry for him if he didn't just try to round me up and haul me off to the damn railway prison, if that even exists.

I run my fingers a bit further through his personal items. A short stack of wallet-sized photos are contained in its plastic sheath. A crinkled stack of old receipts hang limply from the space where the money is supposed to sit. There's not a single greenback inside, but the leather slots are piled thick with plastic. At least half a dozen credit cards. Cards that could get me to Travis and then to Birdland with the magic of a magnetized strip.

A droplet of sweat rolls down the side of my face. The wallet shakes in my unsteady hand. I've never stolen a single thing in my life, but I've also never been a stowaway on a militarized train headed to nowhere. So I break the mold. I slide a single card out of its slot. Just one. I stare at the name, "Harrison J. Smith" at the bottom of the treasure and I take a deep breath because I'm about to do the worst thing I've ever done in my life. Well, second worst, next to sending my brother off the tracks.

I slide the card in the pocket of my jeans and wipe the sweat off my face. It feels wrong, but I know it's just an insurance policy. One that I'll only use if necessary. I toss the rest of the wallet with everything else intact on the floor of the train car, exactly where I'd found it. Then I unzip my bag and reach inside for my phone. My lifeline. There are seven text messages waiting for me, probably more than I've received in the life of the phone combined. The first one is from Mom:

Saw your note. Where are you? We're worried.

I don't bother to scroll through the rest. I assume they get progressively worse and more alarmed, and I realize something. Maybe Emma Rose, no last name, helped me realize—though I'd never give her the satisfaction of knowing it, should our paths cross again—I'm not cut out for the road. I admit it. Maybe I *am* too much of a rookie to finish what I started. Maybe I'm just a boring kid from High Point, North Carolina and there's nothing in the world I can do to change the course of Travis's life or his relationship with Dad. Maybe I am best off hiding away in my bedroom. Cuddled up inside my shell, safe and sound.

I slip my phone inside the pocket of my jeans and inch my way to the doorway. The toes of my Chucks hang over the edge. The ground races past below. I take a deep breath, watch the longleaf pines and the kudzu whip past along the tracks, feel revolt rise up in my stomach. I push it down and wait for the train to slow around a curve in the treeline and begin its labored, agonizing slog up a steep incline in the tracks. That's when I know it's now or never. That's when I close my eyes. Launch off into fresh, country air, suspended in nothingness for what feels like eternity. The iron spokes of the train's wheels whir in the background and the cicadas buzz in the undergrowth.

Everything happens in slow motion.

Until I crash down, and razor-sharp particles of gravel pierce the skin on both knees before my vision turns into a living kaleidoscope: sky, then trees, then ground, then train, then sky again. I lose count after about ten, awkward tumbles from the track to the low point of a shallow ravine.

I don't move, just lie there on my stomach and wiggle my fingers and toes and feel the warm trickle of blood flow from every hard angle on my body and let my lungs inhale and exhale until I slowly and painfully rise up on all fours. And then on two knees. And then to my feet.

I have no idea where I am. Hopped the train in High Point. Been riding for God-knows-how-long. Maybe a couple of hours? Maybe less? All I know is I can call my parents. They'll be pissed, but they'll come and pick me up and this whole stupid ordeal will be over. Without Travis, but with only a few real bumps and bruises.

I reach into my pocket for my phone. It's gone. I check my other pocket. Nothing but the thin piece of plastic I lifted from the train inspector's fallen wallet. I get a weird feeling in my stomach, but I remind myself the phone has to be lying around somewhere. I start my search, using a dead branch to hack my way around the kudzu patches until I see the trademark shine of a touch screen and reach down to grab my saviour. Only my saviour needs a whole lot more saving than me. It's obliterated. The screen is a total spider web. A jagged crack runs through the back of the case and, worst of all, the power button is unresponsive.

I'm screwed.

No way to call home.

No way to get home.

And no clue how far I am from home.

I look to the top of the ravine and see the headlights of a passing car on the highway through the blur of my tears. It's my only real choice. So I begin my hike, limping up the wooded embankment to civilization.

I hope this road points me home.

Rising Sun

I push to the top of the hill, through waist-high brush and spider webs that could swallow a grown man's head. My arms are blotched in dried blood and streaks of Southern, red clay. A legion of mosquito bites rise up through a layer of filth.

I throw one leg over the guard rail and then the other. There's nothing here but me and a single, yellow line between two rivers of black. The reflective hashmark strips vanish into the darkness. A lone road marker pokes up from the guard rail and announces "43.7." That's it. Not even the suggestion of a passing car in the distance. All I can do is walk and think and listen to the scuffling of my Chucks on the blacktop.

If Travis were here he'd know how to keep my mind moving in the right direction. He'd know how to stop me from being so nervous I want to puke. He'd tell me to look at the stars and create my own constellations in the sky. That's something we'd do in High Point when school was out for summer. We'd climb out our window and up to the roof and lie flat on the shingles. I'd find weird stuff every time, like the outline of an interstellar urinal or a bag of alien potato chips. Travis would talk me into creating a myth out of my made-up constellations like they did back in ancient Greece. Thanks to Spud Murphy, I'm pretty sure everyone within a hundred mile radius of my house is pretty aware of my obsession with Greek mythology by now, but it was those nights up on the roof with Travis that probably cranked my ignition for the stuff of lore. I'm talking about Plato and Socrates. I'm talking Homer and *The Odyssey*. I'm talking the original gangstas of studying humanity. Those old cats from ancient Greece spent their entire lives trying to figure out what's with all this living and dying stuff thousands of years before High Point appeared on the map. And I happen to think that's pretty cool. At one time, far in the past, Travis did too. We even used to have a massive poster hanging above our bunk beds of the hideous monster, Medusa, with a row of angry snakes striking out at the viewer from under the creature's crown of gold. I guess that's why he'd take me up to the roof. To pass along the knowledge, or maybe just to freak me out. Whatever. It worked.

We'd head up to our rooftop conservatory, and I'd make up some lame constellation story that didn't sound anything like *The Odyssey* or even make sense, and then I'd see Travis's eyes roll back in his head and the next thing I'd know, Travis would save the day with something like, "I think I see Darth Vader's clarinet up there." He'd then proceed to tell me the story of John "Skywalker" Coltrane's saxophone-playing and how it destroyed the Death Star through the sheer force of music. Which was stupid as hell, but it made us laugh and it was cool because me and Travis, we always had Trane—even after Travis grew out of his mythology phase and ripped the Medusa poster down the summer before he entered high school.

But tonight, there's no music. No Travis. Only the chirping of crickets and a low hum in the distance. A car? Maybe a truck? Maybe my only chance. Twin headlights flash up ahead. A giant semi barrels toward me. All I can do is stand there and swing my arms like a windmill and hope whoever's driving the rig is awake, alert, and willing to take on a passenger.

I stand on the solid, white line like a flesh-covered statue. The roar of the road builds in my chest. The semi approaches but does not slow down. The headlights blind me and my ears approach explosion levels as the WAAAAAaaaarrrUUMMM! erupts from the horn and the truck barrels past. My legs buckle. I dive headlong for the safety of the road's shoulder.

The truck lurches and slides to a stop about fifty yards down the road. The driver pulls the truck into the emergency lane and the door of the cab swings open. He hops straight down to the road from his seat in one heroic swoop. I'm shocked halfway to hell with my chin on the pavement and a jagged collection of pebbles pressed into the side of my face.

Before I can catch my breath, the driver is already hovering over me as I lie there, stunned and motionless, having just had an eighteen-wheeler barrel past with only the width of a Kraft single between me and certain death.

"Hey! You alright?" he shouts.

He drops to one knee and clamps his hands down on both of my shoulders. There's a sense of desperation in his voice. His eyes bulge from their sockets and the whites glow against the dark curtain of night. For a split second, with the moon glowing off the angles of his cheekbones and a slight quiver trembling his thin lips, I almost think it's Travis staring down at me. But then I blink and the image is gone. He's just some guy with a shock of pitch-black hair stretching out from under a beanie cap like a million tiny tentacles. But that doesn't stop him from taking hold of the sleeves of my t-shirt and hoisting me to my feet like he's known me all my life.

"Dude! You okay?! Tell me you're still alive!" he pleads, giving me a rough shake. "Come on! Say something!"

The scent of pine on the roadside hits my nostrils and snaps me back to reality.

"Yeah, I'm…I'm fine!" I push out through terrified lips.

We stare at each other, dumbstruck—me, the scrawny slice of white toast with a mask of freckles and the driver, a tall and ghostly-looking specter with dark, bushy eyebrows, a network of metal hoops and gauges punched through both earlobes, and a sinister-looking tattoo on his forearm.

"Man, you almost gave me a heart attack" the driver groans. He doubles over and fights for air. "What the hell are you doing out here in the middle of nowhere at this hour of the morning?"

"Running," I tell him. I feel my freckles turn into a single, red blotch on my face when I say it. Like, I'm about to face the shame I deserve for my reckless decision. But the shame never comes.

"Everybody's running," he says. "I asked, what the hell are you doing out here on the side of a damn truck route? You got some kind of death wish? Cause nobody's running anywhere when they're dead. You got me?"

"Yeah…I got you," I say, and the phrase rolls off my tongue sort of funny, as if I'd just tried to impersonate a famous actor. And it makes the driver laugh a little. It makes me laugh a little too. And suddenly we're both at ease, like he'd never almost flattened me with his truck on the side of a highway.

"Alekos Winchester" he says, offering his hand. "Not the name I was born with, but it's the one I go by now, although pretty much everybody calls me Cowbird on the CB and at the truck stops. I don't mind if you do the same."

"I'm Cordell. Cordell Wheaton. But everyone…well, my folks call me Cordy."

"Hmmm. So where are you headed, Cordell 'Cordy' Wheaton?"

"Well, I'm done running," I tell him. "My next destination is home."

"Home? I can't say that I ever came across a hitchhiker that was trying to run away back home. I guess you see something new every day out here on the road."

"Well, my plan was to run to Philadelphia, but things got out of control on the train and I ended up here." He smiles and shakes his head, but not in a way that says, "What an idiot!" More like in a way that says, "Yeah…I got you."

"Philly's a pretty far stretch from…where'd you say you're from?"

"High Point. In North Carolina."

Cowbird laughs so hard he nearly blows me out of my shoes, all bent over and gasping for air between fits.

"Did I hear you say High Point?"

"Yes."

Another short burst of laughter.

"Dude, where do you think you are now?"

The laughter goes on for a few seconds before Cowbird realizes I'm not laughing with him. I turn and start to walk away.

"Hey!"

I don't respond.

"Hey, kid! Cordy! C'mon, man, I'm just screwin' with you!"

I keep walking until I hear footsteps close in on me and his icy fingers press down on top of my shoulders.

"What's your plan, kid? To walk off into the dark in the middle of nowhere?" I turn to face him.

"Look. I don't know how to tell you this and hold back a laugh at the same time, but we're only an hour away from High Point. This is Mt. Airy."

My ears heat up and my face gets all blotchy because, well, I'm a dumbass. I spent an entire night. Almost ended up as squirrel meat on the highway. Traveled the equivalent of two or three burgs from my own town.

Pathetic.

It makes me feel stupid for thinking Emma Rose was a loser for only traveling through one state in two weeks. But I can't worry about that because, as I know it, my journey is over. I'm a failure before I started. All I want is to do is curl up under my covers and mindlessly scroll through the social media feed on my laptop for the next few months.

"You know," Cowbird says, "I'm headed in that direction. Due East. Out to New Bern on the coast. I can make room in the cab if you promise not to get car sick on me."

"You'd drive me to High Point?"

"If that's where you're running to," he says. "And, as long as you're cool with the no puking thing. Nobody sets foot inside my rig without agreeing to that."

On one hand, I'm about to accept a ride with a multi-pierced, tattooed truck driver who almost turned me into roadkill. On the other, I dove headfirst out of a moving train, hiked up a kudzu mountain, and shattered my only means of communication into a million, tiny fragments before I got fifty miles from my doorstep. All signs point to heading straight back to said doorstep. If Cowbird is my only means of flight from the middle of nowhere to somewhere I can eat, sleep, and use the bathroom without a million fireflies watching, so be it.

"Thanks!" I say "That'd be great."

"Alright! Well, welcome aboard, Cordell 'Cordy' Wheaton."

I've never been in a Mack truck. Watching movies like *Smokey and the Bandit* and *Convoy* gave me an outdated view on life inside the cockpit, because where I thought there'd be a giant gearshift, a few dials, and a carton or two of smokes, was something more out of a futuristic space vehicle.

"You traveling to the moon or something?" I ask after panning left to right and seeing nothing but levers and switches and dials from wall to wall.

"No shit," Cowbird says. "First time I stepped in one of these rigs I thought I'd been recruited by NASA." He cranks the starter and the rig rumbles to life. He stomps on the clutch, jiggles the gearshift in a thousand different directions, and we're off, winding through the Carolina woods, up and down hills and around sharp curves where jagged cliff face juts out from beneath vegetation and reveals steep drop-offs into no-man's land. All of this with the combined weight of two households trailing behind us while Cowbird holds casual conversation with me like a soccer mom driving her flock to practice in her sensible hatchback.

"So, are you gonna tell me your story?" he asks.

"I'm Cordy Wheaton," I say, "and…well, I don't really have a story."

"Everybody has a story to tell," Cowbird replies. "I guess you just haven't been on the road long enough to find the right words."

"I doubt it. Most people in High Point don't know I exist or if they do, they go out of their way to avoid me. They're not interested in my story."

"Is that why you're out here?"

"No."

"That's why I'm out here. On the road every night hauling milk cartons or sofas or stockpiles of beer that'd flood the street in alcohol for weeks if I ever decided to jacknife this thing."

He takes both hands off the wheel and lets the rig drift along on its own. My grip tightens on the armrest. The wheels hit the rumble strip on the shoulder and the density of the road buzzes up through the seats and fizzes in my spine before Cowbird grabs the wheel and eases us back in the lane. "But I'd never do that to Sally. That's what I call her," he says. He slaps a flat hand on the seat as if it somehow represented the truck's metaphysical shoulder. "Shotgun Sally," he whispers to himself. "You gonna ask me why we call her 'shotgun'?"

"I wasn't gonna, but—"

"We call her 'shotgun' because there's always someone riding shotgun here in the cab. Like you."

I stare at him, motionless.

"It's not a clever name, but I'm sort of a magnet for hitchers. Built a reputation. Guess I don't have the heart to leave a fellow traveler behind."

"Did you also build a reputation for vehicular manslaughter?" I ask, because sometimes I like to give people the business. "Cause you were about a snail's ass from adding to your rep back there."

As soon as I say it, I wish I could swallow up every last syllable.

Cowbird stomps on the brakes. There's a low whine and the next thing I know, old Sally skids to a stop beside the rumble strips. Cowbird's grey eyes are wide as moons.

"Get out, kid. You can walk home," he says in pure monotone.

A watery sting builds behind my eyes. I try to open my mouth, but Cowbird cuts me off with a violent, "Go on! NOW!"

I reach for the door and prepare to launch myself back out into the darkness, and then I hear it. First, a slight squeal like someone squeezed air from the mouth of a balloon. Then complete and outright laughter. Harder than before.

"Dude! You really think I'd do that to you?"

My teeth chatter. I'm shaking and my kneecaps start to rattle off the door panel, so he gets my answer without me saying a word.

"If there's one thing Alekos Katopodi Winchester is good at besides driving trucks, it's busting people's chops!"

He pulls the truck back onto the highway and we're off, this time in silence because I'm not sure I like the kind of jokes this guy pulls. I lean back and watch the road signs whip past the passenger window and notice how they now feature the names of towns I recognize: Winston-Salem, Union Cross, Colfax. And I become painfully aware of how the silence in the cab, those few feet of tension between myself and Cowbird, has grown palpably awkward.

After what feels like an eternity, Cowbird breaks the silence. "Look, I'm trying to get you to lighten up, kid. To feel emotion. Cause you strike me as someone who doesn't exactly get outside his shell too often."

"The tortoise shell," I whisper without realizing I'd said it out loud.

"Could be a tortoise," he says, "or a clam. Doesn't really matter. What I'm saying is—"

"I'm trapped in Plato's cave and you think scaring the shit out of me is the best way to set me free."

"Plato's what?"

"His cave."

"Wait. Are you into that philosophy shit? Like ancient times and all that stuff?"

I look at him funny because I'm not sure how to respond. I mean, first of all, I don't know how having the name Alekos doesn't put your squarely in the middle of a huge pile of that philosophy shit. Second of all, I don't remember a time when I wasn't into that philosophy shit, as Cowbird put it.

"We're Americans," I begin. "We're lucky to live in the greatest country on Earth. But it's not like we invented the wheel. We borrowed most of our best shit from other times, other cultures. As far as I can tell, our most important ones—the ideals that form our identity—can be traced back to the birthplaces of democracy. Ancient Greece and Rome and the Egyptians. Maybe that's what draws me in." Somewhere between the "inventing the wheel" line and the "birthplace of democracy" line, I realize I'm not just feeding Cowbird a bright, shiny object. I'm coming to an understanding about who I am and why I'm like this.

He senses I'm ready to clam up again if he continues busting, so he says, "I guess that's cool. But what does it have to do with a cave?"

I take a deep breath because when I get a chance to talk about something I really know, or at least I *think* I know about, I like to make sure I'm accurate as hell. Accuracy takes a lot of breath you didn't know you had. Especially when you have no friends and the only people who keep you company most nights are the ancient Greek dudes staring back at you from the pages of the books you signed out at High Point Library.

"Plato's cave," I begin, "is an allegorical scenario in which Plato theorizes that if a group of individuals were placed inside a cave with only the light of a fire raging behind their backs and a wall upon which puppeteers can project the shadows of their puppets on the walls in front of these individuals—"

"Wait, wait, wait," Cowbird interrupts. "Dude, you're gonna have to slow things down. Don't go thinking I'm some kind of philosophy nerd like you just because my name happens to be Alekos." I nod. "Let me get this straight. You got a bunch of people locked in some cave, right?"

"Right."

"They have a fire burning behind them and a wall with some puppet master dudes on it?"

"They're not necessarily puppet masters, but—"

"Can the people see the puppeteers?"

"No. They can only stare at the blank wall in the cave."

"So what they see on the wall is a reflection of the shadows from those puppet guys messing with their puppets before the fire?"

"Exactly. Like when you make rabbit ears on the wall with a flashlight." Cowbird thinks about it as he pushes the beanie back a bit on his head to reveal another tangled shock of jet-black hair.

"OK. Yeah. So, what's the point? They see a shitty puppet show?"

"No. They see all they can see of reality. Because they're trapped in a cave. They make judgements about their world based on what their brains can gather through their sense—"

"So it's all about the shapes on the wall. They don't know life's going on without them outside the cave."

"Right! You got it," I say as the sign for Kernersville whips past. One more exit until I'm back in my own bed with the sun rising on the horizon. With any luck, I can convince Mom and Dad I didn't answer my phone because I was busy and then I'll worry about expanding the lie as I go. It's not the best strategy, but it's all I've got.

"You know," Cowbird says, "I think you're right about the cave thing. It kind of reminds me of growing up in Boone looking like this."

"Like what?" I ask.

"Like some kind of creep off the screen of your favorite horror flick, with my dyed-black hair, my tattoos and my band t-shirts…Christian Death…Napalm Death…And You Will Know Us By The Trail of Dead. Whatever I could wear that would scare the ever-loving shit out of people. And…I don't know…maybe there was a time in my life where I fixated on death a little bit too much. But whatever. You get the picture!" He takes one hand off the wheel and gives me this goofy thumbs up that makes him look like a cartoon character for a second, but also helps me see the true Cowbird. The same one from Boone who'd been hiding himself under that arsenal of death-themed tees. "Cordy, I'm gonna tell you one thing and I hope it turns out to be the reason you started this journey. Maybe why you ended it early too."

"Enlighten me," I grumble. I get a satisfied chuckle out of Cowbird this time instead of a finger pointing me out the door in the middle of a dark highway.

"When it started to feel like everyone around me believed I was this, that, or anything other than the young man I am, I took your advice."

"I never gave you advice."

"You said to leave the cave."

"I never said that."

"But Plato. That dude said it. I mean nobody's gonna lock people up in a cave without letting them out at some point."

"It was a theory…but, yeah, he'd let them out. Eventually."

"And then what? They'd lose their damn minds?"

I think about this statement for a second. I mean, I don't know. I left my cave for a few moments tonight and things wound up being semi-okay. Like, not perfect by any means, but I *can* say I have a sliver of my sanity intact.

"They'd adapt," I say. "It'd be weird at first, but I think it would be a relief to know life isn't a bunch of odd shapes and squiggly images on a wall."

"That's exactly why I left Boone," Cowbird says. "Why I travel the nation with Sally, meeting people who think I'm weird as hell." He stares purposely in my direction. "But also lots of people who show me not everyone is the same." His stare melts into a sly smile.

The rig slows down under the weight of Cowbird's crusty, black construction boots and the gears shift lower on the column as he moves old Sally into the right lane. In the distance, I can make out the words High Point in faint, white lettering across a green sign. The morning's first light peaks over the asphalt line on the horizon.

"Sometimes," Cowbird says, "you gotta think about whatever brought you out here in the first place. I don't know what that is for you, but it had to mean something if it scared you out of the cave."

The engine purrs and the needle on the speedometer tips back on the dial as the exit approaches. "Sometimes you make it to the crossroads and you gotta decide," Cowbird says. "Sometimes you let the tide take you where it may. Sometimes—"

And in the moment, in a flash of fear and anger at Travis for having me out here in the first place, and sheer panic at seeing the green exit sign grow larger on the right hand side and an open stretch of road grow smaller on the left, and outright desolation at knowing I'm about to dive right back inside the cave from whence I sprang, the words fumble over my lips without me having the slightest control over them.

"How long do you think you can you put up with me, Mr. Alekos Katopodi Winchester?"

"It's Cowbird," he says with a broad, satisfied grin washing over his lips. "And I can take you as far as the coast. It's a straight shot north to Philly from there. As long as you think you've got what it takes to live outside of that cave you were talking about."

I don't respond, and Cowbird takes a deep, agitated breath. "Cordy, I'm asking if you think what you're trying to find is important enough to put your life in danger. To make your parents worry. To get you in more trouble than you'd encounter in a thousand of your so-called *dreams*."

I turn and look at Cowbird. His pale forehead glistens in the early morning sunlight that now filters through Sally's windshield. His thick eyebrows climb up his face and perch themselves near the hemline of his beanie and his eyes are wide with expectation. I exhale and realize I've been holding my breath for the past half-mile.

"What I'm trying to find," I say in a shaky whisper, "may be the most important thing in the world to me."

A thin smile spreads across Cowbird's lips. He stomps hard on the gas pedal, and I watch the words High Point disintegrate in the side view mirror as Shotgun Sally rumbles over a ribbon of highway headed straight for the rising sun.

Black plastic on the windows. Fingers of murky light fight through a tear along the bottom corner. The usual contents of a warehouse: a work-worn, concrete floor surrounded by cheap, metal walls. A moldy row of ceiling tiles. An echoey drip-drip that's bounced around my skull since my eyes popped open. I try to scream through the rag. I struggle with the ropes until my wrists go raw and bloody.

I hear a voice. "I don't give a shit!" Low. Angry. Snarling.

Another one. "Don't worry. He'll get the money." Screechy. Unsure. Wavering.

A chain jangles. A droplet of sweat rolls down my face. The door explodes open. A tall figure hovers in the threshold. Dressed in black. A knit cap on his head.

He takes two steps, conceals something behind his back. The light twinkles off the object. Metallic. Cylindrical. One more step and he reveals the object. Places one gloved hand on the stock. The other on the trigger.

There's a SNAP! and a POP! as the shotgun is cocked. Held at attention. A warm, wet sensation moves down my legs. Spreads through the fibers of my pants and...

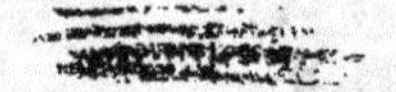

Glue

"Cordy! Dude!"

My eyes flap open. I'm in the cab of old Sally. The sun hangs high above the asphalt, and its rays stare at me through the windshield and make me squint. But I can still see Cowbird. He has one eye on the road and one super-annoyed eye, with a thick eyebrow perched way up in the stratosphere of his forehead, trained on me. "You gonna stop the spill or ruin my seats?"

My pants are soaking wet and it kind of burns a little. The whole cab smells like coffee. Cowbird bought it for us at a rest stop near Greensboro and said, "This will keep us alert. Stronger than motor oil." But, it wasn't strong enough to stop me from seeing them again. The same scenes that have haunted me every night since Travis left.

I grab the wad of paper towels out of Cowbird's hand and mop the spillage from my pants, the seats, and the floor of the cab.

"I'm so sorry, Cowbird. How long was I out?" I ask when Cowbird's grimace drops from his lips and he looks semi-satisfied with my housecleaning skills.

"Not long. I didn't know you were out cold until the river started flowing."

"Sorry," I repeat.

"Don't worry. As long as you don't permanently damage Sally, all is forgiven. I mean, I should have known you were passed out when you started breathing heavy. Sounded like you were running from something up in that gourd of yours."

Cowbird takes one hand off the wheel and points at my head. I don't know what to say so I pretend to sip coffee from an empty cup. Cowbird's trick eyebrow pops up a few notches and I know I'm not getting out of this without a real answer.

"Just a dream," I say.

"A dream?"

Cowbird can smell the bullshit from a mile away, but it's not like I understand the dreams enough to tell him anything of value.

"It's nothing," I say. "For real."

"I know that kind of nothing. It's the kind of nothing that wakes you up in a cold sweat in the middle of the night." The road sign for Burlington whips past us on the shoulder, as Cowbird continues. "I know you don't want to rehash the details. I'm all too familiar with that kind of shit. I remember. And I wouldn't want to share none of it with you or anyone."

"What are you talking about?" I say, as if I don't already know.

All that does is make Cowbird's face soften and then the creepy young man straight from the reels of a horror film, with his scary tattoos and a trillion piercings poking holes through his ears takes on a weird, mother hen vibe. "Cordy. Come on, man. You don't have to spread any bullshit around me."

"They're just dreams."

"Cordy."

"How do you know? I mean, how *could* you know?"

"Take one look at me, Cordy. I've been places. You think a misfit like me doesn't pick up a few ghosts along the way? I spent half my childhood getting shuttled around the state in the foster program. I didn't sleep through a full night until I was twenty years old."

"What happened to your parents?"

"They were immigrants. Came over here from Greece with the clothes on their backs and not much else, but somehow they managed to live out their dreams. They opened a restaurant down on the coast, near Wrightsville Beach. And they had it running pretty well until Alekos came along and money started getting tight. I don't remember any of this, of course, but I do remember the fire. Mostly because I've seen the newspaper clippings and because I remember living the rest of my life without them."

"You mean...they didn't make it out?" I ask, not really knowing what else to say.

"From what I read, it happened pretty late one night after they'd sent the kitchen staff home. I guess they were closing out registers or refilling ketchup bottles or doing any one of the generic tasks you'd have to do if you were new to your country and low on cash and you had a new baby at home with a sitter you had to pay."

"What happened to them?" I ask, not sure I really want to know the final answer.

Cowbird's lips tremble a little. He takes a deep breath and slowly exhales before responding. "There was a gas leak," he says gravely. "The place disappeared in a flash. The only thing left for the newspapers to photograph was the sign that had hung over the front door...Aristotle's. That's what they named it."

My eyes dart over to Cowbird as soon as he says the name and he's already shaking his head at me before I can open my mouth and ask the question. "Before you get all geeked out on me, the Aristotle thing had nothing to do with philosophy. It was my grandfather's name, I think. Or maybe my great grandfather. Whatever. It's a pretty common name in Greece."

I don't know why it deflates me so much to learn that Cowbird's parents hadn't named their restaurant after an ancient Greek philosopher. Maybe it's because of fate. Maybe it's because I want to sit here in the cab of old Sally and think I wound up here for a reason. That there's some master plan in place for me already and that I'm not just out here on the road all alone. That I'm not the only one in control of my destiny.

I lean back in the seat and let Cowbird's story wash over me. About his parents and the fire. About how Cowbird's entire life had gone up in a flash at the same time as the restaurant, and how his destiny seemed out of his control from the start.

Then Cowbird chimes in and breaks into my thoughts. Brings me right back to my nightmares. "I still see the flames sometimes, Cordy," he says. "Even though I wasn't there. I feel the heat on my face and feel the thick fingers of smoke wrap around my lungs, and then I wake up and I'm just staring at the ceiling. And I'm sweating. And I think you know where I going with this."

"They're just dreams," I repeat to him as if it's my dang catch-phrase. A crease forms across Cowbird's forehead, and he gives me this look that tells me I better change the subject unless I want to sit here and dish about my stupid dreams all morning.

"What did they...uhh...do with you?" I ask clumsily. "You know... after the fire."

"Well," he says, "my sitter that night was just some girl in high school that my parents had hired to wait tables at the restaurant. I think her name was Susan, but that's not important. What's important is this poor girl wasn't about to go on raising an orphan kid just because she'd decided to make a few bucks on a Friday night babysitting gig. I mean, who could blame her for that? Certainly not me. Well...Susan...she did the only thing she could do. She handed me over to the police and...well, since I didn't have any family around besides my parents, my jolly tour of foster-vania began. But you know what, Cordy? Not having my parents around? It kind of felt like my life was over at first. That I was finished before I started. But being an orphan at such a young age also set me free in a way. To roam, I guess you could say. Or maybe just to learn. I don't know. It's something I only recently started thinking about."

"So how'd you wind up in Boone?" I ask, as old Sally rumbles past the mass storage units and outlet stores that dot Route 40 near Mebane. The supercenter. A lot full of discount warehouses that represented the farthest point I'd ever truly been from home. Every year Mom would pack Travis and I up in the cab of Dad's pickup and haul us out here for the back to school sales. And every year Travis would get salty about it, like trying on a new pair of sneakers was the worst thing he'd ever done in his life. And he and Mom would argue about the volume of the radio or the sweeping speed of the windshield wipers, or anything at all that happened to be within the realms of their five senses. I never understood any of it, but I sat there in silence in the middle of the bench seat and shielded my face from the spittle. Mom would always say something to Dad about it later like, "I can't wait until he gets out of this phase." But I'm not sure Travis ever did. Seems kind of unimportant now, listening to Cowbird tell me about his experiences. About *real* hardship.

"Got lucky," Cowbird says a moment later. "I burned through so many foster families I lost track. They thought I was too distant, or too private, or too damn weird. All of them. I mean, they thought my music was too loud, or my piercings were too creepy, or that I was out of my mind simply because I'd wear black nail polish once in a while. I ended up with Mrs. Mildred Winchester. Toughest old lady I ever met. She was a widow and she never remarried after thirty years of being alone in Carolina sky country. She wasn't exactly rich, either, since she spent forty years of her life as a schoolteacher." Cowbird wipes his eyes with the back of his hand. "When she retired, a bunch of her former students threw a party and they named her classroom The Lady Winchester Classroom.

Put it on a plaque and everything. I know she was proud of that. Man, old Lady Winchester and me couldn't have been more opposite if we tried. She was this little old lady with frizzy gray hair and then you get me, the the most punk rock looking dude you've ever seen in Boone, a whole foot taller, with a mat of scraggly, black hair and piercings and everything the nice people of Boone weren't ready to accept."

"How old were you when you went to live with Lady Winchester?"

"Sixteen or so. About your age. Only lived with her for two years until I got my license and my rig and I've been on the road ever since. Right where I belong. Lady Winchester...well, she died in her sleep one night when I was way out on the West Coast. I couldn't make it back for the funeral. Completely broke my heart. But I know Mildred wouldn't hold it against me, because she was special."

"She sounds special," I reply.

"Yeah. She was family to me. If I'm being honest, she's the only one I ever had, and we weren't related or even the least bit similar."

"Then how could she be family? I mean, you said you bailed on those other foster families, but you don't consider them family?"

"Nah. First of all, they bailed on me. Second, Mildred Winchester never did. She walked down any street with me no matter how much chatter bounced around town or how strange the folks there thought she was for taking me in. She didn't even care if I played my Minor Threat albums on full blast and let them spill out my bedroom window into the streets of Boone. I would have done anything for that lady. *That's* how I know she's family. It's also how I know she was all that kept me afloat when I thought I was drowning. At a time when I couldn't figure out how I fit into this weird-ass jigsaw puzzle we call life, I had Mildred Winchester on my side...and I had these." Cowbird tugs at his collar and fishes out a gold necklace that'd been hiding under his shirt. A pair of wedding bands dangle from the end of it.

I watch in silence as Cowbird reaches up and rubs a fully formed tear from his eye.

"I think I know what you mean," I say. "I'm trying to find my brother," I say out of nowhere. "He's the reason I'm on this journey."

"He ran away?"

"Yeah. Well my father ran him off, more like."

"Damn. That's some cold shit, Cordy. His own father, his own flesh and blood kicked his ass out?"

"Well, he didn't kick him out as much as shamed him out. Just kind of wore Travis down, I guess. Dad would just sit and stare and judge, until one night, Travis snapped. Travis got into pills and whatnot and I think Dad got embarrassed by all of the gossip around town. He seemed more worried about the gossip than he was about his own son."

"And he moved all the way to Philly?"

"Well, that's why he left High Point. I have a pretty good feeling he headed to Philly because of John Coltrane. I'm not certain. It's more of a hunch."

"The jazz musician? That smooth looking dude with the sax?"

"That sounds like Trane."

"What's a couple of white boys from High Point, North Carolina doing listening to Trane?" One of Cowbird's bushy eyebrows perks up so high it almost disappears under the band of his beanie cap.

"I guess the same thing a dude like you was doing sewing doilies with the Lady Winchester."

The rogue eyebrow falls back into place on Cowbird's browline. He slaps the steering wheel and his cheeks puff up like Dizzy Gillespie's when he blows into his trumpet.

"In a way," I continue, "it's like the philosophy thing. While most everyone else in this world worships the latest gadgets to hit the market, I'm about tracing things to the source. Far as I can tell, jazz is the original American music. Without it, nothing that follows exists. I mean, I like new music and new clothes and new ideas, but it's impossible to beat the original. And I don't think a person needs to be black, white, brown or green to reach that conclusion. Just a human with an open mind and an open heart."

"Well listen up, everyone," Cowbird says in an amplified voice to an imaginary audience that is most definitely not sitting here with us in the cab of old Sally. "The kid from High Point has done it! He's gone and caught me being a goddamn hypocrite!"

He rubs an icy hand over my orange crew cut. "Your boy Hippocrates would be proud."

A sign for Raleigh and Durham pops up along the shoulder and I feel a little spasm in my stomach as I start to realize the distance I'm putting between myself and my parents.

"You do know there's no link between Hippocrates the Greek scholar and a hypocrite, which does happen to define what your Coltrane comment made you."

"I did not know that." The hand finds its way back to Cowbird's own head. "Damn. Now you've caught me being a dumbass *and* a hypocrite!"

That's enough to get both of us laughing.

When the commotion dies down, Cowbird bottoms out his coffee and says, "You ever been to a ballgame?"

"Like, in a real ballpark?"

"What else is there?"

"I mean, I went to a few games at my high school, and Dad and I got to watch the High Point Rockers practice one time after they finished building the new minor league park. But then Travis disappeared and we never got around to watching a game."

"When you mentioned John Coltrane it made me think about baseball."

"That doesn't make sense," I say.

"Sure it does. Sounds to me like Coltrane was the glue. He's what held you and your brother together. If the two of you lost everything in the world, you'd still have Trane. Because his music gets inside you. You can hear it in your molecules."

Cowbird flicks the turn signal and old Sally glides through two lanes and slips off the exit marked Durham. He twists the knob on the dash stereo and it comes to life with a hectic clash of drums and guitar. "Gotta love Pennywise. *Same Old Story.* This song right here made me realize I wasn't cut from the same cloth as everyone else. That I needed to live my own life and not leave my future up to the foster system. That I needed to be me no matter what people said to me or how they looked at me. Lady Winchester...she understood that, and it's probably why we got along so well."

Cowbird chuckles to himself, but I don't play along. Probably because I have no clue what he's talking about. "See, I can relate to what you and Travis seem to have," he continues, "because music saved my life too. And not just any music. All the music. Two white kids like you listening to Coltrane? Man, I have to admit that sounds kind of funny to me. But you know what's funnier? A dude in a death-metal t-shirt rolling down the highway in old Sally listening to Beethoven. And singing along with my own set of made up lyrics too. There's nothing like it! See, Cordy, we all have music. We all have a little jar of the glue right here when we need it." He pats the front console of his dashboard stereo as old Sally rumbles to a stop at a traffic light. The faces of old, Southern-style midrises stare back at us through the windshield.

"What's your point?" I ask. "And where are we going?"

"My point is, we all have something in our lives that makes us tick. Something that we love. And when you share that love, that common bond, with another person who loves it as much as you do...well, it can bind you to that person forever. Simple as that. For some it's music. For others, poetry or food or fashion. For me and Lady Winchester, baseball was as close as you could get to Super Glue."

"You mean the old lady was out there slugging beers and heckling umpires?"

"Noooo! She wasn't one for slugging beers, Cordy. She didn't hardly even talk. Neither of us did. We were just happy to be together, sitting in the sunlight with the crowd buzzing in the background. Sometimes we'd take turns closing our eyes and guessing the outcome of an at-bat based on the sounds we heard alone."

For a moment, neither of us says a word. Cowbird flicks off the radio and we hone in on the sounds of the road and the steady hum of Sally's massive engine as she pulls into the heart of Durham.

"I think I know what you mean," I say. "Maybe that's how I know John Coltrane's music is what my brother needs right now."

Even as I hear the words leave my lips I'm not sure I believe them myself, but then I think about Travis on the night he left. How he placed his saxophone in the case so carefully you'd think it was made of glass. How he lifted the case off the desk and cupped the front of it with his other hand, as if he were protecting it from the evils of the world. How he decided to take the saxophone with him, wherever he intended to go. That had to mean something, right? That had to mean the music and the legend of John Coltrane and High Point, North Carolina, and his lonely-ass brother were still alive and well somewhere inside Travis's heart, even if the pills made it hard for him to recognize us.

All of a sudden, almost in response to my statement, Cowbird pulls the rig into an abandoned lot beside one of the many old tobacco stacks left standing in one of the country's oldest tobacco towns. "You know, Cordy, you gave me an idea," he says. He cuts Sally's engine and lets his seatbelt snap back against the seat. Then he pops open the driver's side door and takes one step out of the cab.

"Come on," he says.

"You never told me where we're going."

"To grab a bite to eat," he says. "On me. Then we're gonna get you to that game. The Bulls have an early one today."

We walk the streets into sleepy, old Durham and stop for a moment to admire the lightbulb-encrusted marquee in front of the famous Carolina Theater. A few blocks away is the American Tobacco Campus where farmers rolled out their bales of dried leaves for sale on the open market, now an open-air collection of shops, restaurants, and a radio studio.

We sit down at a crusty picnic table outside a smoky joint that smells like hickory and serves "pig pickin's." There, I tell Cowbird the fine details of my master plan. The one I hope will bring my family together before it's too late. How I'll hitch my way to the City of Brotherly Love and find the brother who may have forgotten he loves me. How I'll deliver him the special piece of sheet music so he can hear the notes themselves as they spill from the mouth of his sax. How I'll convince him to take the trip with me to New York City. To the place where jazz was born and where Trane made his name. How we'll see a show at the club where Trane became a legend. To Birdland. That's where we'll go. And after that there will be nothing Travis can do but remember to be Travis again.

After I finish laying it out, Cowbird says, "That's a sound plan, Cordy. It's like Birdland's your ballpark, only with a different kind of music." I tell Cowbird I like thinking of it that way and he pays the bill and we head across the street to the legendary fortress, Durham Athletic Park, home of the famous Bulls.

Once we're through the turnstile and across the sticky surface of the concourse, there's nothing but emerald green for miles. Just as Cowbird had described, the low hum of the crowd sits like a comfort inside my chest. Right away I understand what Cowbird meant when he compared Trane's music to the symphony inside one of America's great ballparks.

We find our seats and Cowbird looks at me with his index finger crossed over his lips and his eyes closed. CRACK! A Durham hitter slaps a line drive to deep left field. A roar of appreciation swells around the stadium.

"Sounds like extra bases!" Cowbird says, his eyes still shut tight. The hitter rounds second and dives headfirst into third. There's a millisecond of complete silence in the park as fans' voices dry up in anticipation of the umpire's decision. SAFE! The roar shakes the structure of the stadium and Cowbird opens his eyes to confirm his accuracy.

"The whole secret," he says, "is to *listen* to the game like you'd listen to a song. Just like Trane. Remember, there's an order to it. A swish-pop-roar of the tag, the hit, the celebration. But there's also room to fire off stray riffs. Steal a base out of the blue. Call your own shot and swing for the fences. Any of that sound familiar to you, Cordy Wheaton?"

I nod. "I think it'd sound pretty familiar to Travis too," I say. "At least that's what I'm banking on."

"Have faith, man" Cowbird says, as the next Durham batter steps to the plate.

I lean back in the stadium seat, close my eyes, and pray that the pop and the crack and the simple rhythm of the stadium's rat-tat-tat will be enough to guide me.

The Truth About Cowbird(s)

After the Bulls put the finishing touches on a three to nothing victory, we hop in the rig and Cowbird says, "Strap in. We got to make up time if we're gonna get to the coast by close of business." He twists a nob on the dashboard and I hear a click, followed by the clash of the trumpet and the sax, and the soulful tones of one James Brown. The legend.

Cowbird winks at me. "Looks like Papa's got a brand new bag, today" he says. "You know, he recorded this song in Charlotte, right here in the great state of North Carolina." He nods. Then he stomps on old Sally's pedals so hard I think her engine might shoot through her smokestack, and we rumble down the narrow, Durham streets with the Godfather of Soul urging us on. Cowbird yanks the pulley on the air horn until we're safe and sound on the open surface of I-85.

That's when he locks his hands down on the steering wheel and crouches forward in his seat with both of his grey eyes trained on any stray pebble that dared to cross Sally's path. He doesn't move. Doesn't speak. Just sits there driving, locked in an epic session of trucker meditation with James Brown as his personal musical Yogi. I sit back and relax. I dig it. For two straight hours I only hear two sounds: classic 60's soul music and the various degrees of Southern drawl floating from the receiver of Cowbird's CB, touting handles like The Asphalt Joker and Dovetail and The Dread Pirate and sharing insight ranging from traffic updates, to the sightings of a freak thunderstorm over the Blue Ridge, to a listing of the daily specials at every BBQ joint in the city of Lexington.

That's about the time I see something in the shoulder of the road up ahead. A form. Wavy at first, then more solid. More clear. Saggy shoulders and saggy pants and a long shock of brown hair down the back of his neck. It's Travis! I can tell that from about a thousand feet away and my heart starts racing as we make our approach. I'm already leaning my head out the window, but Cowbird still has the needle pegged like he doesn't notice. Like this hitcher doesn't matter.

We're about two hundred feet away when I shout, "Aren't you gonna stop?" and Cowbird's face goes slack and he starts to pump the brakes and I hear old Sally's tires squeal against the asphalt and her gears grind against the column.

"What the hell, Cordy?" Cowbird hisses, and all I can do is point at Travis on the side of the road as we rumble past him and his cardboard sign with the words "Cordy. Stop! We Need to Talk" scrawled across it in black magic marker.

And then he's gone.

Vanished.

Just like that, he's a patch of dried grass in the side view mirror. Nothing more.

"Goddamn, Cordy," Cowbird says in a hoarse whisper as he starts to feed some gas to Old Sally again. "You alright, dude? Cause maybe you got a little something in your eye back there."

"It was…nothing," I say. "Nothing at all."

Cowbird mumbles something under his breath, but decides to let the matter rest. I mean what else could he do when he's carting around a perfect stranger and that perfect stranger starts seeing shit that isn't there?

Cowbird sinks back into his driving trance, nudging old Sally at needle-pegged speed past a lifetime's-worth of hash marks and mile marker posts until we climb an overpass with a vast body of murky water beneath it.

"You smell that?" he asks, as if I hadn't almost gotten us killed a dozen or so miles back. I take a whiff and catch something that makes me think of clams cooking on a sidewalk.

"Wasn't me," I say.

Cowbird laughs.

"It's marsh grass," he tells me. "Gives off an unpleasant smell this time of year, but it means we're almost there. That reminds me. Maybe it's time I gave you a few tips. My rules of the road or the rail or wherever you find yourself a week, two weeks out. Free of charge."

"Oh. Gee. Thanks," I say trying to sound sarcastic as hell but not laying it on thick enough.

Cowbird rambles right over me. "I've learned three main lessons of the road that have kept me out of trouble. I wouldn't doubt if they kept me from getting myself killed a few times."

"I guess obeying the speed limit is nowhere on this master list," I say.

"Very funny." Cowbird's foot eases off the pedal and old Sally calms down and settles herself in the lane. "First thing to know is don't take your eyes off your stuff. Ever. That bag you got? The one that's filled with marshmallows or some other crap that won't save you out here? Well, I guarantee as soon as that bag isn't with you, the first thing you're gonna need is a marshmallow. You got that?"

"Yep. Squirrel away my marshmallows. Check."

"I'm serious, Cordy. I don't want you taking two steps out of this cab until I'm sure you heard what I have to say. So…are you?"

"Am I what?"

"Willing to listen?"

I don't know why it takes me so long to answer considering I have no clue what I'm doing out here and that, for me, being any distance from High Point is like being on the moon. Maybe it's my stubborn side. Travis told me I have a stubborn side. He would say, "Cordy, you're the kinda kid who'd piss in his own apple juice so no one else could drink it." I don't know if I'd go that far, but maybe he did have a point.

After a few seconds of deafening silence, I give Cowbird an answer. "Yeah. Sure. I'll listen."

"Good, because the second lesson is more important than the first. You ready?"

I nod.

"When you're out on the road you gotta take your chances because you never know when another handout's coming. But you gotta be cautious too. You gotta use *this*." An ice-cold index finger pokes me in the temple. "You're gonna want to use this first." He pats me on the chest. "But, trust me, step back and think it through…before you go hurling yourself out another train car or in front of a big rig like Sally."

"I'll keep that in mind," I reply.

"And finally, the most important lesson of all. When you're on the road, it feels like you're alone. But you're not. In fact, you can't let yourself be alone or you'll never reach the finish line. You get me, Cordy?"

"I do," I say, and this time I believe him.

Cowbird smiles and reaches under his seat with his left hand. He pulls out a small, canvas bag and tosses it in my lap.

"Open it," he says.

I reach in and pull out something cold and steel. A pocket knife with a tortoise shell handle and chrome around the hilt.

"I mean, open it. For real."

I flip the handle and watch the sun sparkle off the blade as it slides out with a click.

"Nice," I say. "Where'd you get this?"

"My lady gave it to me when I started driving. Said she stayed awake at night worrying about me. Wanted me to have insurance in case something happened. Nothing ever did. I want you to have it," he says.

"No. I can't take this," I say.

"You're gonna take it, Cordy. No choice."

"But what am I going to do with a knife?"

"For starters, you could cut things. Like food or rope or something like that. Or you could protect yourself. You'll know what to do if the time comes."

"I'm not taking—"

"Cordy…put the knife in that bag of yours right next to the damn marshmallows or whatever and don't take it out again until you need it. Hopefully that'll be never. You hear me?"

I nod and unzip my bag and watch Cowbird slip the knife inside with my spare undies and my forty bucks. A sign that reads "New Bern: 2 Miles" whips past on the shoulder.

"So what's gonna happen to me when we get there?" I ask. "What happens at the end of the line? You know…for a hitcher?"

"There's no end of the line," Cowbird says. "Only beginnings, cause now you'll really be alone."

All of a sudden, I can't help but notice how much Cowbird sounds like John Coltrane when he said, "There is never any end…there are always new sounds to imagine, new feelings to get at. So that we can see more and more clearly what we are…we have to keep on cleaning the mirror." I'm about to go all philosophical on Cowbird, but he cuts me off before I can start, and it's not with the most comforting news I've ever heard.

"You know, you're not gonna have this mama Cowbird carrying you around any more."

"What? You would kick me out of the nest? Just like that?"

The right eyebrow raises on Cowbird's forehead and he gives me a look that says, "that's exactly what I was thinking." Then he says, "Hear me out. You see, in the wild, the cowbird is a remarkable creature. Maybe the most adaptive bird in all of birdland. See, any good mama cowbird knows in her heart she needs to be free. She's not trying to sit around on a nest three times a year, but she'll still find a way to raise her young. All she does is zip in and drop her eggs in the another bird's nest. And then she catches up with her young down the road...when they've had a chance to write their own journeys. I like that about cowbirds."

"Yeah, I guess I do too," I tell him, as he pulls old Sally off the ramp into New Bern.

"Truth is, I've been dropping eggs in nests as long as I've been driving this rig, so I'm good at finding the right nest for the right bird. I guess I got pretty good at doing what nobody else could do for me."

"You mean...you found a nest for me?" I ask, half-joking.

"Sure did. Only the other bird? She doesn't know about it yet."

"She?"

"Don't get excited. She's an ex-naval officer. Grew up near Wilmington, then spent time in the Arabian Sea helping to command an aircraft carrier that was so close to the Persian Gulf she could probably skip stones into it from the bow." He pauses and gives me this stern look that tells me I should let that information sink in. Then he says, "She's as cool as they come, Cordy, but if you step one inch outta line around her she'll snap your ass in two and toss you overboard faster than a dried-up sardine."

"Sounds promising," I say. "What's her name?"

"Captain Adomi. Her first name's Ayel. Sometimes she even lets me call her that...but I wouldn't push my luck if I were you."

Cowbird steers the rig into the heart of New Bern, racing past ramshackle barns with their dry-rotten foundations obscured by tall reeds until they give way to the lazy glide of kayakers like tiny, neon fishing lures bobbing the surface of the Neuse River, until they give way to great rows of thick-shingled A-frames straight from the American Revolution. Then comes the waterfront. With the scent of marsh grass rising in plumes, the outstretched fingertip of the Atlantic Ocean comes into view.

Cowbird slows Sally to a roll and the tires crunch over gravel as we enter an empty warehouse that smells like rotten fish and reminds me of an airplane hangar from a WWII documentary. Cowbird taps the digital clock on the dashboard. It reads 4:55 pm in green, pixelated lights until my vision blurs out and my hearing goes static and I'm in the echo chamber again for a few seconds:

Almost five

Say goodbye to him for today....

Then the pixelated numbers glow strong—4:56 pm—and I'm back in the cab with my vision and my hearing intact, but with Cowbird's upturned glare scorching a hole through the center of my forehead.

"The hell's a matter with you?" he asks with both eyebrows pointed down toward his nose like darts.

"Noth...nothing," I push out. "I'm...just a little tired."

"You sure?" he asks again. "You're not seeing little green men again are you?"

"No," I lie. "I'm fine. Just...fine."

Cowbird stares at me for a few more agonizing seconds before he's satisfied and gives up the query. "Good," he says. "Then we have less than five minutes to spare, so help me unload and I'll fix you up with the captain. I'd bet half my wage she's got an expedition going out soon."

"An expedition? I thought you said she was done with the Navy."

"She captains a commercial fishing vessel now. The *Ama Kamama*. She told me it's Cherokee for 'water butterfly' which might be the most accurate name I've ever heard."

We hop out of the cab and meet a group of dock workers in grease-stained clothing and scuffed up work boots. The guy up front wears one of those weird back braces that looks like an old man's version of a world wrestling belt.

The guy with the belt bellows, "Hey! Whaddya got for us today, Alekos?" I have to remind myself he's talking to Cowbird.

"Looks like a load of nets," Cowbird says. "Maybe some rigging. Other supplies. The usual." He unlatches the gate and swings the double doors wide open. The men scurry inside like a tiny legion of ants stacking breadcrumbs on their shoulders. Crate after crate comes out of Sally's hold. Each one is set on a portable roller and shuttled off to a distant quadrant of the hangar. It takes no more than ten minutes to clear the freight. I'm drenched in sweat by the time Sally's trailer is empty and, believe me, it's not like I was the most valuable asset on the crew.

Just as Cowbird slams the double doors and swivels old Sally's latch into place, a tall woman with an angular face, a strong jaw and ten inches of long, black hair flowing out the back of her bucket hat sweeps past with a stack of paperwork in hand. There's a smile on her lips, but it's the kind of smile that can go straight any moment. I get the feeling you'd be in pretty deep shit if that moment ever met you.

The dock workers stand rod-straight and stop talking about last Wednesday's poker game. The little fireplug in the back brace unstraps his cruiserweight belt in one motion and hides it behind his dolly.

When the woman reaches Cowbird, he stands at attention with his right hand in full salute and rattles something off like, "Chief Petty Officer Winchester reporting for duty!"

She slaps the stack of paperwork against Cowbird's chest.

"Just sign these, you clown." The thin smile expands to something much closer to one hundred and eighty degrees when she says it and I'm surprised by how one person can seem like they might be two hundred years old in spirit while being, like, thirty years old in real age. That's Ayel Adomi.

As Cowbird scribbles his way through the vast sea of pages, the good captain strides up to me and says, "So, who's the barnacle?"

"Name's Cordy Wheaton," Cowbird mumbles past the pen cap in his mouth. "Straight outta High Point in the Old North State." He says it like he's announcing a boxing legend into the ring rather than some shrimpy dishrag of a kid who's never traveled much beyond his bedroom.

"He know how to make sounds or should I just pack him away with the chum?"

"He talks once in a while," Cowbird says through a chuckle. "Don't you, Cordy?"

I stand there with no clue as to what to say to a war hero who, quite frankly, scares the ever-loving shit out of me. Good thing Cowbird's around for a final assist. "Cordy's trying to get to Philadelphia to find his brother."

"Philly, eh?" she says. "Great town. Spent some time at the shipyard there. You got any idea how far you are from Philadelphia, Private?"

I nod.

"And you're still up for the challenge?"

I nod again.

"You know, my crew is pushing out later tonight. Doing a bit of fishing and bringing the haul into port at Norfolk. You ever been to Virginia, Private Wheaton?"

A burst of hot air hisses out of Cowbird's mouth and the laughter revs up again. "My boy here's never left High Point, North Carolina!" he pushes out through strained lips.

Captain Adomi sizes me up with no sign of a smile on her face. Her dark eyebrows rest on her forehead in jet-black arches, but the eyes underneath pierce right through me like daggers. "That so, Private? You a homebody?"

"A what?" I finally manage.

"A homebody. Some slug that never leaves the house. Never breathes fresh air. That sound like you?"

I stare at her for a moment, not sure how to respond. I mean, on one hand she has me pegged. On the other, I feel that stubborn streak boil up inside me. Kind of makes me want to piss in the apple juice.

"Not anymore," I say. Just like that. Cold as hell, like my words are the knife and that thing Cowbird gave me is some stupid, plastic child's toy.

It's exactly what Captain Adomi wants to hear.

She paces around me in one fully-cadenced loop as I stand there as close to attention as I've ever been in my life. "And you'd be willing to carry your weight on deck and not take more than your fair share of grub?"

I don't know what the hell she's talking about, so I stand there. Silent.

"Of course he would," Cowbird says. "Isn't that right, Cordy?"

"Y-y-yeah," I say, even though I feel like I just signed my life away.

"Welcome aboard," she says. "We push off at twenty-two hundred hours. Pier seventeen. Don't be late."

I hold my hand somewhere between a salute and a handshake and watch the thin lips curve into a full smile and then emit this cute, little mouse laugh you'd expect to hear from a three-year-old. Captain Adomi straightens up and shakes my hand. "Don't be late," she repeats, and then she strides into the hangar office to file the paperwork.

That's when it sinks in that I'll never see Cowbird again. He brought me to the nest and now all he has to do is swoop past and drop me in like a lonely egg. I reach in my bag and take out the knife and hold it in front of Cowbird. Creases form across his forehead.

"What's this?" he asks.

"I can't keep it," I say. "It's too valuable."

"Not as valuable as my peace of mind," he snaps back. "Look, Cordy. You're gonna take that with you for two reasons: one is protection and the other is to help you remember the other things I told you."

He walks over to the driver's side of the cab and climbs half way into the cockpit. "Besides," he says, "you can give it back to me if our routes ever intersect. Deal?"

I slide the knife in my bag and toss it over my shoulder. "Ok. Deal."

Cowbird smiles. He saddles up on the driver's seat and cranks the ignition. Shotgun Sally rumbles to life, only she'll have to ride for at least a short stretch without someone keeping the other side of her seat warm.

"I'm praying for you, Cordy Wheaton. And I wish you all the luck in the world as you start this new part of your life."

"What part is that?" I ask.

"The part that's outside the cave, man."

Cowbird gives me a final wink as Sally roars out of the hangar and back to the roadway—right where she and Cowbird make perfect sense, and where I hope to fit in one day. If I survive.

Experimental Jazz

The hangar is twice as gloomy and a thousand times more empty once old Sally becomes a mere vibration on the sea air. That's not because Cowbird takes up so much space by himself. It's because I'm alone and I have to start over from scratch. Still, it feels good to know Cowbird's out there on the roadway, maybe scooping up another wayward egg he can drop off in another nest at the end of a dark, lonely road.

I don't know how long she's standing there watching me scrape the loading dock grease on the bottom of my sneaker against a patch of clean cement, but a warning light flashes in my head and I realize I'm not alone. I try to play it off like I'm not a social reject with more pimples than friends.

"Just prepping the old sea legs," I say before regretting every word in the sentence. A wrinkle forms on the bridge of Captain Adomi's nose and her eyebrows jut downward like arrows.

"Whatever you say, Private." She laughs and tosses a bag of potato chips and an empty, plastic cup in my direction. I fumble both and step on the cup with every ounce of grease on my sneaker. Not the most graceful start to my service under Captain Ayel Adomi. But she doesn't seem to mind.

"Come on, chatterbox. I have another cup in my office," she says. I follow her across the open hangar floor into an ice cube-sized office that holds a desk you might find in a 1930s schoolhouse, a basin-style sink with a slow leak dribbling from the faucet, and a cot with a scratchy-looking military blanket rolled in a ball on the naked mattress.

Captain Adomi opens a drawer on the desk and plops a loaf of Wonder Bread, a bottle of mustard, and a new plastic cup on the desktop. "The supplies are on deck," she says. "This is all I've got for now. We have a long night ahead of us. I suggest you fill up. Make a bread sandwich or something."

"A bread sandwich?"

She twists the tie off the bread and slides two slices out of the bag. "Yeah, a bread sandwich." She squirts a thick puddle of yellow mustard on one of the slices, covers it up with the other and holds it out to me. "You never heard of one?"

I stare at her for a second, then at the bag of chips in my hand I'd been agile enough to avoid crushing into smithereens, and then back at Captain Adomi. She smiles, but all indications are she's serious about the whole bread sandwich thing. I take a bite. Pure mustard. But it's not bad. For a free ride all the way from New Bern to Norfolk, Virginia, I can choke down a few more of these.

"Get a little R & R," she says. "I have a few things to do before we push off, but I'll be back to get you when it's time, Private."

"Thanks," I tell her through a mouth full of mustard and soggy bread. "And feel free to call me Cordy. Nobody calls me Private."

"I know," she says. "But what fun would that be?"

She stands tall and straight, like a statue, and I find myself trying to do the same thing out of pure instinct, as if I'm a real soldier in Captain Adomi's personal battalion, which is ludicrous but also kind of amusing.

"See you at eighteen-hundred hours, Private Wheaton," she says.

When she's gone, I lean back in the captain's squeaky desk chair and munch on chips, make another bread sandwich, and force down two full cups of warm, coppery-tasting water from the tap. I flip the switch on an old pocket radio that's lying there collecting dust on the desktop, like my father might have had when he was a kid. There's nothing but a wave of static at first, but with a few twists of the dial and a little persistence, I find a station with a signal. It's a jazz station. I recognize the song from hearing it spew out of Travis's headphones in the top bunk. It's Charlie Parker's "Lullaby of Birdland" and it feels like a personal message from the ether. See, Mr. Parker's nickname was "the Birdman." The very same birdman behind the Birdland Jazz Club.

The slow, even rise of his sax rings out in soft, metallic notes and the brushes skitter across the high hat. It reminds me why I started this journey and how far I've come in a single day. And I think about Travis and my father, and how sometimes you can't avoid the things that come at you no matter how hard you try and that sometimes they cause opposing forces to collide and bounce off in opposite directions. But sometimes those things—we'll call them fate because that's what the Greeks would have called them—pull the forces back together like some kind of giant, unseen magnet.

I toss my cup in the trashcan near the captain's desk and carry the radio to my cot. I lie on the mattress and warm up under the scratchy blanket and the smooth melody of Birdman's "Lullaby." As the music washes over me, I feel like I'm where I'm meant to be. It feels good to be connected again, or, rather, disconnected depending on how you look at it. I mean, I haven't thought about celebrities or video games, or any of that nonsense since my smartphone was obliterated at the side of the train tracks. The same smartphone my face would have been glued to, had it been functional, preventing me from stumbling upon the exact song I needed to hear at this exact moment. It's funny how things happen that way. It's also funny how the Greeks recognized the same phenomenon over two thousand years ago.

I lie there with the stale scent of Sally's fumes wafting under the office door, let my tired bones sink into the lumpy mattress, and listen to songs by some of Trane's heroes—Miles Davis, Dizzy Gillespie, and Thelonius Monk—until my eyelids grow heavy and the sounds of the sax trail off behind me, and…

Gas fumes. My eyelids sting from a thousand fallen tears. I blink. Darkness. The chug of the engine eases to an idle. The tires crunch over pebbles and warped asphalt.

I can't move with my hands tied behind me. I can't scream with this fabric tied across my mouth. I can't bite down enough to touch my teeth together.

The radio goes silent. Someone shouts, "How's he gonna find out?"

Then silence until the car is drowned in a million decibels of high-octane music. Something I recognize. Something experimental. Something I'm sure I've heard before.

I lean back and kick the lid of my coffin. The trunk. But I'm trapped. I breathe in and try to heave the sound of my voice out over the gag and the music and…

My eyes spring open. I pop up in the cot so fast the military blanket flies into Captain Adomi's arms as she stands over me. Her eyes are wider than full moons and her bucket hat is clutched in a ball over her mouth. The pocket radio screams out in the background with a calliope of saxophone screeches and uneven chord changes. It's the song from my dream. The one I've heard every night since Travis left. Since the night it all went down.

Captain Adomi leans back in her desk chair as the song fades out. A disc jockey says in an other-worldly voice, "That was *Transition* by the legendary John Coltrane, from his posthumously-released album of the same name." I flick the dial and the office falls silent.

"You ok there, Private?" Captain Adomi asks. She folds the blanket in a neat square and pushes it to the corner of her desk.

I look at her, as I struggle to focus, and try to sound as casual as I can. "Yeah, sure. Just fine, Captain." Another lie.

She doesn't press, but I'm convinced she doesn't believe me. Not after she heard me blubber like a baby or, worse yet, watched me thrash around like a cornered copperhead on the bed while I slept.

Without a word, Captain Adomi tosses my pack from across the room. It smacks me clear in the damn face.

"That's your wake-up call," she says, as she turns to leave.

I follow the captain out of the warehouse and across a narrow street to a pier stretched along the water's edge. A long gangplank trails the bank, its floating docks extended like arms into the harbor. On each arm floats a vessel, many of them battened down in white plastic to shield the decks from harsh weather and the summer sun.

"We're on the end," the captain says after we pass five or ten slips with massive boats attached.

An absolute beauty floats in front of the last slip at the end of the pier. The powder blue sheen of the deck paint mingles with the moonbeams and reflects sparkles of light off the surface of the Neuse River. Three broad-shouldered crewmen stand around a crane that looks like a giant version of one of those metal claw games you see in the arcade. The ones where you spend forty-seven dollars in quarters for a chance to grab a crappy, fifty-cent plush unicorn. Captain Adomi's best men tighten the cables that connect the crane to the vessel's most essential tool: the net. The words *Ama Kamama* stand out in red, script letters on the rear of the boat.

"Water butterfly," I whisper to myself.

"Ah, so he told you."

I nod and the captain shakes her head as we walk the plank to the top deck. "That Cowbird spills the tea. But I'm glad you know."

"You…are?" I ask.

"Sure. I mean, I wouldn't want you to go around thinking I'm nothing but a hard-ass, drill sergeant."

"W-why would I think that?"

"Spend a night on deck, Private, and you'll know what I mean. I'll bet right around this time tomorrow, when your arms are heavy and your belly is as hollow as a kettle drum, you'll look at these words painted on her bow and you'll know what they mean. And they'll give you hope…I guess…that, you know, I'm not a total ogre all of the time. That there's more to me."

I don't say anything for two reasons: One, I'm terrified to the core of Captain Adomi, and Two, I think I get what she's saying. It must be hard to captain a ship, or to captain anything. I mean, I wouldn't know. The only thing I ever lead in my life is this half-baked expedition I'm currently on. Taking control of an entire ship and its crew is nothing like that, and it probably requires you to lose a lot of friends, make a lot of enemies, and become a close confidant to your own solitude. So, I guess knowing the captain is a butterfly in disguise does give me a small amount of hope. Who knows? Maybe I'll even survive the voyage.

"She's beautiful, isn't she?" Captain Adomi asks after we've taken in her ship's splendor.

I nod and continue gazing at sparkling brass rails on the main deck, the various ropes and rigging hanging at uneven intervals, and at the perfect version of the captain's hangar office perched high atop the bridge. The vessel is impeccable. It's tip-top. But what do I know? I'm a landlubber. The closest I've been to a cruise on the seven seas was in the cramped bathtub in my house on Brookside Drive, with my Fisher Price submarine replicas battling the soap suds.

The crewmen approach and I recognize them as the loading dock workers. The older gentleman isn't sporting his WWE-style back brace any more, but he still works with the same intensity as he did in the hangar.

Right away, Captain Adomi feeds me to the wolves.

"I hope you're powered up on bread sandwiches, Private Wheaton, cause it looks like you're about to be kinda busy."

She pats me on the back and strides off to the serenity of her control tower in the sky.

Maybe I was wrong. Maybe this part of the journey *is* going to be as hard as it seems.

Know Thyself

On what might be the lone positive note, I've slept through two nights without winding up in the trunk of a car or on the cold cement of a warehouse. Maybe it's the gentle arms of the sea that rock me to sleep and nudge me awake in the morning. Maybe it's because the sea is the only place in the world where it's cool to be alone. Or maybe it's the work. I mean, the sun-bleached deck of the *Ama Kamama* rivals the Gobi Desert as one of the most unforgiving places on Earth. That's what I discovered over the past two days. I also learned that water travel might be slower than painting a mansion with the end of a toothpick. And a thousand times more tiring too.

The second we push off into the Neuse River, with the docks still in plain sight, Captain Adomi barks orders at us from the heights of Mt. Commando. Under the dim light of the moon, we mend nets and tie up loose rigging and clean buckets full of slimy fish bait for the next morning. The work only stops to catch a few hours sleep in a scratchy hammock and to shove a slice of cheese and some bread down our throats before the routine starts again.

I'm the young buck on the crew. The new guy. Which means my daily routine looks something like this:

> 4:00 am: rise with the gulls and slog buckets of mashed up fish guts we call bait out of the hold and up to the main deck.
>
> 5:00 am: recheck the main net and auxiliary nets for holes and restring with twine.
>
> 6:00 am: wake up the rest of the crew at sunrise and eat a bread sandwich.
>
> 6:30 am: use an instrument the size of a toothbrush to strip salt deposits, barnacles, and seagull droppings (that's shit for you landlubbers) off every square inch of the ship while the rest of the crew does the real job of fishing and Captain Adomi navigates. Mop, clean, scrub, shine. Repeat. Repeat. Repeat.

Noon: eat another bread sandwich.

5:00 pm: crawl into the hold as it shivers with thousands of fish, and help the crew sort and separate the catch by length, weight, and species. Eat yet another bread sandwich.

7:00 pm: cut more bait while the real crew releases the throwback fish.

9:00 pm: free time, which is the naval code name for sleep.

I get along with the crew enough to get the jobs done, I guess, but it pisses me off when they treat me like a freshly-hatched chick because I'm only sixteen and I never ventured more than a stone's throw from my hometown and it's my first time on a commercial fishing boat. It's like stuff I learned about human nature and ancient philosophy hold no merit out here on the open seas, and it's gotten worse since we slipped past Ocracoke, out of the nurturing arms of Pamlico Sound, and into the blood-stained teeth of the Atlantic. The longer we go without seeing land, the more they treat me like a garden-variety scrub.

Part of me wants to spill the next bait bucket I'm handed in the middle of the main deck and tell them to clean it up themselves. But I don't because I'm a guest of Captain Adomi, and because Cowbird vouched for me, and because you don't spend forty-eight hours working next to people without finding out about them and, well, these three guys had some rough stories to share. Each one more harrowing than the last.

There's Juan Suarez, a squatty little buzzard with close-cropped, black hair and a shiny mustache who resents wearing his back brace as much as I resent waking up before sunrise. Old Juan's hometown was Mexico City, but he travelled in each year as a seasonal worker.

"I wouldn't say it was totally legal," he told me as he smoothed out a rogue wire on his stache. "But it's a system, you know. The farmers get the labor they need, and us workers go back home with a bit of security for our family. And no crops are left withering in the fields." Juan said he worked the same couple of farms in Eastern Carolina for about three years straight.

"And then one night, there was a raid," he told me. "Federal agents busted into our campsite with flood lights blazing and bullet proof vests on, all to arrest a few guys who picked turnips and yams for a living."

I asked him what he did with ICE agents rushing at him from all angles. "I ran like crazy," he said. "Walked to the nearest town, which happened to be New Bern, and started looking for something to eat. A place to sleep. You see, everything I owned I left back at camp…and there was no way I was going back. So I found a quiet, unattended warehouse and started snooping around. I'd never stolen anything in my life, but what were my options at that point?"

"So what happened?" I asked him. "Did you break into that place?"

"I never had a chance. I got my assed kicked about two seconds later by this tiny lady who then offered to sponsor my green card and give me a job mending nets on her fishing boat."

"Captain Adomi?" I asked.

Juan nodded, and that's all he had to say, which was kind of perfect because that gave Nassar Tahan a chance to share his story. As far as I could tell, Nasser was sort of the first mate of the expedition. He helped Captain Adomi with navigational tasks just as much as he labored on the deck with Juan and his deckhand, Pierre.

Nasser's story hit me hard and I don't quite know why. He told me he served in the U.S. Navy, on the same carrier as Captain Adomi and that he was from Portland and she'd tease him about being a softy from the West Coast instead of a hard-edged East Coaster like her. "She was kind of like a big sister to me," he told me, "because I wasn't really ready for the responsibility of being a soldier. I was barely eighteen years old when I enlisted, mostly cause I was pissed at my parents all the time and I wanted to give them a real shock. Get them back. I wasn't on the carrier for more than two months before I got discharged."

I asked Nasser what evil thing he'd done to get him kicked out of the Navy and he said, "It was an honorable discharge. I got injured. But not in battle. Just doing my normal duties one morning, and I got my arm pinched between a burst pipe and the bulwark of the ship." He rolled up his shirt sleeve to show off a jagged and chewed-up-looking scar knifing across the front of his bicep and stretching like a lighting bolt up and over his shoulder. "They said I couldn't safely perform my duties."

I asked him how he can perform his shipworthy duties now if he couldn't do them for the Navy and he said, "It wasn't just the injury. It was other…stuff." That's when he told me about how the pain had gotten to him so much that he started digging into the bottle of painkillers he'd been prescribed. But it didn't stop there. "I totally lost control," he told me. "After that, I couldn't keep a job, my family and friends started pushing me away. The only person who managed to get through to me was—"

"Captain Adomi?" I asked, already knowing the answer.

"Yep. And she offered me a job here on the *Ama Kamama*, and the rest is—"

"History?"

Nasser looks at me and a smile spreads on his lips, and that's all he has to say…which naturally opens up the microphone for Pierre Jolicoeur, who tells me right away his name means "jolly heart" in French. It's not exactly a surprising name translation for a man with a face-consuming smile and a tendency to laugh about ten times more than he speaks.

What did surprise me was that a man could keep laughing and smiling like that after surviving a 7.0 magnitude earthquake in his hometown of Port au Prince, Haiti. It was the big one of 2010, and Pierre's mother, father, and four-year-old sister did not make it out alive.

"I became an orphan overnight," Pierre tells me. "I was scared and I had no other family to back me. I was just a ten-year-old kid." But a few organizations came together and helped Pierre file for temporary protected status in the United States. "At first it was great," he says, "but then I got stuck bouncing around the foster system. Wound up in a few homes. Got beat. Got yelled at. One day I just had enough. I decided I was getting on a ship and going back home."

"To Haiti?" I ask.

"Hell yeah," he told me. "Stowed away in the hold of a ship and everything. But I got caught."

"Let me guess," I say to him. "Captain Adomi?"

"She's the best," Pierre says, and then he lets out a good long laugh. "She really is something else."

You know, when you think about how much Captain Adomi has done as both an employer and a friend for all three of these gentlemen, I guess what you have aboard the *Ama Kamama* is America's most diverse and effective family. Plus one. And I happen to be the plus one, so you can imagine how complaining about my official rank of "Low Man on the Totem Pole" might not be the best strategy no matter how much it pisses me off to carry bait buckets. Still, each slippery hunk of fish head that passes through my hands makes it harder to bite my tongue.

As fast as I can think it, I get my first test…and fail miserably.

"Cord-a-leeeeeeto!" Juan sings from his stool before the crane controls. He's taken to calling me Cordalito, which is in no way my name.

It means "little Cordy" and I'll never let it stand. All the air bursts from my lungs at once so it comes out in this annoying sigh that I pray Juan will hear. But my huffing and puffing trails off in the wind and I hear, "Hey! Cordalito! You don't hear me calling you?"

I wipe a layer of seaspray off my face and poke my head up from the rail I'm polishing, but I don't say a word. I figure any kind of acknowledgment is more than Juan deserves. I mean, it's kind of childish and stupid, but so is polishing a rail with a damn toothbrush.

My silence is not lost on him.

"Oh! Look at this. Men! Come quick!"

Nasser and Pierre scuttle across the deck like a couple of crabs. Their eyes pan the ship—at the cloudless sky ablaze in midday sun and the waves rippling against the hull from somewhere beyond the horizon, even down into the grimy hold, now splashing and writhing with life, to make sure it still bears the morning's catch. Neither of them stop for a moment to notice I exist.

"The hell are we looking at?" Pierre asks. He plucks the toothpick—all splintery and wet—from under a slight overbite and cocks his head to one side. Nasser stands there with his long, stringbean arms at his side and awaits further direction.

"It's Cordalito," Juan says in a voice you might use to freak people out at a campfire. "He's…he's just how you young guys like to say it. Look at him. You see it?" Nasser and Pierre stand there confused. They stare at Juan like he's blown a gasket.

I go back to polishing the rail. Try to mind my business. But Juan bursts out laughing and I'm lured back in. "See?" he shouts. "I told you! I think he is ghosting me!" Before I can make another stroke with my polishing tool, Pierre and Nasser are in hysterics. Nasser bends over at the waist and roars, while Pierre rolls on the deck and pounds his hands into the wood like tiny, repeating jackhammers.

I know Cowbird told me there's no such thing as an "end of the line." According to him, you only have beginnings. But right now that statement is a load of crap. Because Juan and Pierre and Nasser reached the end of *my* line two days ago. And now they've gone and crossed it.

That's when something snaps inside of me. I hoist the polishing tool overboard first and then a slimy bucket of chum rains down on the spotless deck and all of a sudden I'm in front of the crane rig taking Juan head on. Like I don't even know who I am anymore.

His eyes flash and he tries to pull back, but I can't stop myself. I fire away, unloading all the anger I've had bottled up in me since we first set sail.

"First of all," I say in a voice I barely recognize, "my name's not, nor has it ever been Cordalito. It's Cordell. Learn it! All of you!" I flash my eyes at Pierre and Nasser. They look even more freaked out than Juan, but it doesn't phase me. I'm rolling. "Second," I continue, "I'm not ghosting you. I'm just opting not to respond because y'all think I'm a shrimp you can bully into doing the shit work you don't want to do." This gets a raised eyebrow and a nod from Juan, who's amused all of a sudden. "Besides, that's not even what ghosting is and, as much as I want to explain how the internet works to you right now..." I jerk my hands around and motion to the open sea. "This doesn't seem like the time or place!" By now, Pierre and Nasser have crowded around Juan and they're listening intently.

"Final note," I say. "When are you gonna let me do some *real* work around here? You know, like, actual fishing instead of scrubbing and smelling like fish guts all day. Like, being a part of the actual crew."

A smile rises under Juan's mustache and the sun sparkles off his eyes in the same way it dances on the rippling tide. "Cordalito? Do I hear you correctly?" He glances back and forth between his two cohorts, who also appear amused. "You say you are ready to do *real* work?"

He fails to conceal a chuckle behind his lips.

"Of course," I say. "How hard can it be?"

Pierre throws his head back and laughs so hard his bandana flips off the back of his head and he has to snatch it off the air before it drifts out to sea.

Juan motions me up onto his stool before the rig. I'm confused, but it's not like I'm in a position to do anything other than accept the responsibility which I demanded.

"Time to check the main net," he says. "You're on the scoop."

"Bu...but—"

"No, no, Cordalito, please. Be my guest," Juan says. "Only one way to see if you are ready. Now...vamanos!"

Pierre and Nasser scuttle back to their positions on the bow of the ship, where their job is to guide the rising nets and the thousands of pounds of wriggling cargo contained inside to the mouth of the hold until the catch can be lowered inside and unloaded. Juan steps down off the rig and grabs a new polishing tool.

"Best deal I ever made," he says as he scuffs at one of the side rails.

I have no clue how to operate the crane, but I'm not about to wuss out in front of the entire crew. Besides, there's only two or three switches and a lever—nothing like the cockpit of old Sally—so how hard can it be?

I crank the key in the rig's ignition and the engine sputters to life. The scent of diesel fuel fills the air. Looks like old Cordalito is about to make apple pie out of this situation and old Juan will be stuck letting the sun turn his ass to shoeleather as he polishes and sweeps, hauls and guts.

But that's when things get kind of tricky. I mean dangerous. I mean downright out of control. That's when I pull back hard on the lever and the chain on the rigging springs to life and the whole boat rocks backward in an aquatic version of popping a wheelie. I panic and push the lever forward. The ropes go slack and the boat settles on the surface of the Atlantic.

Pierre and Nasser shout gibberish at me and I can't make out the words, so I pull back on the lever again. Harder this time. The water behind the boat bubbles until a round, wriggling mass of netting and fish and seaweed breach the surface like a killer whale. The crane creaks and the gears slip and the boat hits a swell and lurches up at an angle that would make Jacques Cousteau puke, and the ropes swing and snap against each other and send all two thousand pounds of netting and fish flesh right at me like a giant, living wrecking ball. My vision goes all foggy for a second, and then I'm in the echo chamber again:

Get him back on there

Help me lift him.

Hold his arms. Steady him!

And then everything comes bursting back the next instant and I'm cold and disoriented. And wet. Bobbing up and down in the swirling Atlantic at least twenty feet behind the boat. My lungs are filled with seawater and a shiner throbs below my eye socket.

With my good eye, I search the deck. I see the forms of Pierre and Nasser and Juan shrinking in the distance as they wave their arms and scream into the blanket of nothingness. Even Captain Adomi evaporates into the distance as she stands at attention on the deck of her crow's nest.

I'm going to die here.

This is how it ends for me.

I'm as good as shark meat.

The gears grind again, and the engine dredges up a mass of whitewater as the ship reverses course. One by one, the three crewmen hurl themselves off the deck and into the drink like penguins from an ice floe. Pierre gets to me first. He wraps both arms around me and kicks off in the opposite direction. Nasser meets us halfway to the boat, and Pierre throws one of my arms up over Nasser's shoulders. The two of them kick as hard as they can against the current until we're floating under the words *Ama Kamama*. Juan meets us there. He's already in the water pushing me aboard by my rump before I can say sorry.

I can tell you, after the qualified crewmembers of the *Ama Kamama* save the resident chum cutter from becoming chum himself, said chum cutter somehow feels he's part of the crew instead of a lowly chum cutter.

Pierre and Nasser and Juan confirm my suspicion by rescuing me in two ways. One is the actual rescue. The other comes by making me laugh about it. I never realized that sometimes the best way—maybe the only way—to handle a difficult or embarrassing situation is to laugh your fool head off.

That's probably why Juan's like, "Hey, Pierre, remember your first week aboard?" and then lets Pierre tell us about the time he got his foot stuck in a chum bucket and was so embarrassed he tried to play it off as a shoe. And why Pierre finishes the tale by saying, "What about little Romeo over there?" and lets Nasser tell us about a time he was so smitten with a girl he'd met in Charleston that he lost track of time and Captain Adomi set sail for New Bern without him. And then Juan tells the topper, about a time he sleep-walked up on deck and walked the plank right into a hold filled with fish.

"You've had your moment. Now back to work, boys!" Captain Adomi shouts from her silent perch on the catwalk deck. She doesn't sound happy. "He could have been killed! Private Wheaton!" I scurry over to the base of the metal staircase leading up to the Captain's chambers. I'm still wrapped in a towel from my swim. She laughs. "Up here now! On the double!"

"Yes, Captain!" I shout.

I drop the towel on the deck and I'm up the catwalk stairs in about three strides. I'm shaking a little and it has nothing to do with being drenched in cold seawater.

"Come inside and get warm," she says, without a trace of emotion in her voice.

I follow Captain Adomi to the control tower, which reminds me of old Sally's cockpit. There's a giant, wooden captain's wheel at the center of the bridge like you'd see in an old pirate movie and a bunch of sonar-looking devices on a panel in front of it.

"Sit down," she tells me. She directs me to a round table with two metal folding chairs set around it. Two cups of steaming coffee and a plate of chocolate chip cookies sit at the middle of the table. "Have some," she says as she makes a peculiar measurement on her map with an even weirder device that looks like a giant protractor from math class. "I always bring cookies on a long cruise. Never share them with the boys, so don't tell them."

"I won't," I say cautiously. "And thanks for having me aboard. I don't know—" She puts a finger to my lips to silence me and then pushes a plastic bag filled with ice against my eye. I wince.

"Hold this on your eye," she says. "And, Cordy, I didn't ask you to come up here to get all apologetic and weepy on me."

"You didn't?"

"No."

"So this isn't about doing the 'man overboard' routine out there a few minutes ago?"

"Nope. Although that was pretty dangerous and stupid. Also entertaining." She smiles and takes a massive bite out of her cookie. "I want to talk to you about sleep," she says through a mouth full of crumbs.

"Sleep? I'm sleeping fine. The sea is like—"

"I'm talking about your dreams. There's something—"

"I don't want to talk about them," I say, cutting her off mid sentence.

"I don't want to talk about the context of the dreams as much as the fact you're having them."

"Well, I am. Sometimes. It's not a big deal."

"It *is* a big deal," she says. "I know that too well."

"You do?"

"Yes. Things weren't easy for me when I got back from the Gulf. You see stuff in war that I don't think anyone should ever see. You hear things too."

I nod and sit up straight in the chair, take a sip of strong, black coffee. "I kept seeing some of those things long after I wish they'd been gone. Sometimes I still do."

She places a hand on my damp shoulder. "You know what I mean?"

I nod, but I'm not ready to talk about it with her. I mean, I barely know her.

"You know, you're not alone. You're not being punished. There are others like you."

"Thanks," I say, because I'm not sure what else there is I *can* say.

"That's it? *Thanks*?" The captain leans back in her chair and downs the rest of her coffee in one shot. "Cordy, I'm only telling you this because of Sun Tzu."

"Who?"

"He wrote *The Art of War*. It's one of my favorite books. I know that sounds weird but, in it, he writes 'if you know the enemy and know yourself, you need not fear the results of one hundred battles.' That's kind of how I feel about your dreams and this whole journey you're on. Does that make sense?"

"Perfect sense," I say. I start to get excited because the conversation is veering right into my wheelhouse. "Sounds like Plato. He kept it simple and said 'know thyself.'"

"Exactly," the captain says. "And I didn't know you were so quick with the Greek philosophy. I'm impressed."

"Not just philosophy," I say. "Also mythology and a whole bunch of other stuff. Like, there's this one story about the necklace of Harmonia that reminds me of my brother, Travis."

"Oh yeah? How does that go?"

"Well, this noble lady inherits a priceless necklace. She thinks it's the greatest gift in the world, only it's cursed by one of the gods and it starts to control her and eventually ends up ruining her life."

"Ouch," she says, "But how does that have anything to do with your brother?"

"Well, Travis inherited his own kind of gift, or, rather, curse that took over his life. Made him into a different person."

"And did it ruin his life?"

I stare at her for a moment and finish the last bite of my cookie. Then I bottom out the coffee. "I'm not sure," I say. "I guess that's what this journey is about."

"Don't lose faith, Cordy. In fact, your brother's story reminds me of mythology from my culture."

"What culture is that?"

"Cherokee Nation. We have a myth about the first man and first woman. They lived together happily for many years until things got tough and they started to argue. So the woman left."

"What happened to her?"

"The first man missed her, so he asked the sun to bring her back. Well, the sun shined down on a spot in the path and a great patch of blackberries sprung up from the ground. The woman passed by it without notice. Then, the sun shined down in another spot, and a great patch of raspberries covered the ground. Once again, the woman passed by without paying it any mind."

"Geez," I say. "She must not have liked fruit very much."

The captain rolls her eyes and continues. "The sun decided to try once more, and it shined its brightest rays on the flattest and most protected spot on the path."

"And what happened?"

"A great patch of strawberries spread across the path and the woman looked upon the glowing, red berries and sat down to have a snack. She liked them so much she forgot what made her angry in the first place and she started back on the path. She didn't get far before she spotted the first man, and they walked back to camp together and never separated for the rest of eternity."

She bites into another cookie and we sit there in silence for a few seconds. "I know, it all sounds a bit fantastical," she says finally.

"No. It's perfect," I tell her.

"Then why do you look so deflated?"

"I don't know," I say. "I guess I hope John Coltrane will prove to be the strawberry Travis doesn't know he's looking for."

A puzzled grin crosses Captain Adomi's mouth. "What does John Coltrane have to do with any of this?" she asks.

"He's my brother's hero," I say. "Mine too. Cowbird seems to think he's the glue that binds Travis and me together. I think I agree. Of course, all I can do is hope John Coltrane proves to be the kind of glue that never dries out. Not like that pasty crap they used to make us use in kindergarten."

"I hope the glue is strong," the captain says, "but there's only one way to find out."

I nod because I know she's right. I just wish she could foretell my future like the ancient prophets of Greek lore. If anyone could use a prophecy right now, it's one Cordell Wheaton.

Safe Passage

Another dreamless night. I wake to the whole ship vibrating under the weight of the *Ama Kamama*'s foghorn. There's a stampede of footsteps shuffling back and forth across the main deck. A sliver of sunlight squeezes through a crack in the face of the trapdoor and pools at the foot of my hammock.

In a scene straight from *Gilligan's Island*, I flip three times in the hammock before it deposits me face-first on the floorboards. I dust myself off and snag a clean t-shirt and dry shorts out of my bag. I slip into them in one motion like I'm jumping inside a potato sack.

I scamper up the ladder. The first crewman I see on deck is Juan. "Look who it is!" he says loud enough to be picked up by any spy submarine in the area. The salty corners of his mouth are jacked up to earlobe level.

"Why didn't you wake me?" I ask.

A lanky arm rests on my back. I turn to meet Nasser's face. It's twisted up in motherly concern. "Ouch," he says, looking at my swollen eye. "We thought you could use the extra rest."

"Yeah, Cordalito," Juan says. "We couldn't bear to look at you while we ate. It's like roast beef or something." He grabs one of my hands and places a jagged hunk of ice in my palm. I press it against my eye. It hurts just enough to make me forget about the softball-sized bruise on my shin from my little train jumping adventure.

Through my good eye, I look over the starboard and notice a faint outline on the horizon. It's obscured by sea mist, but I can make out the razor-sharp angles of highrises and the sparkle of sunlight dancing on their scaly panes of glass.

"You hungry?" Pierre's voice echoes from inside the hold as he splashes around in thigh-high, rubber boots. The thought of another bread sandwich makes me want to jump overboard, but then Pierre says,

"I left a container of my famous red beans and rice. And mango. On Juan's station."

Just as Pierre promised, there's a plastic container filled with rice, and a plastic fork, a bottle of water, and a mango—already peeled, pitted, and sliced—in a small, metal bowl on the dashboard of the rig. Juan takes the ice off my eye, tosses it in the ocean, and stacks Pierre's food in my arms.

"Go eat. We have things under control. Be in Norfolk soon."

I don't know what to say, and then I think about these practical jokers and their unquenchable appetite for busting each other's chops and I start to question the whole thing.

"What are you guys up to?" I ask.

"Up to?" Juan asks. "Why would we be up to something, Cordalito?"

"Because I've been on this boat for three days and I never stopped working for a second, and now I wake up on a freaking Disney cruise?"

Juan wipes a layer of early morning labor off his brow. "You hear that, hermanos? Cordalito thinks we're punking him. Like that show!"

Nasser spits out his water. A deep, echoey cackle rises up from inside the hold. "I'm proud of you, Cordalito," Juan continues.

"Proud? That I almost got myself killed?"

"No. I could have done without that," Juan says. "I'm proud of you for becoming fifty percent less gullible since yesterday. But there's no catch this time. Go. Enjoy your food."

I stare at him, not knowing if I should take my chances and shovel a bunch of rice and beans down my throat only to find they're spiked with metamucil, or guzzle some water to find it's seagull piss or something. Juan sees my struggle and reaches in his pocket. "Look," he says, "we wanted to surprise you. There's no Ashton Kutcher out here. You will not get punked." He stacks a pile of bills on the plastic rice container and, right on cue, my vision lurches and goes blurry. The echoey voices move in on me:

From the congregation.

They took up a collection?

For us?

And then I'm back on the deck of the *Ama Kamama* with Juan, Pierre, and Nasser staring at me like I have three heads. I don't know what to say to them so I ask, "Did y'all just hear that?"

Juan's forehead is all scrunched up with worry and Pierre stares down at the deck as if he's afraid to make eye contact with me and contract whatever kind of weird disease I'm currently afflicted with. Pierre raises a single eyebrow and says, "Man, I don't know what you're talking about. Only gulls out here. You talking to gulls, Cordy?"

I shake my head and try to push past the weirdness of what just happened. I try to play it off as if I'm normal and not the type of dude who happens to hear voices out of thin air and in the middle of the damn Atlantic Ocean.

"So…uhh…what's all this?" I ask.

"About sixty bucks," Nasser interjects. "Give or take."

"We all collected," Juan says. "Even the captain chipped in. Sorry it's not more, but we don't get paid until we get back to New Bern."

"And after we sell all these damn fish!" Pierre splashes and shouts from below.

"Thank you," I exclaim. "But, why? Why would you do this?"

"Because of respect," Juan says. "We gave you a hard time, but not by mistake. You passed."

"I didn't know there was a test."

"Everything's a test," Nasser says.

I pocket the bills and take a forkful of rice, which is easily the greatest thing I've eaten in my life after surviving on bread sandwiches the whole trip.

"He's right!" Pierre shouts from below.

"Cordalito, you did what we all have to do."

"And what's that?"

"You paid your dues, my friend. Sacrificed. Made compromises."

"It sucked."

"Of course it sucked," Juan says through a snicker. "Why do you think all three of us stay away from our families for so long? Just so we can slosh around in a giant, floating fish bowl?"

"I don't know," I say with mango juice running down my chin. "I've been trying to figure that out."

"There comes a time when you've sacrificed enough, Cordalito. You feel it. It burns inside you. And that's when it's time to do something. To take action. To fight for survival."

"That's what I did?" I ask.

"In a way," Juan says, "you grew ten sizes when you stood up to me, even though you made a mess of our rig and your face. We also talked to the captain last night."

I cough up a piece of half-chewed mango when he says it. "What did she tell you?" I ask staring down at the white-washed plank boards all lined up like matchsticks.

"Everything," Nasser says as he swishes a salt-encrusted mop across the deck.

"And we approve," Juan says. "We hope our contribution gets you where you need to go, Cordy."

I'm stunned when he calls me by my actual name instead of passing me off as a wee Cordalito. Juan stands there with the grin of a proud father and one weathered, brown hand extended in front of him. My entire hand is engulfed in his as we shake.

"Good," he says. "Now all we have to do is work on that handshake."

Laughter builds from behind the mop and in deep echoes from the hold. Then the crew snaps to form and resumes the usual tasks of the day.

I sit cross-legged on the bow and eat the last forkfuls of rice and slurp up the excess juice from the mango bowl and down my water and listen to the waves crash against the hull. The view of the shoreline solidifies and the outlines of buildings grow heavy and precise.

I sit there for an hour, feeling the crisp, sea air on my face and the midday sun as a blanket on my body. I'm amazed by how far I am from High Point, out here in the swirling Atlantic, a sea barnacle among men. And I think about how far I still have to go before I reach Philadelphia. Before I can search for Travis. When my journey will truly begin. And I think about Juan and Nasser and Pierre. About how their lives have been pockmarked battlefields from the start and how they've spent every day since trying to avoid the land mines.

I guess that describes everyone's life at some point in time, all with different kinds of landmines producing the same kinds of outcomes. And I think about how strange and uplifting it is to find a group of individuals from diverse backgrounds who can be so much the same that they're on the same boat, at the same time, doing one of the world's oldest jobs under the leadership of someone who descended from one of the original inhabitants of this land.

All of this makes me realize how important it is to crawl out of the shell and go for a wander. Because the shell can't protect you from everything. Nor can it teach you anything. Sometimes the only real protection, or the only lesson, is to run. Or to fight. Or to sacrifice for others.

And if you don't believe me, go ask Juan or Nasser or Pierre.

At that moment, the foghorn of the *Ama Kamama* startles me back to reality, and we begin to drift like a butterfly into the Port of Norfolk. The vast horizon, which not so long ago was just waves and nothing else, is now obscured by the great, white hulls of steamships, and tall cranes that jut up like stalactites from the dockworks, and the shadowy stonework of buildings that rise up from the distant streets like fortresses.

Captain Adomi doesn't descend from the bridge until the *Ama Kamama* is moored. She finds me on the bow and hands me another bag of ice for my eye, and we sit in silence and listen to the sounds of the city—horns blaring and gears slipping and vendors crying out their wares. Alien sounds that assault my ears with an intensity I wouldn't have noticed before three days at sea. Finally, Captain Adomi reaches over and pats me on the knee.

"Did the boys give you anything?" she asks.

I nod. "Yes. Thank you. Y'all really didn't have to—"

"And what? Send our investment out there in the world with nothing?"

"Your investment?"

"Cordy, we didn't risk our lives to save yours so you can go out and become a corpse in ten minutes."

I can't hide my smile. Captain Adomi seems amused by her own joke too. "Thanks," I say. "I'm sure it'll help."

"Should get you pretty close to Philly if you hop a train. Might even get there by morning if you leave now."

I stand up and move toward the captain with my arms outstretched. She takes a step back and I'm left squeezing air. "Let's not get mushy about this, Private," she says with her lips creased into a devilish slash mark of a smile. She raises her hand to her bucket cap in mock salute. I step back and do the same. Then Captain Adomi lurches forward and squeezes me in a bear hug until I think I might die of suffocation.

"Good luck, Private Wheaton," she says.

And that's it. I walk the gangway down to the dock works with my bag slung over my back and wave to my fellow crewmen as I slip into the city and adapt to the feeling of solid ground underfoot.

The train station is a short walk from the dock works, which is good because the last thing I need is to get lost in Norfolk, Virginia. The place in no way resembles the sleepy, little station back on High Street with its roof covered in tiles and the waiting room lined in oak benches. No, this place is straight from the future. Like an alien spaceship landed in the middle of Norfolk and got bought out by Amtrak. The outside blazes in LED lighting and the inside is a triumph of Teflon and other space-age plastics, with round, spinning stools for resting and an automated kiosk for travelers who know what they're doing. Of course, I do not, so I find the lone straight line in the place, hidden among the futuristic curves and planted in front of the ticket booth.

It's manned by an actual man, if you can call him that. I can tell he's a few years older than me because his face is a patchwork quilt of untrimmed whiskers he's apparently, and unsuccessfully, attempting to play off as a full-on, legitimate beard—which it is not. He punches both the keyboard on his smartphone and the keyboard on the magical ticket-printing computer that's jammed in behind plate-glass with him at the same time. He takes a single earbud out of his ear long enough to listen to an annoyed traveler grumble out a destination. Then the bud's in again and he's back to typing and printing out tickets and collecting money all in one motion.

At the window, I'm met with a staticky mish-mash of synthesizers and screaming that floods out of the dude's earbuds, through a hand-sized opening at the bottom of the plate-glass, and right into my face. I can't tell what it is, but it's not Coltrane.

I pull out the cash I got from the crew and set aside enough to get me and Travis through the doors at Birdland. The ticket clerk stares at me from inside his glassy cage. His name tag reads "Chip" and a bushy head of curls spills out from under an Amtrak-approved conductor's hat. He pulls the earbud for a split-second and says in a monotone, disinterested drawl, "Can I help you?"

"How far can I get with—" He holds his palm to the glass like a crossing guard and types something on his phone with the other. Then he waves me on and I continue, "How far will this take me?" I spread the bills against the glass. Chip's eyes dart back to the Amtrak monitor.

"Which direction?"

"North. To Philly," I say. He taps away on the keyboards simultaneously, with both hands moving in opposite directions and the earbuds firmly in place. I start to say something, but he raises an index finger to the glass before anything crosses my lips.

"Harrisburg. There's nothing direct."

I'm not sure how far it is from Harrisburg to Philadelphia, but I know it must be closer than Norfolk. At least Harrisburg is in the same state.

"OK, I'll take it," I say.

"One way to Harrisburg," Chip says a bit too loud over the volume blasting in his own head. "Safe travels." I slip the money through the glass. A ticket emerges from the ticket counter. Chip slides it through to me. "Platform's listed on the bottom," he says. "It's final boarding."

I glance at the ticket. At the bottom, near the perforation, it reads: Platform 7F. I look up on the wall where a bright orange sign reads: Platform 1A. I tear off through the station with my bag bobbing up and down and the hard, metal hilt of Cowbird's knife ringing against the same vertebrae on my back over and over again.

Lucky for me, the station isn't as big as it looks from outside. I shoot up a corridor that looks like it came off the set of *Star Trek* and I'm standing in front of Platform 7F. Outside on the actual platform, the doors on the train cars glide closed. A porter slips a final piece of luggage inside one of the cars before it prepares for take off.

I hand my ticket to a gentleman at the gate in a red, scratchy coat and a weird, bell-hoppy-looking hat. He stares at it, then mumbles a few words into his walkie. He says, "Get on out there," as he motions me to the train and hands me the torn-off half of my ticket.

I don't notice the sweat dripping down my face until I'm in my seat with my backpack stowed in the compartment above. The train whistle sounds its shrill call as I mop my face with the bottom hem of my t-shirt and prepare for a super long, super boring, super bumpy trip without the luxury of my smartphone to occupy me. At least then I could text Mom and Dad and let them know I'm alive, or mindlessly scroll through my social media feed. Anything other than staring at the back of this seat for five hours, stuck with nothing but my thoughts.

My thoughts are deadly. They get me in trouble when I get so caught up in them that I don't know what I should do. And then I do nothing.

And then I'm right back in my shell or my cave or wherever it is people go when they're too scared to fight for change. I can't afford that. Not when my nose is pointed in the right direction. Not now.

But now, that's exactly where I go. Into my head, with the rumble of the track crawling up through my seat and the cattails waving at me as the train whips through the coastal Virginia marshlands. The first thought that comes to mind is Trane and how Travis taught me to listen to his music. To sit there and concentrate on each note, each decision Trane made with his fingers, each millisecond of sound. Travis told me, "If you know how to listen to Trane, his music never leaves your head and you can listen to him anywhere."

Right now, with the reddish afternoon glow giving way to the blues of evening, I hear Travis's song—Trane's song—behind the locomotive's chug-a-lug so it sounds like a full quartet with Trane and Travis and me and even Dad, free of illness, tapping a tambourine on his leg. And for a few moments—before I start to fade off—it feels like that night never happened. It feels like Travis still played his sax every day and had his perfect GPA and never got in his accident and started with the pills. First popping and then pushing. Then both. For a split second it feels like nothing came between us and that I didn't ruin his life, and that maybe, just maybe, my crazy plan might just work.

That song. Again.

Piercing, Squealing, ungodly sounds of screeching brass. It builds. Falls. Rises again in a heartbeat. But it lacks melody. Cadence. The notes fray apart like the end of a rope. Splinter off in tiny, irritating fibers that stick in all the wrong places.

The tires vibrate on rough ground. The music cuts off and both car doors open. Slam shut. Keys jingle against the trunk. The panel pops open. Blinding white. Tears. A blurry figure in black clothing.

I struggle against the ropes. Against fear. But there's no escape. The figure grabs my ankle and the rope. He yanks me from the trunk. My body rolls off the back bumper. Crashes down on soft earth. Down here it smells green. Plentiful. Full of life.

My fingertips drag the concrete as they lift me. Stagger to a door. The masked figure pushes it open with his foot. Nothing but stale air and Darkness. I'm flung in through the open doorway. Crash down on cold cement. The door slams shut. The call of a train whistle grows louder and less distant and...

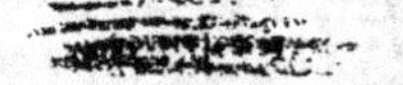

A Girl and Her Guitar

I bolt up in my seat and wipe a trickle of drool off my chin. The train whistle screams like a tea kettle. I take a deep breath, then exhale as I try to get control of my heart rate. I'm drenched in cold sweat. I touch my eye and wince. Still puffy and painful. I don't want to know what it looks like.

Passengers mill around the train car, pulling baggage from their compartments and replacing hats and sports coats as they wait to be spit out on the platform. Then the worst happens. The crackle of a speaker and the sound of a chime. A woman's voice mumbles something incoherent, pauses to make some throat-clearing noises and then says, "Amtrak Express welcomes you to Lynchburg. Welcome travelers. We hope you'll ride with us in the future. Once again, our final stop is Lynchburg, Virginia."

That's when three things happen. First, I check my ticket stub and notice it says "Lynchburg" instead of "Harrisburg" front and center, right at the top. Next, my heart beats a million times per second until my body feels like a giant pressure cooker set to: EXPLODE. Finally, I panic and grab my backpack and push right past the line of business travelers and family rubberneckers in the aisle. I don't come up for air until I'm on a railway platform packed with people.

I push through the sea of arms and legs. I'm at least fifty times more freaked out than anyone around me. A woman in a white hat with a floppy brim grunts when I nudge past her and displace the horizon of her hatline. A man with a briefcase in one hand and a paper folded under his tweed jacket stares me down as I pass, though I can't imagine what he's looking at.

But I don't care. I'm in Lynchburg, Virginia which, I'm pretty sure is even farther from Philadelphia than Norfolk. How could I be so stupid? How could I have been so careless and blind? How could I have let this happen? Only, none of the answers to my questions matter right now.

All that matters is I find a ticket booth and figure out how to make the money I have left—the bread I was supposed to use on Travis—work to my advantage.

I put my head down and crawl through the pack like a hedgehog. I charge up to the ticket kiosk before anyone can stake a claim. I look the ticket agent in the eyes and feed him the biggest load of crap I can come up with at the moment.

"I'd like to lodge a complaint," I say. He rifles through a drawer inside his enclosure and slides an accordion-thick stack of pages under the glass with a pen on top.

"Please fill out the forms, have them notarized and returned within thirty days of the alleged incident," he says in a dry, nasal voice that matches his polka-dotted bow tie and his round, wire spectacles. I lift the stack of papers. It's about the weight of a cinderblock.

"Then what do I do?" I ask.

"The station director reviews your claim and passes it to the regional director if it meets the requirements."

"Then I get my money back?"

He starts to laugh but cuts it short when it becomes clear my question was meant to be a serious one. "No," he says. "The regional director reviews and then decides on the merits."

"Then I get reimbursed?

"No. Then it's passed to the regional board and then to company lawyers and then, maybe, you'll get reimbursed. If you're lucky." He smiles so hard it looks painful.

"How long does that take?" I ask.

"Anywhere from six to twelve weeks."

Since I don't want to sit around in a train station for the next three months wondering where Travis is or if Dad's on his deathbed, I push the stack of forms and the pen back through the glass. I reach in my bag and gather the stack of bills I was saving for Birdland. I shuffle through them.

Thirty-six bucks.

"What's the cheapest fare you have to get to the Philadelphia area?" I ask. The ticket agent pushes his spectacles up on the lumpy bridge of his nose and types on his keyboard with a single, outstretched finger on each hand. As he types, a calm falls over the station. The army of ants have scattered off to a million individual destinations, and the station will be a hollow shell until the next train rumbles in on the platform. The only sounds are the ticket agent's incessant keyboard punches, the sound of a news report coming through the window of the station's bar and grille, and the clopping of nameless footsteps that echo in distant corridors.

"Hmmm," the ticket agent says. "We have a special for seventy-eight. Today only."

"Anything cheaper than that?" I say. As the agent goes back to typing, the words of the news reporter on the TV in the bar stop me dead in my tracks.

"Parents of sixteen-year-old Cordell Wheaton, pictured here," the reporter says as a photo of me in seventh grade—the one Mom keeps in her wallet—flashes on the screen, "are reaching out to citizens throughout the Southeast region tonight in hope that someone has seen their son who's been missing since—"

"We also have one to Pittsburgh for fifty-nine," the ticket agent says over my shoulder.

I'm too frozen to move or breathe, let alone respond.

"Young man?" he says when I don't turn around, but each word the news anchor says pushes me closer to becoming the world's first documented case of spontaneous combustion.

"Police have labeled this a missing persons case," she says, "and are ramping up efforts at the state and local levels to bring this missing child home to High Point, North Carolina where—"

"Young man?" the ticket agent repeats. "Are you alright?"

"Yeah, I'm fine," I say, spinning away from my view of the broadcast. "What did you find?" I expect to see Mr. Efficiency behind his plate-glass window typing me an answer. Instead, he stares at me with his jaw down near his Adam's apple. I catch my reflection in the glass for a second and realize I look so pale someone could mistake me for a warm glass of milk.

The ticket agent takes one look at my face, and I know I better find a quick solution to get me out of here before anyone notices *I'm* the Cordell Wheaton being broadcast on every TV set in the station. That's when my hand hits the side of my jeans pocket and I feel the thin slip of plastic poking out. That's when I remember the patrolman who tried to chase Emma Rose into oblivion and inadvertently left me a rather generous donation.

"Do you take credit?" I ask, trying to stop my voice from quivering and the beads of sweat from rolling down my forehead.

"Of course," the ticket agent replies. "Just slide your card through the glass."

I reach in my pocket and push the stolen card across the transom and into the realms of a possible felony. My heart races a million beats per second as the ticket agent swipes the card through his machine and waits for a receipt and my train ticket to squirt out in response.

But nothing happens. The news reporter keeps rambling on about potential Cordy Wheaton sightings from the bar's TV and the ticket agent stares at the screen of his computer with a slight wrinkle in his brow, and I stand there trying not to soil my shorts in the same way Emma Rose described the nightmarish thrashings she witnessed. Then the ticket agent picks up a phone receiver on his desk and stares out through the glass at me.

"This will just take a second, sir," he reassures me, but I'm not so sure of what he's doing at all. In fact, I'm not so sure I haven't just ended my trip—and maybe my life as a free man—in one swipe of a stolen credit card.

I start to back away from the ticket booth, slowly as not to spook the agent and make him realize I'm just a garden variety crook with absolutely no idea of where to start a life of crime. But he notices me backing away and I hear him mumble, "Hold on," into the receiver before pulling it slightly from his face.

"Young man? Please don't…"

That's when I realize my plan for saving Travis and reuniting my family is toast if I don't get the hell out of here. Like, *now*.

"Thanks for the help," I shout at him, but the ticket agent doesn't hear a word because I'm ten steps away, busting through the empty station house at a full sprint.

"Hey! Stop!" The ticket agent's nasally pleas bounce around the station's hollow corridors. Two security officers immediately pop out of an unmarked door beside a row of water fountains. Their heavy steps pound on the tiles behind me. My legs go woozy and rubber-like as I cut through a line of indoor shrubbery and race through the food court.

The food court is littered with people waiting for trains and taking coffee breaks, but they stop what they're doing and rise from their seats when I race past their tables and leave upended trays of food in my wake and ignore the pursuing officers who warn me to "Stop! At once!" because "You can't escape!"

But, I'm not about to get scooped up in Lynchburg, Virginia after all I've been through. So I take my only chance, and bolt down an access corridor behind the fast food establishments. The officers round a corner behind me firing off warnings like stray bullets.

There's a crack of light ahead. An ounce of hope. A door leans half-open on its hinge, with the chaotic workings of a grease-trap kitchen behind it. I charge through the doorway and crash into a middle-aged fry cook. His entire basket of blazing hot French fries cascades into the air like crispy, golden confetti and the cook's funny, little paper hat flips off and lands on the grill. The officers crash through the doorway next, just as the paper hat goes up in a flash and the whole grill erupts in a grease fire and the kitchen crew scatters around their stations like a buzzing swarm of bees and one of the officers' boots hits a pile of greasy fries and sends him headlong into the other officer, who falls into the fry cook, who collapses into the raging inferno caused by his hat. Meanwhile, I slink away, into the staff bathroom and up onto the trash can stationed below the window.

I climb outside, close the window, and shimmy down to street level on the side of an aluminum drainage pipe attached to the cement wall. I drop the final ten feet to the ground and land in a heap of dust and tiny bits of glass.

On one side of the alley is the station, with its steel beams and space-aged masonry. Even the dumpsters below the food court windows are clean and painted and new. On the other side of the alley is a pile of old gin boxes stacked eight feet high on top of two rusted-out dumpsters aswarm with flies and stench. The pile's so massive it overshadows the cracked, brick walls and the rusty hinges of a seedy-looking establishment behind it. The only nice thing to look at on that side of the alley is the car. Electric blue with a thick, white racing stripe down the middle of the hood, over the roof, and over the tail. A chrome tag on the hood reflects particles of early morning light and reads: Chevelle.

I'm about to move in for a closer look when the back door of the dive bar swings open and a twangy crash of Honky-Tonk pours into the streets of Lynchburg. Then another work of art walks out the door. Maybe the most beautiful lady I've seen in my entire sixteen and some years in this solar system.

Her blond hair is pulled back in a long braid that hangs out from under a Stetson hat like a horse tail. Her boots are sharp-toed and snakeskin. Turquoise, which happens to be an anomaly to nature, but seems kind of fitting as well. She walks to the back of the Chevelle and drops her guitar case on the gravel next to a box filled with assorted odds and ends.

That's when she notices I'm standing there with my chin dragging the ground. She jumps. Scuffs the leather soles of her boots against the street and flattens one palm to her chest like it's the only way to stop her heart from bursting right through. I don't know why I do it, but my first instinct is to stand up as straight as I can and put my hands over my head like I'm caught in a bank hold-up. Then I sputter out something stupid like, "I come in peace," or possibly something even more embarrassing.

I'm guessing that I must have come across as completely harmless and pathetic, which at times can be a good thing, since she just smiles, bats the lashes over blue eyes and says, "well, they sure grow city rats a heckuva lot bigger than country ones." She pauses to laugh at her own joke. I'm too nervous to laugh with her. Also to speak words and/or breathe air near her.

"Ain't you got somewhere to be, Mickey Mouse?" she asks as she fumbles with her keys. "Like school?"

"It's…uhhh…s-s-summer?" I manage to say, which is a lie but sounds a whole lot better than "I got suspended."

"Right," she says. "Makes sense. You forget about stuff like that when you ain't been somewhere for awhile."

"You can't be that old," I say, feeling like maybe it's not all that hard to talk to a girl this way.

"Only twenty-three, sugar. But I've been on the road since I was sixteen." She twists the key in the trunk, but her hand slips. "Dang it! This darn thing!" she shouts. She turns and smashes one of her fists through the face of an empty gin box that was lying there minding its own business.

"Let me try," I say.

"Why not?" She sighs and hands me the key. I slide it in the lock, jiggle it a bit, and then POP! The lid opens in one sweep. I drop the box of odds and ends in the trunk and then reach for the guitar case. The girl grabs my wrist. Hard. Like what you'd expect from someone who just knocked out a gin box ten seconds into Round One.

"That's Lil' Hank Williams," she says. "Nobody touches Lil' Hank but me." I step aside and she lifts the guitar case into the trunk on her own.

Then she's all bubbly and sweet again the next instant. "I do appreciate it though, Mr. Mouse."

"It's Cordy," I say. "Cordy Wh…uhh, Wideman." I hold out my hand like a regular freaking gentleman and we shake.

"Ms. Lula McBride. Country music extraordinaire. At your service. At least someday."

"How do you know that's not today?" I say all suavely.

"Kid, look behind me." She motions to the trash pile. "You think anyone can describe this moment in time as extraordinary?" I want to say "hell yes!" but instead I shake my head.

"My brother's a musician too," I say. "Well, he used to be one. He played the sax."

"That so? I don't know much about horns, but put me behind a microphone with Lil' Hank and I promise I'll have you two-steppin'." She stares at the lump on my eye and her smile fades to something you'd expect to see on a mother's face when she takes her sick kid to the doctor. "You alright?" she asks. I don't say anything and I can tell she realizes I'm stuck and I'm reaching out for help without trying to ask. "What's your story, Cordy Wideman?"

I don't know about this Cordy Wideman kid, but I can tell you Cordy Wheaton sure couldn't stop telling Ms. Lula McBride just about everything from the beginning. About Dad and Travis and my hair-brained plan. About how I have no idea if I'll find him in time or even at all. By the time I finish telling her why the heck I'm in a trash pile in Lynchburg, Virginia instead of in Philadelphia, Pennsylvania there's no way she can get in her Chevelle and watch me disappear in the rear-view.

"Tell you what," she says. "I ain't going anywhere near Philadelphia. But I am going somewhere that's not here. Wanna come along?"

"Where?"

"Nashville. Country music capital of the world. I've got a big-time show at the smallest-time venue in the whole dang town. You in?"

"I don't know," I say.

But Lula says the perfect thing at the moment I need it most.

"Sometimes, you gotta let the currents take you, honey. Stop fighting. You'll find that they'll take you where you need to go."

Stone. Cold. Philosophy.

How did she know she'd get to me that way? Or maybe it was her use of the word *honey* that sealed the deal? Hard to say.

I was going to end up further away from Philadelphia than ever, with thirty-six bucks to my name, but it felt right. Something in my gut told me to just go with her—that Lula was some kind of real-life muse and this was fate—and I'd eventually find my way to Travis if I just let the currents take me there.

I drop my backpack onto the back seat and hop in the passenger side of Lula's electric blue Chevelle.

Lula's Dreamcoat

I'm lost in thought, replaying the news story over and over in my head, worried about my parents, as waves of guilt begin to wash over me, when Lula, with a hypnotist's precision, snaps me back into the present, as she moves on me like a surrogate mother. Somehow, she manages to shift into fifth gear, keep the Chevelle steady in its lane with the nudge of a knee on the steering wheel, and make the engine roar under a lead-weighted cowboy boot—all while cleaning some kind of gunk off the side of my face with a balled-up handkerchief and a little spit-shine.

I shrink away when the fabric hits my cheek, but Lula McBride doesn't do things lightly—not dress or talk or drive—and she takes a sandpapery swipe across my face before I can fend her off. And then I'm suddenly in the echo chamber again. With that voice. One that sounds so much more familiar than before:

Let me have that cloth

I'll keep him cleaned up *Just like way back when*

I took care of him then *and I'll take care of him now...*

Before Lula even notices I'm not there with her for a few moments, I spring back and I'm sitting in the passenger seat of the Chevelle with a wrinkled up old tissue scraping against the side of my face.

"When's the last time you came in contact with soap?" Lula asks. "Cause it smells pretty darned ripe in here!" She rolls the window down. A gust of cool, mountain air washes out my apparent ripeness. The moonbeams shimmer through breaks in the peaks above us. They filter through the windshield and onto the black, leather dash and make the weathered cracks more visible.

"Been a few days," I say, "and my bathtub was the Atlantic Ocean—"

"So, longer than a few days?"

"Yeah," I say. "Too long."

"We'll get you washed up when we get to Nashville. Sound good?" I nod. I mean, I'm excited about the idea of a long, hot shower. Everyone likes to be clean. But I'm not crazy about getting grooming tips from a girl who's not much older than me. It's pathetic, so I try to change the subject.

"So, how'd you go to school and go on tour at the same time?" It's out of the blue, but I'm willing to go any direction as long as it's away from my current state of hygiene.

"School?" A devilish-looking, sideways grin rolls across Lula's face but she doesn't go any further, so I press.

"I mean, you said you were on the road at age sixteen. How'd you do that and still go to school?"

"I didn't," she says, then she flips on the radio to a country station that's more static than music. All I can tell is there's a lady singing and her voice is as twangy as an old tuning fork.

"You didn't go to school?" I ask a third time. Lula cranks the volume on the radio to tune me out. I turn it down and wait for her response.

"Yeah, I went some," she says. "Never finished once I started missing days and getting held back for attendance." She spins the volume to a moderate level and hums along with the tune for a mile or two. Her voice is melodic and beautiful. It seems to roll like the Old Blue Ridge, with rivers and streams and great valleys of sound all tracing back to her as the source.

She stops humming with the music still playing in the background and says, "That's my girl, Tammy Wynette. Bonafide country music superstar."

"I've heard of her," I say, "but never listened."

"That's all I did growing up," she says. "I think Tammy, Dolly, and Patsy were the only people I could count on."

"Dolly and Patsy?"

"Dolly Parton and Patsy Cline," she says through a chuckle. "My heroes, and the first ladies of country music."

"It's good to have heroes," I say.

"Long as you pick the right ones." She pops the glove box and pulls out a pack of Camels and a kerosene lighter with an ace of diamonds etched into its silver case. "You mind?" she asks with a cigarette pressed between her lips. I shrug, because who am I to demand a non-smoking section when I'm hitching a free ride? "I don't do it much," she continues. "Just when I'm storytelling." She takes a long drag and blows the smoke out the driver's side window in one long hiss, careful not to get a stray finger of smoke on the Chevelle's interior. "Feels like we're headed to Storytown." Another long drag and a hiss. "Because you *were* gonna ask me about my poor taste in heroes, weren't you?"

I look at her without the vaguest sense of what she's talking about. "Not really," I say.

She flicks her half-smoked cigarette out the window and the sparks from the butt tumble off behind us on the distant asphalt. "Well, I'm gonna tell you anyway," Lula says. "Because before I got smart and started looking up to people like Tammy and Dolly and Patsy, I didn't know better. I thought it was normal to skip dinner sometimes or to eat baked beans straight from the can or to tell bedtime stories to my mirror or tuck myself in at night. When I was barely old enough to walk I knew Daddy was a musician. That was his life. And he was my hero."

My ears perk up. "Your father was a musician too?"

"Part of the time," she says. "You could hand that man a tin can and a few lengths of fishing twine and he could play any song you wanted to hear. He played in Branson a few times. Even pressed himself a record. Problem was, he spent the rest of his time slumped over bars in every hayseed town from Vicksburg to Charlottesville."

"Did he ever come home?"

"Sometimes. When he needed to sleep something off or make a trip to Willy's Pawn with one of his guitars."

"What'd your mom think about that?"

"Don't know. She left when I was born. Only saw one picture of her and I hope the only thing I inherit from her is her looks."

I feel a sudden impulse to give Lula a suave compliment, but decide it wouldn't have much impact coming from a dude she envisions sitting beside her in a child's safety seat.

Instead, I ask, "Is that why you went on the road?"

She lights another smoke and takes a long drag. "In a round-a-bout way. Since my dad was always on the road or just missing in action, I got sent over to my aunt's house in Martinsville a lot. It wasn't much better over there. She had a string of lowlife boyfriends, one after another. My 'uncles' she'd call them. Well, let's just say that one of these so-called 'uncles' tried to get a little too friendly with me, a little too hands on." She smiles ruefully to herself. "Learned himself a lesson that day. You don't mess with Lula McBride. That's how I ended up with the Chevelle."

My eyes pop wide open. "You stole his car?"

"Didn't steal it as much as I reminded him how much of a scumbag my aunt would know he is if he didn't provide it to me as a 'gift in kind.'"

"Damn, that's cold. And cool as hell. I'm glad."

Lula stomps on the gas and the Chevelle weaves through cars, bouncing from lane to lane with the mountains riding the horizon. "I'm glad too. The son of a bitch had it coming."

I laugh a little, because I'd never want to be the one who crossed Lula McBride. "So, that's all it took?" I ask. "You got yourself a car and you were on the road for good?"

"Not even close. I guess everything kind of traces back to singing old Conway Twitty songs with my Dad…whenever he was around. I got pretty good on my own and started breaking into my daddy's stuff. Played with his old guitars and his ukes. He even had a banjo I'd mess with. I remember one night when he was piss drunk and passed out on the couch I found a plastic crate filled with vinyl albums—Daddy said all the classic country artists are on vinyl—and that's when I learned about Dolly and Patsy and Tammy. Also when I learned about the kind of woman I wanted to be."

"And that's all it took? You got in your car and went on the road armed with the knowledge of a few vinyl albums?"

Lula takes another drag from her smoke. The silence and the slow curve of the road through the pine trees help me notice the harshness of my question.

"No. Of course that's not *it*, Cordy. That's never *it*. There's also the hours of practice, and the shit-ton of courage you have to build up before you place a bet on yourself, and all the sacrifice and the hunger and the people who tell you everyday you can't do it when you know you can. You know any people like that, Cordy?"

I nod. "Does my entire school count?"

"It counted for me," Lula says, tossing most of her cigarette out the window to disappear behind us in another shower of sparks. "First time I built up the courage to tell people in my class I was gonna be the next great country music star…I was in ninth grade and I hated every minute of it…they laughed me out of the classroom. Eva Chatham, who was supposed to be my best friend, told me I was flat-out crazy. You know what I did the next day, Cordy?"

"What?"

"I brought one of my daddy's ukes to school and played Patsy Cline's 'Crazy' just for Eva. Serenaded her in front of her locker. I hit every damn note of that song and you know what she told me when I was done?"

"That you're awesome?"

"That a girl like me couldn't afford to dress up like a country star, let alone be one."

"What'd you say?"

"Nothing. I was too busy cramming her head in a locker."

That breaks the tension and we both laugh until Lula's eyes flash and her hand reaches for the volume. "I love this song," she says. "It's Dolly!"

The engine roars and the Chevelle picks up speed around a sharp corner. We emerge from the shelter of the trees on a straight shock of asphalt that overlooks the orange and brown patchwork of the Tennessee Valley. Lula hums along with a song that tells a story about a girl who's so poor her mom has to piece together her winter coat out of odd scraps of fabric. The end result was apparently a coat of many different colors.

When the song is over, Lula flips off the radio and says, "That song. That's why I left."

"Because you couldn't afford a coat?"

"No. Because once I proved to everyone in Charlottesville I had the talent to chase my dream, well then, most of the people I knew commenced the process of trying to break down that dream."

"What do you mean?"

"If it wasn't because I was poor, it was because I was a girl. Or because I was too weak. Or blond. Or didn't have a mama. Or that my daddy was a drunk. It got to feel like everyone in town was searching for a reason I *couldn't* be a singer and forgetting about the one reason I could. I can sing, Cordy. I have a voice."

"I know," I say. "And I only heard you hum."

She smiles for the first time since she mentioned locker-bombing her ex-best friend. "That's the real reason I left," she says. "Why I'm on my way to Nashville." She pops the glove box and tosses her smokes and the lighter inside. "You hungry?" she asks. "I'm buying."

There's no chance of me passing up a free meal, so Lula pulls off at the next exit and parks the Chevelle outside one of the South's most recognizable landmarks. The Waffle House. We sit at the counter on chrome-plated stools with ripped, vinyl cushions and place our orders. Lula gets a coffee and two eggs over hard with a waffle and a big plate of hash browns. I get a waffle and some bacon, then chow down on Lula's leftover toast because, apparently, I miss my *Ama Kamama*-style bread sandwiches.

The whole time we eat, I can't get that Dolly Parton song out of my head. And I can't stop thinking about heroes, and when I start thinking about heroes, I can't help but come up with stuff from Greek mythology. I mean, the Greeks cornered the market when it comes to heroes, so I can't help myself.

I finish the last swallow of coffee and our waitress refills my mug.

"It's like Helen of Troy," I say, completely out of the blue. "Like in *The Odyssey*."

Lula almost chokes on her coffee. "What are you talking about, Mickey Mouse?"

"Your song. From Dolly Parton."

"You mean 'The Coat of Many Colors'?"

"Yeah. That one. It's straight out of Greek mythology or philosophy… or both."

"You've completely lost me," she says, as she snaps a strip of bacon off my plate. I don't protest because I'm too far in the zone.

"You know the Trojan War?"

"Uhhhh…no."

"The one with the Trojan Horse? Where the soldiers hid inside and—"

"Sneaked into the city while everyone was asleep? Yeah. I know *that* one."

"Well, in the myth, the whole war started over a misunderstanding. All because this goddess, Eris, didn't get invited to the cool kids' wedding."

"Did she crash it?"

"Kind of. She got pissed and tossed a golden apple in the middle of the dance floor. It had the words 'to the fairest' inscribed on it, only in Greek so it was probably a bunch of weird symbols and stuff. None of the guests could figure out who the apple belonged to, though they all wanted to possess it."

"Total blood bath."

"Not yet. First, there was a petty squabble."

"So, like the start of every war in history?"

"Basically. So, these three other goddesses claimed the apple and asked this mortal dude named Paris to judge who was indeed 'the fairest.'"

"Like, a beauty contest? Barf!"

"What's worse is, for three maidens trying to be deemed 'the fairest', they didn't play fair. They bribed the hell out of Paris. Eventually, the dude cracked and named Aphrodite the fairest in exchange for his choice of any wife in the land."

"This keeps getting worse."

"Yep. He chose Helen, who was already married."

"Then war?"

"Uh-huh."

"Makes sense. But how does that connect to Dolly?"

"Think about it," I say. "The reason you'd fight over a stupid apple you can't even eat is the same reason you'd make someone else's life miserable over a coat."

"Oh yeah? And what's that reason, Professor Mouse?"

"Jealousy."

Lula bottoms out her coffee. She drops a few bucks and some loose change on the counter beside our check. "You might just understand me," she says, and for the first time since we left Lynchburg I feel like I'm not being pushed around in my stroller by Mama Lula. For the first time, it's like we're walking side by side...which we do on our way back to the Chevelle, and as Lula revs the engine and we take off toward Nashville.

We don't talk for a long time after leaving the Waffle House. Lula cranks the volume on the country station and we listen to old songs and watch the trunks of the passing pines flick past so fast they merge into a rough streak of wood paneling on the side of the road. The Chevelle weaves in and out of a maze of trucks as big as Old Sally without breaking time with the music.

Out of nowhere, Lula asks, "Did you pick the right hero, Cordy?"

I don't know what to say. I mean, it seems like a trick question. On one hand, there's John Coltrane. I don't think I want to meet anyone who'd tell me John Coltrane isn't a good hero. On the other hand, there's Travis. Of course, the jury's still out on Travis. But I'm not ready to say I chose wrong yet. I'm not ready to accept that my actions may have brought my brother to a place where it's hard for me to say if he's my hero or not.

"I *think* so," I say. "But you never know who's gonna be a hero or a villain until it's time for you to know."

"What the hell does that mean?"

"I have no idea," I say. "I made it up."

Lula laughs and cranks the volume. This time it's a song I recognize. Willie Nelson. "On the Road Again." I remember Dad would blast it in his pickup on the way to the fishing hole and me and Travis would get him fired up and we'd scream out the lyrics at the top of our lungs. It was the most fun I ever saw Travis and Dad have at the same time.

A sign along the guardrail reads "Nashville 80 Miles." It's the only sign Lula and I need to remind us we're on our way, and Willie Nelson is the right guy to help us remember what we've left behind.

Crazy

An early morning haze hangs over Nashville. Lula downshifts and the Chevelle purrs along West End Avenue. It's a variety of Southern smog made of two parts humidity and one part sweet tea. The kind that makes you want to bubble out of your skin like a boiled crawdad. A trillion tons of glass and steel preside over quaint, revival row houses and honky-tonk hangouts. Lula's turquoise boots lose their mastery on the gas pedal. She inches the Chevelle up West End, past the massive Tudor clocktower at Vanderbilt University, and back down Twenty-First Avenue in a bunch of uncoordinated, twitchy bursts—like a person who's lost as hell.

"Lots of cool venues in this town," I say. "So, where's the dream gig?" Lula's blue eyes expand but lose some of the blue. She creeps up in the driver's seat until she's folded over the steering wheel and nudges the Chevelle ahead at the speed of a parade float.

"It's not far," she says in a distant voice that sounds like she's not talking to me at all. "Should be right around…yep." Lula snaps back to reality and pulls the Chevelle to the curb in front of a row of small shops. One looks like a cafe with some picnic tables out front and green, canvas umbrellas poking up from the sidewalk. The sign above the cafe reads: The Bluebird.

"You better wait here," Lula says. She takes a cleansing breath, leaves her guitar case in the trunk and her driver's door wide open, and tucks in through the door of the cafe.

After five minutes of sitting there biting my fingernails, I get out of the Chevelle to stretch my legs. I figure I might as well shut Lula's door before someone walks off the street and takes the Chevelle for a spin. I'm almost to the front of the car when I hear a rrrriiIIINNG! and a bicycle with a full basket of who-knows-what on the handlebars zips past and almost turns me into sidewalk putty. Then my heart stops as I notice a police officer heading right toward me.

What to do? I know I can't outrun him. Fact is, all I can do is stand here and remain as calm and collected as Coltrane in the heat of a solo, and hope he has no idea he's just stumbled upon a teenage runaway who recently committed credit card fraud. My pits turn to liquid about two seconds after I spot him.

"You okay, kid?" the officer says when he's within earshot. "I thought you were done for!" There's an idiotic grin smeared across doughy, red cheeks. His police hat looks like a child's toy perched atop an iceberg.

"Yes, I'm fine, thank you, officer" I reply, pushing the door closed on the Chevelle's driver side.

"This your car?" he asks, sidestepping his grave concern over my near-death experience via bicycle and completely unaware of the fact that he's talking to a living, breathing teenage criminal.

"No," I say. "It's…uhh…my sister's."

"Well, your sister has good taste. A 1965 Chevelle. Couple of hundred horses under that hood. I'd pony up my pension for this here vehicle if I found someone stupid enough to sell it."

I stare at him with a look that says, "Don't you have better places to be?" But he doesn't get the message. "Had a buddy," he continues, "who used to cruise in one of these here rides. Let me tell you, you ain't never—"

Suddenly, he stops and looks me square in the eyes. The veins in his forehead pulse and strain as his boulder-sized head closes in on me. "Hey…don't I know you from somewhere?"

A bead of sweat rises up from my scalp, rolls through the hedgerows of my crew cut, and down the back of my freckled neck.

"No," I reply. "I don't think so."

I try to escape around the side of the car to the safety of the passenger seat, but Officer Melonhead inches toward me every time I inch away.

"I don't know," he says with an index finger tapping his upper lip. "I swear I've seen you somewhere. You go to school with my kid up at Hillsboro? Danny Deacon."

Before I can answer, the cafe door swings open and Lula storms out, boots first. She slams the door behind her with such velocity the cowbell on the handle pops off its rope and clangs on the brickface. Lula doesn't flinch. She sweeps through the picnic table area and makes a beeline for the Chevelle. Tears well up in her eyes and there's a slight quiver in her cheeks. She battles her shakiness behind a clenched-down jaw.

"You alright?" I ask.

Her voice cracks when she says it, but she squeaks out, "Yeah, never better."

That's when old Melonhead thinks it's somehow a good idea for him to chime in.

"You know this young man?" he asks Lula. She nods.

"Here's my sister," I blurt out.

"Yes, he's…" She looks over toward me and I'm sure she can see the look of panic on my face. "He's my brother. Just helping with a sound check."

"Oh. You're a musician," he says. "I should have known out here in front of the Bluebird. Well, break a leg now." He tips his stupid, little toy hat and waddles around the corner. The idiot.

When he's out of sight, Lula says, "Maybe I should ask if *you're* alright. What the heck was that? Why did you look like the guiltiest guy in the prison lineup?"

"Long story," I say.

"Long story or the wrong story?"

"I just don't feel comfortable around cops," I say. "Besides, shouldn't I be the one grilling you about why you came screaming out of that cafe like a live round of ammo?"

Lula hops in the Chevelle and cranks the ignition while I'm still standing on the sidewalk and, out of nowhere…it's that voice again:

Blunt force trauma, I'd say

From inside that damn car

He's lucky…

"Cordy? What's your deal? You gettin' in or not?"

I snap back to reality as Lula revs the engine, and I figure I better get in the car now or start walking. She's so fired up about something she doesn't even notice the crazed look in my eyes from having these weird… moments. The voices in my head that I can't explain. I stagger into the Chevelle and I barely have the door closed when Lula speeds off down Twenty-First Avenue at a thousand times faster than a parade float.

"Goddammit!" she shouts, and I almost jump straight out of the car through the windshield. Streams of mascara run down her cheeks and there's nothing to hold back the sobs. No clenched jaw. No quivering cheeks. Just all-out bawling. And cursing. I grip the corners of my seat and watch Lula double the speed limit and curse and bang her fists against the steering wheel.

It takes a few minutes, but she calms down and the Chevelle slows to normal, non-warp speed levels and Lula pulls over on the curb below an overpass.

"What's going on?" I ask when the silence becomes too awkward to bear.

"There's no gig, Cordy. No gig. You happy?"

"Not really. I was kind of looking forward to—"

"And what's worse is there won't ever be one."

"What are you talking about?"

She grabs an old t-shirt out of the backseat and wipes her face. When she removes the white, cotton shirt it's smudged in the faint outlines of Lula's cheekbones and chin.

"What I'm talking about," she says, "is never having a gig lined up in the first place."

"You mean—"

"I mean I dragged your ass all the way down here from Lynchburg with no gig, no plan, and no chance."

"But I—"

"You were supposed to be going clear in the opposite direction. Up to Philadelphia. Not down here to this musician's hell."

"Lula, there's no—"

"Reason why I'd be so selfish to think it's right to just—"

She's all worked up again to the point where I think we might be in store for another tear-filled joyride from the apocalypse. But I stop her. Put my hand on top of her hand on top of the gear shift.

"Lula," I say, "what happened?"

She takes a breath and her giant-sized blue eyes shrink back to their normal, big blue status. "I thought I'd give it one last shot. Because I can't do the dives anymore. I can't wander around searching for stray sets and finding empty beer cans. I need to make music, Cordy. Real music. For real music fans. Not just background noise for a bunch of drunken conversations. You know what I mean?"

"I do. That's why you think you did something crazy when it was probably the only sane decision you could make."

She pauses and lets my statement rain down on her for a moment.

"You're really into this philosophy stuff, ain't you?" she says. "But maybe you're right. Bunch of stars got discovered right here at the Bluebird and, well, my daddy's known the manager, Chuck, since they strummed their first chords. Didn't think there's a chance in hell he'd turn me down if I showed up in person."

"But he tossed you out on your sorry behind, didn't he?"

"Yep, he sure as hell did," she says, not trying to hold back a sniffling laugh. "Told me he's got a business to run and doesn't have time for no talent shows."

"Sounds like a great guy. I admire his subtlety."

She laughs and I'm aware for the first time in my life I might be making a situation better. But then I'm not sure.

"I'm done, Cordy" she says. "I want you to be the first to know. I'm done running. I'm done putting on an act. I'm just done."

"You mean you're done playing? Cause that would be a crime against humanity," I tell her.

"Nobody's gonna care if the washed-up, has-been Lula McBride never sings another note."

"No," I say. "I'm serious. I mean, look at John Coltrane."

"Your hero, huh?"

I nod. "He faced so many setbacks. Moved all over the place and played his sax for more hours than I've been alive. He could have given up. You know what, Lula? He probably should have given up. But if he did, where would music be today? Think about what you'd be robbing from the world."

For a few seconds there's nothing but the sound of traffic clomping over sections of pavement on the overpass. I sit there amazed that a freckled-up nobody from High Point could have thought of something so damn eloquent to pull out and say to a beautiful country music singer like it's no big deal.

"This might seem weird," she says, "but I miss waking up in Charlottesville. I miss home. I even miss…him."

"Your dad?"

She nods. "You must think I'm crazy," she says.

I think about Dad, sitting in his recliner in High Point, feeling like crap, worried sick about the whereabouts of his two boys. And I think about Mom, and how much she does before the sun comes up each morning just to keep what's left of our family intact. And I think about High Point. The city. The place I drew my first breath. The place that brought me thousands of new sunrises. The scent of freshly-mowed grass on Saturday mornings, the sudden screech of a red-tail hawk hundreds of feet overhead, the smokey sting of a perfect pork barbecue washed down with a bucketful of Cheerwine. *Home.*

And suddenly it's easy to give Lula an honest answer.

"No," I say. "I think you're far from crazy." She smiles and squeezes my hand. Then she leans in and pecks me on the cheek. The same cheek I will never wash again even after I'm done riding the rails and fleeing police.

"If you don't think I'm crazy now, you're gonna in a second."

She hops out of the car and pulls her guitar case from the trunk. I follow her across the sidewalk, to a graffiti-covered wall under the overpass and beside a torn trash bag with scraps of greasy paper, putrid odors, and all kinds of other unidentifiables seeping out.

"I'm playing a show in Nashville, one way or another," she says. She doesn't take a breath before she starts strumming on her guitar. It's one acoustic beauty with a sunburst face and another with platinum, blond braids serenading the whole city of Nashville.

Lula doesn't get more than three or four chords into Patsy Clines' "Crazy" before a lady with two massive grocery bags cradled in her arms shuffles past and drops a bill in her splayed-open guitar case. Then a lady and her toy poodle do the same. And some buff bodybuilder carrying a bucket of chicken. Next thing I know, the pavement is lined up three rows deep with spectators, and Lula's guitar case is littered with crinkled bills and spare change. Each roadside concert-goer hangs on Lula's honey voice and the delicate plucking of each string on Lil' Hank until she hits the last note and the sidewalk erupts in applause. Lula takes a half-bow, then an extra curtsy. She's in her element, playing her music for the purpose it was intended.

She's not done enjoying her moment when one of the spectators shouts, "I think that's Taylor Swift!" and the whole stampede of stargazers rushes away down the street for a chance to see fame with their own eyes.

Lula shrugs and strums a generic progression of twangy, bluesy-sounding chords as she gazes out at the only person left: me. "Guess that's the biz," she says. She gathers the money from her guitar case and places Lil' Hank back inside.

"Well, not too many people can say they closed out their career to a standing ovation in Nashville," I say. "And besides, John Coltrane already said it best. He said, 'Don't ever get so big or important that you can not hear and listen to every other person.' I can tell you there's at least one person in the world who knows you've got that lesson down pat. And that's important, Lula. It's really goddamn important."

Lula smiles and nods to herself as she pops the guitar case in the trunk. She roughs up her hand on my razor-sharp crew cut. "Come on, you," she says.

"Where we going?"

"To Charlottesville," she says. "And I'm buying doughnuts."

She fans the proceeds from her final performance in front of her. It's not enough to retire on, but it's plenty for doughnuts.

"I guess, it's the least you could do," I say.

Lula cranks the ignition and the Chevelle rockets off the curb as we head back toward Virginia, and with each passing second, closer to Philadelphia.

Take Me Home

About an hour or two outside of Nashville, still on our climb up the green steep of the Blue Ridge Mountains, Lula starts to roll out the questions.

First, she's like, "How can you be sure you'll be able to find Travis in Philadelphia?"

I don't answer.

Then she's all, "How do you know Travis wants you to find him?"

Again, I don't answer.

Then she fires off the one that really gets me pissed. "What's the point of saving your money for Birdland?" And then so many others designed to let all the air out of my balloon; to make me have doubts; to make me forget why I started the journey. They rattle off the windows of the Chevelle. They pinch and prick at my skin until I can't take it anymore and I want to burst out of the car and tuck and roll it the rest of the way down the Blue Ridge.

Instead, I get loud. Like, top of my lungs loud. And I rattle off in a single, hot breath, "Damn it, Lula! My brother's an addict and my dad smoked half his lung away! What the hell else can I do?"

She doesn't answer for a long time. Like, eternity long. We sit there in silence until Lula raises a pink, polished fingernail to the dial and flips on the radio. The country station again, getting more staticky by the minute. There's a familiar song playing. One I know because I remember Mom and Dad one time, sitting in the truck after it was parked in the driveway and after Travis and me were waiting under the porch light to listen to the rest of the song. John Denver's "Country Road."

Lula steers the Chevelle and I sit there quiet as a copperhead and watch the roadway sweep up next to steep cliff faces with the pearlescence of mountain streams washing down their mossy faces. John Denver brings us ever closer to home and to Travis, little by little, until Lula has to go and ruin the peace.

She grabs her phone from the glove box and holds it out to me. "You should call home and let them know you're safe."

I stare at her with the phone dangling from her pink-polished fingertips, but she doubles down with a stare that's twice as hard and icy as hell. I take the phone just so I can get her eyes back on the road.

"This isn't necessary," I say.

"Do it. For me." I figure it can't hurt to pretend I've called and got no answer. At least that would appease Lula until we hit Charlottesville. I turn the phone on and the thing explodes with notifications. For a second, there are so many bells and beeps and buzzes going off it sounds like a carnival sprung up inside the Chevelle.

"Yeah," Lula says. "Haven't checked that thing since we left. Guess I was in the zone."

"Yeah," I say, but that's all I get out because one of the notifications is an amber alert. And below it an emergency message. And below that… my picture!

I quickly tap out the notifications and dial in the number 222-222-2222, which Travis and I used to prank call when we were kids because we thought it was hilarious to hear the automated operator repeat back the same, stupid number over and over again.

"Why didn't you leave a message?" Lula asks after I hit the "End" button and hand her the phone.

"Voicemail was full," I lie.

Lula doesn't look convinced, but I'm pretty sure she doesn't want to incur my wrath and hear me scream like an idiot, so she turns up the volume and we admire the landscape and listen to the soft purr of the Chevelle as we glide downhill toward Virginia. It doesn't take much time for the evening sun to touch the side of my face with the right warmth, and for my eyes to bog down with fatigue, and for my mind to wander off…

I sit on the cold cement. My tongue turns to sandpaper under the gag. The vibrations rumble the floor. The train. The rattle and jerk of cars.

A voice breaks the tempo. In the key of a foghorn. "Take that damn thing off!"

It trails. Blends with the rumbling, "how could you—" and gets swallowed by the train whistle.

Then a solo. Nervous and squeaky. "I needed it!" he pleads.

The whistle cries a long, mournful note. Discordant but true.

The foghorn takes over. "Here's your money!"

A splash. Bills tinkle down to Earth as paper raindrops.

The door clangs open. Two outlines stand silhouetted against the light.

"Corrdddy!"

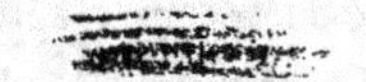

My eyelids fly open.

I'm in the Chevelle with the passenger seat fully reclined. The car sways on its shocks, back and forth a few times, then goes slack. My eyes shoot to the driver's side window. A pair of glowing taillights on a straight, dark road are the only visible signs of the rig that swept past and stirred up the wake.

The driver's seat is vacant. The glove box, wide open. Lula's pack of smokes and her lighter are missing. I rise from the seat like I'm locked in an Old West-style gunfight and I'm afraid I'll take a cheap one between the eyes. The Chevelle's parked in an open lot with a grove of live oaks stationed at each corner of a cracked patch of asphalt. At one end, a squatty-looking cabin sits dressed in its faded, red shingles. The marquee over the door spells out the name "Lou's" in individual light bulbs. Under it, the sign reads: Charlottesville's Best Fried Chicken and there's a space that reads "Tonight" over a big, square patch of bright, white blankness. It makes me wonder if Lou's chicken lives up to the hype.

It also makes me wonder if Lula ever played the stage at Lou's Chicken Pit and what it'd be like to see the name "Lula McBride" shining up there on the marquee. And then I hear boots scuffle across the pavement. The sure-fire spark of flint as a plume of smoke rises from a spot on the far side of the restaurant, near the dumpsters. Nearly out of sight.

I roll down the window without making a sound, and I hang my head half out and cup my hand behind my ear the way Travis taught me after his Boy Scout trips. And I listen. I listen as hard as I can.

Lula's voice rides on the air like silk, but the guy she's talking to—Lou, I'm guessing—speaks in a deep, gargling monotone that sounds like gibberish when it's not amplified in the hollow chambers of the dumpsters and spit out like the recycled echo of a cyclops.

"It's not like that," Lula says, followed by a few grunts and groans from Lou the Cyclops.

He doesn't seem to agree.

Then Lula says, "This has nothing to do with my decision. I would have made it whether I knew or not."

Lou's voice comes through loud and clear. "I don't understand it, Lula. How you can ruin your life twice in one night!"

It goes quiet for a few seconds and I hear Lula sniffling or sobbing, and she says, "I had no idea. I swear. I didn't check my phone." My throat tightens when she says it. My heart drops to the pit of my stomach. I look at my left hand. My empty left hand. The same hand I planned to use to hide Lula's phone, so she couldn't find out about my missing status or the credit card fraud until we parted ways and she was safe with her father in Charlottesville.

I do a quick search around the interior of the Chevelle, but there's no sign of Lula's phone. Just loose change and a spent pack of matches from a dive bar in Memphis named "Eddie's."

Then I hear Lula mumble something behind the dumpsters that sounds like, "He's a good kid, Lou. I don't want to get him in trouble. I'm no snitch."

"You don't have a choice," Lou says. "Ditch the kid and come back. He'll forgive you. He's just a kid."

"I don't know," Lula says, but I already have my hand on the door and I'm already pushing it open nice and slow so the hinges don't squeak. And I already have my backpack over my shoulder. Because I refuse to sit around and find out if Lula is capable of stabbing me in the back. And Travis can't afford it, and Mom and Dad can't either.

I crawl across the asphalt on my belly, with the silence of a snake through a chicken coop, and I charge off through the mud and the brush behind Lou's Chicken Pit.

Alone again.

Cordy is a Rolling Stone

I did nothing that resembled trailblazing after I dashed from Lula's Chevelle and made a break for it through dark, uncharted forest. I mean, there was a narrow trail overgrown with kudzu and bramble, and I guess you could say there was blazing if you count the scent of the hickory logs burning in the pits of downtown Charlottesville. But mostly I crept along, feeling my way through the dark, convincing myself I wouldn't be eaten by a bear.

After what feels like hours, stepping over splintered logs and slogging through stretches of sticky, orange mud and swatting at the three-millionth mosquito of the night, the trail rolls around a bend in the tree line and meets a stream. It's the first break in the canopy since the Chevelle. For a moment, I stand there and let the moonlight wash over my pale skin like milk.

Then I see something move.

Up ahead.

At first, I think I'm finally about to go toe to toe with that black bear or something even more sinister thrown at me by Mother Nature. But then I notice whatever it is stands on two legs. It shimmers in the moonlight, almost transparent against the dark green of the tree line. I creep forward along the trail, with my hand reaching back against my bag because Cowbird's words ring in my ears: *when you need to use it, you'll know it.* But the form remains still, standing idly on the bank of the stream with its luminescent reflection rippling on the water's surface.

As I get closer, the form starts to take a more distinct shape. A tall stringbean of a young man, silent and brooding, with long hair trailing down the back of his neck. I know right away it's my brother. I can see how his left foot leans against his right, the way Travis used to shift his weight back and forth in his marching band days when he was tired of standing in the same place for too long.

I feel a rush rising up through my feet, into my chest. My heart throbs and, before I can stop myself I'm at a full sprint through the bramble and the kudzu.

"Travis!" I shout, and I hear my voice echo through the hollow touching nothing else but the leaves in the trees and the brush underfoot. "Travis?"

I pull up at the edge of the stream and there's nothing there but moonlight. No Travis. No response from the ghostly form. No hope. Nothing at all. Like the mirage I saw on the side of the highway that almost got Cowbird and Shotgun Sally destroyed, and me obliterated. I take a deep breath and pull my hand off the zipper of my backpack with Cowbird's knife still buried deep inside.

On the edge of the stream, a section of granite juts out like a shelf over the water. I climb it and drop my pack. Alone as always. I catch a whiff of myself in the process.

Dang.

It dawns on me I haven't changed my clothes since the *Ama Kamama*. I figure I'll never have a better chance at privacy, so I reach in my bag and pull out my extra t-shirt, jeans, and a pair of boxers. I strip down right there on top of a rock, next to a stream, under the light of a pale moon, somewhere in uncharted Charlottesville, with the real Travis still hundreds of miles away.

I have to tell you, sometimes back in High Point I used to feel alone. Like, all by myself and no one around for miles alone. But you never feel *alone* alone until you're on top of a rock, next to a stream, under the light of a pale moon, somewhere in uncharted Charlottesville…and you're naked as a jaybird. Trust me on this. It's not something you need to experience yourself.

When I'm dressed, I smell at least twenty percent less lethal on the nostrils. I sit cross-legged on the rock and watch the dried oak leaves float past on the current like tiny, crinkled-up canoes and listen to the gentle hooting of a resident barn owl I can't see but I know is watching me.

I don't know if it's the solitude or the calming rush of the water or the soft kiss of the moonlight, but for the first time in days I am able to simply sit and think. To be alone with my thoughts and reflect on the decisions that have brought me here.

Now, if your name is Cordell Wheaton of High Point, North Carolina, this newfound consciousness of thought, this distraction-free moment of peace away from the action and without my eyes going cross in front of a nameless gadget, can be good or bad. Or both at the same time.

Like, right now I could be thinking I'm proud of myself for getting this far and surviving on my own, even though it hasn't yet been a full week. Instead, all I can do is run Lula's questions through my mind over and over again. And I don't like the answers.

"Does Travis know you're coming?"

No.

"Do you have a plan to find him when you get there?"

Not really.

"Do you think Travis wants to see you?"

No idea.

I have to throw a couple of my own questions in there. Ones that have bothered me since I hopped in Cowbird's truck and we rumbled past my hometown and left High Point in the rear view.

"Are my parents worried sick?"

Probably.

"Do they deserve this?"

Probably not.

"Do you think you should go home?"

This is one question for which I don't have an answer.

I stuff my dirty clothes into my bag and a funny thing happens. Almost like fate. Almost like Socrates himself planted Cowbird's knife at just the right angle so it would catch on my hand as I pull it from the bag and slide it out onto the rock. I extend the blade with a click. Watch the moonlight sparkle off the steel face. I examine the handle, worn smooth from years of use and toil on the road, and wonder how many times Cowbird reached the end of his road and yet still found a way to continue the journey.

I reach inside the bag again and feel around until I find it. A small length of rope Captain Adomi let me keep after she taught me how to tie a sailor's knot, which now hangs suspended in time at the center of the twine. I think of the captain's shifting life at sea, at the whims of the tides and the winds and the weather. I wonder how often she had to rely on her most basic skills as a sailor to survive the dominion of Poseidon day in and day out.

I reach in the bag one more time and find the folded-up page, like it jumps into my hand on its own. I unfold it and hold it to the sky, so the tissue-thin paper is backlit by the moon, and I trace my eyes across the scales and the stops and the musical notes. Behind them, I see Travis. In his bunk in our room with a spare reed in his mouth and Dad's headphones wrapped halfway around his face. I see Travis on the fifty-yard line, in his marching band uniform, playing sax with the heavy pound of the bass drum behind him. And then I see Travis with his eyes glazed, like a zombie. With no feeling. Not for his family. Not for his sax. Not for himself. And certainly not for me.

I take one more look behind me at the trail winding its way back to Lou's Cyclops Restaurant, where I know I can talk to big Lou and have him get in touch with Lula. And I can hop in her Chevelle and go to the police station and turn myself in and be done with the whole thing.

But instead I turn and follow the trail, because I know I'm the only one that can get Travis his sheet music. And because I'm the only one who can get him clean. I think even Lula would agree with me. You know what? I *know* Lula would agree with me because, if not, then why did she come back to Charlottesville? Why did she put her dreams on hold? It's because she has a mission. For someone other than herself.

I climb down off the rock and think about how much I'm going to miss Lula McBride. The girl of my dreams right up until she thought about turning on me. Probably after that, too, if I'm really honest. Before I hit the trail, I bend down and pick up the smoothest, roundest stone I can find. It's dove grey and worn down from eons of water rushing up on the banks. I free it from the mud and let the stream wash the muck from its surface. It's a fitting artifact. Like Lula. Just a rolling stone packed down in the Charlottesville mud. Right where it was meant to be.

I toss it in my backpack with the rest of my keepsakes and slog down the trail, moving at a more rapid pace now that I'm cleaner, more rested, and my eyes have adjusted to the pitch of the forest. I follow the trail. It runs parallel to the stream and at a slight incline, which I can't see but I feel in the burn of my leg muscles. I follow it for so long and incur the wrath of so many mosquitos I start to hear the calls of the morning songbirds. First, the tweet-tweet of a chickadee, and then the harsh kirrr-kirrr of a cardinal, and before long I hear the recognizable hush of traffic somewhere in the distance.

The trail terminates in a steep hill. The only marker on the narrow lane above is a rusted length of chain link covered in ivy. I reach the fence at daybreak and wander out of the woods into another parking lot. This one is smaller than the asphalt wasteland in front of Lou's. In fact, this one isn't paved at all. It's covered in the tiniest particles of gravel you've ever seen, and they spill out like drifts of dirty snow on the blacktop of a winding, country lane between the trees.

Two ancient-looking gas pumps poke up from the gravel at the heart of the lot. Set off beside them is a small outbuilding with an A-frame roof. A sort of general store. Neither the pumps nor the store look operational this early, which is weird because I'm used to gas stations and convenience stores staying open around the clock in the century I come from. Safe to say, this establishment is not from the same time period.

I camp out behind the A-frame, between a beat-up plank fence and a dumpster, and wait until I hear the crunch of tires on the gravel. It's the only sign of a vehicle I've seen in the area since I emerged from the brush. I wait fifteen minutes or so and give the store owner time to get the place in order. Figure I'll pop inside for the cheapest snack I can find and maybe a drink—nothing that'll leave me short when I get to Birdland. But mostly, I'll hang around. Haunt the place. Like a ghost. If I move around like a shadow, eventually someone will pop in and maybe I can land a ride into town.

The store is exactly what you'd expect, from the sleigh bells that hang over the door, to the entire wall devoted to locally-made jerky products, to the brown, fuzzy sacks full of boiled peanuts under the register, down to the leathery scent of tobacco that permeates every square inch of the place, this is the store they were talking about when they coined the phrase "general store."

The sleigh bells jingle as I step through the door. The man at the register eyes me from under his bushy, white brows and tightens the knot on his apron. He says, "Can I help you?" He looks at me like he's never seen a person before.

"Just browsing," I say.

"Holler if you need me," he says, and he drifts off behind the pages of a newspaper. I head to the back of the store where a bunch of old-fashioned Coke bottles reach out of an ice-filled cask like glass fingers. I pull one off the ice.

"Don't you think it's a bit early for that?" I hear from behind the register. I pretend not to hear him and bring the bottle to the register. I reach in my bag for a spare bill. Then he says, "If you think you need something like that this early in the morning, there must be a reason. No charge."

"You sure?" I ask, already zipping up my bag.

He lowers the paper and looks me over. He stares at my eye. The one that's feeling better every day but is still purple and puffy and may have a few shades of green or yellow in there by now. "Looks like you could use it," he says. "Just passing through?" He pops the cap off the bottle on the counter with a single, carefully-placed tap on the heel of his palm. He slides the bottle across the counter to me.

"Yeah," I tell him. "Any chance I could bum a ride into town?"

"You're in the wrong place for that. Nobody comes through these parts since they built the new expressway. The ones that do ain't looking to pick up underage hitchers. It's not 1953 out there, you know."

As struck as I am by the irony of his statement, and as much as I want to believe that a luxury tour bus giving out free seats to Philadelphia will stop for gas in the next ten seconds, I get the sense Mr. General Store isn't going to help my cause beyond the Coke. I decide to play it the less honest way, or what some people might call "dirty."

Real dirty. Like, the hiding out in a dumpster kind of dirty. I'll sit and wait for somebody, anybody to show up in that parking lot to get a carton of eggs or to fill up their tank. I don't know how long I sit out there in the hot sun holding my empty Coke bottle in one hand and Lula's stone in the other, before I hear the gravel slide on the other side of the store. And, boy, the ground rumbles good. Something heavy. Something loaded down with diesel fumes.

I creep around the corner of the store. Parked beside the gas pumps is a truck like Cowbird's, only the trailer is smaller and slatted with iron bars. A livestock container. A flat, pink nose pushes through the bars in one of the container units. The whole parking lot smells like a mud pit all of a sudden.

Hogs.

I look through the front window of the general store. A man stands at the register with his back turned to me. His shirt is your ordinary, powder blue mechanic's get-up and when he turns to head for the door

I read the name "Gus" stitched in white on a name tag over his breast pocket.

I lean back against the sidewall of the store, out of sight, and watch the man named Gus lumber across the gravel with the coordination of Humpty Dumpty in a pair of chewed-up work boots splattered in more dried mud than his pigs. He pulls a drag from a squatty-looking cigar as he reaches the vehicle and flicks it, with the cherry still lit, at a pig in the top row. He looks pleased with himself, and lets out a grotesque, little chuckle as he stands on the top step of the cab. Then he stops. Pats down his pockets. Shakes his head and grunts something that sounds like, "Shit!" and then lumbers across the gravel and back in the store.

I know this might be my only chance. Since Gus doesn't seem like the kind of guy who'd offer up his cab like Cowbird, I figure what he doesn't know won't hurt him. I don't have time to deliberate. It's time for action.

I cross the parking lot and pull frantically at each cage, praying one will open and I can climb inside and disappear among the hogs. The jingle bell on the door tinkles and Gus takes his first lumbering step onto the gravel. I pull and strain and lift at each individual bar, hoping for a weak one, praying for pure luck. I reach the last cube of empty cages near the front of the truck. Behind Gus's cab. I rattle the bars. Footsteps on the other side of the truck. My hand hits a bar that sounds kind of hollow. It rattles and I pull with all of my might. The whole thing pops off in my hand. I squeeze myself inside the cage as Gus tromps up the steps and into the cab. The door slams shut. The engine rumbles. It roars and there's the crunchy sound of tires on gravel. Then the smooth roll of asphalt.

And we're off.

Circe

The stench of hog shit rises up around me in clouds until my nose goes blind to it. For a few minutes, as Gus bucks the old truck over rough patches of asphalt and around sharp bends with the cages rattling against each other like backwoods castanets, I get a false sense of security that, hey, maybe I won't smell like a pile of brown sludge in the back of a pig pen—the one with all the flies buzzing around it. Then I take a whiff of my t-shirt and come back to reality—the one in which a quick dip at the local sewage treatment plant might improve my odor.

The gears grind and a plume of thick, white smoke bursts from the stack over the cab. The weight of gravity and the pull of friction bears down on the old truck as Gus points the tires up a steep incline and struggles to keep them on the right side of a double yellow line. We whip around a sharp, right-hand curve. The cages and the hogs and the rail-thin redhead with a million freckles (that's me) tilt back and brace themselves against the force of gravity, as if braving the opening leg of a record-setting roller coaster.

I narrowly escape—that is, from getting flattened between two heavy cages that contain even heavier livestock before they collide with a cataclysmic clang. I catch my breath and remember one particular scene from an old movie I love where a super adventurous archeologist dude named Indiana Jones escapes at least four million booby traps and has to slip under a door on his belly before it slams shut and seals him inside the temple forever.

When the adrenaline stops pumping and I settle myself in a safer spot between two less mobile cages, I catch a glimpse of the road, and of the wide open vastness of the valley below.

On one side, through the jailhouse pattern of vertical bars, the mountains rest like snoozing giants on the horizon—just dark outlines shrouded in bluish haze. On the other side, I'm planted in a patch of sweaty hogs with their pinkish skin tangled up in wiry peach fuzz and dried mud.

In front of me, however, is a much more hideous sight—the small bald patch on the top of Gus's head through the sliding window at the back of the cab. He's got his radio tuned to a local news station with a rash of high-altitude static drowning out every other sentence the reporter reads. I can't make out what is being said, but I can see the strain build in the wrinkled folds of Gus's chin, so I know what he hears pisses him off.

All of a sudden, Gus pounds one of his flabby palms down on the steering wheel and shouts something like, "Well whaddya know!?" It startles me, and I lose my balance and smash flat-backed against the cage behind me. There's a loud CLAP! and, all at once, the fat hogs with their million little white spots unleash a prolonged and collective screech.

The truck lurches and slows down. I dive down on my belly and follow Gus's eyes in his reflection on the windshield, panning back and forth over the heads of his livestock until he's sure they'd been startled by a bump in the road instead of a freckle-faced stowaway.

I lift myself into a crouched position and resume the stakeout, watching the clouds sweep past like giant, floating cotton balls that wrap their ghostlike arms around the craggy rock faces of the surrounding peaks. Then I pan back inward to watch Gus cram foot-long lengths of red whip licorice behind his seven or eight yellowed-out teeth and produce masses of red saliva he spits into a growing collection of sugary, bodily fluid he keeps in a dixie cup on the dashboard.

Meanwhile, the hogs bed themselves down like bacon-flavored angels and enjoy a more civilized road trip up Virginia's world famous Skyline Drive.

To kill time, I think about all sorts of crap—like Mom, Dad, Travis and Cowbird. I wonder what they're doing at this exact moment and if they might be wondering the same thing about me. I figure this, if nothing else, is the one way we can be connected when we're thousands of miles apart, like tiny sewing needles traveling across the vast haystack of America.

It's funny, because here I am in the back of a hog truck driven by a farmer whose entire existence is based in the care he provides to his livestock. And they're in here with me, in a prison of sorts, a few feet behind the guy who was supposed to take care of them and now he's mindlessly driving them off to slaughter with a mouth full of licorice and not a shred of guilt. Makes me feel lucky, because at least I have a connection somewhere. It may not be here, on this winding mountain road with the stench of pig shit all over me, but at least I'm not like these hogs. And at least I'm no Gus.

It reminds me of *The Odyssey*. I know that probably wouldn't surprise most people I've met, but every time I look through Gus's dust-covered back window I can't help but think about the Greek sorceress Circe. She lived alone on a beautiful island in the middle of the Aegean Sea, and when sailors ran aground on her shore she'd entice them with her beauty and her hospitality. She'd sit them down to a massive banquet and feed the men all the food they could eat. Except she was kind of like one of those douchey, teenage fast-food workers who drops a gooey lugey in your burger and doesn't tell you until after you've eaten the whole thing. Only, her gooey lugey was a potion that turned her dinner guests into animals; and not just any animals. Animals whose personalities matched those of the men who devoured her food. I guess it's no surprise that Odysseus's entire crew was transformed into pigs or that Odysseus had to plot and plan and strategize to trick Circe into turning them back into humans.

The only thing about the story that does surprise me is how, in my current instance, the driver of the truck isn't the hog and all the captives riding in cages on the flatbed the upright, moral beings.

As I'm lost in this bizarre thought, I hear another crackle over the airwaves and see Gus's chubby hand reach down to crank the volume on his radio. It's faint, but I hear the staccato voice of a male reporter say something like, "The boy's whereabouts are unknown, but police last spotted him in the vicinity of Lynchburg, Virginia and believe he has not left the state. A reward is being offered…" which is the exact moment my eyes go all blurry again and I'm back in that weird echo chamber I have no way of explaining. The bass-drenched voices wash over me like a slowed-down record:

Where is he right now?

We can't say

Will he ever

come back?

I snap back to reality just as Gus's hand reaches down to lower the volume on the radio. His bushy eyebrows rise to the top of his forehead.

Great. I'm trapped on the back of a moving pig prison and the warden is on the lookout for escaped prisoners—namely, me. But what can I do? Jump off the truck and roll my way about three thousand feet to safety at the bottom of a gorge? I've tried something like that already and I've come to the painful conclusion it's not the most effective strategy.

The best I can do is lie flat on my back between the cages. Out of sight. Out of mind. And, after feeling the soft vibration of the truck roll up through my spine, out of energy. I close my eyes to rest for a few seconds and…

I hack once or twice. Try to scream, but the sound gets swallowed up by the gag.

All is silent. A sliver of white light widens between the hinges and the door frame. Becomes a blinding beam of fury..

A silhouette glides through the light. Then another. Strands of long hair wisp out from under a wool cap. Then a third form.

I know I'm in trouble. Heat tingles the tips of my earlobes. Tears stream down in the folds of the handkerchief. A weird sound behind the footsteps. Something dry and papery.

"What's wrong?"

"He's short."

The giant races to the doorway. Grabs the third form by the throat. He buckles. Falls to his knees.

"Where's the rest?"

Frantic sniffing. The third form fumbles around on the cement. Fights for air.

"Bring him outside!"

The door clangs shut and...

There's a sharp clang as the two hog cages overhead clash and the muddy hooves of the livestock struggle against the bars. Fifty rolls of back fat battle inertia.

My eyes are open, but I'm not awake.

I lie on my back and wonder if things will ever feel real again or if the rest of my life will be spent stuck in this loop—in an epic journey with no money, no destination, no food, and a shaky grasp of my own reality.

Gus downshifts the truck. A plume of black smoke filters from the stack above the cab and the gears rattle against each other in a calliope of madness. A vibration rises through the tires, through the frame of the truck, and into my spine as it strains against the steel frame of the freight bed. Gravel pitter-patters off the front bumper and rattles around in the mud-encrusted wheel wells. A wet, hacking cough gurgles up from within Gus's tobacco-stained lungs and he slows the truck to a stop.

There's a short squeak and then a long, wailing squeal as Gus dismounts his cracked, vinyl seat and lumbers down the steps. He teeters across the parking lot and into another roadside convenience store that rises up out of the middle of the Virginia wilderness.

I don't want to be the dude who can't prevent himself from poking his head out of his hiding spot only to have it blown off by a double-barrel shotgun, but my stomach won't cooperate. It's on empty. Like the hog truck. The gurgling sounds make it clear my body is eating itself from the inside. I guess this may have been how Travis felt. And Trane. How a substance could take hold of your body and compel you to do its bidding. To put yourself in danger and do whatever it takes to hold the substance in your hand and swallow it or shoot it or snort it or smoke it without a second thought.

I want to lie there hidden under a few thousand pounds of future hog meat, but my belly rumbles louder than Shotgun Sally's engine. It's so empty I can't think of anything besides those sweet, red whips of pseudo-licorice. I mean, I'm pretty sure I can make it to the cab and back before Gus notices. But what if he sees me? What if he figures me out as the missing kid from the radio report and decides to play Johnny Hero? What happens then? Will I ever see Travis? Will he get his chance to patch things up with Dad?

So I stay concealed. But only for another second or two until my belly groans and I sit upright with the orange fuzz on my head bristling the bars of a cage. I peer out beyond the pigs. See the outlines of old-time gas pumps with a squatty attendant standing sentry in a pair of overalls and a brown leather stetson. A greasy rag hangs from the attendant's oversized pocket. Behind him, the convenience store reminds me of the storage shed Dad built and set on top of an old pallet we swiped from the local Home Depot on North Main Street. Back in High Point. Where I was never hungry, or tired, or alone—even all those times I thought I was.

It's weird how when you're huddled under a pile of hogs trying to swipe a ten cent piece of candy from a literal hogman, your hometown—the same hometown you wailed about for almost seventeen years of life because you didn't know any better—suddenly feels like an oasis in the middle of the desert. But I don't have time to long for High Point or shed tears over how much I miss Mom's biscuits, hot and fresh on the counter each morning, or hear Dad's boots scuffle across the linoleum in our foyer after work. I mean Gus moves pretty slow, but he's not a freaking sloth.

In a flash of overconfidence and hunger, I pop up from between two hog cages and slide off the side of the flatbed. My knees buckle when I hit gravel. The soreness in my back and shoulders throbs with the full weight of gravity. I don't want to get hawked by the pump attendant, so I flatten my back against the side of the truck and ease my way to the cab in the same way a building jumper maneuvers the crumbling ledge of a skyscraper.

My hand hits the door handle. I close my eyes and pray Gus is as stupid as he looks and he doesn't believe in locks. I pull. Click! The full sweep of the door swings past my ear in a haze of rusted-out squeakiness. My eyes pan the parking lot. Still quiet. Nothing but smoke rings drifting over the pump attendant and the top tier of his Stetson rising above the sports section of the paper.

Easy pickings. I'll hop in the cab, snag a few strips of red whip goodness and retreat to the sheltering flab of my new family—the hogs.

My grubby, pig fingers dart in and out of the Twizzler bag with my lips peeled back like a Great White Shark. Then I hear it. CRUNCH! The slow, steady interplay between a large man's heels and the groaning gravel beneath.

The blood rushes from my face. I drop the bag of Twizzlers on the tobacco-stained floor of the cab and try to stuff two lengths of strawberry-flavored rope behind my teeth. I bypass both steps leading up to the cab and descend straight down to the gravel surface with a long strand of red saliva dripping off the second of two Twizzlers—the one I can't quite fit in my mouth.

I grab the bottom rail of the flat bed and prepare to launch myself inside with my swine friends. But I'm too late. The gravel crunches behind me in the way it might crunch if, say, an elephant happened to stroll past. The scent of French roast rides the breeze and reaches my nose before I can turn around and face inevitable doom. It smells delicious for a second before the wind shifts and everything reverts to pig shit.

"What the hell?" Gus growls through a mouthful of powdered doughnut. The hem of my shirt strains under the pressure of Gus's chapped hand. I spin around and immediately wish I hadn't because the fishy crapulence of his humid breath on my face is almost more than I can take. "Hey, you stealin' from me?" he growls, his cheeks broiling up to tomato-level shades of red and pink and orange.

"I…I…I…" I have no idea what to say. On one hand, yes, I had been stealing from him, but I managed to swallow at least half of the second Twizzler whole before Gus gripped my shirt and spun me around to sample his halitosis. On the other hand, it might be better if he thinks I stole a stale piece of candy from his truck instead of realizing I'd been chilling with the livestock since I snuck aboard in Charlottesville.

"Well…spit it out. You steal something or what?"

It takes a few seconds before I realize he wants me to spit out my explanation and not the half-digested Twizzlers now burning a hole in my stomach.

"No, sir," I say barely loud enough to outshine the light breeze. "I'm no thief. I was…uhhh…admiring your hogs."

Gus stares down at my cruddy sneakers covered in pig slop. His eyes trace their way up my body, taking in various shades of dried mud, grass stains, and who-knows-what-else.

"Where the hell you come from, boy?" he asks as he takes a swig of coffee in one side of his mouth and spits a load of tobacco juice out the opposite side.

"I…uhhh…I'm local," I say. "I'm from right here in…uhhh…this town."

"Oh yeah? And what town is that?"

I fake a chuckle; try to play Gus's question off as a joke, but his eyes don't budge. His lips flatten into a thin, straight line. He doesn't blink. Just sits there waiting for an answer that will never come because I'm sure saying "Virginia" would not qualify me as either a geography scholar or a local.

Gus takes another swig of coffee and deposits more tobacco-flavored mouth juice on the gravel. "Looks like you been travelling quite a ways," he says. "'bout sixteen, maybe seventeen years old I 'spect. That right?" I nod because, hey, maybe the dude's training to be one of those carnival barkers who guesses people's weights and birthdates. But Gus is not training to be a carnival barker. No. He's too busy putting two and two together to even attend a dang carnival.

And then he says it.

"You're that boy on the radio, ain't ya?"

Oh shit. I scrunch up my face and try to look as confused as possible. "What? What kid?"

"You're him! I know it."

"Sir, I have no idea what you're talking about."

That's when Gus does something that tells me all I need to know about his humanity and his treatment of his own livestock and how he's able to raise a bunch of living creatures he plans to up and kill when they grow to be fat enough. In one motion, this disgusting swine of a human being reaches out and grabs me by one of my ears. So hard the cartilage twists and burns and threatens to leave the actual surface of my head.

"You move an inch and this ear's gettin' fed to them hogs," he whispers, so close to my face I think his breath might melt my skin. He drags me to the back of the truck with my ear in one hand and a brass ring of about a million keys in the other.

I try to scream for help, try to kick gravel in the pump attendant's direction, but the more I squirm and fight, the harder Gus tears and twists at my ear until the searing heat is so intense I give up before the guy transforms me into a teenage version of Vincent Van Gogh. The whole time the pump attendant sits there puffing his cigar behind his newspaper on a wooden stool next to the diesel pump. It's no use. I'm better off saving my hearing and letting Gus do whatever the hell he's gonna do.

That's when he jams an odd-shaped key in one of the locks at the back of the truck. A door swings open on a rusty cage barely large enough to house a ferret let alone a pig. But no pig is going in this cage.

"Get in," Gus whispers. He gives my ear a sharp twist until I swear it's no longer attached to my head. I hop up on the tailgate and Gus shoves me inside the cage with a single, hearty push. The door clangs shut and Gus weaves a chain through the latch hole and battens it down with one of those locks you get in gym class. The ones I have no chance of opening without a special key or a combination, of which I have neither.

"What are you gonna do with me?" I ask in a stunted whisper that sounds like Cordy Wheaton, age four.

"I'm gonna git my reward, you thievin' little son of a bitch."

He lets out a hideous snort and, on cue, a chorus of hog squeals rain down on me from the surrounding cages.

I'm stuck in the mud. Literally. And all I can do is watch Gus lumber back over to the convenience store to make the phone call. The one that will end my journey and end all hope of the Wheaton family becoming whole again.

Orpheus

I can be a fighter sometimes. That's what Travis used to say. After we'd return from trick-or-treating in one of the wealthy neighborhoods in High Point—the ones close to the golf courses—he'd rip my pillowcase full of candy from my hands before we slipped out of our costumes. He'd dump it on his bed and hunt for my Reese's Cups and try to stuff every one of them in his bag.

I wasn't about to stand for it because, if there's two things I've learned in life, it's that you don't mess with another man's family and you don't mess with another kid's Reese's Cups. Especially on Halloween. So, I'd punch and bite and claw my way into Travis's bag and steal back as many Reese's as I could—which was never as many as I'd collected. Travis would get a kick out of it. He was always bigger than me by virtue of being born four years earlier, so he took my beatings and laughed his fool head off knowing whatever happened, he'd finish with a net positive in Reese's Cups, which are obviously the marquee bargaining chips when it comes to Halloween candy.

I never enjoyed the routine as much as Travis. It never made sense why he was putting me through the torture. Probably didn't occur to Travis either, beyond the fact he was adding to his Halloween candy empire. But, you know, maybe subconsciously Travis was preparing me for something. Maybe somewhere in the back of his mind he knew it was his responsibility to toughen me up; to get me ready for a moment when I needed to fight and translate my superhuman skills of survival into reality. Maybe he wanted me to understand the limits of what I'd accept as justice and learn to battle anyone who tried to steal that justice from me. Maybe he prepared me for this exact moment, and maybe it was Dad who'd put him up to it—not consciously, but through all the times he'd force us to do things we didn't want to do, like stacking the wood pile for the fireplace or cleaning all the unused crap out of our garage, or how he'd leave it up to me and Travis to band together and fight for our right to be lazy. They were fights we never won, but we waged them. This moment—the one where I'm trapped in some kind of freaking gerbil cage on a truck loaded down with future pig parts—is hopefully not gonna take the same track.

I unleash all of my fury at once—all the rage I have against Travis for leaving me stranded in High Point, and against High Point for leaving me stranded in my room everyday, and against Dad for smoking so many cigarettes he might well leave Mom and me stranded for good. I lean back and drop-kick the door of the cage with all of my weight.

Nothing happens.

I grab the bars with both hands and shake them senseless until my knuckles are pure white and my palms are ragged and sore.

Still nothing.

The pump attendant looks up from his paper, figures pigs are noisy creatures, and dives back into his reading. There's not much I can do but sit back and let the bars bite into my skin and wait for the sirens and the flashing lights, and then get driven off to some distant precinct where Mom and Dad will pay a fine and drive me back to our tiny colonial on Brookside Drive where this whole failed experiment had been hatched.

My vision starts to blur, as I stare through tears—tears of grief and frustration—for failing my family, myself, and Captain Adomi, Juan, Nasser, and Pierre. For failing Cowbird. I mean, what would Cowbird say if he could see me now, packed into this tiny cage loaded down with a thousand pounds of swine meat and pig shit? I can almost hear his trick eyebrow creep to the top of his forehead from hundreds of miles away. I can see him shake his bald head so slowly it's like watching a mannequin move behind the display glass of a department store. And I can see him with the knife outstretched in his hand, forcing it into my backpack, and the twinkle of light off its silver-plated hilt and…then it hits me. The knife!

I hear Cowbird's sage words of advice again: *you'll know when it's time.*

Cowbird's words ring loud and clear, even while I'm mired under the weight of a million slices of bacon. Even if the last time I used a knife was to butter a burnt slice of toast in Mom's kitchen. Even as my hands shake so hard I might lose a finger if I flash my only form of defense.

But what choice do I have? Wait in silence until Gus returns? Wait for the police to arrive? Tell Mom and Dad I only started this stupid journey because I barely recognize them any more? That I barely recognize myself anymore without a Coltrane song playing in my ear buds?

None of that will work. None of that will keep me out of the cave. None of that will heal. So, I feel around in my backpack until the steel hits my palm. I flick the hilt and the blade swings open. The metal captures the morning light in a single flash. My right hand wavers like a dry leaf. I steady my wrist with my left hand to prevent the knife from falling through the bars and down into the Virginia mud.

The lock is small enough to swing inside the bars, so I pull it through and examine the odd-shaped slot on its bottom, just below the black, spinning dial and the rounded hammer on top. I jam the tip of the blade into the mouth of the slot and jiggle it around, the way crooks on TV open locks in, like, two seconds flat.

Nothing happens. The lock hangs victorious from its position at the center of the cage door.

Then something jingles. A newspaper crinkles. My eyes shoot to the convenience store as Gus starts to lumber out. The pump attendant lends him a quick glance then retreats behind his newspaper. Gus spits a shower of brown juice into a paper cup and wipes the excess dribble from his porky lips with the sleeve of his mechanic's shirt. A ragged smile rises on his face when his eyes lock on mine and the first faint whine of sirens becomes audible in the distance.

My hands start to move at warp speed, twitching back and forth through gaps in the bars. Pulling. Twisting. Tugging. Yanking. The knife moves at awkward angles and grates against the back of the lock. The sirens grow louder and more distinct until I feel them ping off every gray wrinkle of my brain. My hands move so quickly and shake so wildly I can't figure out where the knife ends and my hand begins, until the blade slips and jumps off the lock and slashes a harsh line of liquid red across the back of my left hand. I wince. Feel the slow trickle of blood ooze down my wrist and over the tiny, hairs on the back of my arm.

I lose my grip on the knife. It bounces off the bottom of the cage and lodges itself between two bars on the cage below me. Gus tosses his paper cup full of nasty, dip spit in a wastebasket beside the gas pumps. The crunching of the gravel and the high-pitched squeal of the sirens pollute the air like noxious fumes. I reach down through the bars, straining and stretching beyond capacity. The tips of my fingers make subtle contact with the hilt of the knife. The sirens are right on top of me. Gus's rancid mouth-breathing closes in on the cage.

And right then, as if in slow motion, my panic dissolves. The fog lifts from my eyes. The sting dissipates from the wound on my hand. The uncontrollable shaking in my hands steadies to a surgeon-like composure. In one motion, like a freaking red-headed superhero, I grab the knife between two fingers and slide it back through the bars. My hands feel for the lock. I push the tip of the blade into the slot and…CLICK!

The hammer pops and the lock slides off the door, clangs against a cage below and thuds down onto the gravel. My eyes meet Gus's eyes and turn to narrow slits in synchrony with the pigman's—like we're revving the engines of our muscle cars at a traffic light, waiting to blast off down a straightaway and leave the other chump in the dust. I *do* blast off. Right out of the cage and down the side of the truck faster than your friendly, neighborhood Spiderman. I hit the gravel feet-first and roll forward on my hands, leaving a trail of blood and a litany of curse words piled high behind Gus's pork-filled paddy wagon.

"Hey! You little son of a bitch!" Gus bellows. From where he is, he has no chance in hell of catching me. There's a patch of dense woods behind the convenience store. I remember my experience at Lou's Chicken Pit when I had to break out on my own and bid a hasty goodbye to Lula. I figure it worked before, so I might as well dive into the bush and re-emerge on the other side, safer and less identifiable to police.

Then my eardrums start to throb under the intimidating weight of the sirens and the catastrophic swoosh of tires rolling up in the gravel lot. I squeeze the straps of my backpack and dive through the withered brush behind the convenience store. I catch a glimpse of the police cruisers pulling up beside Gus's hog truck before I'm hidden under the canopy of backwoods Virginia, bounding down a narrow trail overgrown with creeper and poison oak and enough milk thistle to feed an army's-worth of butterflies. If only one of those butterflies was the *Ama Kamama*. Then I could hop the main deck and let Juan, Nasser, and Pierre stuff me in the hold like a dead fish and stay hunkered down until Captain Adomi sailed me to safety.

Instead, the brush rustles on my heels and the hollow thud of footsteps rushes up behind me on the trail. My lungs are on fire. The jagged cut on my hand is swollen and raw. Long streaks of dried, brown blood stain the front of my t-shirt and the lap of my jeans. I know the police are on my tail, even if they're not yet in sight. All I can do is pull my backpack tight against my body and run as fast as a kid who just sprung himself from a hog cage can run.

The trees and the brush thin out ahead and there's a gate. An arch made of wrought iron and inscribed with a bunch of Latin phrases I can't make out except for the word "mortem"—DEATH. It seems fitting that I should be forced to run for my life through this archway with Virginia's finest on my heels. It seems doubly fitting once I'm through the gate to the other side which, instead of being lined by oak trees and kudzu, is piled high with gravestones and carnations. A cemetery. An old and spooky one with stone markers that jut up from the craggy earth at odd angles, and the faint scent of incense in the air.

Behind me, an officer shouts something into his walkie like, "Requesting backup!" All I can do is flop onto my belly with my head leaning against a gravestone in a position I never want to be in again until I'm actually dead. There's more movement on the other side of the iron arch. I know this may be the only chance I'll have to escape. I'm hoping all those hours I spent playing *Frogger* on my phone may prove useful if everything goes according to the plan I just sketched out in my head.

I mean, I guess what's really in my head right now is how this could be the end of the line for me? Not my metaphysical end or anything, cause if the police did happen to haul me in, it's not as if they'd treat me like Socrates and accuse me of moral corruption and make me drink a poisonous hemlock beverage just because I talk philosophy. No. It would simply be the end of my journey. Which would end any chance of reconciliation for Dad and Travis. Which would effectively end the debate on whether or not my family exists. Which would make lying here in this cemetery with my head on a gravestone and my hands folded across my chest a fitting and convenient destination.

But I'm not about to drink the hemlock on Travis and Dad and Mom. I'm not about to be taken down by some bloated, tobacco-juiced pig farmer because I hawked a few strips of licorice and a shit-smelling ride.

It's time to move. And quick! I roll to one side and slither across the grass like a serpent, careful to keep a row of gravestones between myself and the police. When I'm at least a hundred yards away from the officers, I pop up on one knee and tumblesault behind the Grecian columns of a dilapidated crypt I'm sure no one has visited—alive or dead—since before the Civil War. I am desperate to peek my head out and check on the progress of the search team, but I'm reminded of my experience in Lula's Chevelle before I trucked off into the woods. And then I can't help but think about Orpheus and Eurydice.

See, Orpheus was this Greek dude who could play a mean harp and Eurydice was his wife until Hades, lord of the underworld, took one look at her and thought, dang…I need to have this girl down in the pits of hell with me. She's too beautiful to sit around collecting dust with these pitiful mortals on Earth. So he kidnapped her and imprisoned her in the Land of the Dead. But Orpheus wasn't about to play that way. The dude searched and searched until he found the hidden gates to Hades—which I imagine looked a lot like the gate outside this cemetery—and he snuck down there and got himself a meeting with the God of the Dead! Hades was impressed by Orpheus' powers of persuasion, so he decided to strike a deal. He said, "Orpheus, I'll return your wife if you leave at once and trust that she'll be right behind you at all times. But if you don't trust me—if you so much as turn around one time to check on Eurydice's whereabouts, she'll be sucked back down into the bowels of hell where she'll remain for eternity."

Orpheus made it all the way to the gates before he couldn't stand it any longer. He turned to steal one, quick glance. And there she was, his wife Eurydice, whom he was able to see for about two tenths of a second before Hades yanked her back into the underworld forever. Orpheus learned the shittiest lesson of his life—never look back—which is the exact lesson I'm trying *not* to learn right now.

So, I take off at a full sprint, ducking gnarled tree limbs and crouching behind gravestones. And to my relief, the *Frogger* routine works. I reach the other side of the graveyard, slowly and carefully lift the latch on the front-side gate, and slip out, softer than a spring breeze while the police are still staging their plan of attack on the opposite side.

But what now? I'm in the open. I'm too freaked out to stand around in broad daylight and plan my next move. I see some kind of outhouse and an old pickup truck loaded with what appears to be a large mound of dirt or mulch covered by a tarp. Within a split second, I'm on the truck bed. I pull the tarp over me and lay there still, trying to catch my breath.

Next thing I know, the door of the truck opens, then slams shut. The ignition cranks, the engine roars, and the truck pushes off to parts unknown.

Arete

I'm exhausted, but I fight the urge to drift off in the back of a random pickup truck with no idea where it's headed. The mound of soil under the tarp is dank and earthy. It reeks of earthworms and damp clay and death. It's not enough. I'm still locked in an epic battle with my eyelids as they droop low on the ridge of my eyelashes and flap open each time I start to drift away to nightmare land.

The truck had zipped away from the graveyard area, bouncing over patches of lumpy grass and rock, onto a smooth ribbon of highway with the wind ruffling the tarp and the side panels of the flatbed. It then slowed and fell into a recognizable stop, start, stop, start pattern before navigating a downhill semi-circle and pushing out into a sea of car exhaust, shrieking horns, and the broken-down syllables of human voices.

My heart does little flip-flops in my chest. At first, I'm not sure why. I mean, the police cruisers are long gone and, as far as I can tell, the driver of the truck has no clue I'm crouched in the flatbed. Still, the nerves rise from my gut and into my heart and spill into my bloodstream as molecules of panic.

Where in the world are we headed? Will I end up somewhere in Florida or Texas or California or on the surface of the dang moon—like, fifty million miles away from Philadelphia and Birdland and any chance of reuniting my family? Is the dude driving this smelly hunk of metal as unhinged—or possibly even MORE unhinged—than Gus, the maniacal hogman, or does he have an invisible road map like Lula McBride? Are these sudden stops and jerks and detours just slow, steady checkpoints on the way to the end of my journey, or will I pop out from my muddy hiding spot and find myself in the parking lot of a police precinct?

I can't take the suspense. The pressure. Just like Orpheus, the intrigue of not knowing what I can't see is too much to bear. The next time the truck slows down and the long screech warms up in the wheel wells, I make my move. A risky one. One that makes me so nervous I want to puke.

I roll out from under the tarp and heave myself over the sidewall of the flatbed. I stand there like a complete fool in the middle of a jam-packed intersection in the middle of a city I kind of recognize, even though I know in my gut I've never been here.

The traffic light is red—lucky me—but the driver in the black BMW directly behind the pickup stares in shock when she sees me emerge from under the tarp in my mud-encrusted jeans with my blood-caked hand draped at my side. She leans on the horn—apparently to alert every other commuter at the intersection to my presence.

The light turns green. I dodge a car and stumble over the curb. The sidewalk is loaded with people in their ties and their business suits. I stick out like a sore thumb, so I catapult myself over a cement half-wall and through a sparse line of ancient oak trees and into a cement-covered clearing that looks like a racetrack encircling a long, rectangular pool. The water is flat and clear. Not a ripple in it. The only thing that reveals itself in the mirror-like glaze of the pool is a reflection in the scratchy texture of masonry.

My eyes trace the reflection the length of the pond until they're drawn upward. The structure rises up like an obelisk from the grounds of the mall and stretches to the heavens. It is instantly recognizable. The Washington Monument. I'd seen it hundreds of times on the pages of my history textbooks, on the covers of magazines, and on commercials that run in the weeks leading up to the Fourth of July. I had somehow just landed in our nation's capital. Washington, DC. The cradle of American democracy and closer to Philadelphia than ever.

I feel lighter. As though an enormous weight has been lifted off my shoulders. As though the wave of panic I experienced in the flatbed was indeed a sign. From the fates. That I better get my ass out of the truck and my feet on the ground because I'm here—in a place that's within striking distance of the most important destination of my life.

My legs unwind. My feet stop feeling like useless blocks of Swiss cheese, and I let the warmth of the sun cast down on the back of my neck as I stroll the length of the world-famous reflecting pool. I reach a place I've always wanted to visit. A monument that rises above all others in the city. The monument of monuments. The Lincoln Memorial, with its columns mined directly out of classical lore and its endless stack of steps like the multi-faceted tiers of a giant wedding cake.

I know there's someone inside I need to see. Someone who stands almost twenty feet high and is chiseled from marble. Someone whose spirit and integrity has been woven into the fabric of what makes this nation a miracle. What forever gives it the potential to be different and great and promising and hopeful to all who enter, despite their beliefs or who their daddies were or how much money they have in their pockets, so long as its people follow the examples set by a man who knew how to call the country out when it was wrong.

Without giving my legs a command, my body glides up the four score and seven steps, all eighty-seven of them one by one. On the top level of the masterpiece is a series of gaps between the columns. I step inside, and I'm struck by how much bigger Lincoln's chamber is than it appears from the street.

The memorial is crawling with tourists—moms in baggy sweats and t-shirts heralding the DC attractions they've visited, and dads pushing strollers with snoozing toddlers and their sticky, lollipop fingers stuffed inside. I lean back against one of the columns and take in the scene. Notice the taught jawline of our fearless captain who, in his time, stood for all that was good and right and just even though it meant he'd pay for it with his life. The eyes serene and brooding, the hands stretched out on the armrest of his great American throne, and the weight of an entire country's hopes and dreams and fears shining through in the gravity of the crease marks on his forehead.

I'm reminded of the Trane statue back in High Point. Travis's statue. The one of the man as musician standing resolutely in the path of his achievement. Like Lincoln, fearing everything and nothing at once, and pushing onward regardless of the obstacles before him. It gives me an empty feeling in the pit of my stomach because I know all the tourists snapping vacation pictures think a quick status update that shows them standing in front of a statue is somehow a substitute for supporting the man's ideals in words and deeds. At least that's what I saw sometimes back home in High Point. Who knows? Maybe I'm not the best judge of this type of trial. But, then again, maybe I am. Maybe the past few days have catapulted me further outside the cave than folks who think they have the world figured out. Maybe I'm the perfect judge in this case.

Look, I know I haven't seen much of the world in a little over sixteen years, but from what I have seen, there's plenty of room for improvement.

For one, I can't understand why humans have such an obsession with the concept of control. Over others. Over themselves. Over things that don't seem to make much of a positive difference in the world when you really think about them. Like Travis's pills or Dad's pack of smokes or my obsession with anything I can scroll through on a screen. It's like, shouldn't we band together and protect each other from the evils that attack us on the inside instead of attacking each other over clothes we wear on the outside and possessions we own on the outside or skin that drapes over our outsides?

You know, like Lincoln tried to do before he got shot trying to sit and enjoy a damn play.

Even after a hero like Abraham Lincoln pays the ultimate price to bring us together, why is it so hard for geniuses and doctors and artists—folks who happen to look like Trane—to break through and share their contributions with society so many years after Lincoln delivered his proclamation? And why is it so hard for a strung-out ferret with a ponytail and a saxophone to make amends with his father after so many years of eating meals around the same table? And why is it so hard for a red-headed, teenage nothing with a face full of freckles and an interest in philosophy to find a few friends in his own hometown to help him navigate a path out of the cave once and for all?

Although I have yet to see them myself, it makes me happy to know that places like Harlem and Birdland exist. Places where birds of all feathers reach out with both talons and snatch their creations; to invent; to lead; to make music; to simply walk down a street without fearing for their lives; to weave memories that form the tapestry of society.

Even Plato, back in ancient times, had the sense to classify people according to their virtue instead of the randomness of genetic characteristics. And, sure, the great philosopher recognized people were different. He noticed the Thracians and the Phoenicians and many other races of people his countrymen may have warred against and labeled savages—but he felt the measure of a human being should be based on virtue alone—that is, the contribution one can impress upon the world at large. The Greek poet, Homer, called it "Arete" and I think I'm gonna spend the rest of my life searching for the Arete in everyone I meet. If the serenity in Lincoln's eyes are any indication, I'd say the tall man in the stovepipe hat would agree.

The consistent drone of chatter in Lincoln's chamber is shattered by the sharpness of a loud and mechanical voice. When I crane my neck around the column and squint my eyes to view a group of people perched on the bottom step of the wedding cake, I realize I'm not far off in my assessment. It's a bullhorn. And it's in the hands of a man in a threadbare, military field jacket, mossy green and pockmarked with a collection of iron-on patches, dangling medals, and political buttons pinned on in no particular order.

He wears black, knit gloves sliced off at the knuckles so his bare fingers poke through the ends. Probably for better grip on the bullhorn, which he depresses and holds to his face. "Are we not Americans?" he shouts. His voice filters through the circuits of the bullhorn and floats out in mechanized notes above the mall. The crowd of twenty or so followers shout, "Yes! We! Are!" and the man with the bullhorn rattles off another question. "Are we not heroes!?"

"Yes! We! Are!"

"And do we not bleed!?"

"Yes! We! Do!"

"And do we not deserve to be healthy!?"

"Yes! We! Do!"

From the heights of Mt. Lincoln, I can't make out everything this group of protestors stands for, but it's clear they possess a specific type of Arete I can't quite place. I leave Mr. Lincoln to the comfort of his chamber and make my way back down the steps under the power of some strange force I can only describe as fate. The closer I get to the group, the louder and more vociferous becomes the speaker's shrill, mechanical tones.

"Have we been forgotten!?"

"Yes! We! Have!"

"And do we deserve respect!?"

"Yes! We! Do!"

The protestors are dressed in fatigues identical to the horn man. From this distance, the purpose of the protest becomes clear, as many of the activists wave cardboard signs with messages on them like "Vets For Peace" and "Ho Chi Minh Was HELL, HELL, HELL" and "FUND THE VA!" Most of the activists bear an identical symbol on their uniforms—one I recognize from war movies—hanging like a metal teardrop above their left breast. The Purple Heart Medal. Maybe the most heroic recognition a soldier can earn because it stands for sacrifice. It means the soldier suffered personal injury—often catastrophic and life-changing in nature—to preserve the lives of fellow platoon mates and the fabric of our freedom.

I absorb the scene, watch the activists mix and mingle with ordinary Americans who wake up each morning and eat their bacon and their scrambled eggs and trudge off to work to the safety of their office buildings without having to hide in a trench or step over landmines or watch the blood gurgle out of their best friend's mouth as he takes a final breath.

These activists distribute pamphlets with the letters POW-MIA standing out in boldface letters across the top. I listen to their words, their pleas to ordinary, voting Americans to remember the sacrifices soldiers made during the many American conflicts around the globe that history often succeeds in forgetting. I'm struck by how alone these injured souls seem even as they attempt to communicate with throngs of ordinary people—those who never have to see atrocities flash through their nightmares. Still, the Arete swirling around this group of forgotten warriors is so palpable I almost have to scrape it away like shower steam on a bathroom mirror.

The man with the bullhorn startles me with a half-gloved hand on my shoulder. I jump a little and the man steps back and holds up both hands in jest like I'm robbing him. "Woah there, buddy!" He says it like I'm a frightened colt bucking around in my enclosure. "I don't bite. Just want to share some literature with you." He hands me a pamphlet. I fold the pages back. There are so many bullet-pointed statistics on the first page it makes my head hurt.

"Are you ok there, bud?" he asks, seeing my clothes caked in mud and streaked with blood. He catches a quick whiff of the pig shit encrusted on my shoes and takes a noticeable step back.

"Yeah, I'm fine, thanks," I reply, adding, "so, are you a war veteran?" I feel like an absolute dumbass as soon as the words leave my mouth.

"What gave it away?" he shoots back, flicking the tiny Purple Heart back and forth with an index finger. "Served from sixty-eight to seventy-two. Heart of Saigon. One of only three men in my platoon to make it out."

I look at the man's face. Years of pain and anguish are wallpapered across his brow. His eyes are soft brown and narrow. They hug the thick bridge of his nose and accentuate the blocky squarishness of a jawline dappled in bristly, white whiskers—not a full beard, just a heavy frosting like you might see on an elderly version of Fred Flintstone. He takes two steps in my direction and I can't help but notice the way he shuffles when he walks. Like, his left leg moves free of impediment, but his right doesn't lift as high off the sidewalk and the black sole of his combat boot scrapes the pavement. He catches me noticing his limp before I can snap my eyes away.

"Took some shrapnel," he says, pulling the pant leg of his blue jeans up to knee level. There's a jagged scar and a patch of chewed-up skin on the side of his calf muscle. "Would have lost the whole thing if Sammy hadn't dragged me out."

I look around the collection of veterans huddled at the base of Lincoln's steps, but no one stands out or looks old enough to be Sammy.

"No point looking for him," he says. "Didn't make it. Most of my platoon got picked off by a sniper."

"Sorry to hear that," I say, and I'm not just saying it to be polite. I mean it with every ounce of Arete I have in my body.

"Don't mention it," he says, then he holds out one of his hands and we shake. "Name's Giacomo Annunzio, but people call me "Jack" because apparently Army grunts don't speak Italian. Those dudes hate syllables. And vowels."

I laugh because the Army grunts Jack speaks of must have all come from High Point, North Carolina where a name like Giacomo is about as common as a flying saucer. "I'm Cordy," I tell him. "Cordy Wheaton. From High Point, North Carolina."

"It's a pleasure to meet you, Carolina Wheaton." He winks. I notice a sparkle in his eyes. "That's what your nickname'd be if you made it through basic."

"Basic?"

"Training. Fort Dix. Maybe the longest six weeks of my life—unless you count the nightmare I woke up from the day I left Saigon. I don't. I try to forget that part."

"This protest probably doesn't help you accomplish your goal," I say in one of those famously-regrettable comments I make that I immediately wish had never crossed my lips.

I see the man smile for the first time. His bullhorn swings down to his side. "No," he says through a chuckle. "It definitely does not. But I'm the only one who owns a freaking bullhorn, so they kind of need me."

"What are y'all doing out here?" I ask.

"We're being Americans," he tells me. "And Americans make their voices heard when they face injustice. Otherwise, what's the point of people like me heading overseas and jumping out of planes or tanks and risking our lives?"

"For freedom?"

"Exactly. But this is what freedom looks like, Carolina. It's not pretty pictures and amber fields of grain all the time."

I nod because he pretty much described my life for the past few days and I know my plan is completely based on Jack Annunzio's concept of freedom, which in my estimation means standing for what you know is right even when it's the least convenient thing in the world.

"So what are y'all fighting for?" I ask him.

"Respect," Jack says. "We fought for this country and we watched our friends die. Some of us wake up in a cold sweat each night for the past forty-some years. But it's like people hardly remember we exist. Like the past has become disposable, and nobody thinks about who made it possible for them to buy a Starbucks at all four corners of an intersection or carry all the information in the world around on a tiny device that fits in your pocket."

It's true. I don't remember the last time I questioned any of the conveniences I'm blessed to enjoy as an American, and if I did, guys like Bill Gates and Steve Jobs would come to mind instead of shabbily dressed bullhorn blowers like Giacomo "Jack" Annunzio.

"So," Jack continues, "we're trying to remind people that veterans do exist and that we're still suffering all the mental and physical wounds we brought back with us from any one of those goddamned wars…pardon my French."

"Believe me," I say, "I've heard much worse than a few damns and hells. It's actually kind of amazing people still fight over dirty words before they think about people like you."

Jack's face softens. "We're cut from the same cloth, Carolina. Maybe you should give this thing a try." He holds the bullhorn out in front of him with both hands, like an offering. "Take a spin," he says.

"I wouldn't know what to say," I start to tell him, but the bullhorn is already crammed in my bread basket before I finish the sentence.

"You'll figure it out," Jack tells me with another sparkle-eyed wink.

I inch myself up on the bottom step of the wedding cake. My knees wobble as my finger grazes the intercom button and a loud shriek echoes across the mall. All of the activists, along with every pedestrian and tourist in sight, stop and turn their heads toward me. I push the intercom button, this time with more grace, and say, "Are we…uhh…not humans?"

"Yes! We! Are!"

"And…do we not bleed?"

"Yes! We! Do!"

"Then what do we need for our veterans?"

"Fund the V-A!!"

The activists erupt in raucous applause. They hoist handmade protest signs over their heads and chant competing slogans that blend into one messy, indistinguishable—but beautiful—voice. Like jazz.

I step down off my soapbox and Jack takes the bullhorn. He shuffles another step closer and the soft fabric of his cut-off gloves press down on my shoulder. He smiles and says, "Carolina Wheaton, we could use a soldier like you. We're heading to Baltimore this afternoon. How'd you like to come along?"

It doesn't take much for me to realize Jack's offer is about the luckiest thing to happen to me in days, so I'm like, "I'd love to," before the poor guy finishes extending the invitation.

"Great," he says. "You can ride with me."

We file in behind a throng of veterans all voicing their concerns about a country in search of its Arete. The fortress of the Lincoln Memorial recedes behind us into the patchwork of our capital city, and I can't help but feel like I've found my way again. All it took was a few dozen war heroes and our legendary captain—one of America's greatest presidents—to help me right the ship.

Complete darkness. The prickling sensation of fear crawls up my spine. The drip-drip and the musty scent of rodent piss. My throat tanned like rawhide. Voices.

"I swear we'll do it!"

A dull thud. The crawl of two knees as they drag across gravel.

"You'll get it."

A new voice. Haggard. Slow. Wrapped in a wheezing, strangulated cough. Familiar but distant. Something I can't grasp, like a name or a phone number I've dialed all my life but can't recall.

"This ain't no game!" The deep voice. A CRACK! as the back of a hand strikes cheekbone. The wheezing takes over. Hideous, wracking coughs from the chambers of corroded lungs.

The gravel stirs outside. A car door opens. Slams shut. "I swear to God you'll get it." The haggard voice.

An engine roars to life. Gravel sprays out from encumbered wheel wells. The tires emit an antagonized squeal and...

Shadows

I'm jolted awake by the screech of the air brakes on a large semi as it blows past the passenger side window and forces my vital organs into my throat. The afternoon sun blasts through the windshield of Jack's Prius and leaves tiny, floating white spots before my eyes. Squinting, I catch the look on Jack's face as he navigates the car along a stretch of highway stacked with vehicles on their way to the harbor. His mouth puckers. His wrinkled face spawns a few extra wrinkles.

"You okay there, Carolina?" he asks.

I'm stunned, stuck on the sound of the ragged cough from my dream as I search every inch of my brain for an identity. "Yeah," I say. "I'm fine, thanks. Just tired."

"I noticed," Jack says. "Maybe more tired than you let on."

He flicks the right turn signal and pulls the emerald green Prius, with all of its fuel-efficient might, off the next exit ramp beside a road sign that reads Inner Harbor. From atop the ramp, we look down on a humble, yet distinct, city skyline with midsize highrises butted up against the glassy surface of the harbor. The Chesapeake reaches her silky finger into the main artery of downtown Baltimore. The white sails of small clippers flash and wink at us from the bay and heave their wake against the starboard bow of a larger ship fastened to its bulwarks. Pedestrians scurry across a red-brick walkway that circles the waterfront. They travel as a single line of army ants and bottle-neck in front of a building that resembles some sort of space station.

"National Aquarium right there, Carolina. Pretty cool place if you're into fish. You into fish?"

"I guess so," I reply. "Never really thought about them past those little fried sticks Mom plops on my plate when she doesn't feel like cooking."

"Yeah…well, these fish do not trust the Gorton's Fisherman," Jack says. I laugh. "But that's not where we're headed."

"Where are we going, exactly?" I ask.

"To the harbor. We're gonna use our voices on the street. Where the crowds can hear our message. And where we won't get locked up."

"Not that I'm trying to get arrested or anything, but doesn't that sound kind of…well…wimpy?" I ask. Jack's head pops up for a second and a puff of air releases through his mouth. It's like my remark stabbed him right between the ribs. He's silent. Thinking. Brooding. Deciding whether or not it's worth vocalizing the ideas he's mulling over in his mind. His lips curl. He takes a deep breath.

"You know, courage has nothing to do with acting like a hard ass in front of police or trying to get away with things that break the norm." I don't respond. Just kind of stare at him for a second with a blank look on my face. "You think I'm full of shit," Jack says, looking amused.

"I never said that," I tell him. "It's just, I always thought true courage had more to do with standing up against the man. Like, physically."

"You're right," Jack says. "Except I think that 'man' you're talking about is yourself."

"That doesn't make sense. What's the point of standing up to myself?"

"Standing up to yourself is one of the hardest things a human being can do. Believe me. You might already know a thing or two about what I mean."

"I doubt it," I say, "considering I have no clue what you're talking about."

Jack pulls the Prius up beside a fancy hotel and backs it in along the curb in one swoop like he's the absolute king of parallel parking. He cuts the engine and locks the doors before I can grab the handle and get out. He stares at me for a moment and says, "I think you know exactly what I'm talking about."

"I don't," I say. "Not even a little bit."

"The dreams," he says. "Or should I say nightmares?"

"I still don't know what you're saying."

"Come on, Carolina. I sat here driving this car for twenty minutes watching you bounce around in the passenger seat like a damn racquetball, and you're gonna sit here and pretend you were dreaming about gumdrops and lollipops?"

"Who said I was dreaming?" I snipe back with an edge that's sharper than Cowbird's knife.

Jack slaps his hand down on the steering wheel and bursts out into a wild cackle that's half anger and half amusement. "Look who you're talking to, man!" He flicks the Purple Heart medal back and forth. "You think I don't know about being haunted? About being trailed by visions I can't touch? Ones that stab me every time I close my eyes? You think I'm both blind and stupid, Carolina?"

I don't answer. For one, I'm kind of startled by his blatant accuracy and by the speed with which he flipped the whole conversation about courage around on me. For a few seconds, I don't know how to answer. I mean, I barely know the guy and the last thing I want to do is talk about a bunch of weird shit I'm going through that even *I* don't understand.

"No, of course not" I say finally. "I don't think you're blind or stupid."

"Then tell me about the nightmares," he says.

"They're not important," I tell him. "Just dreams."

"They are vitally important. They are the precise tools you can use to figure out what's haunting you. Until you face those demons, you'll never know the real definition of courage."

"I don't have demons," I shoot back, with a maelstrom of fear and rage swirling in the pit of my stomach.

"We both know that's untrue. But I get it. I understand how it feels to pretend there's nothing wrong. That the visions will pass and life will go on like normal. That you never experienced trauma."

He pulls a slice of Doublemint gum from his breast pocket and pops it in his mouth. He offers the pack to me, but I decline because somehow it doesn't feel right all of a sudden. Nothing feels right anymore except this desire I have to crash through the passenger window and disappear into downtown Baltimore.

Jack doesn't let the argument die. "Take me," he says. "In Nam, I saw some shit I don't even want to put into words. It hurts too much. But one specific event—one I started telling you about in DC—sticks with me. I see it every night and almost every waking day, too, if I'm not careful with my thoughts."

"What is it?"

"The sniper. I can still see the tiny flash off the barrel. Hear the single burst from the battery as another one of my platoon-mates explodes in red and slumps, lifeless, on the jungle floor. I can hear his cries and the muffled gurgles of his final breaths. Can feel the humidity of a Saigon summer trickling off my face in droplets. The bone-splitting sickness of my leg shattering into a million, tiny fragments. And the feeling of sheer terror and helplessness. Lying there, alone, under a pile of bodies. In a foreign land, thousands of miles from home. With the warmth of blood soaking through the fibers of my uniform. Waiting and praying and hoping for a miracle."

He pulls a tissue from a travel size pack on the dash and dabs the moisture from the corners of his eyes.

I'm speechless.

"*These* are the images I see every night, Carolina. In violent flashes consumed by artillery fire and the boom of air cover. They've never left me, but I face them and question them anyway."

"How can you live this way?" I ask.

"Courage," he says. "First, I had to admit to myself I had a problem. I had to make amends with the fact that my service to this country—at least right after I returned—was a matter of scorn to some of my fellow countrymen, that my plight was not something that even registered with most Americans. And that I had to seek help."

"Help? From where?"

"Doctors, my friend. One after another after another."

"And what did they tell you?"

"That I had some newfangled disease not many people were talking about back then. Caused by a natural response to extreme stress and trauma. My war buddies called it "shell-shock" back in the day. The doctors called it Post Traumatic Stress Disorder."

"PTSD," I say under my breath.

"You've heard of it," Jack says. "It's pretty common now, at least in terms of diagnosis."

He pauses and blows a tiny bubble with his gum. When it pops, he looks at me and asks, "Have you ever experienced trauma?"

The little hairs rise on the back of my neck and, for a second, I feel like I might be sick. Then it happens again. The echo chamber. The voices in the back of my mind, calling out:

I could kill him for putting us here

It's all his fault

Never should have

Turned a blind eye *and now this…*

In a flash I'm right back in the passenger seat of Jack's Prius, and he's waiting for an answer. I steady myself and lock my jaw down tight. I fiddle with the POW/MIA button Jack pinned on my shirt pocket when we hopped in the Prius back in DC. I can't for the life of me understand why I react this way to a simple question. I just want to say "NO!" or look at him with my eyes crossed and pretend I don't know what the word "trauma" means. But I can't. Because I can't remember. All I see is fog and red and nightmares from which I can't wake up. So, I don't say a word. Just sit there and pick at the shiny film on the face of the button until Jack breaks the silence.

"You don't have to talk about it. All you have to do is listen. Know you're not alone."

He pauses to blow a quick bubble. "But you'll figure it out. And you'll stop blaming yourself too."

He snaps the gum between his teeth the second he finishes the sentence, and then he winks at me. I want to punch him, but I realize he's dead-on accurate. All this stuff about finding Travis and giving him the sheet music and taking him to Birdland? It's because it's my fault. It's my fault Dad smoked a carton of cigs a week and I never said a goddamn word to him. It's my fault I watched Travis pop a percocet, then two, and then four, all because of some stupid leg injury. I kept my head down, carried on with school, did my homework, watched TV, then went to sleep while he was turning into a full-blown addict right there in the bunk above me. It's my fault I don't have a single friend, or a single enemy, or anyone who cared enough either way to ask me what the hell was going on in my life so I didn't have to get so tired of being the one to ask that question of myself.

Yes, it's my fault. All of it.

My cheeks are wet with tears and my shoulders start to rock and I'm breathing in stunted, half-breaths all of a sudden. Out of nowhere. Jack rests a hand on the back of my neck and gives me a towel. "For your hand," he says. I force back the tears and wipe the dried blood off the back of my hand with a clean, white towel that reeks of rubbing alcohol. The thin slice from Cowbird's knife stings, and I wince a little before Jack hands me a bandage. I strap it over the wound.

"It's not that I don't want to talk about it," I say through sniffles. "It's that I don't know *what* to talk about. It's like a shadow I can't reach."

"Except in your dreams."

I nod.

"I understand," he says. "Believe me, I understand."

"What can I do?" I ask, hoping Jack knows some kind of world-changing secret that can help repair whatever it is that's wrong with me.

"You continue the journey."

"That's it? Just keep going?"

"That and you stop trying to forget."

I straighten the button on my shirt pocket and meet Jack's gaze for the first time since the conversation veered off into this weird little parallel-parking heart-to-heart session.

"That might be a little harder than the journey part," I say.

He laughs and reaches into the back seat for his bullhorn. "That's where you're wrong," he says. "The remembering part IS the journey. It's how you get there that's the hard part."

"I don't know what the hell you're talking about," I say.

Jack hits the power locks on the doors and drops the bullhorn into my lap.

"Come on," he says. "First step is to get you out from behind those shadows."

"Me?" I ask, staring down at the bullhorn.

Jack's mouth opens into a wide, satisfied grin. He nods.

And that's how I become the voice of a group of always-heroic but sometimes voiceless Americans for the second time that day. And how my journey begins to fall right back in line with fate.

Infinite Resonance

The whole time we're raising hell in Baltimore Harbor with the war vets, Jack doesn't say a thing about our shadows. He doesn't pat me on the shoulder every five minutes like some creepy support counselor. He doesn't press. He keeps his distance. He lifts a protest sign and joins the only chant I learned in my five hours as a political activist. My voice belts out through the wide mouth of the bullhorn and over the rippling waves of the harbor, ripe with paddle boats, until the message is raw and hoarse.

We gather around the harbor in groups of four or five and watch the street performers juggle bowling pins while perched on unicycles or feed roasted peanuts from brown paper bags to the fearless, Inner Harbor squirrel population.

The calm is shattered when we get back to Jack's Prius. As soon as my ass hits the upholstery. It's like old Giacomo went and hit the "start" button on the video game controller and unpaused the conversation at the exact point we left off before the protest.

"So, come on, Carolina. What's your story?" he asks. "And what the hell are you doing out here smelling like a heaping pile of horse shit?"

It's a reasonable set of questions, and I owe the guy answers. I mean, he's taken me under his wing and driven me at least fifty miles closer to Travis without wondering if I were some kind of axe murderer on the run, so I figure I can respect the guy's curiosity.

I tell him everything. How I'm almost seventeen years old and how I've been traveling on a shoestring for days since I left High Point. I tell him about Gus the hogman. I tell him about Travis and Mom and Dad and the Birdland Jazz Club. About Trane and my brother's sheet music and how I'm gonna bring the Wheaton family back together so it's not just me and Mom weeping into our microwave mac n' cheese every night.

When I'm done telling Jack my plan—which is much less of a plan and much more of a throw-shit-at-the-wall-and-see-what-sticks sort of approach—all he does is nod, put the key in the ignition, and crank the engine as much as one can in a Prius.

"Well, then you're coming with me," he says.

He pulls the car from the curb and rips off down the cobblestone street before I can respond.

"Where are we going?" I ask, as Jack pulls the Prius back on the highway.

"Home. To Rehoboth Beach. In the great state of Delaware."

"Delaware?" I say half to myself and half out loud. "Delaware's good."

"Delaware *is* good, especially when you're on an epic odyssey to Philadelphia."

He pops another slice of Doublemint in his mouth, presumably to refresh the old one he's still chewing from earlier.

"You know, I shouldn't be carting underage runaways around in my car like this—"

"I'm also wanted by the police," I tell him. "I may have…uhh… ripped off some poor slob's credit card or something."

He shakes his head and rubs one of his weathered hands through his white whiskers.

"He's also wanted by police," he repeats under his breath. "I shouldn't be doing this, but what the hell, I'm gonna do it anyway."

"I don't get it," I say. "Why do you keep helping me?"

He goes on a mini tear of blowing bubbles and popping them in quick succession like a minty fresh machine gun.

"I honestly don't know," he says after literally thinking and chewing gum at the same time for at least a full minute. "Maybe it's the soldier in me? Always trying to be the hero. Or maybe it's, like, a fatherly instinct or something? Who knows? But you shouldn't question charity, kid. Didn't your parents tell you that?"

"My parents don't tell me anything," I say. "Especially not since Travis left. They pretty much go about their days moving back and forth like robots on an assembly line. We mostly communicate through the walls in our house."

"Every family has its challenges," he says.

"What about your family?"

"What *about* my family?"

"Does it have challenges?"

I don't know what sets him off, but Jack cackles like a madman, smacking the steering wheel and fighting for breath as something—my question, apparently—brings tears to his eyes.

"What's so funny?" I ask.

"Yes, my family sure did face challenges. You can definitely say that."

"Your kids?"

"Never had any."

"Wife?"

"Nope, no wife, either."

"Your parents then? Were they real pains in the ass?"

"Well, they weren't happy with my choices, I can tell you that much."

"Was it because you never married or had kids?"

"That may have played into it," he says, "but I thought we were talking about *your* family, Carolina."

I steal a slice of Doublemint from Jack's pack on the dashboard and pop it in my mouth. "It's my fault," I say.

"What?"

"My family fell apart because of me. I screwed up. Let things get out of control. Just sat by and watched it happen."

Jack takes one hand off the steering wheel and presses it down on my forearm. "You can't blame yourself for other people's decisions."

"But I could have stopped him."

"You didn't drop the pills in Travis's mouth, did you?"

"No. But I could have told someone. I could have made him stop!" The agitation in my voice is evident, and I'm aware of it, but I have no control.

"Travis is the only one who could make Travis stop."

"What do you know?" I shout. "What does a guy who's never had kids know about anything?" It comes out twice as nasty and twisted as I intended, and I want to gobble up the words and swallow them, but it's too late.

Jack's lips go thin and taut. His eyes sink back in their sockets. A grave shadow sweeps down his cheekbones. Without saying a word, he rips open the glove box and rifles through it with one hand as he steers the Prius with the other. I sit there, stiff as a board, in the passenger seat and pray my big mouth isn't the deciding factor in whether or not I become an instant crash test dummy.

Jack plucks an old polaroid photograph—cracked and yellowed at the edges—from a tangle of receipts and car manuals in the glove box, and he settles back into a safer position for driving a vehicle. He looks like he wants to explode, but when he speaks it's in soft, deliberate tones.

"You think reproduction is like a certification card to understanding life?" I'm too stunned to say anything, so I sit there like I'm part of the seat. "Cause if you do," he says, "you have more to learn than you think."

He holds the photo against the clear glass of the windshield and smiles. "You want to know why I never got married? Have a look."

He hands me the photo. "Only person on Earth I ever truly loved. Take a good look."

The photo is worn and blurry. I have to squint and hold it at an angle to the passing streetlamps to make out the form. When I do, I see a stocky gentleman with broad shoulders in a street cop's uniform. His bushy, black eyebrows sit like caterpillars on his forehead and look like twin, miniature versions of his scratchy-looking mustache.

"I don't get it," I say. "Who is this guy?"

"That, my friend, is Sergeant Frederick P. Johnson, Baltimore P.D. Bravest son of a bitch I ever met. Of course, I just called him Freddy."

"So…what? He a cousin of your's or something? A platoon-mate?"

Jack rolls his window down and spits his gum out in disgust. "No… he was not a cousin. Or a platoon-mate."

He stares at me and I stare back with the blankest and most desolate expression of all time. "Don't you see, Carolina?"

"Not really."

"Back in those days, it's not like we could have been married. And children? Well…."

"You mean?" Suddenly, everything starts to line up for me and I feel stupid and incredibly awkward at the same time. "So you mean you're—"

"Gay," he says. "I'm gay, son. Let's not let it ruin our lives or anything."

He snatches the polaroid out of my hands and stuffs it back in the glove box with the rest of his paperwork.

I stare straight ahead through the windshield and watch the hash marks on the highway whip past, without a clue of what to say next. I mean, it's not like I have anything against someone just because they're gay. That'd be stupid. And it's not like I think Jack is some kind of different species of human being. It's just that I've never been around anyone who is gay. At least, not when I was aware of it, and now I'm not sure how to act, or if there's ever a different way to act when you find out a person doesn't match your original notions. It's what happens, I guess, when you spend all your time in the shell instead of out in the world enjoying the journey and learning what life looks like through a variety of lenses.

Once the awkwardness inside the Prius gets to an unsustainable level and I'm on the verge of tossing myself out onto the highway to ease the torture, I build up the courage to say, "I'm not afraid of you or anything," which is easily the stupidest thing I've ever said in my life. But somehow it works. Because Jack can't help but laugh in my face.

"Well thank you, Carolina! I'm so glad to hear that I'm not a threat to your safety!" he blurts out, and I realize how stupid I sound.

"I'm sorry," I say. "It's just that…well…these sorts of things aren't talked about where I come from—or at least not from the pulpit of the Wheaton household. You caught me off guard, that's all."

"I won't hold it against you," he says, "especially since you mention religion. I know that can make things interesting. Trust me, I'm Catholic."

"What does that have to do with anything?"

"It means I know what it's like to feel like I'm guilty most of the time."

"Guilty of what?" I ask.

"There's plenty, Carolina. It's not like I'm perfect or anything. It's just that religion seems to always find a way to remind me of that fact. For better and for worse, I guess."

I pause to consider Jack's point. I don't know why, but it leads me right back to Dad.

"You know, I thought it was weird how my father was so busy telling people how to save their souls, he forgot that those souls belonged to individual people with different lives and their own unique set of issues."

"Yeah, I hear you. Never saw much room for individuality in religion," Jack says, "but maybe that's not a bad thing all of the time."

"Just most of the time," I shoot back, and get a rising chuckle out of Jack.

"Reminds me of my experience in the service," he says. "Always hiding my true identity even from the brothers I swore my life to."

"That must have been horrible," I tell him.

Jack nods and grunts his agreement. "You know, when we were in the jungle with bullets whizzing by, it's funny how quickly we forget our differences...how survival, our fundamental goal on this planet, becomes a whole lot more important than our differences."

"John Coltrane knew that," I say.

"The jazz man? Is that right?"

"Yes. Travis told me that Trane respected *all* religions, that he was spiritual, but not exclusionary."

"Exclusionary, eh? That's a mighty big word there, Carolina."

"Travis told me Trane thought every religion had at least something right and you could make the world a better place if you were open-minded enough to blend together all the good parts and filter out the bad."

"Sounds like a pretty smart fellow," Jack says. "Probably why he made such beautiful music."

"Exactly," I say, and I feel myself going on a roll. "He was famous for bringing together all kinds of music—from bebop to avant-garde to indigenous—because he believed bringing together all forms of beauty made something even more beautiful."

"Sounds simple, and yet we seldom make it our mission to do just that."

"Trane did it," I tell him, "because he knew it's the only way to survive. As a human race. Together. That's why he said 'music can create the changes we see in the thinking of people.' It's the only proof anyone needs to understand how bringing things together instead of pulling them apart is the essence of creation. Trane called it 'infinite resonance.' Well...that's what Travis told me, anyway."

"I tend to agree with him," Jack says.

"Me too," I reply.

And, in that moment, I feel as stupid as I've ever felt in my life for allowing myself to see Jack as anything other than the war-ravaged vet I met on the steps of the Lincoln Memorial. The guy who gave me my first real shot at finding my voice and speaking the truth. And the guy who may well have shown me how to take my first step out from behind the shadows.

I'm not sure how long we drive in silence after crossing the Delaware state line, but it doesn't matter. It's no longer an awkward silence. Instead, it's a productive one. One of those rare moments when you start to notice things you didn't notice before, with your brain all bottled up in anxiety. Like the smooth, steady sweep of the highway as it banks through pine forest, or the intermittent pinecone tossed down from the needly heights of a conifer onto the narrow shoulder below. Like the sheer expanse of the galaxies winking back at us through the windshield or the twinkling red light of a single, passing airplane ushering dozens of passengers on a thousand separate journeys just like mine. Or the feeling of *comfort*. Simple comfort. The kind you feel when two people can simply sit there beside each other as equal participants in this crazy race we all run—the one with a starting line, no clear finish, and a course that runs directly through lava.

Just as my eyelids start to feel heavy, Jack flicks on the turn signal and eases off the gas. A road sign marks the exit for Rehoboth Beach. I shake the sleep from my eyes and thank the galaxies above for helping me avoid another nightmare. At least for now.

Jack nudges me with his elbow and says, "Almost at the end of the road here, Carolina."

The first thing that comes to mind is Cowbird telling me that the road never ends, it only begins. But I don't repeat it to Jack, because it's pretty clear he already learned that lesson.

Instead I say, "Yeah. And with only a few hundred miles to go."

"Maybe I can help," he says.

"What? You plan to keep driving for a few more hours? Jack, you've done enough."

"No, not a chance," he says through laughter. "Us old folks need our rest to help us stave off the big sleep. You're a young buck. I figure it won't pain you much to continue your journey right away."

"That's my intention," I say.

"Here. Take this." He hands me a few wrinkled-up bills and then flicks the turn signal and pulls the Prius up a street that runs parallel to the bay. Choppy, brown waves broil up on the surface beyond the cattails and other assorted marsh grasses that border the roadway.

"What's this?" I ask, holding the bills—two fives and a twenty—in front of my face.

"The Cape May Ferry," he says, pulling the Prius into a large, open parking lot. Two massive, white ships float breathlessly at the end of a long pier on the far end of the lot. "Quickest way from here to New Jersey, and you don't even have to be awake."

"That might not be preferable."

"Drink a few cups of coffee, Carolina. Now head on out there. Last trip of the evening leaves in about ten minutes."

"You're serious? You're paying my fare?"

"Do you want to get to Philly or not?"

"Of course I want to—"

"Then get going," he replies. "What are you waiting for?"

I reach for my bag in the back seat of the Prius and hook the straps over my shoulders.

"But, Jack? I don't want to take your money. I can find my own—"

"Take it, Carolina. What am I gonna do with it? Spend it on my grandkids?"

He stares at me for a moment, expressionless. Then the corners of his mouth rise and his eyes go all sparkly and his whole face explodes in a toothy grin. I can't fight back the smile. Our arms wrap around each other and, for a second, it feels like I'm hugging Dad.

"Thank you, Jack."

Jack waves it off as if to say, "it's nothing, get out of here." He then says, "You take care out there, Carolina, and see that you reach your destination."

I hop out of the Prius and cross the parking lot toward the two hulking vessels.

About halfway between the Prius and the pier, a loud metallic crackle fills the still, salt air. "Carolina Wheaton!" Jack's voice blares through his bullhorn. "Two promises!" I turn to face him.

"Stop trying to forget!"

I give him a thumbs-up.

"And be sure to step out of the shadows once in a while!"

I stand at attention and salute Jack, then wave.

I hear the metallic crackle for the last time, followed by the electronic whoosh of a power window rolling up to its closed position.

I turn back toward the ferry and make my way over the sun-bleached timbers of the pier, and aboard the massive, floating taxi cab that will take me closer to Travis than I've been all year.

Crumbs

From the top deck of the Cape May ferry, the harbor at Rehoboth stretches across the night horizon for an eternity. A trail of moonlight casts a glittering pathway over the choppy waves of the bay. The foghorn blows its nasally tone as we drift away from port into the vastness of the Atlantic, yet not so far that I can't make out the on-and-off flicker of Jack's hi-beams in the parking lot. His way of saying goodbye, I guess.

The first thing I do when I get on deck is find a bathroom. I wash off in front of a bay of old sinks and rinse the pig shit off my sneakers. I change into my last pair of underwear and wipe as much grease off my jeans as possible before drying under the air blower. I still wreak like a rancid dumpster, but it's at least a hundred times less rotten than I must have smelled in Jack's Prius.

I take the change I have left from purchasing my ticket and buy an extra-large order of soggy French fries and a bucket of cola from the snack stand on the second deck. I sit on a rail-side bench near the bow of the ship and feast.

Up on the top deck, I'm surrounded by day-shoppers loaded down with bags from the army of outlet stores dotted up and down the Delaware beach line. Two young moms sit on a bench a few feet away and discuss the once-in-a-lifetime bargains they'd stumbled into that day. Their two toddlers tumble around on the deck like a couple of sea trout, jamming their greasy, French fried fingers in their mouths and then immediately crawling around on the grimy deck.

I look down at my own fingers, wipe them off with a napkin, and decide to use my fork on the rest of the fries. One of the ladies reaches into her purse and pulls out a hunk of tin foil shaped like a swan. Weird. She tears a small hole in the neck of the aluminum bird and pulls out a half-eaten dinner roll. She breaks it into a million tiny crumbles.

She then says, "Come here, Timmy," in this sweet, sing-songy voice that apparently isn't appropriate for talking about sidewalk sales but is like a dang siren's song to a toddler. Little Timmy ambles over with half his diaper sticking out of the back of his pants and who-knows-what loaded down inside. "Take this and toss it on the floor as hard as you can," sidewalk sale lady says in the same key as a tea kettle.

Timmy Toddler's eyes go so wide they almost swallow his face. He takes the breadcrumbs in one hand and spikes them at the feet of his toddler girlfriend, who squeals and bounces around a bit on the tippy-tops of her tiny Nikes.

That's about the time I hear the first ruffling of feathers. Then a loud CAW! When I look up at the night sky it's draped in white and spiraling down on us in a scene reminiscent of a Hitchcock film. Seagulls. Everywhere. Flapping and scraping and pecking at each other for a chance to pounce on a single, tasty morsel at the feet of Timmy Toddler.

For the first few seconds of the aerial assault, I'm shocked by the sudden appearance of this swarm of screeching gulls and their tenacity to overlook the fall of night and the basic laws of nature to maraud the deck of a ship at the tiniest flicker of a crumb. Then a squadron of angry gulls swoops right through my sight line, and I can tell they've locked in on my fries.

I stuff the whole basket under my shirt and curl up in a ball against the railing of the bench, trying to make myself the smallest possible target while Timmy Toddler and his pint-sized playdate scream bloody murder and the two sidewalk shoppers run around like their hair is on fire—which it is not. It's just loaded down with gull feathers and gull droppings.

As I sit there crouched in my best defensive pose and endure the repetitive thrashing of dive-bombing beaks, I gather a sense of calm. Like an out of body experience where I'm somewhere else—maybe on a bench not under threat of bombs—watching myself and the sidewalk shoppers and the toddlers and the gulls connect in a way we never expected and, frankly, never wanted.

And I think about Travis and his addiction. How he'd brave the uncertainty of night and the warnings of nature to get his crumbs. And I marvel at the way these gulls, addicted to their gluten-filled bursts of sweet, sweet dopamine, can become so focused on a tiny scrap of nothingness, one that couldn't sustain their lives for more than a few seconds. How they could fight tooth and nail for a tiny crumb and see it as a necessary means to survival when they're literally surrounded by an ocean's-worth of bounty. How they could fool themselves into thinking nothing else matters but the crumbs at a toddler's feet.

And somewhere between the shrieks of Timmy and his playdate, and the swooshing of feathers, the crumbs disappear and with them the gulls. I uncurl myself from the fetal position and resume the chore of forcing the nastiest French fries in history past my teeth and down my throat.

Somewhere between forcing down the French fries and the steady rise and fall of the mighty Atlantic, I start to feel kind of green. The kind of green where the bench moves on you when you know it's bolted to the deck. The kind of green that forces you inside to the mezzanine deck, where the horizon stays in the same place and the benches are more or less stationary.

I find an empty set of three padded-vinyl seats in a row and sprawl myself over all three of them with my backpack under my head as a pillow. I'm so nauseous I don't care about the hilt of Cowbird's knife jabbing me behind the ear. I close my eyes and try to steady my equilibrium and…

Dry thirst. The chafing of the handkerchief at the corners of my mouth.

My jaw throbs. A shiver rakes my body.

Then I hear it. Low and distant at first. Then a rumble. A long and pronounced CHOOOOOO!

It grows closer. Rattles the metal panels. Churns up through the cold concrete.

CHOOOOOO! It grows. In my memory. Behind the shadows.

CHOOOOO! Clearer. A train.

The train. CHOOOOOOOOOOOOOO!

Trane...

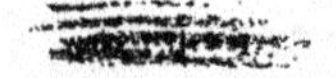

My shoulder hits the deck. My eyes spring open. They're met by a line of concerned expressions on the faces of people in the seats opposite. The ship's foghorn blows its nose on the sea air for a second time. Then a third. I squint my eyes at the gawkers as if to say, "What? You never saw a kid do gymnastics in his sleep?" which works because they all look in different directions like they hadn't witnessed my unconscious break-dancing routine a few seconds ago.

I grab my backpack and follow the flow of passengers to the main deck as the captain fires up the reverse engines and coasts the vessel into port at Cape May, New Jersey. It's pretty late by the time all three hundred or so passengers are on dry land. There's a small width of wooden planks—a boardwalk, if you will—set up in a winding border along the street side of the beach, with old-timey shops and brightly-painted Victorians looming over it.

Most of the shops are dark, and the beach is vacant but for the rolling tide. In an instant, all three hundred passengers aboard the ferry disappear into their cars or up side streets, or into their waterside homes. One minute I'm standing in a crowd and the next I'm alone on a desolate street with the threat of rolling tumbleweed on the approaching tide. Not a car, nor a person in sight. No place to ask for directions. Nothing but sand and surf with a small strip of concrete running through the middle.

I walk. But I don't get far before that famous Cordy Wheaton fit of panic starts to build in the arch of my neck. I walk faster. And then faster still with no sense of where I'm headed.

Within a few minutes, I literally reach the end of the line. The City of Cape May just stops. Like, it ends—at the foot of this annoying-looking jughandle in the road that leads directly into Davy Jones's Locker. The only thing that resembles hope in any form is the beach rental shop at the corner of the street. The lights are off and the sidewalk in front of the shop is littered with a row of baby blue beach cruisers with baskets on the handlebars. I walk up to one and lay a flat palm on the banana seat. There's not a lock or chain in sight.

That's when I give in to my desperation and my anxiety. That's when I do something I never thought I'd do again. I steal. A bike. Right off the rack and out from under the jolly, yellow awning with the words "Copacabana Adventures" scrawled across it and a little grass hut in place of the letter "A."

I drop my backpack in the basket, slide my ass up on the banana seat, and pedal as fast as I can around the jughandle and out of Cape May into the vastness of the ocean's unknown—which amounts to a long, straight ribbon of two-lane highway between heaving bodies of water—the bay, partially obscured by dense marsh grass on my left, and the rambling ocean as it kisses the white sands of New Jersey on my right. A cable of low-hanging fog reaches across the roadway from the bay side, beckoning the ocean onward with an outstretched finger. Beneath it, a strange twinkling of bluish light, pulsing slightly in the darkness. Creeping up off the sand and onto the edge of the asphalt. Its form solidifies as I approach. This time, I know at once who I'm looking at.

Travis.

With his crinkled-up, cardboard sign from the side of Route 40, a message scrawled out in black magic marker that simply reads: *This Way, Cordy*. And there's an arrow pointing in the direction I'm already headed on the desolate stretch of coastal roadway.

What kind of a game is he trying to play? Is this some kind of big joke?

This time I'm hell-bent on catching up to him. Of pulling up alongside my brother and wrapping my arms around his shoulders and never letting him go until we're back in High Point with Mom and Dad. Until I'm sure he's Travis again and not some withering hologram on the side of the road. In the depths of my mind. Somewhere deep down inside my burning hatred for everything my life and the Wheaton's life has become.

So I pedal harder and faster than I've ever pedaled a bike in my life. Maybe harder and faster than any crappy, archaic beach cruiser of this kind has ever traveled before because, as I approach my brother with his messy nest of brown hair trailing down the back of his neck and his cardboard sign held high over his head, I feel something pop and the pedals go all slack and the front wheel skids across a patch of sand as I flip over the handlebars and land in the dunes beside the road. The beach cruiser ghost rides itself a few more feet before it sputters and twists and takes a massive nose dive.

I sit up and dust myself off, shaking half the beach out of my shirt. The glowing form of Travis has vanished, replaced on the roadway with nothing but salt air and darkness. All that stands between myself and a clear stretch of asphalt between the crashing waves and the rippling bay is a weather-beaten road sign that reads: Welcome to Wildwood Crest.

I'm afraid to see what I did to the poor bike and, boy, is it bad. For starters, the chain hangs loose on the axle, which wouldn't be a big deal if the back tire wasn't hopelessly deflated—which could also be repaired if it weren't for the front wheel being bent into the shape of an "S." The thing is totaled. There's nothing I can do for the old girl but retire her now, so I lean the mangled beach cruiser up against the signpost, strap my backpack over my shoulders, and continue into town on foot.

I walk for at least twenty minutes, passing the same four models of cookie-cutter suburban, beach homes in their rectangular communities with their gold-plated gatehouses set up in front. Everything looks the same. Nobody's awake. There's nothing I can do but wander around until morning like a creepy night-stalker and hope I don't attract attention.

Each step I take pounds in my ears and raises my anxiety level by a factor of ten. Then twenty. Then a hundred. Then I escape the suburbs and find a stretch of the main strip—Ocean Boulevard—that looks like it's part of an actual city. But not like any city in this country, or even in this time period. No. This city is straight out of the fifties, like a scene from Mom's favorite movie, *Grease*. It's ablaze in neon, with tiny motels dressed up to look like they're on safari, or at the foot of Mt. Kilauea, or on the sunset beach of a desert island.

I sit on the curb under a neon sign that reads: *Biscayne Motel* in bright blue letters. Not only am I stuck in a town that is definitely not Philadelphia, but I also happened to land in the wrong time period with no idea of how to travel back to the present. I bury my face in my hands and let the tears stream down in warm, wet dollops for the second time that day.

I wish I'd never taken a dime from Jack Annunzio, and stayed hidden behind the safety net of my own shadows.

The Circle of Coltrane

I sit on the curb under the twinkling, neon sign with my knees pressed to my chest and the warmth of my tears spilling through my fingers until my butt goes numb and the prickling pain of pins and needles flows down through my feet. Every minute or so, a car or a bike with one of those old-school bells attached to the handlebars whisks by. I try to cover my eyes to conceal the shame, but all that does is make me feel more alone and farther away from Travis, and Mom and Dad, and the Birdland Jazz Club—and all that does is make the tears fall faster.

I'm startled by the staccato beat of high heels on the pavement behind me. I rub my sleeve over my eyelids to hide the evidence, but it's too late. Her arm drapes over my shoulder and the scent of her perfume—some kind of coconut—puts me in a trance.

"Hey, why you out here all alone in the dead of night?" she asks.

A faint crease folds across her forehead. I can tell she's gone straight to motherly mode the same way Lula had when we first met. I don't answer at first. Just pop up from the curb and spit out an unintelligible burst of sniffles and sobs and unrelated words that hold no meaning.

She leans in so close that one of her long braids hangs down over my chest and dips its frizzy edge into the front pocket of my t-shirt. "You gonna be okay," she coos in the soft tones of a mourning dove. "Ms. Elsa's here now. No need to worry." She wraps both arms around me and cradles my head in the crook of her elbow and strokes the fuzzy redness of my crew cut with long, slender fingers loaded down with rings of every shape, size, and color. "What's your name?" she asks in a whisper.

I take a deep breath and fight hard to swallow the sniffles. "I'm Cordy," I say flatly, like a machine. "I'm from High Point, North Carolina."

Ms. Elsa jumps back and holds me at arm's length. Her eyes are wide, and the whites sparkle in the blue glaze of the neon. In this light, I can tell she's not much older than Travis—maybe mid-twenties—but every inch of her exudes the wisdom of an old soul. Like she's seen things. Heard things. Experienced life with a higher level of emotion.

"North Carolina?"

I stare at her until I realize she's looking for an actual response.

I fumble my words and sputter out something like, "Ran away… going to Philadelphia…Travis," which makes no sense to anyone not residing inside my head. Ms. Elsa looks puzzled and also kind of worried at the same time.

"Mmmhmm," she mumbles with her gaze still cast on me and her eyes unblinking. "Well, you're a long way from home. You know that?"

I nod and wipe a final, lingering tear from my cheek.

"You know, Philly ain't that far from here if that's where you're headed. Hell of a lot closer than your hometown."

I nod again, and Ms. Elsa's easy-going smile collapses into a frown. "Boy, you really don't say much, do you?"

I want to tell her everything so I don't seem like a sniveling lunatic, but instead opt for, "I'm just tired. Been travelling for over a week now and I'm still not where I need to be. All I want to do is find my brother, Travis."

"He in Philly?"

"I think so."

"You don't sound so sure."

"It's the only place he could be," I say. "I mean, if he's not in Philadelphia, I guess he's lost."

"Lost? Seems to me the only one around here that's lost is standing in front of the Biscayne Motel and spilling his eyes out."

"That's a good point," I say. I give in and tell her about Dad and his malfunctioning lungs and how he and Travis may never speak to each other again, and how Mom and I will be alone and about my plan and Birdland and John Coltrane. The second I mention the name John Coltrane, Ms. Elsa's eyes sparkle in the blue light and her frown turns back into an easy-going smile with two big dimples that pop out of nowhere in the middle of her cheeks.

"Coltrane?" She says it loud enough for anyone walking the strip of Ocean Boulevard and maybe anyone sailing out in the actual ocean to hear. "What's some skinny-ass white boy like you doing with the words 'John' and 'Coltrane' on your tongue?"

"He's my hero," I say without having to think. "And Travis's, too. Trane grew up in my hometown."

Ms. Elsa's head snaps back and her braids bounce and swing in a thick tangle. She lets out a high-pitched wheeze of a laugh, bends over at the waist, and makes a huge display of trying to catch her breath between fits of laughter.

Just then, a door opens in the middle of the white stucco of the Biscayne, right between the glass-paneled lobby all suited up in its art-deco glory and a foamy-looking, outdoor pool with a spiral slide. The clatter of glasses and boisterous, drunken voices escape along with the crash of a cymbal and the lowdown funk of a bass guitar. Three gentlemen dressed in sharp suits stroll out and stride toward us as if riding an invisible conveyor belt. Ms. Elsa stops laughing long enough to motion them over.

"Hey y'all!" she shrieks through the laughter and the wheezing. "This little dude's out here talking about Trane being his hero!"

Everyone, including Ms. Elsa, goes deadpan for a moment. The three gentlemen move in around me and inspect me like I'm one of Gus's prized hogs. The tall string bean with the green, velvet fedora pulls a splintery toothpick from between his front teeth and says, "Hell no," in a bass tone that's deeper and darker than a spoonful of molasses, which sets the rest of the group on fire again and breaks the silence of the night.

The waterworks build again behind my eyes. I pull the straps on my backpack a little tighter and fidget with the frayed edges of the adjustment bands, thinking I might want to slip out behind the Biscayne sign and maybe drown myself in the motel kiddie pool.

Ms. Elsa rests one of her slender hands on my shoulder. "Boys, this here's Cordy from High Point, North Carolina. And he don't need to feel no shame over likin' Trane." Her braids jingle down over a tanned, leather blouse that's tied super tight like a corset from Elizabethan England.

The man with the bass-drenched voice holds out one of his bony hands and waits for me to accept it. When I do, he shakes it and says, "High Point, North Carolina…that's Trane's hometown." I nod. "Then I guess you've got as much right as anyone to ride the Col-Train," he says.

"You mean, you're fans?" I ask, thinking that maybe this random meeting with a group of late-night strangers might not be so random. That maybe fate has intervened.

"Hell yeah we're fans," one of the other gentlemen says, a short dude in a blue suit with a paisley print embroidered into the material. His tie hangs at half mast. The first two buttons on his dress shirt are popped open to reveal a thin chain with a cross hanging on it. His pointy, black shoes poke out from under the hem of his pants. I can tell he's not wearing socks because his ankles poke out when he moves and the hems of his pants rise to mark the tides. "We ain't just fans," he says. "We're living monuments to Trane's legend."

"You mean like the statue that stands in downtown High Point?"

"Do we look like statues to you?" asks the third man in a voice that sounds like he's got a clothespin clamped down over his schnaz. He takes a massive bite out of a salami sandwich and jumps out of the way before half his lettuce and a glob of mustard lands on one of his gray, leather shoes.

"We're musicians, Cordy. We sing together," Ms. Elsa adds. "And, by day, we take classes at the art college in Philly."

"Philly?" I reply, as a lightbulb goes on in my head and my heart starts to beat faster. But then I start to think for a second and my hackles start to raise because even a philosophy nerd like me has limits when it comes to believing in the intervention of fate. "Hold on," I say, "Did Travis put you up to this?"

There is pure silence and a congregation of blank faces staring back at me when I ask the question, so I try to prod them on still thinking about how I saw him on the side of the road with his makeshift sign in hand. "My brother," I continue. "Travis. He's in on this. Right?" Still nothing but the sound of the ocean lapping up on the shore.

Elsa looks at me with sheer confusion in her eyes. I notice all three gentlemen gazing down at the street and I can tell they must think I've lost my marbles, so I quickly jump back into the conversation as if I never mentioned Travis in the first place.

"So…uhh…what kinds of classes do y'all take?"

"Music theory," the nasally voice says with bits of chewed-up bread spraying from his mouth.

"Yeah, we know all the inside shit," the bass-drenched voice adds, "and we also know a thing or two about mister John Coltrane."

"We even named our group in his honor, being that he's a son of Philadelphia and all," the man with the missing socks says. "We call ourselves The Coltrane Circle because we stick together…but, you know, we're also a bit like Trane because we don't like sticking to no hard and fast rules."

"We *do* like to improvise," Ms. Elsa says.

"That's a cool name," I say. "I feel like I've heard it before, but I can't figure out where. What does it mean?"

The bass-drenched dude clears his throat.

"Well, John Coltrane didn't want to play no recycled garbage other people already played. But when you're playing saxophone in backstreet bars like the one we just stepped out of, you don't get to play original work all that often. So Trane made everything his own. Even songs you heard a million times over sounded like his own creation."

He pauses to light a smoke and take a long drag, and I think about Travis's sheet music—how I've heard the song a trillion times, performed by a million different performers, but how it always sounds new whenever I hear Trane's version.

The tall string bean puffs a cloud of smoke over his head. I watch it wisp and curl like swirling ghosts up into the blue-tinted, neon night. "You see," he continues, "that old boy was the king of improv. He'd drop a bunch of high speed arpeggios and outright glissandos up in there in the middle of a song and it'd sound like Trane was landing on a million different notes one after another until he had you in his trance. He called it a sheet of sound. You know where I'm coming from?"

"I think I do," I say. And I'm not completely lying. Sure, glissandos and arpeggios are like gibberish to me, but I've listened to Trane enough times, and Travis taught me how to hear all the individual notes and appreciate them like they were their own tropical islands. "So how does this all line up with the Circle of Coltrane thing?"

The dude with the sandwich holds an index finger in the air and we watch him finish chewing his last bite before he says, "I'll take this one." He dabs a bit of mustard off his mouth with a paper napkin. "See, the whole reason Trane was able to improvise so quickly and produce the kind of sound worthy of a damn god was because he understood music. And not just like a musician. No, that man understood music like a mathematician."

"That's it!" I cut in suddenly, and the sandwich dude's face deflates a little because he wants to keep rolling.

"What do you mean, that's it?" he says sullenly.

"Mathematics," I tell him. "I remember where I heard the term 'Coltrane Circle' before. It was from Travis."

"His missing brother," Ms. Elsa chimes in to inform the rest of the group on Travis's status.

"Yeah," I say. "My brother had a physics teacher who used to talk about how the rules of math and music were almost interchangeable and he taught Travis about the Coltrane Circle and then he couldn't stop talking about Coltrane and jazz and mathematical equations for, like, weeks."

"Well, that makes a lot of sense because Trane did study up on some of Einstein's theories and even found ways to use the damn laws of physics to take his compositions to a higher level."

"Mmmhmm," Ms. Elsa says. "He sent his sound straight into the heavens."

"And he did it all," the sandwich dude mumbles with a fresh bite of salami in his mouth, "by using the Circle of Fifths."

All of a sudden, I'm so confused my eyes start to float around in their sockets. "Circle of Fifths?" I ask. "I thought you said it was a Circle of Coltrane."

The bass-drenched dude steps in and says, "That was after Trane got his hands on it. See, the Circle of Fifths is just a circular chart of all the major tones used in a composition. Like, if you were a painter, you see… then you'd use a color wheel to figure out which colors blended together to make the most appealing tones. Same thing with the Circle of Fifths, except for music."

"That man," says Elsa, "reinvented the whole damn thing. First he noticed all kinds of subtle interactions between the tones that no one else knew existed, and then he went ahead and documented it."

"Yeah," the sandwich dude cuts in, "and he actually went out and played that shit in front of an audience to prove his theories were tight."

"Man was a damn genius," the string bean adds. "So you should have no trouble understanding why we chose the name for our group."

"No trouble at all," I say. And this time I'm sure of it.

"Good," Ms. Elsa says. "Then I guess you're worthy."

"Worthy?" I ask. "Of what?"

"Of being in our presence," she says. At first, I think she's being serious, but then she goes and smiles again—that broad, warm smile—and I know she's trying to pull a fast one on me, just like Cowbird had.

"How'd you get here anyway?" the man with the nasally voice whines through his sandwich.

"Trains…hitchhiking…a boat…a hog truck. Whatever I find that can move, I'm on it. Rode a rental bike into town from Cape May until I crashed the dang thing."

"Where you headed?" the string bean asks.

"Philly," Elsa chimes in before I can answer. "He's looking for that brother of his."

"Philly?" the man with no socks asks.

"Damn," the string bean says, "you ain't gonna get nowhere near Philly riding around on a damn tricycle, my man." This causes a mini-swirl of laughter to rise back up from the whirlpool of flashy coats and weird shoes.

Then Elsa says, "Cordy, it's only an hour's drive into the city. Maybe a little more. Why don't you ride with us in the van?"

She points to a black van with tinted-out windows parked across the street from the Biscayne. It is unmarked except for a single cleft note—painted purple—on the rear end of the driver's side door.

"You mean it?" I ask. "You'll take me with you to Philadelphia?"

"Sure," Elsa says. "Long as these boys don't mind."

She gives a stern look to each of the gentlemen in turn, and I figure out that Ms. Elsa is sweet as honey but you best not get on her bad side. The other three members of The Coltrane Circle seemed to have learned the lesson long ago.

"Fine with me," the string bean says.

"I'm cool," the sockless dude says.

The man with the half-mast tie shoves the last bit of sandwich past his teeth and grunts something I can't understand but which apparently means I'm good to go, because Ms. Elsa grabs my elbow and escorts me to the van.

The man with the half-mast tie wheels an amp and carries a microphone stand to the back of the van as he finishes chewing his salami, and sockless dude and string bean move in behind him to load the equipment.

As I make my way toward the back of the van, the string bean looks at me and holds out his hand. I take it and shake, and he says, "We haven't had a proper introduction. Name's Siggy Genko. I sing the bass parts."

"I kind of figured that," I say.

He nods and lowers his voice at least ninety-seven octaves and says, "That's my specialty," in a way that makes him sound like he's speaking underwater or amplifying his words through a tuba. Then his voice bounces back to normal—which is still deeper and darker than a cup of coffee—and he continues. "This here joker is Mr. Grover Sanchez, who shares not only his name but also his height with a certain Sesame Street character."

The sockless man leans forward and shakes my hand. "Very funny, Siggy," he says to the string bean before he tosses another mic stand in the back of the van.

"Ms. Elsa May Kingston—prettiest damn voice this side of the mighty Mississ-SIP—is up there in the driver's seat, and this here fool is Billy Hillman. We call him Hilly." The man with the salami sandwich leans in with a greasy hand and shakes mine.

"Why do they call you Hilly?" I ask.

Grover steps in close and puts his arm around my shoulders. "Don't go spreading this to anyone, but you catch the gut on this dude?"

"Shut up, Grover," Hilly says in his patented nasal tone.

"He ain't never met a meal he couldn't eat," Siggy chimes in through a laugh.

"Shut up, Siggy," Hilly retorts, this time less nasally and more resigned to the fact that he inhaled a salami sandwich right in front of me in under five minutes.

"It's great to meet y'all," I start to say, but I'm interrupted by the long drone of a car horn.

"Get going or be gone!" Elsa shouts.

The rest of the group hops-to like a bunch of schoolchildren called in for dinnertime by their mothers. I don't relish the thought of "being gone," so I pile in behind them and grab a seat in the back row, next to a pile of cables and mixers and other assorted electronic musical equipment. Ms. Elsa May is busy reaming out Siggy, Grover, and Hilly by the time I'm strapped in my seatbelt.

"You boys are about as slow as hogs in mud," she says in her worried mother voice. "No. You know what? You're slower than that damn tortoise people always lie about and pretend he can outrace a hare."

"But he did beat the hare," Siggy says.

"Slow and steady," Hilly mumbles through a mouthful of chewed-up potato chips he'd pulled out of thin air.

"You can keep believing the bullshit," Elsa says. "But I can also just go ahead and prove my point."

She cranks the ignition and stomps her foot on the gas pedal. The van lurches away from the curb, and a bunch of frayed cables slide across the floor of the van and tangle under my seat. I lock my hands down on the armrest as Elsa launches the van out of Wildwood Crest, past a tightly-woven patchwork of old-fashioned ice cream parlors and miniature golf courses, and over a small drawbridge with the stench of marsh grass and the rippling water of the bay on both sides.

No one says a word until the van crosses the foot of the bridge and sweeps across a toll booth where Elsa drops a few coins in a basket to raise the mechanical arm. The van fires off past a sign that reads: New Jersey Parkway. The road is straight and flat and hunkered down between endless stands of gnarled pine trees that seem, from here, to cover every square inch of the Garden State. The whole journey from the Biscayne Motel to the ribbon of asphalt that'll lead me to Travis takes less than five minutes with Elsa May's lead foot on the pedal. She then picks up the conversation right where she left off.

"See? That's why you ain't gonna see a tortoise outrunning no damn hare," she says before flicking on the radio to Philly's smooth jazz station. My heart does flip-flops in my chest when the radio DJ signs off at the top of the hour with call letters that include a "P" an "H" and an "L" for Philadelphia.

We're so close to Travis that we could well be listening to the same song on the same station at this very moment.

Nobody bothers to argue with Elsa May because I'm pretty sure they're afraid of her. But I pipe up and say something stupid. As usual. Something like, "There's no fault in being a tortoise if you come out of the shell sometimes."

Typical me, dropping philosophy on people I've known for a grand total of twenty minutes.

The other boys react in a long bout of silence and shifty-eyed glances in all directions except at each other or me, like I'm the first person in history to question Elsa May's judgement.

But Elsa May doesn't play. She shoots her eyes to the rearview mirror. Gives me this hard-ass gaze you might get from your teacher if you farted in the middle of class but she can't prove it was you even if she's pretty sure it was.

Siggy, Grover, and Hilly sit in their seats like they're expecting a volcano to erupt and a whole mess of lava to spill over them—like those poor fools who lived at the foot of Mt. Vesuvius.

But the eruption never comes.

Instead, I get the wide smile and the sweep of a single hand across the rearview as Elsa pushes a braid behind her ear.

"You some kind of oracle or a prophet or something?" she asks with the sheen of passing headlights reflecting on her forehead. "You got a crystal ball in that backpack?"

"So, kid?" Grover asks. "Like…what the hell are you talking about?"

My palms go sweaty and my brain goes blank because I can't remember where I was going with all the tortoise shell garbage, but then I hear the trademark sound of the sax call me from the van's speakers and I know it's Trane. Not just any Trane song. It's Travis's song. The breath pours back into my lungs and the cogs spin in my head.

"The tortoise shell," I say. "Much like the hare who loses the race because he curls up like a dumbass and passes out before the finish line, totally blind to real life happening around him, the tortoise would have no chance of winning if he loafs around in his shell."

The three boys glance at each other, eyebrows raised. "Little dude's got a point," Siggy says. "You some kind of ancient philosopher?"

"Course he's a philosopher," Elsa May says before I can answer. "Ain't no…wait, how old did you say you were?"

"Sixteen and three quarters," I say. Elsa's eyes do a loop around her sockets and her braids scrape across her shoulders as her head shakes slowly.

"Like I said, ain't no sixteen-year-old kid gonna know a damn thing about John Coltrane unless he knows a whole lot about life. No secret there."

It's the best compliment I've ever received. Still, I'm not sure Ms. Elsa meant it as one. But I'll take what I can get, like Cowbird taught me.

"Thanks," I say. "I always wanted—" But I don't finish the sentence because Elsa breaks into the most beautiful tones that have ever left the boundaries of human lips. Where Trane's version of Travis's song is purely instrumental, Ms. Elsa May Kingston fills in with a lyrical power that punches you in the gut and floats off on the night air like the fragrance of a jasmine flower.

"Theeeese are a fewwww of my faaaav-or-ite things!" she croons. The boys back her up in three-piece harmony that flows with the strength of a single, super-powered voice, both steady and cataclysmic at the same time. A true work of art, and a testament to the Greeks' idea of fate—because what else can explain how I ended up in a van with Trane on the radio and a drop-dead gorgeous group of voices known as The Coltrane Circle?

I give them a round of applause when the song ends. Siggy tips his green fedora, Grover tightens the knot on his tie, and Hilly takes a vicious bite of his beef jerky. I figure it's the perfect moment to show them something, so I reach in my bag and pull out the slip of sheet music. I pass it up to Elsa May, and I tell them everything I know about Travis. About his saxophone playing and his dream to be the next great musical innovator. About the statue and his love of Trane and how he taught me everything I know about the man and his music. About Dad and his illness. And about Travis's addiction, and how Dad and Travis may never talk to each other again. And when I'm finished digging through the fine details of a plan I've never let boil, the signs start popping up beside the highway until the word "Philadelphia" appears with startling frequency. The faint outline of a massive skyline—nothing like the ones I saw in Nashville or Baltimore or even Washington, DC—comes into focus. A single tower stands above the rest with its zig-zaggy, Charlie Brown-looking pattern of lights etched across a sharp steeple.

"There she is," Siggy says. "City of Brotherly Love."

"Let's hope so," Elsa May says. "For this little philosopher's sake."

Her remark gets a few laughs, but Elsa is quick to silence the group. She says, "Is that the real reason you like Coltrane?"

"What do you mean?" I ask.

"I mean, the Trane. He's a symbol for you and Travis."

"A symbol? I thought he was—"

"You bet he's a symbol," she says. "Be honest. A part of you sees Coltrane as the boy down the street in High Point, North Carolina. Like every other boy except he can see things others can't…and he can hear things the other boys can't hear. And he can create. He can create music, oh yes, but more important to you is that he found a way to escape. From that tortoise shell."

"Damn, Elsa, where the hell did you pull that from?" Grover asks.

"There's more than one philosopher in this van," Elsa retorts. "Now, all I need is for Mr. Cordy here to tell me I'm right."

The van goes silent and Elsa lowers the volume on the radio to put me under the spotlight and make the sweat roll out into the pits of my t-shirt. "I…I, uh—"

"Spit it out," Hilly snaps in one of the most ironic statements of all time.

"I don't know," I say. "I mean, on one hand, I really do love John Coltrane's music and I look up to him as a man. He's my hero. But Ms. Elsa has a point. I mean, I never would have heard of Trane if it weren't for Travis. So yeah, in a way, I guess a part of me sees the two of them as one and the same."

"Like, how one goes so goes the other?" Siggy asks.

"Kind of," I say. "I mean, sometimes I see Trane as a test case. Like, if he could make it out of High Point and kick his bad habits and become a musical legend, then maybe Travis could too."

"And if Travis could do it," Elsa says, "Then so could you?"

A tear streams down one of my cheeks when she says it, and I'm not sure why. Then it hits me. "Yeah," I say. "I guess Travis is the barometer as to what your garden-variety Wheaton might be capable of accomplishing. So far the results haven't made me feel all that great about my future."

The whole group groans at the same time, which may have sounded like a beautiful and cohesive melody if it weren't directed at me. "You kidding?" Siggy says with both hands pulling his fedora down tight against his head.

"That's the biggest load of crap I ever heard," Grover adds, and Hilly shakes his head and pops the last nugget of his jerky in his mouth.

"Listen to these boys," Elsa May says. The van takes a sharp curve on the highway and mounts the incline of a steep, blue suspension bridge.

"Why? They think they can teach me how to be a Wheaton?"

"No," Elsa May says. "But they can teach you how to be a person. About how you ain't defined by your DNA for better OR for worse."

"What are you talking about?" I ask, getting more confused by the second.

"I'm talking about our unique stories. Ones that have nothing to do with who our brothers and sisters may be or what they've done."

The van rumbles over the bridge and through another toll booth, and then we're in the canyons of a bustling city loaded down with modern art sculptures and colorful murals that stand five stories high on the red-bricked faces of burnt out buildings.

"Take me for instance," Elsa continues. "You think I'm about to give up my dreams? Think I'll turn off my voice because my big brother's a pediatrician and my parents worship him? You think singing a damn song to a bunch of winos in some bar in Wildwood's as important as saving kids' lives everyday?"

"Kind of," I say.

"See! That's why I like you," Elsa says through a broad smile, maybe broader than ever. "But that's not my family. They think what I do for a living is some kind of childish phase. But you know what?"

"What?"

"Well, I choose not to give a damn. Gonna be me."

The three gentlemen sit there in silence. Their eyes are trained directly on me. It only takes a slight nod from Siggy for all three of them to communicate the same message. That every word Elsa had shared with me was drenched in truth, and that I needed to keep on listening.

"Point is," Elsa says, "you don't need anyone telling you who to be but Cordell Wheaton. He's the one who knows who he wants to be. And the only one with the power to become that man in real life."

I don't say anything because, for the first time in my philosophical life, I have no further philosophical statement to make. Mostly because everything has been said. But Elsa breaks the silence for me. "Look here," she says. "If you don't know where to start becoming the human you want to be, then this is as good a place as any in the world."

"Where are we?" I ask, staring down the length of a street that's paved in cobblestone and flanked on both sides by brickface row homes. They look like they landed on a time machine that traveled from colonial times. Then I find out they had.

"Elfreth's Alley," Siggy says. "Oldest residential street in America. It's where democracy was born."

"No shit?" I ask.

"Absolutely none," Hilly says. "People been living on this street for almost two hundred and fifty years and it still looks the same."

"This is where your search begins," Elsa says.

Grover reaches over and unlatches the sliding door and holds his palm up as if to say, "After you, fine sir."

I tighten the straps of my backpack and step out onto cobblestone. "Thank you for getting me pointed in the right direction," I say.

"Don't mention it," Elsa says. Her broad smile straightens and a film of moisture glistens on the lenses of her eyes.

"And, Cordy," Siggy says, "I don't think I need to tell you this, but my man Trane would want you to remember what he learned from the teachings of Gandhi."

"Oh yeah? What's that?"

"Be the change you want to see in the world, my friend. Be the change you want to see."

I smile and shake Siggy's hand. I give a slight nod to Elsa May, Grover, and Hilly. They each nod back their acknowledgements—that we've only known each other for a little over two hours, but they were filled with the kinds of knowledge and understanding that were two thousand years in the making. The kinds of knowledge and understanding that sustain you on the journey and keep you headed toward a vision of the person you've always hoped to be.

The van door slides shut and I'm left there on the streets of our nation's birthplace. Alone. Again. I don't know the time, but I can tell it's either late or super early depending on how you look at it. The street lamps buzz above me and the narrow chasm that is Elfreth's Alley is drenched in dark. I figure there's not much point in searching for Travis at this hour. He'll either be asleep or maybe he will be so high he won't recognize me. Plus, it tends to look conspicuous when a kid my age wanders an alien city with nothing but a stained t-shirt and a marshmallow-filled pack on his back. Police tend to notice these types of things, especially when you're a missing child case and a potential credit card felon.

I walk a half a block up the road, placing Elfreth's Alley at my back. The buzz of celebration rings from a window on the second floor of a squatty colonial. A sign pokes out from the sill. It reads Patty's Pub. I slip down an alley between the bar and the building next to it and bed myself down beneath a stack of old wine crates. I'll wait here until first light, with the harshness of concrete crawling up my spine and rats gnawing at odd scraps of refuse all around me. But then fatigue overtakes my body. My legs tingle from being at rest for more than a few minutes. My eyes burn. They take on the weight of my exhaustion and then…

DELIRIUM. The drip-drip wracks my brain. Time doesn't exist. No light. No visitors. Nothing but fire in my throat and the adhesion of dried blood on my wrists.

The door swings open. White light rushes in. Assaults my pupils. Renders me blind. He reaches for me. The rancid scent of old whiskey bristles my nose hair.

Fabric is forced over my eyes. Tied around the back of my head. He jerks me to my feet. Drags me across cement. Outside air hits my face. Revives me. Then a hand smashes into the small of my back. I'm airborne. I crash down on gravel. A slow, warm trickle soaks the sleeve of my shirt.

"Let him go!" An older voice. Distinct. Familiar.

"Dad?" A stiff jab hits my ribs. I'm silent.

The boot eases off my neck. The weight lifts.

My eyes flip open and the ground spins. I wipe the fog away and squint as the sun's morning rays stretch through the wooden slats of the wine crates. A man in a pair of green coveralls stands above me. The toe of his boot nudges my ribs. "You alive down there?" he asks.

I pop up from the sidewalk and the man jumps back a full step. His eyes twitch and his face turns paler than a glass of milk. He retreats to the back step of a garbage truck before it rumbles off down the street.

It's not exactly the way I want to wake up on my first morning in our nation's birthplace. But I'm here. Finally. In the city that holds the keys to my journey, my search for the brotherly love I long feared might well be lost forever.

Pea Soup

With the benefit of daylight, I decide to explore the oldest street in America. Elfreth's Alley is lined in red brick that climbs the faces of the colonials and crawls behind massive shutters painted bright red, green, and white. The street is covered in cobblestone so it trails off into another era. A Union Jack flag on one side of the road is rivaled by Old Glory waving to and fro on the other. The air smells old—a mingling of car exhaust, mildewy masonry, and incense. Actors in colonial clothes patrol the scene, completing daily tasks as if King George III had never been deposed by our forefathers some two hundred and fifty years prior.

After a brief tour through history, I cross the street and walk toward the tallest buildings on the skyline, hoping my venture into modern America will yield a long-lost brother. I mean, I have no clue where Travis might be or if he's within the city limits at all, but there's something in my gut that makes me think he's close.

And just like that, I'm met with a thirty-foot-tall message from the fates. It comes in the form of a mural painted on the tired brickface of a distant apartment building—a testament to the legend. John Coltrane. Standing there as resolutely as the statue in High Point, his saxophone tipped forward and a few buttons of his dress shirt unfastened to show the collar of a white tee underneath. In the background, Trane's band members and his adopted city float like musical notes on a sheet of sound in the celestial shadows of a legend.

There's no doubt in my mind that Trane is speaking to me. Telling me I've come to the right place. That Travis is close, and he'll see me and we'll talk about Dad, hop the next bus to New York City and watch a show at Birdland—and everything will turn out fine for the Wheaton family.

I stop for a moment in front of a tiny, stone house that's so small it looks like it could have been made for a Hobbit. Outside the door is a wooden placard that reads: Betsy Ross House. I peer through the window and notice her famous thirteen-star flag hanging on the far wall with a network of old cross-stitchings swarming around the individual stars and stripes. A warm, jittery sensation moves across my stomach when I realize I'm standing ten feet away from the most iconic flag in our nation's history. I wonder if Travis stood in this exact spot or if Trane stood here, too, admiring the handiwork of a woman who was centuries ahead of her time.

I curl around the back of the tiny house and hang a left on Fifth Street, where modern high-rise buildings mingle with colonial structures on one side and an expanse of grass and trees line the other. The sidewalks are crowded with street vendors, and folks in business suits with briefcases in their hands, and lines of schoolchildren waiting to enter the many museums dotted up and down the thoroughfare.

I zig-zag my way through the throng, crossing an innumerable number of intersections until I'm standing in front of one of the most famous structures in American history. Independence Hall. The place where it all began. Where a bunch of revolutionary types we now call the Founding Fathers decided they were tired of eating shit all of the time and made a pact to start a whole new nation. One that was based on the undeniable rights of life, liberty, and the pursuit of happiness. One that was meant to afford justice to *all* people who entered its shores.

I stand there for a few moments and stare at the famous tower in the middle of the brick-lined square, and I think about the fifty-five British citizens who signed a declaration one summer day in 1776 and how they formed a brand new experiment. And I wonder if those fifty-five original Americans would feel like their words still rang true for this nation so many years later. If they thought folks like Travis and John Coltrane and Cowbird and Lula McBride and even Emma Rose No Last Name enjoy the same kind of liberty today they wrote about under their powdered wigs in the heat of a Philadelphia summer. And it makes me kind of shake my head a little and stare down at my shoes because it's the first time in my life I don't know if the answer is yes. It's the first time I think maybe our Founding Fathers wouldn't be so proud of a nation so willing to toss the Travis Wheatons of the world on the scrap heap just for falling victim to his own addiction, or a nation that would ignore the daily struggles of a girl like Emma Rose even as the bruises form and the tears dry up and she's forced to be a homeless runaway just to provide herself with some semblance of safety.

The whole damn concept of injustice makes me feel uncomfortable. No, it makes me feel downright angry every time I think about it. And then I get depressed because let's be clear, I don't even know if I can get my own brother to talk to me these days, let alone solve the most pressing issues facing our nation. Which in turn makes me feel weak. It makes me doubt myself again and question what it was that made me ever think I could complete this journey.

But then I hear it.

The squeal of a sax.

It trails off in tinny notes from down a distant avenue.

It beckons me to find the source.

I leave Independence Hall in the background and wander past another intersection onto South Street. It's a never-ending stream of eclectic shops—from tattoo parlors to pizza parlors to parlor rooms meant for nothing more than sipping jet-black coffee from tiny mugs and puffing on fat cigars over games of chess. The buildings on South Street are nothing like those on Elfreth's Alley. They forego the ancient look and scream modern, their faces covered in mosaics constructed from scraps of broken pottery and clay from the surrounding art collectives. Even the people are different. Instead of Ben Franklin look-a-likes sweeping sidewalks in front of colonial storefronts, the streets are filled with people of all persuasions—from artsy, professor types with wire-rimmed glasses and fuzzy, little goatees to soccer moms loaded down with shopping bags, to rough-handed tradesman in one-piece work uniforms delivering cold beer or Italian water ice to the vendors.

It's not a quiet street. No, it's littered with the consistent murmur of human voice and the ever-present screeching of bored toddlers overwrought with the day's shopping regimens. Still, I can hear the one, singular sound rise above the racket. The tinny brass of my brother's sax, bouncing off row homes. Amplifying sweet vocalizations onto South Street.

My heart races as the sound grows closer and more distinct. The soles of my Chucks scuffle on the pavement until the sound of the sax overwhelms me, squeezing its tune through the narrow chasm of a side street.

I take a breath as I reach the corner. In my head, I've been rehearsing what I'll say the first time I see him, but every word of it dissolves and trails off into the gutter and down a Philadelphia drainage pipe into the Delaware. I guess a simple "hey" is all I'm armed with now.

I whip around the corner and there he is, slumped down on an upside-down paint bucket with the sax case splayed out before him and a long, skinny ponytail diving out from the back of an engineer's cap. I start to open my mouth, but the words crawl right back inside. My throat gets all scratchy and tight. I start fidgeting with the stretched-out collar of my t-shirt and I think about everything that can go wrong in a moment like this. The pay-off, where my whole journey either amounts to me being a hero or me having wasted my time and risked my life for nothing. I mean, Travis could turn around and not even recognize me. He could pull out a phone and call the cops on me right there on the spot. He could tell me to go straight to hell for all I know.

Or he could smile.

He could spin around and put me in a headlock and rough his knuckles up against my scalp, and we could buy a pair of bus tickets, and be in New York by nightfall, and catch our show at Birdland. And then everything could go back to normal. Like the way things used to be. Like the way I want them to be again.

So I do the only thing that feels right in the moment. The thing that reminds me most of being in our room with the cracked ceilings and the bunk beds on Brookside Drive. The thing that reminds me most of home. I walk up behind him and grab his ponytail, like I used to do on our walks to school before Travis left me alone in High Point.

I tug.

Hard.

And that's when he spins around—and I realize it's not Travis at all. He's…just some dude I've never seen before in my life. And he's as surprised as I am when he spins around and my gaze meets the fuzzy, salt and pepper beard of a man who's much closer in age to Trane—the actual Trane—than my brother, Travis.

"What the hell, kid?" he snipes with the reed of his saxophone silent and dipped down a few inches from his chapped lips.

"Oh…uhhh…I'm…uhh…sorry," I say as my heart flips around in my throat. The man adjusts the brim of his cap and moistens the reed between his lips. His eyebrows knife across a furrowed brow line. He shakes his head and resumes his wailing through the horn like it's a physical extension of his mood—shrieky and somewhat off-key. I reach in my bag and fish out a wrinkled dollar bill. I drop it in the man's saxophone case. His brow releases and he winks at me before his cheeks go full and he blows a long, sullen note that floats over South Street.

"Hey!" I ask over his tune. "You happen to know any other sax players in the area?" The man's brow crinkles again, and he shakes his head in time with the somber rhythm of his song. "His name's Travis," I sputter out in desperation. "Please tell me you know someone named Travis!"

The man looks confused at first. Then he scowls and takes one hand off the sax to shoo me away. His other hand keeps working the brassy keys, pushing heavy, ominous bursts of sound through the mouth of the instrument until I feel my vision start to blur and I'm right back in the damn echo chamber again:

It's worth a try

Do you think he'll recognize it?

Do you think it'll work?

Hope *is all we have left....*

And then, just like that, I'm right back at Independence Hall, with the street musician's notes floating above me like storm clouds as I stand there and let the shame wash over me like a patchwork quilt.

I'm mortified.

At mistaking this poor, random dude for my own brother. At unleashing my panic on him for no reason at all. And for thinking the first musician I happened to find in a city the size of Philadelphia would somehow be Travis. I feel like an idiot, but I also know I have no real choice but to keep searching. So I scurry off down the street, passing old row homes with withered, wooden window frames and little trap doors in the sidewalks that lead down to the bowels of the city.

After walking a few blocks, I notice I've somehow managed to complete an enormous loop, because the back side of the public square surrounding Independence Hall now stands before me at the junction of two intersections. Colonial brickwork regains its total domination over the neighborhood with a few neat rows of cherry trees, now disrobed of their pink flowers, tucked in between. From here, I have a better view of the rounded archway in the hall's central portico, its ancient clock face and its rounded dome, rich with hundreds of years of patina, as it stretches a pointed steeple to the heavens.

Then I hear it again.

Music.

A rash of brassy notes that filters out from behind the great hall of democracy. It is somber. Heavy. Filled with all the sadness and tears and grief of a lifetime. This time it has to be Travis. I hop the single-link chain and navigate a tight, cobblestone pathway that leads to another open courtyard beside the building.

The brassy notes are on top of me now, ringing out from a shady spot under an ancient maple tree. The saxophonist, or what I thought was one, is seated at a park bench—but it's obviously not Travis. And he's definitely not playing a saxophone. It's just an old boom box tuned to Philly's jazz station. And I don't have to yank the dude's hair or anything to find out for sure, because I can tell from fifty yards away the man is black—not snowdrift white, like Travis.

I continue my journey through Old City Philadelphia in search of my brother, with a growing sense that my plan to find Travis might not be the soundest plan I've ever concocted. That finding a skinny saxophone player on the streets of Philadelphia would be about as easy as pinpointing a specific blade of grass on a football field.

I walk until I can't walk any further—not because of fatigue, but because I reach another impasse. This time the barrier is geographical—a river teeming with steamships and tugboats and cargo liners and draped in the stench of swampiness and gasoline. I can tell it's the Delaware—the same river George Washington traversed before a fateful siege on the Red Coats at Valley Forge—because the street sign on the corner reads: Delaware Avenue. Lined up along the murky straight of brown water are floating restaurants on piers awash in the sounds of clinking glasses and silverware. A massive, WWII-era steamship snoozes on the banks with ropes thicker than drainage pipes reaching down off its decks, mooring the vessel to the massive bulkheads of its pier. Further along Delaware Avenue, a fortress rises up from the sidewalk with a glittery marquee that reads "Harrah's Casino" in a million twinkling light bulbs.

I venture no further. Not because I'm afraid or tired, but because I hear another screaming saxophone note on the breeze, which must be the universal sound of fate. The sweet notes of improvisational jazz swirl up from the sidewalk on the corner of the block. A young man in a pair of blue jeans, ragged at the cuffs, puffs his cheeks and blows life into the instrument, and all I can do is move toward the sound. My heart races again. A few droplets of sweat form at the small of my back and pool into the band of my underwear, but it's all for nothing. The closer I get, the more it becomes clear that my eyes are fogged with the ghosts of my past. I'm seeing the images I want to see through eyes that are more hopeful than realistic…and they probably have been since my journey began. Since I started seeing Travis with his wrinkled, old cardboard sign back in North Carolina.

This young man with a saxophone in his hand is definitely not Travis and, in fact, he doesn't even look that much like him. I take a deep and resentful breath and ready myself to keep walking for however long it might take to find my brother.

But then my heart stops dead.

I hear the slow, staccato beat of a bass drum, and I squint my eyes down hard and clench my teeth and try to filter every one of my five senses through my ears so I can determine its source.

And then I see him.

Unbeknownst to the rogue sax player on the street corner, he's not playing a solo concert at all. He's being accompanied by a drummer… of sorts. The drummer sits on the top step of a neighborhood stoop on the other side of the street, and he's pounding out a rhythm on an upturned bucket with both of his hands. This drummer, however, is not your traditional drummer intent on maintaining tempo. Nope. This drummer seems oblivious to the beautiful music cascading around him and, instead, plays completely to his own self-centered beat.

I take one look at him and I know right away it's Travis.

There's no doubt about it. No mirage or a figment of my imagination this time. It's Travis, for real.

I watch with a mixture of confusion, shock, and awe. My throat starts to tighten again and my heart beats so fast I feel faint. But I take a deep breath because this time my brother is sitting right in front of me. And I know this time I have a real chance to make things right.

I pull a few bucks from my bag and cross the street. My eyes remain locked on Travis as he stops drumming for no apparent reason and begins to rock to a fro on the top step. He stares hauntingly down at his hands as if he longs for them to depress the shining keys of his instrument instead of pound incessantly on a plastic drum.

When I reach the base of the steps, the first thing I notice is the saxophone case resting midway up the stone stairway. There's no doubt it's Travis's saxophone case, with the adhesive strip of red plastic from my cheesy label maker sprawled out across the handle and the words "Travis Wheaton" staring back at me. The case is splayed wide to reveal an open wound where a saxophone once rested. My brother, the humble musician, lingers above it on the top step with his eyelids squeezed shut and his cheeks half-inflated with the last breath of music he never got to blow.

I drop the bills I'd been holding and watch them flutter into the sax case like autumn leaves. When the paper makes contact with the naked interior of the case, Travis's eyes pop wide open and he stares at me as if he's never seen his own brother before. The edges of his eyelids are rimmed in red and match the lightning streaks that crackle through the whites of his eyes. I can tell he's high as a kite. Like before. It takes him a few seconds of squinting and thinking before he realizes what the hell's happening. He stares right at me with a tiny glint of recognition in his eyes, but still he says nothing.

"Travis," I say.

The faint hint of recognition steadies and the fog starts to lift. His eyes open wide. "Cordy?" He hops up off the crate, rushes over to me, grabs me by the neck, and starts to rub my scalp. "Dude! What's happening my little man?"

All of a sudden he's acting like he just saw me yesterday and there's nothing odd about my sudden appearance in Philadelphia, hundreds of miles from home.

"Dudes!" he announces to an imaginary audience that is nowhere in sight. "This here's my little brother, Cordy. He's…oh how old are you, bro?" He looks directly at me as if he's waiting for me to announce my age to a lounge packed with concert-goers when the only beings in our immediate vicinity are me, Travis, and a couple of street pigeons.

I'm too stunned by his erratic behavior to answer. A maelstrom of emotions—from anger, to pity, to sheer confusion—swirls around inside me, as the notes of the sax player across the street wash away on the wind.

"Where's your saxophone?" is the very first question I have for him, and it comes out in a harsh monotone that does nothing to hide my concern or my disbelief at the current situation.

"That's what you came to ask me?" he says. "About a stupid instrument?" He tries to put his arm around me again and jostle me around like we're best bros, but I shrug him away and that's all it takes for

Travis to flip his emotions on a dime

"Look, I sold the damn thing, Cordy," he snaps at me. "You happy?"

"Why would I be—"

"Cordy…you want to stop the bullshit and tell me what in the hell you're doing here?"

"I'm here looking for you," I say, remembering the script that ran through my head on a loop ever since my journey began. "You and the ghost of John Coltrane," I say, which sounded a lot smoother when I rehearsed it back in High Point.

"John Coltrane? Cordy, what the hell are you talking about? And, seriously, what the hell are you doing here?!" He pops up from his perch on the step and begins to pace back and forth with his hands cupped around the back of his head. He's muttering all kinds of weird shit that I can't make out, but he's animated enough to make a few strangers on the sidewalk stop to take notice. Then Travis really starts to lose it. He pulls the rubber band out of his ponytail and takes two jerky steps in my direction. He gathers his balance on the edge of the bottom step for a moment, then shouts something at me like, "I swear…you people can't just let me live my life, can you? My God, Cordy, what would ever—"

"Travis!" I shout, and it spooks the hell out of him because I don't think he's ever heard me raise my voice and I sure as hell can't remember ever pushing back on my own brother with such fury. I squint my eyes down and motion over my shoulder with a slight nod of my chin. Travis stops and notices all the strangers gawking at us from the sidewalk, their jaws dropped open as if they expect my own brother to attack me.

Travis rolls his eyes and takes a deep breath. "Look, maybe we can go somewhere and talk for a bit," he says. "Like, in private."

"Sure," I say. "Let's go to your place." For some reason, Travis jumps a little when I say it, and then he mutters something under his breath that sounds a little like, "For fuck's sake."

Travis collects himself and watches the crowd of three or four onlookers move on down the street. Then he says, "You know what? Let's grab a bite to eat. You hungry?" I nod. "Good. I know a place."

A few minutes later we're seated in a booth inside a noisy, jam-packed diner named the Melrose. It's kind of old school, bedecked in stainless steel counters with appliances behind them, and stocked with sturdy waitresses in pastel uniforms who buzz around the dining room taking orders.

"This place has a famous bowl of split-pea soup," Travis tells me from behind a massive, laminated menu. His hands shake, causing the menu to waver a bit as he speaks.

"I'll have a bowl of that," I tell our waitress, Marge, whose name I know from reading the blue script lettering on her striped blouse.

"Make that two," Travis says. "And two waters. Water's free, right?" The waitress scowls and nods her head before scribbling some chicken scratch on our order ticket and heading to the kitchen.

"So," Travis says, "here you are." All of his initial excitement and surprise at seeing me a few minutes ago has completely disappeared. He's agitated, like having to worry about his little brother all of a sudden has ruined his life even more than he's already ruined it himself.

"Yes, here I am," I reply.

"And you're here…because?" He drags out the 'cause' in 'because' as a way of letting me know I have no business here in Philadelphia.

I take a deep breath and get ready to tell him the heavy stuff. About Dad and his illness. About me running away and the cops and my face on the TV news and all that crap.

"Well…" I say.

But that's as far as I get before Travis's glazed-over eyes rise to meet the glare of a man in a black, leather jacket as he enters the diner. Travis's eyes follow the man to the back of the restaurant, to a tiny hallway where the restrooms are hidden.

"Hold that thought, little bro," Travis says, and all of a sudden he's talking to me in that sing-songy voice again.

He rises from the table and goes in search of the leather-clad stranger.

"Wait!" I call after him. "Where are you going?" But Travis either ignores me or doesn't hear me as he disappears behind the counter.

I stare at the rings of steam billowing off our bowls of soup until the green sludge grows thicker and colder, and as Marge comes to visit the table not once, not twice, but three times with every waitress's trademark catchphrase, "Can I get you anything else?"

"Just the check," I tell her, figuring I might as well pay for the bowls of soup since it doesn't seem like Travis is in any position to do so. Then I slump back against the window on the inside of our booth and wait. The sun filters through the glass and warms the back of my neck and sends little tingles down my spine and raises patches of goose pimples on my arms and makes me wonder how I can be this exhausted after getting the first decent night's sleep I've had since my journey began. And then I wonder how effective a night of sleep can be when it happens on a sidewalk and under a pile of crates and in one of the noisiest, busiest cities in the United States. My body longs for a night of peaceful, uninterrupted rest. The kind I used to get in my room on Brookside Drive. Back when Travis practiced his sax in the top bunk and the biggest problem the Wheatons faced was High Point's resident mosquito population.

My eyelids cede to the weight of fatigue and I drift off right there at our table in the Melrose Diner...

"Run!"

Dad hoists me off the ground. Drags me to the pickup. "Get in!"

Dad cranks the ignition. Stomps on the pedal. The truck lurches. Whines. The tires kick up a mushroom cloud of dust. Tiny pieces of gravel shoot behind the truck in a million, coppery bullets.

My eyes find the rear view. In time to see the dust clear. In time to see my captors scramble after their money. In time to see the scrawny captor lift his ski mask. Wipe the sweat from his brow. In time to discover why his voice sounded familiar.

In time to see my own brother.

Travis.

I slam my fist on the dashboard. Watch the loose change and the spent cigarette butts flip through the air. They rain down in a clatter of metal and ash. I grab Dad's hand on the gear shift and his fingers clamp around mine. A calm rushes over my body.

RELIEF.

The first time I'm able to breathe without a gag or my own tears washing down over my mouth.

I look in the rearview one more time. Just to see Travis before he disappears into eternity.

And that's when I see my brother's accomplice pop up off the ground.

The flash of sunlight on gunmetal.

Then a second flash as the glass explodes in the back window of Dad's truck.

Betrayal

A tray's-worth of plates, mugs, and silverware clash together. My eyes pop open. My face is pressed on the grimy front window of the Melrose Diner. The green carpeted floor beside our table is littered with forks, knives, and a big, round wet spot that might be orange juice or coffee.

"My bad," Marge says. She stoops below table level to clean the mess. I head down there with her to offer my assistance. Just then Travis emerges from the restroom followed by the stranger in the black jacket, and I forget all about the pile of plates and forks. The blood boils in my veins. Intense heat rises from my belly and collects in the pale, white sheet of my cheeks.

The man in the black jacket slips past the counter and out the front door without ordering so much as a cold Danish, and Travis slides into the booth across from me like everything is normal. Like nothing traumatic ever happened between us. Like his betrayal was an ordinary part of brotherhood.

But things are far from normal. In fact, from this point forward, things will never be anything close to normal between Travis and me. I know that now. I know this whole pilgrimage to Philadelphia has been a waste of time and a pointless strain on my parents who have no clue where I am, what I'm doing, or when I'm ever coming back.

"*Have you ever experienced trauma?*" Giacomo had asked me back in DC.

Well, yes, I sure as hell have, Jack. You got that? I sure as hell have. The image of Travis outside that warehouse with his cheesy McBurglar's mask pulled back to reveal his stupid face flashes past my eyes and pastes itself over the current version of Travis.

"What's up with you?" Travis asks when he notices the flaming balls of hot magma exploding from my eyes.

"Why should something be up?" I shoot back in monotone, swishing my ice-cold soup around in the bowl with a water-stained spoon.

"You look like you saw a ghost."

I grunt and float a few oyster crackers on the surface of the split-pea so I don't have to look at my brother's stupid face. The so-called greatest split-pea in the world, now all green and congealed like a big bowl of alien puke that will cause instant death if it touches my lips.

"You come all the way here," Travis says, "and now you just sit there playing with your food? Sometimes you make no sense at all, Cordy."

I reach into my backpack and pull out the scrap of sheet music—the one that launched me on this voyage and gave me hope that my brother had not, in fact, been replaced by a strange being I didn't recognize. That he was still the Travis I knew from home. The one who played music to me and took me to breakfast at Alex's House and walked me to school. The one who used to be my friend and not put my life in danger for a few lousy bucks.

I slap the paper down on the table and push it across to Travis. "Actually," I say. "I came to give you this." He stares at the page for a second, and then his eyes grow a little wider and a barely visible smile begins to form on his lips. But then it disappears as quickly as it rises.

"This is it?" he asks, and he says it like he's talking to someone he's never met before instead of his own brother. "You came all the way up here to give me a piece of wrinkled paper?"

I know they shouldn't, but his words strike me like daggers and I can feel all of my guts spilling out on the floor of the Melrose Diner. Only they're not my guts. They're my emotions. They're all my fears and my darkest nightmares spilling forth from my pores and thickening up like a bowl of Melrose split-pea soup. "But…but it's your song," I say. "It's John Coltrane and you always said—"

A sudden cough and the fine mist of coughed-up water cuts me off mid-sentence. I look at Travis and there's a crooked grin on his face. And he's laughing. He's literally laughing in my face.

"I don't think you get it," he says. "I really don't give a damn about John Coltrane anymore."

Travis pulls a paper napkin from the tableside dispenser and dabs a few drops of water off his chin. "Hasn't it dawned on you yet, Cordy? Haven't you realized I don't want anything to do with my old life? Not High Point. Not Dad or Mom. Not even—"

He pauses and stares at me for a few seconds. There's a weird sparkle in his eyes. Not the kind that comes from being stoned out of your mind, but the kind that comes from being human. I know exactly what Travis wants to say to me, and I hope to hell he doesn't come out and say it.

"Cordy," he says, and he's struggling. He's struggling real hard not to tell me how little I matter to him. His own goddamn brother. "Look, I know you think you're being a big hero and you're here to rescue me or something. But the truth is, I don't need you here. Nobody needs you to be here. Nobody asked you. You understand?"

All I want to do is grab a stray fork from under our table—out from under Marge's scuffed up Stride Rites—and jab it right in my brother's eyes. But I'm too civilized for that. Too principled. Too faithful to age-old philosophy meant to steer us toward humanity. And humility. So I stab him, instead, with a stark dose of reality. Unimpeded. No filter. Just straight up real life. The kind that melts the souls of those who won't poke their heads out of the shell from time to time and try to understand.

"Dad's dying," I say. Just like that. Cold as hell.

Travis's eyelids flap back and the half-smirk on his face oozes into a grimace.

"He has lung cancer. He doesn't have much time."

"What are you talking about?"

"You heard me!"

Travis goes silent. Stirs his spoon around in the bowl like he has no intention of eating a drop of the green slop inside. "Seriously?" he asks after a minute or so of staring at his soup. I nod and imagine myself in a dark cloak delivering the message with the shadows of death parked in circles below my eye sockets—like the world's first teenage grim reaper.

"You need to talk to him," I say. "That's the real reason I'm here."

Travis leans back in the booth and smacks his spoon flat on the table. He stares at the ceiling for a long time, and I trace the red streaks running the lengths of his lower eyelids as he gathers himself. Finally, he says "Nah! I'm the last person he'd want to see."

"You'd be surprised how much a person can forgive," I reply, even though I'm not fully convinced of that myself.

"Forgive?!" Travis grabs the hem of his collar between his thumb and forefinger and tugs it forward, releasing a gust of heat from the trunk of his body. A single trail of sweat snakes its way down the side of his face and disappears under the collar of his shirt. "What do you mean? Forgive what?"

I stare into his brown eyes and feel the fire of a thousand nightmares flare inside me. "Look, Travis. I know..." I say flatly, "...about everything. The warehouse..."

Travis's eyes shoot down to the tabletop for a split second, then his brow wrinkles and his eyebrows raise as he falls on a secondary strategy.

"I have no idea what you're talking about," he says.

"Then turn out your pockets," I reply.

"What? I'm not..."

"I said turn them out, Travis!" I shout it across the dining room. Two or three heads in the adjoining booths spin around, but I don't care.

"Cordy," Travis grunts through clenched teeth. "Keep your freakin' voice down, man. We're in a restaurant."

"No shit," I say. "Now show me what's in your pockets or I'll ask that police officer to do it for me."

My eyes shoot across the dining room to a uniformed cop sipping coffee at the counter on his break. It doesn't occur to me in this moment that he may recognize me and haul me in. Maybe because it doesn't matter any more.

"You wouldn't..."

I stand up and take a few steps toward the counter. Travis's hand snaps around my wrist and pulls me back to the booth.

"Fine," he says reaching in his pockets. Seconds later, there's a pile of clear sandwich bags on the table behind the shade and security of an upturned menu. Each bag is packed with pills of every shape, size, and color.

"Get rid of them," I say.

"Cordy! You know how much money—"

"You'll never change," I say. I feel a sharp pain in my chest when I say it because I'm sure the words hurt me more than they do Travis. "You're not my brother," I add.

"Come on. This is crazy."

"You want crazy?" I say. "Crazy is never learning your lesson. Crazy is putting your own brother in the trunk of a car and stealing money from your father to save your own sorry ass. Crazy is thinking firearms are used as mere threats and not for all-out war. You're the one who destroyed our family, Travis. It was *you*!"

His eyes transform into fish bowls on his face as it dawns on him that I do remember. That I stopped forcing myself to forget. That I know what he did.

"You don't understand. He was gonna kill me. I never meant for you to get hurt. I never meant for any of it to happen. I swear. It was just for a few bucks. To get out of trouble. Cordy, you have to believe me!"

My eyes narrow to heartless slits and I stare at Travis with the intensity of a ten-alarm blaze. "That's the problem," I tell him, "I *do* believe you."

"What the hell is that supposed to mean?"

"It means I'm the only one, Travis. The only one who hasn't given up on you. The only one who thinks you're still human and not some kind of strung out zombie."

"That's ridiculous. I'm fine. I'm—"

"No," I say. "You're far from fine. Look at you. You're high right now. But you want to know what's ridiculous? *Me!* I thought I could find you and give you your sheet music and take you to Birdland Jazz Club and make you remember how important John Coltrane is and how you used to be like him. But you know what? You're nothing like John Coltrane."

"Is that right?" he says with a sarcastic snicker, as if me and my father and my hero are nothing to him.

I'm immediately reminded of John Coltrane's personal promise. A promise he made to himself and to the remainder of his journey through life. He said, "I know that there are bad forces, forces that bring suffering to others and misery to the world. I want to be the opposite force. I want to be the force which is truly for good." It takes less than a second for me to realize this sounds nothing like the man my brother has become. I can't even look Travis in the eyes as the words bubble up from within my gut and struggle to escape the inside of my lips.

"Yeah, that is right," I reply. "To be like John Coltrane, you'd need a *soul*. And you'd need a *conscience*."

That's when I toss my spoon in the green bowl of sludge and shove the inventory of bagged-up pills off the table, and expect to watch Travis scramble down like a squawking seagull to retrieve his breadcrumbs before the police officer at the counter finishes his coffee and notices there's a freaking drug dealer in his midst.

But that's not what happens.

What happens is I rake my arm across the diner table and push every fork, spoon, cup, and bowl off that table and onto the spotless floor beneath. There are no bags of pills. There is no Travis. My vision sharpens and I notice I'm standing there all alone with a puddle of green slop, a pile of ice cubes, and service for one on the floor at my feet.

The police officer at the lunch counter has his eyes trained directly on me. Not on Travis, who had never been with me in the first place, but on me…the teen runaway and potential credit card felon who can no longer separate his nightmares from reality. They've become one and the same. They've trapped me for good.

And while every eye, including the police officer's, is trained on me and I feel the redness swelling up in my cheeks and the panic start to rise in my throat, I do the only thing I can think to do in the moment. I drop a few bucks down on the table to foot my bill, fly from the booth, say "sorry… I'm really sorry" to nobody in particular, just into the air, and sprint out the double doors of the Melrose Diner onto the streets of Philadelphia.

Alone. Again. Like I always have been, I guess.

Only this time it feels more permanent. More real.

Rumspringa

There's a moment—that split second before the shit hits the fan and splatters back in your face; before the silverware rains down from the table and you expect to see a vision of your brother scrambling around, fishing pills off the floor of a diner and you realize, instead, you're just flat-out losing your mind. A moment when your senses tighten and you don't think about the deadly rot in your father's lungs or how the time you spent evading the police was a waste of time. And, in that moment, when the mirage fades and you're left staring reality in its stupid, sneering, despicable face—that's when everything makes sense. That's when scraps of mental waste unfurl themselves and spill from the cranial waste bin.

First in small flashes.

The masked men. The heavy scent of last night's whisky. The explosion of red and the blanket of darkness that enveloped me an instant later.

Then in bursts.

The doors of the Melrose. The police officer's expression of shock. The pitiful plea that squeezes through the door as it slams.

"Cordy, wait!" is all I hear in Travis's desperate tones. But it's all in my head. I know that now. I know finding my brother out here on the streets of Philadelphia is a fruitless endeavor. Because I know Travis doesn't want to be found, and even if I did find the *real* Travis instead of just running into the wavering, holographic version of him I have stored in my mind, that it'd be pointless. That he'd still be popping those pills in his mouth and forgetting about who he used to be and how much he owes me. How much he's hurt me. And how much he's taken from Mom and Dad.

So I push his stupid voice out of my head.

Maybe forever.

But even as the white rubber of my Chucks makes firm contact with sticky, Philadelphia pavement, I find myself right back at the warehouse. Back inside my nightmare, if only for an instant. If only in the base of my eardrums, where the desperate cry of my brother matches a distinct signature from another time. A time so embroidered on my soul I can't rid myself of it if I ripped out every stitch, burned them, and swallowed the ashes. And all I did was refuse to forget. Like Giacomo told me. Come out of the shadows. Let the memories flood back. Confirm all I wished to deny since the night it happened.

It's how I know Travis is gone and there will be no saving him. Because how can you save something that doesn't exist? To be perfectly honest, it feels liberating. To not have to feel like my family's future rests on my shoulders. It makes my feet fall harder—more surely—on the sidewalk as I race past coffee shops and convenience stores and dodge people walking with their faces glued to the screens of their phones.

I put ten blocks between myself and the Melrose Diner, but I didn't like the looks of that police officer at the counter, and the echo of Travis's primal scream reverberating through my mind doesn't do me any favors either. So I decide not to take any chances. I veer off the main stretch with the shops and the people and the possibility of police officers, and I duck down an alleyway between two brick-faced rowhomes. The walls are crumbling and barely wide enough to pass through without scraping my shoulders on the cinderblock.

What had once been a sunny day with clear skies turns to twilight, with all modes of light choked out by the surrounding buildings and a patchwork canopy of ivy and electrical lines with tennis shoes dangling from their laces. I hurdle a wooden crate, all worm-eaten and soft on one corner, and land in a puddle of murky liquid I hope is rainwater from a recent storm. Plastic packages crinkle under foot. A brown bottle kicks up and shatters behind me. Above, on a stone-chiseled windowsill, sits an angry-looking street cat with glowing, yellow eyes. She licks her paw casually as I race past and surge toward the crack of light at the far end of the alley.

Another street.

I reach the edge of the wall and the warmth of the sun falls on my face. I whip out of the alley like one of those cars on the old Tilt-a-Whirl rides that'd roll through High Point with the traveling carnivals. I skid out on the sidewalk, trying to look casual—not like a dude who just crashed through an alleyway and waded through a pond full of raw sewage.

Then it hits me.

Something hard. Something that grunts and curses and carries a load of vinyl albums down a city street. Something human. And yet solid enough to send me tumbling onto my back. I roll to a stop between the curb and the chrome-spoked front wheel of a Cadillac. Bright spots float past my eyes. I try to take a breath but it's like the first time I tried to blow into Travis's saxophone and was surprised by how much force it took to make a sound.

The sidewalk is littered with vinyl albums bundled in protective shrink wrap with their orange sale stickers standing out like badges of vintage honor. The stickers herald the ranks of each album in the form of cut-rate pricing. Six ninety-nine for a Private Class copy of Metallica's black album. An even ten spot for the distinguished lieutenant—AC/DC's "Back in Black." A lofty twelve fifty for the ranking general of the battalion, Mr. Iggy Pop.

Before I can see straight and peel myself up off the pavement, the human flagpole I crashed into has a stack of the albums under his arms and his hand on my shoulder.

"You okay, friend?" he asks in a voice that's more like a mouse than a monster. "All my fault," he goes on. He hoists me to my feet and dusts the street pebbles off my back. "I should have taken an extra trip with this load, but I was running short on time and, well, I'm sorry for—"

"Woah. Woah," I say when I catch my breath. "You say *you're* sorry?"

He looks at me funny, which is odd because the kid doesn't exactly look normal. At least not in the way I've come to know normal, which might not be normal at all. But still. This dude cocks his head to one side and places his thumb on the base of his chin and starts plucking at the long, bushy sideburns pouring out from under a black, wide-brimmed hat.

"Sure," he says. "Course I'm sorry. Don't you accept my apology?"

He shrinks back a step and fiddles with a strap on his suspenders. His t-shirt is flat black with the words "AC/DC" printed on the front in white, block lettering—which clashes in both style and historical time period with the pair of straight-cut slacks and hand-sewn, leather boots that cover his bottom half.

I laugh. "No, man," I say. "I mean you shouldn't apologize when you've done nothing wrong. It's all my fault. I'm the one who exploded from that alley like a stealth bomber."

"That some kind of athletic outfit here in the city? The Stealth Bombers?"

Now it's my turn to look at *him* funny. I try to make the whole thing feel less awkward by ignoring his question and bending down to recover the few albums that remain on the sidewalk. One is a copy of *A Love Supreme* by John Coltrane. I'm not into talking Coltrane right now because of Travis, but I can't resist telling the kid, "You have good taste."

"Thanks," he says as I hand him the Coltrane album. "Haven't heard any of his music yet, but Jimmy down at the record store says I'm missing out if I never get a chance to hear America's greatest invention. Jazz. Jimmy said Coltrane's a great introduction."

"Sounds like Jimmy's a smart guy. Like he knows how important jazz is to this country. How it signifies a break from the past, a nod to the present, and an ever-present eye toward the future. It's freedom within confines. It's the central story in an American mythology."

"Sounds familiar," he says. His blue eyes surge with a thousand volts of electricity and a thin smile spreads out beneath a mass of scraggly facial hair—the kind that's not yet beard but is more than nothing. "He's been helping me get acquainted with the city since I started taking the trip."

"You're not from around here," I say. "So maybe we have more in common than just sharing the same square foot of sidewalk for one painful second."

His brow furrows as he analyzes my comment.

"Oh yeah?" he replies holding out his free hand. "Name's Levi Kurtz. I'm from Lancaster, in the great state of Pennsylvania."

"You *are* aware we're in Philadelphia," I say. "Isn't that in the great state of Pennsylvania too? It hasn't moved, has it?"

"Not that I'm aware," Levi says, stuffing the stray albums from under his arms back in the plastic crate that, at one time, had probably been loaded down with cartons of milk and stacked in the back of a truck like Old Sally.

"Then why say something so formal like 'the great state of Pennsylvania' when you haven't traveled more than a few dozen miles?"

Levi lays the crate down on the chrome bumper of a Chevy Impala, at least thirty years old and without a lick of paint left on a naked body. He twists a strand or two from his bushy sideburns and meditates on my question. Slow seems to be Levi's only operational speed. It gives me an odd sense of comfort to know he's not rolling off answers without relying on a dose of reason from upstairs in his own attic.

He rests one of his black boots on the bumper beside the crate full of albums and leans forward with one fist resting under his chin, kind of like the famous sculpture. A puff of air rushes through his nostrils as if the machine in his brain were about to dispense a long, paper slip with the printed results. "I suppose I say it all formal because where I come from feels a whole lot different than this place. It's a whole different world with its own rules."

I'm confused because Pennsylvania sure as hell doesn't sound like an exotic location to me. Since I brewed up the courage to leave the shell and see what's outside, I've found most any place on the East Coast—and maybe in the country—is not too dissimilar to the next. More similarities than differences, at least.

But Levi Kurtz stands in front of me with his lambchop sideburns, suspenders, and homemade boots—and his homespun way of thinking things through long and hard before he gets nailed down to an answer—and I'm suddenly not sure if maybe there isn't a place flopped down in the middle of Pennsylvania that's unique to anywhere else.

"So, Lancaster," I say awkwardly. "Mind filling me in on how it's this secret Utopia hidden beyond the suburbs of Philadelphia?"

"I don't know if I'd call it Utopia," Levi says, but then he stares down at the scratched and dented trunk of the Impala and goes into one of his thoughtful trances. "I guess it could be," he says after a long pause. "But I'm just not sure. That's kind of why I'm here."

"You came to Philadelphia to find out if your hometown is worth something? Man, I can relate to that."

"Not to see if Lancaster is worth anything. More to see if there's something else out here. To see if our way of life is the kind of life I want to keep living."

"Sounds pretty serious," I say. "But I don't get it. Why do you have to drive to Philadelphia to buy some old albums? Don't they have music where you come from??"

"Yes, of course. But nothing with electric guitars or anything like that. Best we have back in Lancaster is Mother's harpsichord and she only brings it out for weddings."

"You sure Lancaster is a real place and not a pencil sketch in a history book?"

Levi jingles a set of keys out of the pocket of his work slacks and pops the trunk. It squeaks open on its hinges before he places the crate inside and slams it shut. "Sure feels like that sometimes," he says. "Especially since I've been showing up at Jimmy's shop."

I can't figure out what to make of this kid. I wonder what Cowbird would have said to a young man hauling around a pair of such heavy sideburns with him wherever he goes or if he'd just nod and treat him like the other odd-shaped eggs he's carried with him in the cab of Old Sally. I stand there for so long Levi notices I'm staring at him like he has tentacles for arms. He breaks the silence.

"You know, I'm not a space alien or anything. Just Amish."

"Amish?" I ask. "You mean like one of those dudes who drives a horse and buggy and wears a funny-looking, broad-rimmed—"

I catch myself before I finish the sentence. Levi smiles and tips his funny-looking, broad-rimmed hat. "Yep. I'm the kind of dude you're talking about. Only I've hit a fork in the road. My family says what I'm going through is normal. Mostly everyone in our community has doubts at some point."

"About being Amish?"

"In a sense. Although I guess I'll always be Amish, whether I decide to leave the community completely or stick around and get baptized."

"You can do that?"

"It's not easy. It comes with obstacles and hardships."

"What would they do to you?"

"For one, I'd be shunned."

"What the hell does that mean?"

A grimace crosses Levi's lips when I say the word "hell." Then it's gone. "Being shunned means you don't exist. The community stops recognizing you as one of its own."

"What about your family?"

"Sometimes they're shunned for allowing their child to make a bad decision. Most of the time, families do the same as the other community members."

"They ignore you?"

"You're getting it."

I pull my backpack tighter on its straps. It occurs to me I'm somehow talking religion and Amish tradition with a stranger in Philadelphia I'd plowed into a few minutes earlier. And the weird part, after all I've seen in the past few days, is that I'm not surprised. I've come to expect this sort of interaction with perfect strangers since I dragged my ass out of the cave. In fact, listening to Levi talk about how his flesh and blood could wake up one morning and pretend he never existed because the kid wants to use electricity once in a while makes me realize how lucky I am to have Mom and Dad. They'd never deny my existence, even if I threw my life away on drugs and had my brother held at gunpoint to pay off my debts to a drug dealer.

Like Travis.

Even after he did what he did and gave Mom and Dad every reason to shun the living hell out of him, they know Travis is Travis. I'd bet a million dollars they'd let him walk right through the door on Brookside Drive and sleep in his own bed with no questions asked if he ever decided to rejoin his "community." Levi Kurtz doesn't have that kind of opportunity; that kind of choice. Instead, he is stuck with a decision between tradition, family, and desire. If it were me I don't know which one would win out.

"So, has the big city helped you make a decision?" I ask.

"Not yet," Levi says. "To be honest, I'm taking a risk coming here every week."

"What do you mean?"

"Well, lots of Amish communities observe a period of time in a young person's life, right around the age of sixteen, as sacred. They see it as a time for experience and decision making. As a time for growing up."

"Like a rite of passage," I say.

"I've never heard that term."

"A rite of passage," I say. "It's an event or challenge you go through that builds maturity and character. It helps you grow up. It changes you. Like getting a driver's license or enlisting in the Marines."

"Yes," Levi says. "Sort of like that. The Amish call it Rumspringa. It's Pennsylvania Dutch for 'running around.'"

"So that's what you're doing? Running around?"

"More like sneaking around," Levi says. "My community doesn't observe Rumspringa. The elders think a good Amish lad should give himself to God on day one and remain true for the rest of eternity."

"So what are you doing out here with a stack of vinyl and what I assume is a vehicle with an actual combustion engine." I point to the Impala.

"Oh, she runs," Levi says. "Fixed her myself when I decided I'd observe Rumspringa whether the elders liked it or not."

"Wow," I say. "What I don't understand is how you managed to play mechanic without everyone in the community noticing?"

"The farmer who owns the land next to ours is anything but Amish. Nice guy, but he's got himself six, seven different vehicles scattered around his land. He told me I could have the car if I could get it running and off his property, so I found a secluded little spot in the woods that's loaded down with brush and hid her there. Any time I can break free, I take a drive to Jimmy's."

"All for music," I say under my breath with an air of respect. Then I ask, "How do you even listen to those albums? I thought the Amish were anti-electricity."

"Got an 80s-style record player from Jimmy. It's a hunk of scrap with cartoon characters printed on the case, and it runs on batteries. But it works, and that's all that matters."

"You got it all figured out," I say. "Maybe more than you know."

I hook my fingers in the straps of my backpack and give Levi a nod. He opens the driver's side door and mounts a seat with faded burgundy cloth that's shredded down to the metal. I start to head off in the opposite direction.

"Hey, where you going?" Levi shouts from behind me. "I never got your name."

I turn and take a few steps toward the car. "I'm Cordy Wheaton. From High Point, North Carolina. In the great state of John Coltrane."

Levi's eyes grow three times in size. He pushes the hat back off his forehead to reveal a straight-edged bowl cut on the sawdust-colored bangs suspended from his forehead. "North Carolina," he says. "That's a world away from here. Tell me, Cordy Wheaton, what's a Southern boy like you doing in one of the biggest cities in America looking like you got trampled by a draught horse?"

My hand rises to my eye, which is no longer swollen but still smarts under the pressure of my touch. It's been so long since I used a mirror or had a chance to see my own face staring back at me from the screen of my phone, I'd forgotten how much of a disheveled monstrosity I've become. It comes out in a stutter at first, but by the end of the sentence I'm sure of what I mean. "I…I, uhh…really don't know why I'm here anymore," I say. "I'd rather be anywhere else to be honest."

Levi's eyes sparkle. He reaches over to unlock the passenger door. "Bible says we should help a stranger in need," he says. "You're not a stranger anymore, but I know when I see a person who needs a hand. Wanna catch a lift to Lancaster?"

"In the great state of Pennsylvania?" I ask through a devilish grin.

"The very same," Levi says.

"Will it get me any closer to New York City?" I ask, feeling the impression of the folded up bills in my pocket.

"New York City? What do you want to do there?"

"I have a show to see." I hop in the passenger side and toss my bag in the backseat. "I'll tell you about it on the ride."

"You know, Lancaster isn't as close to New York as you think."

"It's close enough," I say. "And it fits the description of 'anywhere else.'"

Levi tips the brim of his hat and cranks the ignition. Several minutes later, we're on a winding stretch of the Pennsylvania Turnpike with the bright reflections of boathouses on the Delaware River trailing off behind us into the heart of a shrinking skyline.

We drive in silence. Levi grinds the corroded gears of the Impala as he downshifts through patches of automotive congestion and smacks on a massive chunk of grape bubblegum. The scratchiness of the cloth seat gnaws at the back of my neck. Images of Travis grip my mind, like a film reel of our childhood. An establishing shot of the humble bungalow on Brookside with Dad unloading lengths of lumber from the scuffed up payload of his pickup. A close-up shot of Travis with his eyes squinted, his brow furrowed, and the wrinkled sheet of Coltrane music sprawled across his lap. A bird's-eye shot of Penn Griffin High School, with Travis and I the size of fire ants scurrying around campus together on a lazy Saturday morning. A series of shots in a kaleidoscope of action, with Travis slamming the front door and Dad standing alone in the hallway, his eyes glassy and moist, followed up by an unrelenting burst of strobing, painful scenes from inside the warehouse. And then the closing shot, that moment before the credits roll, with Travis's pitiful, red-eyed face staring back at me from the floor of the diner with pills strewn around him. My own image. The one that cements my memory of Travis forever, even if it's one I concocted in my own head.

Levi cracks a massive bubble and the purple gum flips over the corners of his mouth so he has to stuff it back inside with his hand.

The slideshow in my mind skitters free from its reel. The screen goes bright white and I'm thrust back into the passenger seat on a stretch of Pennsylvania roadway that's more cornfield than concrete.

"You okay?" Levi asks when he notices my hands shaking.

"Yeah," I say. "I'm fine. Got a lot on my mind."

"Don't we all," Levi replies. "My pa says when your brain feels so heavy you can't hold your head up anymore, you let someone help you carry it."

I stare at him for a second, dumbfounded. "Did you ask him what the hell he was talking about?"

Levi winces a little and leans farther back in the driver's seat when I dare to utter the word "hell," but then he collects himself and moves on without attempting to scold me or wash my mouth out with soap. "He meant it's best to talk about things when they bother you," he says.

"Then why didn't he say that?"

This question strikes Levi as being more logical than he expected. He smiles for the first time since he scraped me off the sidewalk and says, "Good question. I suppose Pa's one of those people stuck on formality."

"Sounds like he's stuck on something."

"He's stuck on lots of things. But he's no different than any of the other folk in my community. They have a way of doing things that's served them for hundreds of years."

"Sounds like a tortoise shell situation," I say, only half-way under my breath.

Right away I wish I hadn't said it because, for once, I'm not interested in talking philosophy. Not with all that's bouncing around my skull and the uncertainty that lies ahead. I mean, how in the world did I expect to get from Lancaster, Pennsylvania to New York City without a plan or a map or any reason to go other than the feeling I have inside me that once—just this one time in my life—I want to finish something?

But I can't ignore Levi and go on sitting next to him in the passenger seat as he carts me along on an adventure he's no part of, so I decide a quick lesson on Plato's ideology is in order.

Levi's eyes are squinted and his browlines are creased into the ultimate version of origami confusion, so I say, "Don't worry. You're not going insane. I did say 'tortoise shell.'"

"That's what I thought, and yet I have no idea what my pa and a tortoise shell have in common, other than a hard exterior and maybe a bit hollow inside."

"I never thought of that," I say, thinking maybe Levi Kurtz should be teaching me a thing or two instead of the other way around. "But that's not what I meant. I meant your, or rather, one's community is a tortoise shell. Kind of like the cave to your Plato, or the High Point, North Carolina to your Cordy Wheaton."

"Plato? You mean that weird goop that comes in plastic containers that kids either eat or roll it into snakes?"

I burst out laughing because this Levi kid is a riot, but then I look at him and see the straight line of his lips across his face and realize he's not kidding. He's never heard of the most famous philosopher in history. At least he understands Play-Doh!

"No, not Play-Doh! Plato! Plato was a philosopher in Ancient Greece. He had this weird theory that if a bunch of people were trapped in a cave, they'd only be able to base their reality on what they see in front of them."

"Sounds creepy," Levi says. "I've never been in a cave before, but I imagine they're cold, wet, and full of bats."

"Not the point," I say. "Point is, if you never leave the cave, then you have no idea what's on the outside, or if there even is an outside."

Levi leans back in his seat and flicks the turn signal before drifting into the left lane. His hands flutter on the steering wheel as if he's nervous or trying to move massive boulders with only the power of his mind. "Well," he says finally, "I don't see a problem."

"You don't?" I'm confused because I've yet to find anyone I've told about Plato's cave who didn't find me downright brilliant. "If you don't leave, how can you live life? How can you understand how the world works? How can you progress?"

"Pa says progress is overrated unless it builds you a chicken coop or a new house or gets the crops planted in the fields."

Levi flicks the turn signal again and pulls the Impala off the next exit. A thick tree line shades the left-hand side of the ramp and blocks our view of the remaining stretch of highway. The right-hand side of the ramp, and basically every other square inch in view, is dotted with cornfields and cow pastures. He slips the toll ticket out from under his sun visor and tosses a coin in the basket. A mechanical arm lifts and Levi rolls the Impala down a stretch of road that's not too far west of Philadelphia, but thousands of miles from the twenty-first century.

A row of houses with white-washed, wooden planks across their faces stare back at us through eyes with no pupils—which is just another way of saying they don't have curtains in the windows. A young man around Levi's age and dressed in the same, old-fashioned clothing sits atop a chestnut-colored horse in the distance, rounding up a small pack of four floppy-eared hounds as they race through the hedgerows. A buggy straight from the 1800s rolls past with a grey-bearded driver straddled across its stage, the reins hanging from his withered hands.

I'm struck dumb because here I was thinking High Point, North Carolina was the most old-fashioned tortoise shell of a place in the world, and I come to find out Lancaster, Pennsylvania makes it look like a freaking space colony on the surface of Neptune.

"Your pa makes a good point," I concede when it's clear I'm talking to a time traveler who's only recently found his way to the future—which, in this case, is a code name for the present. "But one thing your pa doesn't mention is you never know your capabilities—what might excite or interest you—until you have experiences. You may never understand what truth is unless you have the tools to decide what's real and what's not."

"That's why I have faith."

"You mean *blind* faith," I say, placing emphasis on the word "blind."

"Ain't nothing blind about it," Levi responds through a chuckle. "You can't work from sun up to sun down without your eyes wide open. You live life with the Amish, you know what to expect and what you're gonna take from it."

"It sounds good when you put it that way."

"It is. Except I do see where you're coming from with the whole cave thing, too. Otherwise, I wouldn't be hauling this hunk of scrap back and forth to the city to see how other folks live."

He pulls the Impala off the main stretch of paved road and onto a dusty, dirt pathway with the gnarled trunks of oak trees blocking the late afternoon light on both sides.

"Where are we going?" I ask, alarmed by the harsh change of scenery.

He pats his hand on the steering wheel. "Gotta hide this thing. Then I'll take you home to meet Pa." I'm quiet as I try to right myself in the seat against the bucking and broncking of the Impala on its less-than-stellar suspension.

But I can't resist asking the million-dollar question. "Will you get baptized after you've seen the world and officially join your community?"

"Don't know," he shouts over the commotion of the shocks against the uneven disaster that is the pathway. "I'm kind of leaning that way."

"You mean after seeing all this new stuff and listening to folks like John Coltrane, the whole rumspringa thing might be a waste of time?"

"Not a waste of time," he says, "because I had a chance to experience something that's not Amish, and yet I still get the feeling when I walk through the gates of Pa's farm that this is *home*. You know what I mean?"

"I do," I say. And, for once in my life, I'm telling the truth. About High Point. I miss it. I never thought I'd say it, but I miss the train whistles late at night while I'm lying in the bottom bunk, and Dad's footsteps on the floor when he comes home from work, and Mom's chicken and dumplings on a cold, December day, and the Coltrane statue staring back at me from Hamilton Street with the legend's easy-going expression of understanding. I miss the pine trees and the smell of tobacco growing in the fields and the simplicity. I miss home, even if it's the heaviest tortoise shell I'll ever carry.

"Course, I haven't heard John Coltrane's music yet," Levi reminds me, "so maybe I'll change my mind about the whole baptism thing and give you a call. We can ride the rails together."

That makes me laugh. It also makes me glad I ran into Levi Kurtz, both literally and figuratively.

"You know," I say as Levi maneuvers the Impala through a stand of trees into the density of the forest, "you remind me of John Coltrane, as weird as that sounds."

"That does sound weird."

"Well, Coltrane once said, 'You can play a shoestring if you're sincere.'"

"What on earth does that mean?"

"Well, if you're true to yourself, it means you can do anything and be anything. If you can figure out the person you were meant to be. It also means Trane could blow a fart through a kazoo and it'd sound like silk. I swear, you're gonna love that album."

"I can't wait to—" but that's as far as Levi gets before his eyes shoot out of his head and his foot stomps down on the brake and a cloud of dust swirls up around the Impala and I bounce off my seat and nearly crash head-first through the windshield.

"Jesus Christ, Levi! What the—" but then I look through the glass and see the most terrifying man I've ever seen in my life. He stands there with a leather belt hanging limply from one hand. Levi and I sit frozen in our seats as the engine idles. The man closes in on us one slow step at a time.

"Is that your father?" I ask.

"Yep." Levi reaches for the door handle and cautiously dismounts the driver's seat. "Stay here," he says, but I don't listen. I pop out of the passenger side and stand there in the dusty road, scared half to death, but at least I've got Levi's back. Kind of.

"Appears you have some explaining to do," Pa says to Levi. His black eyes don't break with Levi's soul for a second, and the bushy beard that cascades down his face does nothing to soften the severity of his features, all angles and cheekbones and deep, dark eye sockets.

"Yessir," Levi says with his eyes cast down on the dirt.

"Well?!"

"I…uhhh…I…"

"He was giving me a ride," I say. "Car's mine."

"Then why aren't you driving?" Pa asks without bothering to look in my direction.

"Because…I…uhhh…I—"

"No more lies!" Pa bellows. Levi and I bounce a full step backward.

"Levi," Pa says, "give me the keys."

Levi reaches in his pocket and tosses the keys to Pa. He lets them pound him square in the chest and fall to the ground in a jangled-up mess. He bends down and picks them up. Fires them about fifty yards into the thick of the forest. "You didn't think I'd find your hiding spot, did you?" Levi shakes his head. His face is grave. Pale white. Pa holds the belt in front of his chest and Levi nods, ready to accept his punishment.

"Cordy," he says, "You oughta go."

"Where am I gonna go?" I ask. I immediately know by Pa's low grunt that I never should have asked such a stupid question.

"Anywhere but here," Levi says. "Go play a shoestring." He winks at me from across the width of the car's hood and I know I have already worn out my welcome.

"Don't get cold in the cave," I say to him. "Too many bats in there."

Levi nods.

"About a mile down the road," Pa says, pointing down a desolate stretch of dusty terrain, "you'll hit the center of town. Plenty of transportation there."

And that's it. No more talk. Only silence, except for the sound of my Chucks scuffling through the dirt, and the rush of a soft breeze through the corn as I inch my way ever closer to Birdland.

I hope it's worth the walk.

Character is Destiny

I walk toward a pale-pink horizon, hemmed in by sprawling oaks and tall, skinny conifers. Levi and his father and the beat-up jalopy are gone. Like they never existed, or melted as the last vestiges of snow on a spring day. Into the richness of the forest. Into traditions that hold them tight and safe in their crisp, tidy A-frames. The way they intended for themselves and their folk.

I drag the toes of my Chucks across the rain-scarred trail, kicking up plumes of dust that engulf me in a personal smoke-screen, like a trick some evil wizard might conceal in the sleeves of his robe. It's weird because it reminds me of being in sixth grade, which is not often a time in one's life we want to relive. But that's where I am these days. Stuck in my head, in my past, even as I trek across new lands and have experiences I never dreamed possible when I lay in the bottom bunk and stared up at the ceiling on Brookside Drive.

The particular hue of pink in the sky, combined with the thickness of the dust and the silence of the trail, sends me back to my hometown, where my memory lands upon an obsession I had when I was too alone to know any better. I'm talking about the Freedom Rangers. You know, those geeky action figures kids used to play with and collect and scream bloody murder over until their parents fought through crowds at the toy store to secure the last package or two in the whole state. The ones that caused mini-riots in local malls leading up to the Christmas season and became the subjects of a cheesy, Saturday morning cartoon I'd watch every week. The ones the cool kids—the kids who had real friends and didn't need to play with pieces of plastic meant to represent actual heroes—ridiculed with relentless abandon. The ones that got me in a whole mess of trouble.

I used to take my action figures out for a spin from time to time, which beat sitting in my room by myself and forcing all five Freedom Rangers to emancipate the same area for a millionth time. It gave me the impression I had things to do and friends who didn't come wrapped in plastic. But I didn't. Just the Freedom Rangers, some rope, and a desire to watch them conquer faraway lands that were so distant from my parents' property I could barely see them through the bathroom window with my naked eye. I'd plop all five rangers in a toy dump truck that was deemed "too childish" for me to still be playing with by my sixth-grade classmates.

After setting the green and orange rangers—my favorite two because they had the benefit of super-stretch arms—in the front of the truck and the yellow, blue, and purple rangers in an orderly row behind the real heroes, I'd roll them across the patchy nutgrass in my backyard and dredge up great plumes of orange dust from the North Carolina clays. I'd whirl them around in combative fury until the entire yard resembled the battlements of a World War I bunker. Then I'd force my heroic, ranger friends to retreat through a crooked gap in the back fence—one that led down to the depths of the Carolina woodlands.

After living out this battle for the fiftieth time, I decided the Freedom Rangers needed more freedom in their lives. Maybe I did too. So I pulled the tangle of twine from my pocket and pushed the dump truck, complete with a full payload of heroes, into the woods. Deeper and farther away from my house than any of us had been known to explore. Out there, beyond a trickling creek that sometimes transformed into a raging river after the most tropical of our summer thunderstorms, I found the gnarled trunk of a live oak with its branches spread over the forest floor.

I packed all five of my Freedom Rangers in various pockets and took hold of the bottom branch, scuttling up the side of the trunk like a squirrel. I climbed and climbed, paying no attention to the time or the fatigue in my arms, until I reached the top. The first thing I did when I got there was look down, which was enough to make my eyes pop out of my head and my lunch nearly spew out of my mouth.

But I steadied myself and took a deep breath. I tied one end of the rope to the sturdy crotch between two branches, and the other end around the waist of the orange ranger. I pulled him behind my head and fired him out past the branch line, watching him snap back on the rope, just like I'd planned, and spin itself again and again around the end of the branch until it was hopelessly tangled—something I hadn't planned.

I didn't freak out at first. I tugged on the rope and noticed the orange ranger was stuck tighter than a snagged lure on the banks of Dad's favorite fishing hole. Then I moved on to Plan B—a real rescue mission—which consisted of me tossing each of my rangers in order of color at their orange friend in an effort to knock him free. One by one, I watched the other four rangers plummet to their deaths at the base of the tree. But I kept my cool.

I knew I had two options: either climb out there myself and untangle my favorite ranger from an eternity of hanging fifty feet up in a Carolina forest, or leave him there to face the elements until he grew brittle and cracked and died an unheroic death. He was my favorite ranger, so I chose option one.

I flipped both feet over the branch and held on with my hands as I inched out. The main benefit was I couldn't look down and notice how easy it would have been to lose my grip, drop fifty feet like a nosediving bowling ball, and explode on impact like a ripe watermelon. The downfall was I couldn't look down and realize I'd done the stupidest, most idiotic, and ludicrous thing I'd ever done in my life. I was stuck. Hopelessly and endlessly.

And that's when I started to panic.

I screamed and cried for what seemed like hours, until the pinkish hue on the horizon evaporated into blackness and the headlights of cars—like tiny stars in the sky—danced down distant streets oblivious to my existence.

My hands were shredded, my feet sore and cramped. My breaths came out in stifled whimpers and I reached a point where I was sure this would be my death. My hands would give out and my feet would slip and that'd be the end of old Cordell Wheaton.

But then I heard a rustling in the leaves. The snap of a twig and the uneven, hobbling light from a pocket flashlight. Then a high-pitched, cracking voice that could only come from an adolescent boy. "Corrrrdy!"

"Travis?" I shouted. "I'm here!"

"Where are you?"

"Up here!" The flashlight bobbed over the branches until my dangling, ridiculous form hung like a pitiful silhouette in the spotlight.

"What are you doing up there?"

"Just get me down, Travis! I'm stuck!"

That's all Travis needed to hear before he was up in the tree, climbing faster than any squirrel I'd ever seen, until he stood on the crotch of the branch in question. "Come on! Grab my hand!" I reached out with one hand, but came nowhere near touching Travis's outstretched fingers.

Then, I felt his hands lock around my ankles. "Let go!" Travis shouted.

"What? Are you crazy?"

"I won't drop you. Just let go. Now!!"

My hands slipped off the branch and then my feet and, for half a second, I was engaged in an epic free fall that would have resulted in catastrophe. Then Travis's hands tugged me back, and all the blood rushed to my brain in one swift wash, and Travis wrapped his arms around my waist and hauled me back to where I could shimmy down the trunk while mouthing words of prayer I never thought I'd known.

"You okay?" Travis shouted from the treetop as my feet pressed down on sweet earth.

"I'm fine!"

But I wasn't alone. Travis was still up there. And all it took was some miniscule slip up—a bungle on his shoelaces or a maybe split-second lapse of concentration—before I heard branches cracking. Travis came crashing down, landing in a sickening heap in the brush beside me.

I reach the end of the dirt trail at the front gate of Levi's farm as twilight clicks off into night, and I walk the pebble-covered shoulder of a two-lane highway with forest on both sides.

All I can think about is Travis.

On one hand, I hate him for losing the battle. For losing himself and his family in pursuit of the devil in pill form. On the other hand, I hate myself for giving him the wrong map. For causing him to become lost in the first place. For sitting in the hospital that night back in sixth grade and listening to the diagnosis: two cracked ribs and a fractured tibia. Nothing that a quick cast, eight weeks of recovery time, and a little bit of physical rehab couldn't mend.

"And he can take one of these every four hours for pain," the doctor had said.

I didn't say a word. Nobody did.

And I didn't say a word when Travis bottomed out the bottle in under two weeks, or when a new, mysterious bottle appeared on Travis's desktop, or when that one disappeared and a new one showed up, or when Travis started acting differently—more distant, annoyed, tired all the time. I said nothing. The same way I stood by and let my brother get so lost he could never find his way back.

The way I caused the great train derailment in my brother's life.

For a short time, as I walk the desolate stretch of Pennsylvania roadway with only the moon and the stars to keep me company, I start to feel sorry for Travis all over again. I want to turn around and head back to Philadelphia and continue my search.

He has to be there. *Somewhere.*

I want to talk sense into him and make him complete the journey with me. The way I intended. But then I remember Levi. How he could have taken that beat-up Impala and left Lancaster forever. How he could have slammed the gear shift in reverse when he saw his father in the middle of the trail with his belt hanging limp and a look of anger on his face. How he could have hit one of a thousand corner barber shops in Philadelphia with the swirly red and white striped poles outside and shaved all that God-for-saken beaver fur off his face. How he could have driven off to California with the needle of his battery-powered record player screeching across vinyl as he prepped himself for the surfer lifestyle, or the movie star lifestyle, or any lifestyle that didn't require you to forget your individuality in exchange for cold comfort.

But he didn't.

He didn't leave. He didn't revolt. He didn't even allow a half-assed smirk to cross his lips when we stepped out of the Impala to face the kind of music he'd never find at Jimmy's record shop. He didn't do any of that. Because if Levi Kurtz is one thing in this life, it's committed. Something John Coltrane exuded in every note of jazz he ever played. Commitment. The act of applying oneself to the task at hand and never bothering to look up until true mastery has been achieved. John Coltrane had it. Levi definitely had it when it came to respecting and revering the way of life that shaped him into the young man he'd become.

Travis Wheaton had lost his grip on commitment long ago—unless you count his absolute dedication to his new friends. The ones that come sealed in capsule form in a brown bottle with a child's safety cap and a whole crapload of gibberish printed on the side. Long gone were the days when Travis would sit on the top bunk with his feet dangling over the side and his face buried in a piece of sheet music and refuse to look at me until the notes were mastered. Now I couldn't count on my brother to rediscover the tiniest shred of commitment even with his own father on his deathbed. In fact, I couldn't even find the dude. Like he stopped existing altogether on that fateful night back in High Point.

It's kind of pathetic.

Because I understand commitment. This journey has proven that to anyone who thought I was just a lazy, house-dwelling geek with nothing to offer. And this journey has proven it to me. I'm committed. I *will* finish. I *will* see a show at Birdland. And I will do it alone.

There's a lesser known philosopher in Greek lore named Heraclitus. In fact, he was known as The Obscure back in ancient times. Thinking of him as I do now adds a bit of cushion between the flat soles of my sneakers and the rock hard asphalt. Makes each step a bit easier; a bit smoother. Makes it possible to quicken my pace and watch the tree line whir past as the candlelit houses give way to electrified ones with Venetian blinds in the windows and novelty mailboxes at the feet of paved driveways. Makes the bright line of modern buildings on the horizon seem closer. Because Heraclitus understood me. He never met me, but he understood me. I know this because he once uttered the phrase, "Character is destiny."

The phrase is simpler in speech than in practice. Of that I can assure you, but I'm not about to cop out on my philosopher friend. And I'm not about to cop out on myself. Because if there's one person who needs to make it to Birdland, with or without Travis, it's Cordell Wheaton. The geeky, redheaded loser from High Point who embarked on his own version of an Amish rumspringa without knowing it started—and who now needs to see it through to the end.

I reach the top of a hill and emerge out of Amish country into the familiar confines of a city. Lancaster. At first, it looks like a miniature version of Philadelphia, with lines of colonial-style pubhouses pushed up against high-rises and residential row homes to spawn a hodge-podge of past meets present. Kind of like me and Levi.

The first thing I see as I emerge from the forest is a set of train tracks that runs behind the trees into the heart of town. This is my only map, and one I must follow, so I waste no time allowing it to guide me past gilded streetlamps and traffic lights wobbling on their wires. Past coffee shops and bakeries and homespun department stores all dark on the inside with their "Closed" signs hanging in the storefronts.

The city is quiet, and the night is crisp and cool for early summer. Not a soul stirs on the streets. A few cars whip past as I climb the steps of the station house and start to form a plan. The first thing I do is count my dough. Thirty-three bucks, which is amazing considering I've traveled, like, a thousand miles and I'm only six bucks short of what I started with—all thanks to the kindness of strangers, I guess.

My eyes pan up to a departure board that spans an entire wall behind the ticket booth. The only ticket I can afford is a train bound for Reading, Pennsylvania, which I take as a sign because I remember the Reading Railroad being one of my favorite spots to buy on the Monopoly board. It's also the train that leaves the soonest. In just fifteen minutes.

I fan through my bills and take a step toward the line. But then I stop. I think about my strategy and realize I'd have no way of eating or getting to New York if I spend my cash traveling from Amish country to railroad country.

I push through the door of the station and jog back down the steps two at a time until I'm back at street level in jolly, downtown Lancaster. Then I race around the block to the train yard, where old boxcars and pitiful-looking engines go to die, and where the rats and hobos roam.

Tonight, I'm lucky because I'm the only rat in town and there's not a hobo in sight. On the other side of the yard, across jagged cracks in the cement and sticky splotches of axle grease, is a chain-link fence. I reach into my backpack and pull out Cowbird's knife. I squat down beside a metal post and the mesh fencing it holds up. It looks like a stiff breeze or a half-hearted kick could topple the thing, but I'm more of a craftsman than that.

I flip the blade and wedge it between the hooks that hold the fence to the post and SNAP! I pry them loose in under a minute. I pull back on the mesh and the whole fence goes slack in the middle, enough to leave a gap between the ground and the jagged bottom. I squeeze through and find a spot beneath the platform where I can hide and wait for the train.

But I hear a voice. Then a loud CLANG! as if a heavy wrench dropped down through the workings of an engine. Then two voices. Footsteps move in close behind me. I'm frozen in the shadows between a crate that smells like rancid milk and an old tractor that hasn't run since 1940. The words "John Deere" are faded and barely legible on its face.

"George?" I hear one of the voices say somewhere close to the fence. "You see this?" The footsteps move closer.

"Looks like the work of a hitcher," another voice grumbles. "Couldn't a been more'n an hour ago cause I already checked it off on the log."

"We better go in then. Tell the boss."

I wait for the footsteps to shrink away until they sound like raindrops on a distant windshield, and then I pop out of the shadows and search the scene for a mode of escape. The only way out is through the yard or across the tracks and into the wilderness. Or, maybe, up on the platform? But that'd be insane, right? That'd be like diving into a pool of Great White Sharks with a bunch of tuna steaks strapped to my chest. That'd be like... my only viable option.

Shit.

At that moment, the doors open on the platform and a herd of people push through onto the open, cement pasture of railway departures. I have to make my move now, amid the cacophony of rolling luggage and squealing children, and the crackly voice on the speaker announcing, "Lancaster to Reading, arriving in two minutes!"

I scramble up a steel ladder below the platform, then try to casually mingle in with the crowd of passengers as best I can. No one notices the kid with dried up mud splattered on his jeans and axle grease caked on the white shell-top of his Chucks who crawls up from below the platform like a damn spider monkey.

I file into the pack behind a middle-aged couple and, I assume, their daughter, who looks to be around nine or ten-years-old. The lady cups her hand on the puffy, blue shoulders of the girl's dress and stares at the fine print on her ticket as she drifts to the end of the platform. Her husband, in his brown corduroys and sweater vest, looks like your typical absent-minded professor. He pushes the tortoise-rimmed glasses up on the bridge of his nose and fights through the crowd to remain connected to his family and keep three mobile suitcases gliding on their wheels behind him.

I stay close because, for once in my life, I have a plan.

All I have to do is stay close to this wholesome, everyday, American family and no one will suspect me of not having a ticket. Just then I hear the screech of the train whistle and the high-pitched squeal of the air brakes lock down on the tracks. The red lights on the gangway flicker and flash, and the intercom crackles to life with a nasally voice that repeats, "Lancaster to Reading approaching the station. Lancaster to Reading. Please stand clear of the tracks and behind the yellow safety line on the platform."

I'm about as close to my foster family as I can get without opening up their luggage and crawling inside. The train ambles up then screeches to a stop. The doors slide open. A portly gentleman, hole puncher in hand, steps out in his red coat with brass buttons and his rounded Amtrak cap.

"All a-BOARD!" he shouts. The entire mass of people flows forward like a school of salmon fighting its way upstream. The ticket taker snaps tickets out of hands and clips them with his contraption in one motion as the passengers board the train.

I approach with my new "family," being careful to keep the professor and his wife between myself and the ticket taker. My ninja-like evasion techniques are no match for a set of sixty-year-old eyes behind a pair of thick lenses. My heart races at a million beats per minute as I squeeze through the doors, hang a quick left through a train car that bustles with passengers stowing their luggage overhead and underfoot, and slip into the bathroom. I lock the door and wait, knowing the ticket taker will make another round in a moment or two, going seat to seat to confirm each passenger has paid the fare.

After the whistle sounds once and the train is fully up to speed, I decide it's safe to venture outside. I slide the bathroom door open and poke my head out. There's nothing in sight but passengers snoozing on pillows and toddlers jamming goldfish crackers in their mouths, so I give myself the all clear and march down the aisle like any normal passenger who shelled out the thirty bucks for a ticket. Instead, I think I'll spend some of the money I saved in the bar car.

The bar car is several carriages ahead, which I find after strolling down a couple of vacant aisles and passing through the heavy doors at the end of each vehicle, feeling the cool rush of wind through the gaps between each one as I pass to another. I don't notice a single Amtrak employee on my way to the bar, and when I get there I start to feel pretty sure of myself—like, a bonafide badass.

I take a stool on the side of the bar and order a can of Pepsi—straight outta North Carolina—and a chicken salad sandwich on a croissant. I lean back and watch the lights of a distant, nameless, Pennsylvania coal town rush past through the trees beyond the long, portrait window behind the bar. I take a few bites of the sandwich and wash it down with long gulps of Pepsi. I even start to relax a little and enjoy the journey. That is, until a hand clamps down on my shoulder and a gravelly voice behind me says, "May I see your ticket, please?"

The only words I didn't want to hear.

I cock my head back and rise from the stool. The man's hand slips from my shoulder as I turn to face him, reaching into my pockets—really searching for a ticket that never existed. I put on a good show, scouring my back pockets, the inside of my backpack and even under the elastic band of my socks. The ticket taker grows restless. His lips sit crooked and perturbed under a thin, black mustache. Beads of perspiration glisten under the smooth, plastic bill of his cap.

"Son, can I help you find your ticket?" he asks with a sigh.

"Uhh...sure," I say when I realize I'm down to the Hail Mary pass part of the game. "Maybe it fell under the bar?" The ticket taker shoots me a look of disbelief, then relents and plays along.

I wait for him to bend down and poke his pointy nose around under the stool. That's when I tip the stool over and take off running, like I'm involved in a damn prison break and the snipers on the towers have every rifle trained on me.

I'm through the end of the car before Secret Ticket Agent Man is back on his feet. I fire through the next two train cars and two after that, pushing past passengers as they attempt to pull cell phones or makeup kits from the overhead luggage. They cast shocked expressions on me like I'm some kind of international criminal on the run from federal agents.

I have no clue what my endgame is, though the image of me heaving my own body off a moving train—like I did back in Carolina—flashes through my mind as I run. It may well be my best—and only—option. If I can get to the front of the train, I might have a better chance of gaining leverage on the jump—or maybe that's what I keep telling myself as I delay the inevitable pain and potential death that's about to come my way if I'm lucky enough to escape the ticket ninja.

"Stop him!" someone shouts—presumably my ticket-taking friend—as I hit another door and scurry between one car and into the next. I'm well ahead of my pursuer now. There's no way in hell he'll catch me if I can keep moving at the same speed I'm—

And that's when something slides out in the aisle. A flash. Something I can't decipher in the split second before it slams into my feet and takes my legs out from under me. My shoulder crashes down on the carpeted aisle and, before I can plant my hands on the ground for an attempt at a second flight, I'm screwed. Pinned to the deck with my chin on the floor and the weight of three ticket takers on top of me. My eyes are trained on the bottoms of seats and scuffed up shoes and the dastardly object that prevented my escape and guaranteed my capture.

A small, blue suitcase. I stare at it as a hand reaches down and nudges it back under a seat. A seat that's occupied by a middle-aged man in tortoise shell spectacles, brown corduroys, and a nerdy-looking sweater vest.

A Bird in Hand

"Son, we'll need identification if you want out," the frosty-haired gentleman says. I grind my molars together so hard it's like two porcelain platters rattling against each other in the dishwasher. I don't budge. Don't blink. I barely have the energy to breathe, but I'm sure as hell not about to share my identity with a couple of railroad heavies who'd spent the last twenty minutes dragging me across the railway platform and through a crowded station house with a million traveling spectators training their eyes on me. I'm not about to sell myself out like Travis had or twice as fast as my fake, foster family had, so these two keystone cops can lock me up in a holding cell reserved for odd stowaways and supreme badasses like myself.

All I do is stare down at the surface of the plastic folding table and trace the tiny patterns of concentric circles that'd been melted into its fibers in the factory. The frosty-haired train inspector stares at me, his brown eyes soft and expectant, his eyebrows rounded and serene, waiting for a response that will never come.

His counterpart, the bad cop, is different. He stands over the frosty-haired inspector with a chunky fist planted on the table, his nostrils flared wide, and the tiny blood vessels in his eyes pulsing and twitching on end. After ten more seconds of watching me sit there in silence staring at the table, the bad cop loses his cool and pounds his fist on a stack of folders sitting beside him. A trail of sweat rolls down the side of his face, over a neck that's so thick and rough-skinned it's like his head is balanced atop a fire hydrant, and soaks into the powder blue collar of his Amtrak-approved dress shirt.

"You don't know your own name, son?" he bellows as I lean back in my chair.

I don't say a word.

"You don't have a ticket. Don't have a wallet or a phone or even a goddamn set of initials written by your mama in magic marker on your underwear band? You got nothing! A puny, little twerpy nothin' like you who can't be bothered to pay for a ticket, and you expect me to believe you can't say your goddamn name out loud? That's a load of bull—"

"Now hold on there, Hal," the frosty-haired gentleman says in a calm and soothing voice. "Let's give the young man a chance. He's nervous. That right, son? Nerves got your tongue?"

I clamp my jaw shut tighter than before and trace circles on the table like I'm there all alone. That's when big, bad Hal loses his shit.

"God damn it!" he shouts. He tries to push past the frosty haired official and reach across the table to squeeze the life out of me. "Get off me, Wally! Let me at him! I'll—"

His voice breaks off and he goes icy cool. He wipes the sweat from his thick upper lip with the back of a hairy forearm.

"Son," he continues in a tone just above a whisper, "we don't take kindly to thieves and stowaways here at Amtrak." His voice rises in volume by one click on each subsequent word until the anger boils out of his ears again. "Now tell me your name, you little son of a bitch! Do it now or the real police will have you in the slammer in two seconds! You listening to me, son?! Your goddamn name is BLANK! Fill in the blank, you little thief!"

The monster named Hal is fit to explode. All the veins bulge from his porky neck. His face is blood red. My eyes glisten with the tears I've been holding back since I crashed face-first in the aisle and felt the weight of three fully-grown ticket takers pounce on me. Hal rambles right through them like they feed his rage. Wally sits half-smiling, half-yawning in his chair as if this sort of thing happens every day in the Reading station house.

"You think crocodile tears'll save you? Not today!" Hal screams. "Not on my watch! Now, open that filthy mouth and spit out that worthless name of yours!"

I don't budge.

"I said NOW!"...

An explosion from the chamber.

Slow motion.

Travis struggles with the shooter. Knocks the gun from his hands in the time it travels to us.

The bullet.

Meant for a tire or a fender. Meant as a warning. An act of pointless, macho rage.

The world splinters into a million shards of glass. They strangle me. Cut off my air. Constrict until my chest is heavy and tight.

"CooRRRDY! No! No! CORRRRDY!!!"

Dad slams the brakes.

I instinctively raise my hand to the back of my head. It feels warm and wet. Something is not right. Adrenaline kicks in. Then fear and panic. My eyes grow wide as I begin to mouth the words "Oh my god ..."

Then darkness.

The interrogation room flicks back into view. My hands clamp down on the table with white-knuckled terror. Hal and Wally are silent. Wide-eyed. Terrified. Neither of them move or speak as I kick and twist and throw jabs. I'm somehow aware of a high-pitched, wailing screech that is unrelenting and unidentifiable until it rings in my own voice box and I realize I'm the only possible producer of the sound. And I can't seem to stop myself.

Hal and Wally spring into motion, more careful and less verbally-abusive than before. Wally's frosty hair bobs up and down as he spins around the table, grabs both of my arms and tries to pin them behind me. I slither around and feel my knuckles slap against something hard before Hal dives on me with all his weight. The air rushes from my lungs. All goes silent until I scream my head off again. The two officials scramble around with me on the tile floor. They pin my hands flat.

Shit gets so out of hand as I'm screaming and cursing that it takes a second or two for me or either of the officials to notice the door of the interrogation room swing open and an imposing shadow to loom over us.

Then I hear it.

"Cordy?"

All three of us stop squirming on the floor and look to the doorway.

"What the hell are you doing under there?"

The voice is welcome, reassuring, and instantly recognizable. I know right away it's Cowbird.

Hal and Wally recognize the voice too, because they pop off the tiles and rush to the doorway like they're about to salute a five-star general. Which is weird.

I lie there under the table fighting for breath, trying to figure out what the hell just happened and whether or not Cowbird's really standing there in the doorway of a railway station interrogation room in Reading, Pennsylvania or if I've gone full-blown crazy.

"Mr. Winchester," Hal says in a jolly voice that's more fit for a shopping mall Santa Claus than some maniac who, moments ago, wanted me dead and buried. "Friend, I haven't seen you in months. Where you been hiding?"

"Here and there," Cowbird says, trying not to play into the random small talk. I lift myself off the floor and find the comfort of the folding chair. Cowbird makes eye contact with me. He doesn't say a word, but his glare shoots straight through to my soul. He shakes his head slow enough to make me feel like a total idiot and a traveling fraud. Hal and Wally notice the interchange and find their way back on topic.

"You know this boy?" Wally asks Cowbird. "Cause a coupla the crew from Lancaster caught him riding without a ticket. Brazen about it too. Just sitting there in the bar car sipping cola like he owns the damn train company."

"Course I know this boy," Cowbird says. The gold hoops in both ears twinkle from the doorway. His lanky arms and the eagle tattoo on his forearm hang out from under the sleeves of a bright orange t-shirt with the words "Love Everyone" printed on the front in white letters. "He's supposed to be traveling with me. Don't know how we got separated."

"That so?" Hal asks. "You mean you take responsibility for him?"

"Yes, sir."

"And you'll pay his fare?"

Cowbird reaches into his pocket and peels off a few bills. "Keep the change," he says, "for your trouble."

Hal smooths the bills between his fingers. He pockets them and turns to face me. "You're lucky," he says, "to have fine, hard-working people looking out for you. Or else things might not have gone so…smoothly."

"It's a good thing," Wally adds, "that we happen to know Mr. Winchester here. Been making deliveries to the station for…oh, how long'd you say?"

"Long enough to make friends." He nods at Wally and Hal. They nod back.

"Well, ok. I guess you're free to go," Hal says to me. "But, son?"

I don't say a word because I'm completely freaked out of my mind.

"The gentleman here asked you a question, Cordell. Are you going to answer him?"

"Uhhh….yessir?"

"Son," Hal continues, "don't let me catch you riding through my station again. Paid or unpaid. I couldn't care less. You hear?"

"Yessir," I reply in the voice of a chipmunk.

"Good. Now get out of here before I change my mind."

I grab my backpack from the corner of the room and throw it over my shoulders. When I approach the doorway, Cowbird hooks one of his thumbs through one of my shoulder straps and pulls me tight to his hip. He hustles me out of there, down a long, dark hallway deep in the bowels of the station.

"I didn't think—"

"Shhhh!" Cowbird hisses at me.

"But I didn't want to—"

"I said SHHHHH!"

Cowbird tightens his grip on the strap and quickens our pace until we hit a door at the end of the hallway. We pop out in a trucking lot abuzz with idling engines and ripe with diesel fumes. Old Sally is parked at the far end. As soon as the cool air hits our faces, Cowbird springs back to life, and he's not in a great mood.

"Cordy," he snipes, "what the hell are you doing here?"

"I didn't—"

"SHHH....not done yet," he chirps. "Man, I went and gift-wrapped this journey. Sent you halfway up the East Coast for free. With room and board! And this is where I find you! Out here in the Pennsylvania corn fields? And now you're sneaking on trains and shit?"

"I had no choice," I say. Then I think for a second. About honesty and reality. "Well, I guess I did have a choice, but I made the wrong one. I thought—"

"Thought? Shit. There's not an ounce of thinking going on in that head of yours." He pokes my left temple with his index finger. "Where's all that philosophy shit you were spouting now, huh? What about the dude who said that thing about 'Character is—'"

"Destiny?"

Cowbird shakes his head and stifles a laugh as we approach the truck.

"You know everything about these ancient dudes, don't you?"

"It's Heraclitus, and he—"

"Well I bet Heraclitus sure as hell doesn't think your destiny is worth a damn at this point."

"I wouldn't expect—"

"Because there aren't too many folks stealing fares from Amtrak with enough character to stay out of prison. You hear me?" I nod. "It's a good thing I got enough character for the both of us. Good thing I cashed some of it in or your face would still be attached to that tile back there. It's a good thing you're stupid enough to almost get run over by Old Sally way back in Mt. Airy or you'd be—"

At this point, Cowbird stops, because he notices the faucet has turned on again and I can't stop it.

I collapse on the bottom step below Old Sally's cab, and Cowbird squeezes in next to me. We sit there for a few minutes in silence, tears streaming down my face and sobs wracking my body. Cowbird pats my back and lets me unload all the guilt, sadness, and frustration I've been holding inside ever since I found out about Dad's illness and realized we'd never be the Wheatons again unless I did something.

"I'm sorry," I tell him.

"Oh yeah?" Cowbird asks. "For what?"

"For having no character. For getting in the way of my destiny. For crying. For everything."

"You don't need to apologize to me," he says. "Only one person can forgive you for something like this."

"Who's that?"

Cowbird pats me on my knee and smiles. "I thought *you* were the philosopher. Shouldn't you already know the answer?"

"But you had to save my life…again."

He lets out a short burst of laugher. "Save your life? From those two dudes?" He lets out another quick laugh and shakes his head before he goes serious again. "Cordy, you think the road runs in a straight line?"

"No," I say. "Roads wind. They go uphill. Downhill. Through tunnels. Over bridges. Roads are anything but straight."

"Think about that, Mr. Philosophy Man. But do it in the cab. I have a schedule to keep."

I get off my butt and start up the stairs. "Where are we going?"

"Montclair, New Jersey, about thirty minutes outside of New York City…oh, and I forgot to mention, it might get a little crowded on your side of the cab."

I turn to face Cowbird with my hand about to pull open the door. He shrugs and I finish the job. I squeeze in the cab next to a bunch of coats and blankets piled in the middle of the seat. I poke it with my index finger and the thing springs to life. The center of the pile opens up and a head pops out like a Jill in a Jack-in-the-Box.

"You have gotta be kidding me!" she says when she sees my face.

"You?" I gasp.

"Let's not make this a thing, OK?" Emma Rose, no last name, says. "We have a long drive ahead. I don't need to hear a bunch of whining and self-loathing for the next couple of hours."

Great. Maybe I should have let Cowbird feed me to the Amtrak wolves.

How to Listen to a Ballgame

We're about a hundred feet out of the trucking lot when Emma Rose, no last name, starts in on me. It's like our conversation never ended in those annoying moments we shared before I flung myself from a moving train. Like she hadn't taken a breath since the last time we met.

"I see we're back to saving our little man here from falling on his bum-bum and getting a boo-boo," she says to no one in particular. No one responds, so Emma Rose pours it on extra thick. "Let's give him his bah-bah and help him sit straight in his high chair."

"For God's sake, will you please shut the hell up?" I say. "It's been five minutes and I'm already tired of hearing your voice."

"Let me guess," Cowbird says, flicking the turn signal and pulling Old Sally back on the interstate, "you know each other."

"Affirmative," Emma Rose says.

"Interesting," Cowbird says. "You mind if I ask how?"

Neither one of us says a word, our arms folded flat across our chests. We stare through the windshield at the dark hills above the city of Reading. On the horizon, I can see the sharp outline of a Chinese-style pagoda perched on a ridge, its edges trimmed in brilliant, red light, like an exotic fortress guarding the city. Beside it, carved into the tree line, is a bald-faced rock structure that looks like the final phase of a stone quarry. At some point in time, a brave graffiti artist had scaled the rock face to paint a massive peace symbol that stands three stories high. It projects itself over the city like a pacifistic Batman signal. I take this as a personal message and decide to make a peace-keeping attempt between me and Emma Rose, if for nothing else than to make the next few hours less annoying.

"We met on a train," I tell Cowbird. "The one I hopped right before I met you."

"You mean the one you departed in a dying swan dive?" Cowbird interjects, not missing his chance to stir the pot.

"Yep, that one," I reply, nonchalantly.

"Wait," Emma Rose says. There's a sparkle in her eyes. "You said you *jumped* off that train? Like, onto the ground?"

"Uh-huh." I say it all cool, like I leap off trains for a living.

Emma Rose is impressed even as she wraps herself tighter in the blanket to hide her obvious fascination with the superhero sitting beside her.

"You mean, while it was moving?" Now she's grinning from ear to ear.

"Yep." I keep reeling her in. Carefully, the way you'd fight a marlin.

"Ha! What a dumbass!" she cackles like a Halloween witch.

For a second, I think Cowbird's about to jump in and cool the conversation down and tell Emma Rose, no last name, I'm anything but a dumbass. That I'm a damn philosophy scholar. But that doesn't happen.

"Dude *is* pretty dumb sometimes," Cowbird says.

He shoots me a discreet wink. Emma Rose doesn't notice because she's busy laughing her lungs up through her throat.

"Y'all should have left me at the train station," I say, tracing the red outlines of the pagoda on its reflection in the passenger window.

"Come on, Cordy, man" Cowbird says. "We're just messing with you."

"I'm not," Emma Rose says.

"Well, some of us are," Cowbird shoots back.

He snipes an unlit cigarette out of Emma Rose's mouth before she lights it in the cab. "And I told you already! You want to kill yourself, that's your own damn business. But you're not filling my lungs up with smoke, and you're not making Sally smell like a damn pool hall."

"Okay, fine," she says under her breath. "I'll wait."

"Damn right, you will," Cowbird says.

I laugh because it's nice when someone else is the dumbass for a change.

"You think it's real funny, don't you toddler boy?" Emma Rose asks, because she knows how to dish it but has never been one to take it.

"Who's talking about toddlers?" I ask. "Tell me, how long have you been in the nest?"

"The nest? What are you talking about?"

"He's talking about Old Sally here," Cowbird says. "Little story I told him about my name and the hitchers I tend to transport. I'm sort of like a hitcher-magnet."

Emma Rose's eyes go wide like she's about to say something. Something explosive. Something cutting and rude. The usual. But then she swallows most of the words. All that comes out is a soft and sullen, "Oh."

"Oh?" I ask. "That's it?"

She mumbles something into the blanket.

"What's that? I couldn't hear you under all the—"

"Since Wheeling," she blurts out. "West Virginia. You happy now? We've been on the road a few days. Maybe more."

I give her plenty of time to see the smug grin rise on my lips. "What's with the look?" she asks.

Cowbird jumps in the middle of us and says, "It means you two have more in common than you want to admit." I nod. "Also means the two of you better clamp your damn beaks down tight, cause it sounds like a bunch of seagulls flew in the window, and I'm not throwing y'all no bread crumbs."

Cowbird revs Old Sally's twin, diesel engines and barrels down the highway, while Emma Rose and I wallow in silence, watching the shale-faced inclines of Pennsylvania coal country roll down from the hills and crash at the foot of the road.

We sit in quiet contemplation for several minutes before it dawns on me we're actually at the unmistakable crossroads of a truce. One that has the potential to put a permanent lid on the mindless bickering and the chest-thumping. Cowbird's right. Behind the endless travel and the skimpy meals and the body aches from sleeping in shapes better fit for pretzels than people, Emma Rose is just like me. Alone. Abandoned. Terrified of what lies ahead and what she left behind.

"So...you ready to tell me the long version?" I ask Emma Rose. "Because I might be ready to listen."

"The long version?" she asks. "Of what?"

"On the train. Back in Carolina. You told me there was a long version of the story behind you running away and taking a machete to your last name."

Her eyes shoot down to her lap, and the fear she's been hiding behind her mask of courage is revealed, like an orange traffic cone smack in the middle of an intersection.

She looks to Cowbird like she's drowning in a squall and needs a life preserver. The famous eyebrow rises above Cowbird's left eye. "What are you waiting for? Cordy's trying to pass the olive branch. You'd better take it before he rambles on about old Greek dudes for the rest of the trip."

"Old Greek dudes?" she says, confused.

"Just tell him your story. The long version."

Emma Rose takes a deep breath and mummifies herself in the blanket. "I showed you the bruises," she says, finally making eye contact with me. "But there's more."

"More than getting beaten by a grown man?"

"Yeah…a lot more," she says. "When I finish, you won't question why I don't want to touch my last name with a five-hundred-foot pole. But you have to promise not to make jokes, Cordy. Because this is gonna be hard."

I'm startled when Emma Rose calls me by name, but my surprise turns to concern when I see her eyes. I mean, I really see them. Not like when you notice the grey flecks behind the sea of blue or the perfect ovalness of each eye sitting atop the angles of her cheek bones. Not like that. Not like the first time I looked at Emma Rose's face and knew she was more fragile than she'd ever admit. No. This is different. This is like when you look through the windows of a ritzy mansion and see the furniture covered in dust and dirty clothes strewn across the floors. This is the moment when you realize something is wrong. Really wrong. Maybe even more wrong than having an addict for a brother and a walking dead man as a father.

"I promise," I tell her. "No jokes." And I mean it.

Emma Rose takes a deep breath and exhales long and hard like she's trying to rid her body of an infectious disease. "The night I left," she says, "was the worst night of my life, and it had nothing to do with the beatings or the bruises. That stuff's been happening for as long as I can remember. I've learned to deal with it, even if it's me pretending."

"Pretending?" I ask.

"Pretending it doesn't hurt. Pretending he's not related to me. Pretending I lived a different life than the one I was stuck in."

I nod and wait for Emma Rose to wipe her eyes on the edge of the blanket.

"That night was different from all the times I answered him back or left dishes in the sink or forgot a homework assignment, and I'd take a few cracks from his belt and we'd call it even. That night, I guess I stayed up a bit later than my luck, because apparently that runs out around 11:45 pm. About the same time he came home from Sully's."

"One of his friends?" I ask.

"No. It's a dive bar in downtown Columbia. He's a regular."

Cowbird grunts. The scowl covertly disappears from his face and his jaw goes tense.

"When he got home, he was drunk as hell. Reeked something God awful, like he'd done laps in a bourbon-filled pool. I tried to steer clear of him. Locked my bedroom door, climbed into bed, and hid under the covers. Kinda like I'm doing now."

"He didn't go to bed, did he?" Cowbird asks, knowing where to coax Emma Rose at just the right moments in a story he's most likely heard since he picked Emma Rose up in Wheeling.

"No," she says. "He went to the garage and got his sledgehammer. Next thing I knew he was crashing through my bedroom door. I didn't know what to do, but I knew I was no match for a drunk asshole swinging a sledgehammer."

"How'd you escape?"

"I didn't. All I could do was let him beat the door down and take my chances. Like, maybe he'd be too drunk to do any damage."

"Was he?"

"No. He was raving mad. Worst I ever saw him. Screaming at me about how there's no locked doors in his house and how I'm his daughter so I *belong* to him."

"What an asshole," I say, not so much under my breath.

"Truly," Emma Rose says. "Well, he rushed at me while I was in bed and he got hold of one of my legs. I remember the back of his hand coming down in slow motion and cracking me across the top of my head. All I could do was kick with my one free leg and swing my arms like a windmill. I don't know how many times I hit him or he hit me because it just kept going on and on. It felt like forever. Like I was gonna die right there in that moment. Then I kicked him square in the junk. It was a lucky shot, I guess, but he let go of my leg and I was out of that bed so fast I think I went airborne for a few seconds."

"And then you ran?" I ask.

"I wish," she says. "But I was cornered. All I could do was shrink behind a dresser with all of my hair products on it and my books and a lamp. He charged me again. This time I had no protection. Not a blanket or my hands or even my feet, because he got me in a bear hug and pushed me against the wall with all of his weight and then…then…he…"

Her voice breaks off and she buries her face in the blanket until all that's left is a pile of sobbing fleece propped on Old Sally's seat.

Without thinking, my hand reaches over to rub her back. To console her. Make her feel like she's not alone. I feel her tense up, but then she grabs my hand. Her fingers interlace with mine and squeeze so tightly I think maybe I'm holding hands with Cowbird instead of Emma Rose.

Emma Rose's sobs subside to sniffling and then she's out from under the blanket with fire in her eyes. "That son of a bitch touched me," she says. "He touched me, Cordy! His own daughter!! That sickening, horrible piece of trash laid his dirty, drunken hands on me. Told me I was beautiful…how I reminded him of Mom…how any guy would be lucky to have me. I can still smell his disgusting, stale breath…can still feel the sharp whiskers on my face as he whispered in my ear."

I sit in stunned silence and watch the tears roll down her cheeks. One by one, and then too many to count all at once.

"You know what I did then, Cordy?"

"You kicked his ass," I say flatly, because I've never been more sure of something in my life. I mean, this is Emma Rose, no last name, we're talking about.

She smiles and lets out a sniffly laugh that breaks the tension in the cab. "You bet your ass I did. Got one of my hands free and smashed that lamp to bits right over the bastard's head."

"Then you ran," I say.

"Never looked back. He may be dead for all I know. Not my problem."

She releases my hand and I turn to face her. "Emma Rose?"

"Oh Lord," she grumbles. "What now?"

"Last names are overrated," I say. "And…I'm sorry."

"So am I," Cowbird adds. "No one should have to carry that kind of burden."

Emma Rose smiles, then grasps at her chance to change the subject as quickly as possible.

"So, what about you, Mr. Journeyman?"

"What *about* me?"

"You never told me why you're out here before we got interrupted and you did a half-gainer over the train tracks."

"Yeah," I say. "I kind of like it that way." I sneak a glance at Cowbird as a barometer check and notice the trick eyebrow is half way up his forehead, so I know I'm not getting out of telling my story.

"Cordy," he says just loud enough to make my skin tingle.

"Oh, alright," I say. "But then it's Greek mythology from here to Montclair."

"Not if you actually want to make it all the way to Montclair," Cowbird says with a sly grin.

"Fine," I say. "Just the story."

I tell Emma Rose about Travis and his addiction and the big showdown with my father and how he flew the nest to Philly so he could worship his pharmaceutical goddesses in the privacy of his own city. And I tell her about High Point and the John Coltrane statue and how it persuaded me, in the early hours on the morning we'd met, to poke my head out of the cave and try to bring Travis's sheet music to him and then make a pilgrimage to Birdland Jazz Club where all the problems in the Wheaton family would evaporate and everything would go back to normal.

After I brief her on the major objectives of my journey, and even some of the finer points of my trip, like the first-class ride I took in Gus's hog truck, Emma Rose asks, "So…where exactly *is* your brother? I mean, did you ever find him in Philly?"

"Yeah," I say. "I guess I did find him…in a way."

"Well…where the hell is he? Aren't you and Travis supposed to be on the way to Birdland right about now?"

"Look," I tell her, "let's just say I realized Travis wasn't the right man for the trip."

"What the hell are you talking about? Wasn't Travis the whole point of you diving out your bedroom window and off a moving train and wallowing in pig shit?"

"Yeah. He *was*. But that was before I remembered a few things about him."

For once, Emma Rose is silent with her face scrunched up in a puzzled grimace instead of her normal look of disinterest. Cowbird reaches across from the driver's seat and pats me on the knee.

"Sounds like you had a cup of Joe and some of Captain Adomi's cookies," Cowbird says.

I nod.

"Good," he says. "It's important to remember. That's the first step in allowing yourself to move on. And finding the strength to forgive."

"Forgive?" Emma Rose exclaims. "Am I the only one who has absolutely no idea what you're talking about right now?"

"Yep," I say, and Cowbird lets out a hearty chuckle, the kind where his head whips back and he slaps one of his hands down on the steering wheel.

"Look," Emma Rose says, "are you gonna let me in on the secret or am I gonna have to rattle off annoying questions for the next two hours until I force it out of you?"

I wince. "Anything but that. OK, I'll tell you."

That's when I take Cowbird and Emma Rose on a short trip through my dreams. To the warehouse. With the ropes tied around my wrists and the sting of the fiber burns forming below my hands. To the trunk of the car and to the end of a double-barreled shotgun. To the point where the masks lift off the two men and I identify the smaller one—the less dominant one—as Travis, my brother.

"Wait," Emma Rose says when my voice falls silent, "you mean your brother tried to extort his own father?"

"Yep."

"And he got the money?"

"I think so."

"And you were…a hostage?"

I don't answer this time. The silence in the cab grows heavy and thickens around us as we unwind the forbidding grasp of evil that had reached its bony fingers in each of our directions and sent our lives careening in unpredictable directions. Out of the cave, but to where? We could not tell. And, maybe, we'd never know.

That's when Cowbird pulls out his phone and passes it to me.

"I already told you," I say. "I'm not ready to call them."

"I think you are," he says, "but that's not why you're holding that thing."

"Then why?"

"Take a look."

I tap the screen. Staring back at me is an image I've seen so many times it's burned into my brain. The album cover for one of John Coltrane's most celebrated works, *Live at Birdland.*

"Fitting," I say.

Cowbird nods and says, "Plug it in and hit 'play.' I'm not just showing you pictures. I got you a surprise."

"You bought the album?" I ask. "Did I have something to do with this?"

"Don't let your head get all swelled when you hear this, Cordy, but I may have missed you a little after I dropped you in New Bern."

I smile, but I don't gloat because I'm not about to test a guy who once pulled Old Sally up on the rumble strips and told me to get out and walk right there on a desolate stretch of highway. "Go ahead," he says. "Play song number four."

"Alabama," I whisper.

"You know it?" Cowbird asks.

"Who doesn't?" I say.

"Uhhh…me," Emma Rose says when she can't take not being the center of the conversation. I decide she can use a quick education on Trane's legend, starting with one of his most important songs. I hit "play" on Cowbird's phone and lean back in the seat to let the opening notes of sadness wash over the cab before I start my lecture.

Then I say, "Trane wrote this song in 1963, a few months after the bombing of an Alabama church."

"Not just any church," Cowbird grunts. "A black church. In the heart of Dixie."

"Killed four, young girls," I say, "and got the attention of Dr. Martin Luther King, Jr."

"Dr. King delivered the eulogies of those four lost souls like they were his own daughters," Cowbird says.

As he says this, Trane blows forlorn notes of somber reality through his tenor sax while the rest of the band rattles off responses to his cries on the keys of the piano, the strings of a stand-up bass, and the tight vellum of a drum.

"Scholars say Trane took Dr. King's speech and translated it into music," I say. "That he captured the reverend's voice in notes and measures, and created an anthem for the Civil Rights Movement." The cymbals crash and Trane's saxophone rises out of mourning and comes to life with a high-pitched squeal drenched in honey and a lightning-quick key change. "See right there?" I say to Emma Rose. "He's coming out of his funk."

"Like Dr. King," Cowbird says. "Always bringing people to life. Bringing them together. Giving them hope in the face of despair."

"Pulling them out of the mud?" Emma Rose asks.

"Exactly," I say. "And Dr. King knew Trane had the gifts to make it happen. A great philosopher, Dr. King—"

"Here we go with another philosophy lesson," Cowbird says with a sly smirk rising on his lips. But I don't let it stop me. I'm on a roll.

"He once said, 'Jazz speaks for life, and if you think for a moment you'll realize it takes the hardest realities of life and puts them into music. Triumphant music.'"

"Then you know why I wanted you to hear the song," Cowbird says.

"I do," I tell him.

"I don't," Emma Rose says a second later.

"It's because evil is something that's never going to disappear from this world, and it ain't choosy neither. It can pop up from below or drop down from above. Doesn't matter who you are, the color of your skin, how much money you have or anything. And it'll take a great big bite out of your ass from time to time. There's no avoiding it."

"But you have to keep on going," I say. "You've got to keep on moving."

"Yes, you gotta keep on moving," Cowbird repeats.

Emma Rose wraps the blanket around her again and the weight of her head presses down on my shoulder as the last few notes of Trane's "Alabama" ring out through Sally's speakers.

"You don't mind, do you?" she asks. I feel Emma Rose's warmth against my skin. My eyes grow heavy and then…

I pop out from under the small section of blanket Emma Rose afforded me. She has me by both shoulders and is shaking me like a ragdoll. I feel my eyes roll around in the sockets a few times.

Beside the train tracks. Familiar. Walking. The dry brush swishes against the back of my legs.

I'm drawn to the door of a warehouse. Fixated. Like a tractor beam urges me forward.

My hand hits the latch and I push inside.

Something moves in the corner. A struggle in human form. Faceless in the dim light. I approach. Listen to the heavy breaths. The occasional sniffle. A phlegmy COUGH! that jolts electricity through my body.

He's blindfolded. Both hands tied behind his back. A line of dried blood under one nostril. I lift the blindfold.

It's Travis.

I reach down to untie him. To run him from this place I've come to know well. But he's far away. Further than I can reach. The warehouse floor expands. Fills in with cement. Travis and I drift apart.

I stretch. Reach for his fingertips. Press against the weight of inertia and dread and loss.

Inches away. Then centimeters. Then millimeters. Then a hand reaches in from behind. It clamps around my throat ... and I know he's gone.

"Alright!" I shout out of nowhere. "I'm up!"

Emma Rose takes a deep breath and exhales through puffed-out cheeks. Cowbird shakes his head like he's seen this routine before. Because he has.

They glance at each other, but neither of them says a word. Their looks say it all. And all I can do is quickly look away so I don't have to tell them what I'd just awakened from. I gaze straight ahead at nothing in particular and wait for the remnants of fog to lift from my eyes.

The massive, stone outline of an arena is framed by the windshield. Maybe a stadium? I can't tell.

"Last stop," he says. "City of Montclair, New Jersey. Home of the Jackals."

"Who are the Jackals?" Emma Rose asks.

"Baseball! One of my favorite teams," Cowbird exclaims, "cause nothing helps you forget all the bullshit like a game of baseball."

"Come on," I say to Emma Rose. I help her down from the cab and we file in behind Cowbird. "I'll teach you how to listen to a ballgame."

As we walk the cement gangway to Yogi Berra Stadium—one of America's great public squares where music and sport converge to form a national identity—I walk with my head held high and a broad grin across my face.

I know I'm now a stone's throw from my ultimate destination.

Nothing is Something

It's probably no surprise I failed to teach Emma Rose how to listen to a baseball game. It wasn't that she lacked a desire to learn the ancient gift Cowbird passed down to me, or that she didn't understand the game or anything. It was…well, it kind of went like this:

"So…you close your eyes as the batter steps in the box. Right before the pitch," I say as the Jackals three-hole hitter digs into the batter's box and glares at the lanky lefty on the mound. Cowbird and I fall right into the cadence. Through sheer instinct, we find ourselves balanced on the front edge of our seats as the pitcher rubs his hand over the word Quebec that's stitched across his chest in light blue script and stares back in at the hitter. Emma Rose doesn't flinch. She appears completely unmoved by the drama. You might even say bored.

"Like this?" she squeaks out in this sing-songy voice that makes me think there's no hope of her ever taking this kind of thing seriously. Then she closes her eyes so tight I think her eyeballs might pop out of her ears.

"Yeah," I say, suddenly hopeful. "Just like that. Then you clear your senses, let your ears and your mind paint the picture."

"Paint a picture?" she asks with her eyes still clamped shut and her lips curling into a sneer. "You're serious?"

"It works," I say. "All you have to do is listen, picture it, and guess what's happening in the game."

Her eyes are wide open now and she stares at me like I'm the world's most obvious moron. "And you're sure we can't, like, just watch the game instead?"

"The whole point is—"

She snaps a hand over my mouth. Her eyelids clamp shut as the batter swings and CRACK! The crowd erupts.

"Double in the left center field gap," Emma Rose grumbles in unaffected monotone.

Quebec's center fielder tosses the ball to the cutoff man from the warning track. The Jackals baserunner pulls up at second base and adjusts his belt buckle.

"Damn," I say. "You're good."

"You never asked if I played baseball," she says.

Cowbird rocks back in his seat and laughs so hard he almost chokes on his popcorn.

"How long did you play softball?" I ask.

"Baseball," she says. "Since I was three. About the only thing that worthless sack of shit did for me."

After that, I kind of figured Emma Rose was up to speed on the whole "listening to a ballgame" thing and I spend the rest of the game testing my skills with Cowbird and smiling on the inside each time I look over and catch Emma Rose digging the game.

We had fun, which is more than I can say about most of my days in recent memory. Maybe Cowbird's right about the game of baseball. Maybe it is the best medicine to help you forget the bullshit. At least for nine innings. Until you walk back through the turnstiles and loosen yourself from the grip of the entire spectacle—the crowd, the banter, the feeling of camaraderie, and the game itself—and you cross the vast ocean of blacktop in the parking lot and wash up in front of Old Sally with the shadows of your only two friends stretching past you under the streetlights. And then the bullshit rushes back in at you. Gets in your face. Because it stinks to the high heavens you won't ever see them again.

"I'm headed west," Cowbird says in the heat of the solemness and silence that blankets us. "It doesn't make sense to come with me since Birdland is in the opposite direction. Looks like this is goodbye, Mr. Cordy. Time to drop you off at another nest."

I nod. It's all I can do because I'm choking back tears, and the words I want to say are knotted up in the back of my throat like a ball of tangled yarn.

"You know," Cowbird says, "sometimes I think it'd be easier to stomp on the gas pedal when I see someone on the side of the road. Just keep going and ignore the fact I saw them. But then I'd just be lying to myself. I was born to care for people. Even with my surroundings changing from minute to minute, mile to mile, it's how I do my part. It's how I make sure others have it easier than I did."

"You do it well," I say, forcing the words out like machine gun fire before they spark tears.

"Promise you'll remember to adapt to your surroundings, Cordy, cause that's the only way you'll overcome your obstacles."

"I promise," I say.

"And remember, it's hard to adapt when you can't balance on the ground beneath your feet. When you can't tell the color of the sky overhead. But I don't need to tell you that because it looks like you got all that cave shit figured out already."

"Yessir," I say. "You know you sound kind of like John Dewey right now? He'd be proud."

"The Dewey decimal system dude?" Emma Rose blurts out.

"No," I say. "That's Melvil Dewey. John Dewey was a psychologist and a brilliant philosopher from, like, a hundred years ago. He said, 'experience is what people do and suffer, desire and enjoy, see, believe, imagine.'"

"Oh yeah?" Emma Rose says. "And what the hell does that have to do with Cowbird?"

"Because he's saying the people we bump into by chance, and the things we decide to do, are what make meaning for us in the world. A world that can change overnight."

I reach out to shake Cowbird's hand for the last time, but instead he hands me his phone.

"We're not finished yet," he says.

I know what he's suggesting—that I call Mom and Dad and tell them I'm alive and I'll be home soon and everything will be alright. The whole time I sat there watching the Jackals beat the crap out of the Capitales, I knew this moment would come. But now it's here—and I have no clue what to say to my parents.

I give Cowbird a look that says, "Really?"

He raises the trick eyebrow and nods.

No words. Just action.

I dial the number to our house on Brookside Drive and listen to the phone ring. Once. My heart pounds. I wonder if the spectators piling out of Yogi Berra Stadium will be able to hear Mom's voice shouting at me through my end of the receiver. Twice. The edges of my eyelids tingle and burn as I struggle to hold back the waterworks. Three times. And that's it. The voicemail answers and I hear the long BEEEP! I stand there like a sphinx until I realize I can record a quick message and push this nightmare off into the future—at least for another day or two.

"Mom…Dad," I say. "It's Cordy…Cordy Wheaton…uh, your son. I'm okay, and I want you to know I'll be home soon. I miss you—BEEEP!" The voicemail cuts me off, but Cowbird and Emma Rose don't know that. They look somewhat satisfied by my attempt.

"They weren't home," I tell them. "I left a message."

"Better than nothing," Cowbird says.

"Barely," Emma Rose adds.

Without even thinking about it, I throw my arms around her and squeeze her to my chest before she gets a chance to fire off any more commentary. When I try to pull away she holds on. Refuses to let go, which is weird at first, until I realize she has no one in the world except me. And Cowbird, I guess, but both Emma Rose and I know he's a lone bird despite his love of all forms of life.

"How'd you like to see a show?" I ask with her arms still draped behind my neck. "At Birdland. Not, like, a date or anything. Just, like—"

"You mean it?" she asks. "You'd invite me to your, like, secret lair?"

"I don't know if I'd call it a secret lair," I say, "but, yeah, I could use a partner. I mean, someone who's willing to listen to my Trane stories and talk philosophy and stuff."

"I can do that," she says.

"I guess you'll do," I say.

Emma Rose lets out a fake, little gasp as I wriggle away from her and pretend to smooth out the wrinkles in my clothes—like I'm mildly annoyed to have her tag along with me to Birdland instead of downright thrilled. Emma Rose rolls her eyes at me, so I'm pretty sure she doesn't buy my act.

I reach in my bag and pull out Cowbird's knife. "Came in handy," I say. "Just like you told me."

"Well, good," he says, taking it from my outstretched hand and admiring the rounded smoothness of the handle. He slips the knife in his pocket and pulls out a wad of bills.

"Now to buy me some insurance," he says.

"We don't need your—"

"Nonsense," he tells me. "I want to be sure both of my eggs make it to the right nest this time."

He hands me a few bills and motions for me to pocket them.

"Bus stop's at the end of this driveway. Right along Route 3. Jump on the next one. Tell the driver you're headed to the city. You'll know it when you get there. If you're lucky, you'll get there for the late show at Birdland. And if you're really lucky, they might even let you in."

We spend a few minutes saying our goodbyes and taking a final sit inside Old Sally's cab, before Emma Rose and I watch Cowbird's dependable old lady curl around the corner and speed off past Yogi Berra Stadium. With a honk of the horn, Sally shrinks into the distance until she's a low rumble on the horizon.

We hop on the next bus along the bustling, four-lane highway that is Route 3, just as Cowbird instructed. We pay the fare to Port Authority Station in Midtown Manhattan.

It's weird. Emma Rose usually has no problem holding up her end of a conversation. Most of the time, she finds a way to step right past her side and steal a huge chunk of someone else's conversation. But she doesn't say much as we sit there on the back of a Septa cruiseliner and watch the strip malls and the full-size malls and the auto malls slide past beyond the shoulder of the road.

In fact, she doesn't say a word. Not even when the roadway winds through murky islands of North Jersey marshland with the probing heads of the feather grasses nodding to and fro, or when the bus dips below the Hudson River and into a white-tiled tube filled with bluish light known as the Lincoln Tunnel, or when we pop out on the other side and the bus rolls into the massive bus and train depot on Forty-Second Street in the heart of New York City. She grips my hand until I think the circulation will be cut off and stares at the back of her seat like she's lost deep inside her head.

"You okay?" I ask when the air brakes lock down and the passengers pile past us down the aisle.

Emma Rose's eyelids flicker. She comes to life and releases my hand from her death grip.

"I'm good," she says, subdued but at least conscious. Once we're out of the bus and fighting our way through a crowd of travelers in the main terminal, Emma Rose decides to open up to me about what had her looking so dang catatonic on the bus earlier.

"It's weird without him," she says over the sound of rampant footsteps and random announcements on the terminal.

"You mean Cowbird?"

"Yeah, it's like I don't know how to act around you," she says.

"That didn't bother you before you met Cowbird. You didn't exactly hold back."

I direct Emma Rose past a never-ending line of fast-food restaurants, cell phone stores, and unmarked office space until we hit the main entrance and spill out onto Forty-Second Street—the epicenter of the free world. Times Square sits before us draped in neon lights that crawl so far up the buildings and into the clouds that we have to crane our necks at ninety-degree angles to take it all in.

On the sidewalk right in front of the bus terminal, a crowd gathers around a group of teens and their boombox and cheer the group on as they twist and spin and stand on their heads right there on the asphalt.

Across the street, a man in a cowboy hat and not much else strums an unrecognizable country ditty into an acoustic guitar. Men and women in business suits with fancy, leather briefcases swim past like salmon.

The traffic is a stream of moving machinery and blaring car horns. A constant chorus. But there's a pattern. It's not as random as it may sound to a traveler who never learned how to listen. To really listen.

Like Cowbird taught me.

And like Travis taught me.

There's the underbrush of leather soles on the sidewalk—the percussive swoosh that sets it all in motion. Then the background bass of the boombox sets the time at street level. The brakes of a taxi squeal and it's the long drone of a horn. The sound floats on the exhaust fumes. Up and down the cavern of brownstones and high rises, and spirals into the clouds.

It's jazz.

Every waking second of it.

Every vehicle provides a unique note, and the city helps it to congeal and to combine and to push its way through concrete arteries in one, fluid melody.

It's New York City.

It's jazz music.

It's no wonder Trane found a way to heal his soul here.

I grab Emma Rose's wrist and lead her to the curb, where a vendor with a pointy goatee and a frayed Yankees cap stands in front of a cart with a yellow beach umbrella sticking up from the sidewalk. "What can I get you?" he spits out at warp speed.

"Two dogs with mustard, please" I tell him.

"Two dirty water dogs, coming up," he says. In three seconds flat, the dogs are in the buns, wrapped in wax paper, slathered in mustard, and in our hands. I slip the vendor a few bucks and Emma Rose and I lean against the wall of the Port Authority terminal and dig in.

"I never knew a hot dog could taste so good," I say with my mouth stuffed.

"Blame it on the famine," she says, and it suddenly starts to feel like she's back. The old, annoying, witty, sarcastic Emma Rose I kind of missed more than I ever thought possible.

"Listen," she says. "I'm sorry I got weird and freaked out after Cowbird left. I got used to feeling safe for a while, and then it dawned on me I'd have to sharpen my claws again. Be on high alert."

"I can protect you," I say.

"Oh boy. I thought you were trying to make me feel better," she says—and that's when I know she's officially back to badass status.

"Shut up," I say, then I grab her hot dog and take a big bite out of it. Her face gets twisted and she mouths the word "gross," but I know she's as hungry as I am, so she gratefully accepts the half-eaten dog when I hand it back to her.

"Do you agree with what Cowbird said?" Emma Rose asks. "All that adapting crap? About how our interactions have some kind of purpose that leads us places."

"Yeah, of course," I say. "I mean, everything I've seen and done since I left High Point adds up to what Cowbird said word for word. Why doubt him?"

"I don't know," she says. "I guess I got to thinking how we're all just aimlessly wandering around on this floating rock and how we keep randomly bumping into each other and pissing each other off. Like us two," she says with a wink.

"You're talking about nihilism," I reply. "The belief that *nothing* matters. That all of our efforts are ultimately pointless, and that nothing we do or say makes a difference."

"Yep. That sounds about right," Emma Rose says. "Write that up, put it between a hardcover and title it 'Nihilism: The Biography of Emma Rose' and you'll have yourself a bestseller."

"Not if you tell the truth," I snap back.

"Don't start, Cordy. I told you my story. If you think I'm full of shit let me walk back inside that—"

"No, no…I don't think you're full of shit. I just don't think life is pointless."

She stares at me with a look of perplexion.

"I mean…you're here. Right? And I'm here. I may have lost Travis and my family turned to shit, but I ran into you…and Cowbird…and a lot of other people I never would have met and learned from…and that's definitely not nothing. I mean, it's something, isn't it?"

She smiles at me from behind her hot dog bun. "Yeah," she says. "I guess it is something."

"And who's to say whether any of that is random. It could be fate. Like the ancient Greeks…"

But before I can finish my sentence, we hear a whistle. And the fog drapes over my eyes again—just for an instant—and my hearing goes dull and the echoes:

Remember this one?

Travis always

used to play…

The street flashes back a split-second later, and I realize it's not a train whistle nor the screech of brakes or the honey-drenched squeal of a saxophone. Nope, it's a whistle-whistle. The ones you see in the mouths of police officers as they rush through the doors of the Port Authority bus terminal, pointing and shouting and training their eyes directly on you.

"Shit. They found us!" Emma Rose exclaims as my eyes bug out of my head.

"Run!" I shout.

Our half-eaten hot dogs splatter on the sidewalk as we start to race down the most crowded thoroughfare in America. Our only hope is to make it to Birdland before the police catch up with us.

On the Way to Birdland

My hand tightens around Emma Rose's wrist and I drag her down Forty-Second Street with New York City's finest on our tails. The sidewalk is packed with pedestrians, but the commotion and the police whistles split them down the seam and give Emma Rose and I the dubious, yet Moses-like ability to part the sea with the wave of our hands. The bystanders huddle against skyscraper walls on one side and cower behind parking meters on the other. Some of them cheer us on and I catch one person shouting "hell yeah, stick it to the man!" as we rush past.

I yank Emma Rose's arm and we sprint over old fliers and newspapers, food cartons, and stray scraps of discarded food. We push through a pocket of onlookers and race down a narrow alleyway between a hotel and an Irish pub.

Our footsteps echo off the brickface as the flashes of doorside lanterns whip past like hashmarks on the highway. A hundred feet back, at the opening of the alley, the cops make a conspicuous appearance like a herd of wild buffalo trampling through Manhattan.

I spot a deserted stairwell on the street corner that leads down to the crapworks of the city. The New York City subway system. A modern marvel, and a perfect cover for two idiot kids trying to blend in with their surroundings.

"Down here!" I shout, twisting my head back to check the alley. No cops in sight, so we're in luck for now.

I bound down the stairs two at a time, with Emma Rose on my heels until we reach a turnstile. A group of transit cops swarm the front of the train platform, so the last thing we want to do is jump the gate and draw attention to ourselves. At the same time, the clock is ticking and our officer friends are bound to rumble down the subway stairs at any moment.

A ripped-up beach blanket lies on the ground beside the turnstile with a bunch of knock-off merchandise spread upon it. A man with a scratchy voice barks out his wares, as he tries to spark conversation with anyone who will listen, scratching out sales to make his living.

"Check it out, man" he says to me. "I got your blenders, your t-shirts, authentic handbags. Anything you need. Hats, gloves—"

"You say you got hats?" I ask him.

"What are you doing, Cordy?" Emma Rose exclaims, panicked. "We—"

"I'll give you five bucks for two of those," I say to the street vendor, pointing at a pair of baseball caps with the word *Yankies* embroidered on the front in white, thread lettering.

"Five each," he says. I hand him a ten-dollar bill and keep my fingers crossed it won't cut into my Birdland stash.

"Here," I tell Emma Rose. I hand her one of the caps. "Tuck your hair in. All of it."

"What? Why?"

"The police think they were just chasing a boy with short hair and a girl with long hair."

"Seems like a pretty big stretch," Emma Rose says.

"You have a better idea?"

She smashes the hat down over her hair. She doesn't look at all like a boy, but it's better than nothing, and it helps us blend in more among the sea of real New Yorkers.

"So much for buying tickets at Birdland," Emma Rose grumbles as the screech of a police whistle rings from the top of the stairs.

"We can't worry about that," I say to Emma Rose. "Fate will take care of us."

My hands shake, but I manage to slide a five-dollar bill and a single into the automatic ticket kiosk. Two metro cards pop out. I hand one to Emma Rose and we move toward the gate with the roving band of officers at our backs. The vast tunnel beyond the platform rumbles. A train rolls up and screeches to a stop. DING! The doors slide open. Pedestrians stream in through the many openings up and down the platform.

We slide our metrocards through the turnstile, carefully maintaining our new personas as "Yankies" fans and hiding our faces from the officers. I watch several officers comb through the crowd as we vanish inside a subway car. The doors slide shut behind us. DING! The train revs its engine and lifts off from the platform.

As the train shuttles out of the station, one of the cops makes eye contact with me through the window. He stares at Emma Rose and his eyes grow wide. He points. We watch him fumble for his whistle helplessly, as Emma Rose takes her hand out of her pocket and blows him a kiss. Just as the train shoots into the dark tunnel at lightning speed.

Thirty seconds later, we're at the next stop. The train squeals to a halt along the platform at Grand Central Station. The doors part in the middle and I grab Emma Rose's wrist and whisk her off the train.

"After one stop?"

"Better believe it," I say.

We're like trapped rats on this train. And we have no real idea where the track will lead. I mean, we were only a few blocks from Birdland when we got off the bus. Hopefully, one stop on the subway will shake the fuzz off our tails and keep us in the general neighborhood of the club at the same time.

"What about money?" Emma Rose asks, as we climb the stairs and emerge in Grand Central Station. I don't answer. Just keep dragging her behind me through the crowded network of tunnels until we reach the iconic heart of the New York City Subway System.

A massive, domed ceiling presides over the central atrium, its cement transformed into a sky-blue canvas and painted with the legends of astrological lore. Cancer the Crab and Pisces the Fish. Orion the Hunter swings his wooden club in the direction of Taurus the Bull. Carefully-placed LED lights twinkle down in the places where actual stars would have dotted these ancient constellations. These prophecies from the past. These symbols of my fate in the present. They wink at me as if they knew I'd wind up here from the start. As if this legendary railway station—this intersection between the trains and the Trane—had always been some kind of gateway. Between wherever the hell I am and wherever I end up. Between these crisp images and the fog that sweeps in and clouds my eyes. That dulls my hearing. The echoes:

Come on, Cordy!   Come on!

You're almost…

My vision sharpens. The police are on our trail. I'm holding Emma's hand in the atrium of Grand Central Station. On one side, a winding staircase sweeps its way up the wall to a restaurant at the base of the celestial ceiling. A baby grand piano sits below the stairs ablaze in improvised jazz that surges like electricity from the fingertips of a rail-thin pianist, his scalp an explosion of braids. A pair of dark shades covers his eyes and he's dressed in a tuxedo with the tails of his coat draped over the back of the piano bench.

Emma Rose and I stand there, mesmerized, as the notes of the piano wash over us. Then Emma Rose does something stupid. She scratches an itch. On her head. She removes her "Yankies" cap and allows her long hair to cascade down her shoulders. My eyes grow wide and I try to say something like, "Put that back on! Are you crazy?" but my words get drowned out by a piercing whistle that sounds nothing like improvised jazz.

I grab Emma Rose's wrist and surge forward. We take three or four steps before an entire cavalry's-worth of uniformed police officers moves in from in front of us. I spin around and smash foreheads with Emma Rose.

"Ouch!" she says.

Stars float past my vision. A group of four burly officers flanks us on the left. My vision clears. The police whistles intensify. Footsteps chatter off the patent leather shoes and grow closer. Emma Rose and I stare at each other—then, in a flash, and without exchanging a word, we make our move.

"Now!" I shout. We shoot off in opposite directions. Emma Rose jukes left, disappearing beneath the weight of a dozen loaded shopping bags that hang from the shoulders of a group of bus-touring shoppers. I run the opposite way, glancing over my shoulder while weaving around small children in strollers and trash cans and tables packed down with cookies and coffee mugs. I lose sight of Emma Rose, who's planted so deep in the field of tourists it's like trying to pick out a single corn cob among a thousand stalks. I know she can take care of herself. I just hope she can find her way to Birdland.

Meanwhile, the footsteps gain on me. Two officers breathe down my neck and two more close in from the front and bracket me into the cafe. The whistles drown out the piano until the pianist gives up and smashes both hands down on the keys in one discordant super note. I'm almost out of escape routes now, surrounded by tables packed down with diners who spring from their chairs when the whistles screech past, knocking cutlery and dishes to the floor. Spoons clang together. Knives tinkle off plates. A full glass of ice water splashes off a table and washes down the front of my shirt.

"Stop!" an officer barks close behind me. The kitchen doors are directly ahead. I hop a chair and slide over the surface of a table on my ass, taking the tablecloth and a full basket of dinner rolls with me. My feet hit the marble floor and I'm off across the cafe again with the officers in hot pursuit. Only a few more steps to the kitchen doors where I might be able to find a back exit.

I hit the double doors. They don't budge. I push again. Nothing. Two of the officers swing around the nearest table with their arms outstretched. A forearm lands squarely across my face. I wince and spin off the blow and duck the impending bear hug of his partner. I hop on the piano bench and then up on the keys. The soles of my Chucks tinkle out a hideous tune as I race across the ivories and dive over the front railing onto the staircase.

The officers hit the bottom of the stairs as I peel myself off the far wall. I turn and book it up the stairs toward the gourmet restaurant. I barrel right through the host without stopping to check if I'd killed him. He flails around and crashes down on his back with a full stock of insulting-sounding French phrases spewing from his mouth. I circumvent the dining room, dodging waiters with trays stacked with assorted delectables and collections of martini glasses. And then I'm screwed. I reach a dead end. A marble railing about waist high that overlooks the baby grand piano and the cafe and the fifty feet of unbridled air between myself and the ground.

The cops are gathered now. They see I'm cornered, so they move in. They talk to me in soft tones, imploring me not to do anything stupid, trying not to spook me over the edge. But I have no choice. I lift myself up on the railing and stand straight, allowing the rubber soles of my Chucks to bend around the curve of the top bar. I wobble and then catch my balance before I fall to my death. The diners gasp in one collective breath. Something reverberates down from the domed ceiling above. An echo. No, a voice:

Breathe, Cordy!

You're coming back.

You're almost . . .

And then it's gone. Just the buzz of frightened diners and the urging of the police officers telling me not to jump. But I want to jump. I *have* to jump. For Christ's sake, if I don't jump I'll never see Birdland and I'll never prove to anyone I can finish what I started—and I'll never be able to recall this journey as anything other than an enormous failure.

The officers move in. They surround me. My only option is to go. Over the edge. There's nothing more I can do.

"Don't do it, son," one of the officers says when my intention becomes clear to him. "It's not worth it. You're gonna be in real bad shape if you make that choice."

The muscles in my legs twitch and jerk as I steady myself on the rail. I bend at the knees. Get myself in position. Think about how my body felt as it flipped and spun through the air on its descent from a moving train car. Surely it couldn't be worse than that. Could it?

"Come on, son," the officer says, softer and more contrite than before. "Step down off that rail. Be smart."

I bend down to my ankles, feel the torque build in my thighs and tense up in my knees. I'm ready. Just one breath and I'll spring out over the cafe and hope for the best.

Hope for the best.

I'll just hope for the best.

"Don't do it, son!"

I spin around. My Chucks touch down on the floor of the restaurant. Three of the officers grab me and pull me away from the railing. The commotion, of voices and cutlery and glasses rattling on trays, builds to a deafening crescendo and then all goes silent. All goes blurry. The voices pour down from the celestial ceiling in echoes only I can hear:

He's not there yet   *he's*

He's almost...   *no!*   *NO!!*

                                        CORDDDDDDDDDDDDDY!!

I come to again with the officers encircling me. They stare down their noses in shock, beads of sweat rolling down their faces. I hold my hands together and stretch them out in front of me, expecting the worst—the cold steel of the cuffs and the humiliation of a perp walk through Grand Central Station and a night in the slammer, followed by deportation back to my parents' bungalow on Brookside Drive to face the music and receive life imprisonment in the confines of my room.

"What are you doing?" the lone vocal officer asks me as I continue to hold out my hands.

"Aren't you gonna cuff me?" I ask.

"Cuff you? You're not under arrest. You're Cordell Wheaton, right?"

"Yeah. Well, Cordy, actually" I say.

"Well, Cordy, lots of people have been worried sick over you. Your parents are at the top of the list. But, thank god, we found you."

"And now you're gonna book me," I say.

"Book you?" he says, laughing, as he and the officers escort me through the restaurant, down the stairs, and through Grand Central Station. A line of police cruisers, lights blazing, sits waiting when we reach street level. "Son, I think you've been watching too many police dramas on the TV. We're not gonna book you. You're underage, for one thing. And you haven't committed a crime."

I immediately think about the stolen credit card but decide not to say anything.

"I don't consider myself a child," I say flatly. "Not anymore."

"That's great, son," he tells me. "But the law states otherwise. So get in."

I hop in the back seat of the police cruiser and notice it's empty. No Emma Rose, which means she escaped and can continue my journey without me ruining it. I don't know how I'll be able to thank her for putting up with my nonsense, or for placing herself in harm's way, or for giving me a hard time and making me realize how important it is to have people in our lives willing to say the things you may not want to hear but need to hear. I don't know how I'll do it, but as I sit in the back seat of the cruiser, I start to hatch plans for a future Cordy Wheaton epic journey. One that will reunite me with Emma Rose, no last name.

My thoughts shatter when the driver's-side door opens and the officer climbs in. "Staff Sergeant William O'Rourke," he says with his eyes trained on me in the rear-view. "We're going down to the station, Cordy. Sit tight. You're in no danger."

"Thanks," I say, though thanking him is the last thing I want to do. I mean, I know he's doing his job, but he could have left Emma Rose and I alone for another few hours, so at least if I'm destined to be a humiliated pseudo-criminal, I'd be a humiliated pseudo-criminal who'd seen a show at Birdland.

"Nothing to worry about," Sergeant O'Rourke says while my mind wanders.

The cruiser pushes from the curb and blasts into the heat of traffic on Park Avenue.

"We're gonna get a report written and then hand you off to your parents. They're gonna be thrilled to see you."

He hangs a left on Forty-Fourth Street. My eyes light up as I remember the address of Birdland Jazz Club: 315 W. 44th Street, New York, New York. We can't be far. Maybe I'll even catch a glimpse of the marquee before I get pseudo-booked and shipped back to High Point.

"But we have to make a stop first," O'Rourke says all of a sudden.

He pulls the cruiser along the curb and gets out. He opens the back door and motions for me to slide across the seat and follow him. Once I'm outside, the glowing, red marquee lords over us in the night:

Birdland Jazz Club.

My heart sputters. I take a deep breath and manage to spit out four words: "How. Did. You. Know?"

He nods toward the ticket booth, a slightly rounded depression that curves inward off Forty-Fourth Street. A group of three tourists stands outside with their backs to us.

"I don't get it," I say.

"Go and say hello," he tells me.

"What? I'm not walking up to a group of strangers in the middle of New York City."

"Strangers?"

He laughs as one of the "tourists" spins to face us. It's Travis! The other two turn around. Mom and Dad. My eyes meet Sergeant O'Rourke's. He smiles. Then he nods. He reaches forward in the police cruiser and clicks on the radio. It's the song. Travis's song, and my song, and Trane's song. The one from the sheet music. The smooth sound of Trane's sax accompanied by the honey-sweet voice of Ms. Elsa May Kingston play on a loop inside my head even after I hop out of the back of the cruiser and feel my legs wobble as I hit the sidewalk.

I have made it.

To Birdland.

With Travis. And with Mom and Dad.

Despite the odds, here we are.

And I did it, for the most part, on my own—well, maybe with the help of a whole bunch of perfect strangers along the way. People like Cowbird, who could never leave an egg outside a cozy nest, and Ayel Adomi, who could read the tides with her eyes closed, but could also read into the mind of someone in need. And folks like Juan and Nasser and Pierre, who decide to give unto others even when there's barely enough for themselves. And true philosophers like Jack Annunzio and Levi Kurtz, who help you see the world in ways you never imagined.

Without them—all of them—where would I be? Not here in New York City. Not standing in front of Birdland Jazz Club. Without them, I'd have no measure of the capacity for one human being to care for another. Without them I wouldn't understand what the world truly has to offer, and I'd never be able to move forward. To move on.

"Cordy!" Travis shouts. I don't hesitate. I run to him like when I was five years old and couldn't wait for my big brother to come home from school. Travis wraps his arms around me so tightly I think he might bust one of my ribs. Mom and Dad move in and join us—right there in front of Trane's kingdom in the middle of Forty-Fourth Street in New York City.

We make our way over to the lobby—each one of us changed. Different from the cave dwellers we'd been not long ago. Away from home, but always homebound. Aware of our surroundings but longing for the ones we'd come to know and love. Even as we stand in the heart of the busiest city on Earth, we're somehow back in High Point, North Carolina. Home of the legendary John Coltrane. Where the grass is just as green. And maybe even greener.

"Four tickets, please," Dad says.

As the ticket clerk punches out the tickets, one, two, three, four—I think about fate. And I think about *choice*. And I realize it was choice—*my* choice—that led me to poke my head from the cave. To leave my tortoise shell beside the road. To find my courage. To get outside and explore all this world has to offer.

Yes, I made a choice. It took me hundreds of miles from High Point on a journey that could have got me killed. But it sure made a whole world of difference. Because it made me truly understand the meaning of home.

In an instant, the pain and the heartache and the drugs and the abuse fade away, and all that matters is we're here. The Wheatons. Each and every one of us.

At Birdland.

Together.

We make our way over toward the doors that stand between us and the Birdland stage. I open one of the doors and am instantly hit with an intense, blinding light. I turn to mouth the words "what is happening"—but no words come out. I can barely see Mom, Dad and Travis. My head starts to spin…and then I'm back in the echo chamber—only this time it's worse.

Much worse . . .

"Hey! Cordalito! You don't **hear me** calling you?"

"I think he's **ghosting** me.

"Dude! What's happening my little man?"
"Wind instruments give me wood!"
"You the preacher's boy?"
"There's nothing they can do. It's all in my lungs. Up to God now."
"Have you ever experienced trauma?"
Cordy?
"If you need to go bad enough, you'll find a way."
"So, what's got you running then, rookie?"
"You move an inch and this ear's gettin' fed to them hogs,"
"My name's not kid. It's Cordy. And I'm off to Philadelphia."

"Cordy...I've had enough...
I'm following the sound."
"Does **Travis** know you're coming?"
"**Trane**. He's a symbol for you and Travis."
" **Birdland** is your ballpark, only with a different kind of music."
"On the road, everybody's **running** from something."
"Damn it, Lula! My brother's **an addict**!"
Cordy?
"Did you pick the right **hero**, Cordy?"
"Coltrane was the **glue.** He's what held you and your brother together."
"We're **living monuments** to Trane's legend."
"To be like **John Coltrane**, you'd need a **soul**. And you'd need a **conscience**."
Cordy?

Cordy?
"He'll get the **money**."
"Do you think Travis wants to **see you**?"
"Sometimes you make it to the **crossroads**. You gotta make a decision."
"Sometimes, you gotta let the currents take you, honey. **Stop fighting**."
"Stop trying to **forget**!"
"Everybody has a **story** to tell... I guess you just haven't been on the road long enough to find the right words."
"The remembering part **IS** the **journey**. It's how you get there that's the hard part."
"Step out of the **shadows** once in a while!"
"This is what **freedom** looks like, Carolina."
"I never meant for you to get **hurt**. I never meant for any of this to happen."
Cordy?
"You'll know when **it's time**, Cordy."
"Breathe, Cordy. **Breathe!**"
"Cordy...**Cordy!** He's just not ready yet."

"CooRRRDY!!! No.
No. **CORRRRDY**!"

I open my eyes.

Birdland is gone.

I am staring up at a beige ceiling.
Cold, clinical, silent.

Faces staring at me. Mom. Dad.

"Where am I?"
I try to mouth the words in my head.
But nothing comes out.

"Cordy, honey!"
Mom's arm around me.
Her head on my shoulder, sobbing.

I try to talk.
"Mom, what happened to Emma Rose? Mom, where's Emma?"
Still no sound.

"Nurse! I think he's trying to talk! Nurse, nurse!"

Darkness . . .

I open my eyes and immediately close them.

The light is too bright.

I hear a voice.

"Yes, ma'am. It's normal procedure . . ."

Home

What I've come to learn during my travels—maybe the most important thing I've ever learned—is that what you envision for yourself is not often the way things turn out. But that shouldn't stop you from wishing. From dreaming. From having the courage to take chances. From stretching your head as far as you can outside of the shell and getting a good view of life happening around you. From letting the song play out like a skilled jazz musician. Like Trane, improvising riffs to drown out the bad parts and always finding a thread to lead him back to the beginning. Back to where the song started.

Back home.

That's what I did. And even though I have the memory of Sergeant O'Rourke driving the police cruiser down Forty-Fourth Street with me in the back, and even though the lightbulb-encrusted marquee of the famous Birdland Jazz Club rose up from the sidewalk and greeted me through the side window with its brilliant red glare, and even though I squinted my eyes down to narrow slits in the hope I'd see Mom and Dad and Travis standing at the ticket booth waiting for my arrival, the cruiser never slowed down. It never pulled along the curb and stopped. Sergeant O'Rourke never pushed the driver's side door open and welcomed me out of the squad car.

None of it ever happened—not one single experience—except within the confines of my skull, where the fates of Greek lore have been known to come and play, leaving behind the traces of prophetic fantasy. Shadows. Memories. Associations. The outlines of my reality all rolled into the form of an epic journey through my own emotion. Through the things I wanted to forget but which lingered around long enough to suffocate me.

To make me miserable. To stop me from living.

Of course, I couldn't have known that until I opened my eyes. Until they were flooded in fluorescent light and I was surrounded by windows and lab-coated onlookers gawking at me through the glass. Watching my every move. Monitoring everything from my heart rate to my blood pressure to my brain waves. Treating me like a fragile piece of crystal as I lay there on the hospital bed and note the stinging scent of antiseptic on the air and the chill in my bones and the deep, hollow soreness behind my left ear.

Under the bandages.

Beneath staples and stitches and cauterized skin.

My entire body, aside from the patched-up wound on my head, is so numb I can barely feel my eyes blink, but I can tell they're here with me. Mom and Dad. In the room. At the foot of the hospital bed beside a man in light blue scrubs and a surgical mask. A stethoscope hangs from his ears as he moves in and places the cold metal cylinder on my chest.

"He's stabilizing and seems to be coming out of it just fine," I hear him say to my parents, and his voice is calm, measured, and familiar. It brings me right back into the echo chamber.

Can you hear me? Cordell. Cordell?

He pulls a small penlight out of the breast pocket of his lab coat and flicks it on. He shines it in both of my eyes, moving it back and forth, examining my pupils.

Cordy? Can you see this? Can you follow it with your eyes?

He doesn't actually say these words out loud, but I hear them anyway, somewhere deep in the back of my mind where Emma Rose lives, and where Cowbird and Shotgun Sally rumble across an asphalt wasteland, and where a dude named Juan insists my name is Cordalito.

The doctor backs away and allows my parents to approach from the foot of the bed. I open my mouth and try to push out a sound, but it's all bottled up inside of me like that first time I tried to blow a note through Travis's saxophone. Mom notices my struggle and the trademark lines of worry wrinkle across her forehead like when I'd stay home from school with the flu and she'd feed me bowls of chicken noodle soup and saltine crackers. She grabs a wet cloth from the basin beside my bed and wrings out the excess moisture. She pushes it against my forehead and the coolness starts to jolt me back to life. Back to the moment. To reality.

Let me have that cloth. I'll keep him cleaned up. Just like way back.

I lay back as Mom sponges the sweat off my forehead and I start to notice the repetitive swoosh-swoosh of a record player in the corner of the room, its needle spinning pointlessly around the label of a vinyl album. Dad walks over and sets the needle back in its groove and the undeniable squeal of a tenor saxophone spills out on the antiseptic air. It's Trane playing "A Love Supreme" from the only vinyl record Travis had ever bothered to add to his collection.

Do you think he'll recognize it? Do you think it'll work?

"Yes," I finally manage to choke out. My voice is strained and scratchy, like I'd swallowed a pound of sand. But this time, they hear me. They definitely hear me because I see the pain lift from their faces in an instant. Mom lifts the cloth from my forehead. Dad steps around her and hangs his head directly over mine, his eyes so wide with delight they've nearly taken over his forehead. He squeezes my hand in his.

"Son?" he whispers. "You still there, Cordy? Keep talking to us."

"It worked," I manage to scratch out. "Trane."

Dad locks eyes with Mom and they glance at Travis's thrift shop record player sitting on a table in the corner of the room. A smile rises on Mom's lips and her eyes begin to well up. Dad's grip on my hand gets tighter and he heaves in a deep breath and releases it in a short sob that he tries to cover up with one of his trademark coughs.

"Hey, Dad. Promise me you'll quit the cigarettes," I whisper.

Dad nods and rests his head against my chest, and I can feel the warmth of his tears soaking through the scratchy cotton of my hospital gown.

"I promise," he says with his voice muffled out by the tears and my gown. "Yeah, I promise." He says it over and over again, with Mom leaning in over him and resting her hand on my knee. And we stay there, all huddled together as Wheatons, sobbing and squeezing each other and promising all the promises of time until Trane's saxophone dies out and the needle scratches across the label and the repetitive swoosh-swoosh of a skipped-out record player fills the room again. Until it dawns on me something is missing. Something just isn't complete.

"Where's Travis?"

I watch as Dad glances over toward Mom—the concern, sadness, and hesitation all evident in his eyes. Then I see him nod.

"Oh honey, Cordy…he's….he's gone," Mom says softly.

"We don't know where," Dad says.

His lips begin to tremble, and I know what he's about to say to me is simply too hard to put into words. But he tries.

"Cordy? Don't you…I mean…do you know what he—"

"I know, Dad" I tell him. "I…remember. I was hoping maybe I'd dreamt that part too."

Dad reaches down and grabs my hand again. He squeezes it tightly and wraps one of his arms around Mom. He smiles and tells me, "We can talk more about it when we get you home."

For the first time, I become aware of how dang lucky I am to be awake. To be *alive*. To be able to one day leave this hospital bed and walk up our driveway on Brookside Drive on my own two legs. And, even though the bullet glanced off the base of my skull and may have left me with some irreparable hearing loss and a long road to full recovery, I have to wonder if there was some kind of divine intervention at work—some clever meddling by the fates—that changed the bullet's trajectory by a millimeter or two. Just enough to ensure it didn't embed itself in my brain and end my life in that instant. Just enough to ensure I'd survive my trauma long enough to remember. And to reflect. And to heal.

"I'd like that," I say, as the first signs of movement come back to my body in the muscles around my mouth, as my lips curl upward into the first real smile I've felt in a long time.

Because I know I'm finally going home.

But I know this time, everything will be different. The people who never knew I existed will now know I exist. The church congregation who judged my family off of Travis's mistakes will have nothing left to judge because their verdict will be meaningless. The town that was my shell for over sixteen years will be split down the middle and oozing with everything I've ever needed. The nightmares will have no dominion in my mind and sleep will prevail. And Mom and Dad and I will talk again. Not via text message or through the paper-thin walls in our house, but at the dinner table with the buttery scent of Mom's biscuits blanketing the kitchen in goodness.

I will always care for, and worry about, my brother, Travis. As will Mom and Dad. Our door will always be open because we're not giving up on him. But no longer will I let Travis or his actions define me, because I'm Cordell Wheaton.

I have found my way out of the cave. And I'm never going back.

Questions for Classroom/ Book Club Discussion

1. What motivates Cordy Wheaton to embark on his journey? What theme(s) do his actions demonstrate?

2. What kind of journey does Cordy Wheaton take (both externally and internally)? How does this journey create noticeable change in his character from the first page to the end of the novel?

3. What characteristics do all of the "mentors" Cordy meets on his journey seem to have in common? Why do you think these characters make an entrance in Cordy's life at precisely the right times?

4. Which of Cordy Wheaton's many "mentors" do you relate to the most? Why?

5. How does the legendary career and life of jazz icon, John Coltrane, relate any one of the themes you noticed in your reading of *On the Way to Birdland*?

6. What are your thoughts on the purpose of the many instances where bird imagery and symbolism is used by the author? How do these images help to reveal hidden themes in the novel?

7. What comparisons can you make between the characters Cordy Wheaton and Emma Rose, No Last Name?

8. What is the relevance of the title On the Way to Birdland to Cordy Wheaton's journey on both a physical and a mental level?

9. What events may shock or surprise the reader? How does this shock value impact the way in which any of the themes in the novel are explored?

10. What are the most important pieces of dialogue from the book? Why is each quote significant?

11. If we view the character Travis Wheaton from a figurative standpoint, what might he symbolize in Cordy's life?

12. Compare and contrast the character, Travis Wheaton, with the jazz legend, John Coltrane. Why do you think Cordy is so obsessed with forming a connection between these two figures in the story?

13. What do you think Cordy Wheaton learns about himself over the course of his journey?

14. What is one important philosophical principle you've learned from your reading of *On the Way to Birdland*? How does this principle relate to a major plot point in the novel? How can you use it in your own life?

15. What effects might the trauma Cordy Wheaton has experienced have on his future life after the novel's completion?

Acknowledgements

Writing a book is, in many ways, like trying to chef up a signature dish. It's the product of numerous inspirations from the most unpredictable places, its essence ultimately an amalgamation of your own instincts and the special ingredients procured by the other chefs in the kitchen—those indispensable and unsung heroes in every writer's life who make it possible to sling words at the page.

Folks like Jon Wilson, my publisher at Fish Out of Water Books, who seems to always find a way to trick me into elevating my work. Brilliant folks, like my friends Marty Brown, Birdie Thompson, the McGinnis family, Alyssa DeLio, Jaime English and our cover designer Bailey McGinn, whose varied insights shaped *On the Way to Birdland* in essential ways that can never be measured. Talented authors and treasured friends in the writing community, like Diana Rodriguez Wallach and R.J. Fox, whose honesty and expertise inspired me to transform a novel I already loved into something I never imagined it could be.

The list of contributors, both oblivious and aware, could go on for pages: my wonderful students who ignite my passion for learning every day; my family for believing in possibilities; my teaching colleagues for saving the freaking world on a daily basis and still finding time to show up at book events and cover my classes and drop stray cupcakes on my desk; Ms. Alex Frey for simply tolerating me when I'm in obsessive writer mode, which is most of the time.

But, most of all, I want to thank John Coltrane and the City of High Point, North Carolina. Both of you beckoned me out of the big city over fifteen years ago to come and reshape my entire life in a place that, at first, fit me like a pair of size two sneakers. But coming to High Point and following the life experiences of John Coltrane, one of the town's favorite sons, provided me with my "escape from the cave" moment. It helped me find the light of the outside world. It was surprising and refreshing and infinitely beautiful. And, for me, it has made all the difference.

Writing and creating have always been essential avenues in author Frank Morelli's life. As an eight-year-old, Morelli would hole himself up in his room paging through the *National Geographic* books he'd lifted from his grandfather's barbershop. He would sit at his desk and write brand-new storylines to his favorite video games, complete with the most awful pencil sketches you've ever seen, and he'd store them in a barrel-shaped piggy bank he'd won playing Skee-ball on the New Jersey boardwalk. Morelli never put a dime in that bank, but it was always overflowing with crinkled pages and future ideas.

Morelli's debut young adult novel, *No Sad Songs* (2018), was a YALSA Quick Picks for Reluctant Readers nominee, a VOX top Hopepunk title, and winner of a 2019 American Fiction Award for best coming-of-age story. His fiction and essays have been featured in *The Saturday Evening Post*, *Cobalt Review*, *Philadelphia Stories*, *Boog City Review*, and *Highlights Magazine*. Morelli lives in High Point, NC with his best friend, their obnoxious alley cats, and two hundred pounds worth of dog. Connect with him on Twitter @frankmoewriter, on Instagram @frankmorelliauthor, or at his author site frankmorelliwrites.com.